OUTER
BANKS

Also by Anne Rivers Siddons
in Thorndike Large Print

King's Oak

This Large Print Book carries the
Seal of Approval of N.A.V.H.

OUTER BANKS

Anne Rivers Siddons

Thorndike Press • Thorndike, Maine

Library of Congress Cataloging in Publication Data:

Siddons, Anne Rivers.
    Outer banks : a novel / by Anne Rivers Siddons.
       p. cm.
    ISBN 1-56054-282-9 (alk. paper : lg. print)
    ISBN 1-56054-946-7 (alk. paper : lg. print : pbk.)
    1. Large type books. I. Title.
[PS3569.I28O87   1991]   91-35569
813'.54—dc20   CIP

Copyright acknowledgments on page 624.

Thorndike Press Large Print edition published in 1992
by arrangement with HarperCollins Publishers, Inc.

Cover design © by Will Williams/Stansbury,
Ronsaville, Wood Inc.
Cover illustration © by Greg Harlin.

The tree indicium is a trademark of Thorndike Press.

This book is printed on acid-free, high opacity paper.

To the Duck Seven
And most especially to Gee Gee

Shall I part my hair behind? Do I dare to
  eat a peach?
I shall wear white flannel trousers, and walk
  upon the beach.
I have heard the mermaids singing, each to
  each.

I do not think that they will sing to me.

I have seen them riding seaward on the waves
Combing the white hair of the waves blown
  back
When the wind blows the water white and
  black.

We have lingered in the chambers of the
  sea
By sea-girls wreathed with seaweed red and
  brown
Till human voices wake us, and we drown.

"The Love Song of J. Alfred Prufrock"
                                  T. S. ELIOT

CHAPTER ONE

On the Outer Banks of North Carolina there is a legend about the ships that have come to grief in the great autumn storms off those hungry shoals. Over the centuries there have been many; the Banks have more than earned their reputation as the Graveyard of the Atlantic. Most of the graves are in Diamond Shoals, just off the point of Cape Hatteras, but the entire hundred-odd-mile sweep of coast has devoured its measure of wood and flesh. Myths and spectres and apparitions lie as thick as sea fog over the Banks, but the one that I have always remembered is the one Ginger Fowler told us all . . . Cecie, Fig, Paul Sibley, and me . . . the September of my last year in college, when we were visiting her between quarters.

"They say that whenever a ship is going to go down you can hear something like singing in the wind," she said. "Bankers say it's mermaids, calling the sailors. Lots of them claim to have heard it. It's not like wind or anything. They say when you hear it, you have no choice but to follow it, and you end up on the shoals. A few of the sailors who've been rescued swear to it."

We were sitting on the front veranda of the Fowlers' house on the dunes on Nag's Head beach, watching the twilight die over the Atlantic. On either side of us hulked the great, black-weathered, two- and three-story cottages that made up what the Bankers call the Unpainted Aristocracy — a long line of huge, weather-stained wooden summer houses that had been built in the early days of the century by the very rich. When they were first built, the houses reigned alone on that lordly line of dunes, owning by sheer *force majeure* the wild, empty beach. Now they are surrounded by flealike armies of bungalows and time-shares and fishing piers and umbrella and float rentals, like mastodons beset by pygmies. But even now, when you are on the front porches or verandas, you have no sense of the graceless, idiot hoards nibbling at their skirts. Only of wind and sun and emptiness, and the endless sea.

I remember that I felt a small *frisson* that might have been night wind on sunburned flesh, and reached for Paul's hand. He squeezed it, but did not turn to look at me. He was looking intently at Ginger's sweet, snub face, stained red by the sun setting behind us over Roanoke Sound and by the long, golden days in the sun. Autumn on the Outer Banks is purely a sorcerer's spell:

so clear you can see each grain of sand on the great dunes, and bathed in a light that is indescribable. We had stayed on the beach from dawn to sunset for the past four days, and all of us wore the stigmata on our cheeks and shoulders. But Ginger was the red-brown of cast bronze all over. The freckles on her broad cheekbones had merged in a copper mask, and her eyelashes and tow head had whitened. She looked like a piece of Mayan statuary in her faded cotton bathing suit with the boy-cut legs, squat and abundant and solid as the earth.

I thought she looked almost perfectly a piece of the old house and the older coast, but in fact her father had only bought the house two summers before, from an imperious old widow who was going, most reluctantly, to live with her children in Wilmington. Before that Ginger had summered at Gulf Shores, on the Alabama coast, and lived with her family in a small north Alabama town called, appropriately, Fowler. It consisted of a huge textile mill, a mill village and store, and little else, all of which belonged to Ginger's father. The Fowlers were newly, enormously, and to us, almost inconceivably rich. Ginger worked very hard to conceal the fact, and succeeded so well that until we went to visit her on the Outer Banks, and saw the house, we did not really comprehend it. Fig had told us when she proposed Ginger for sisterhood in Tri Omega that Ginger had a trust fund of her own approaching five million dollars; in those days that was a breathtaking sum of money. But since none of us paid much attention to what Fig said, we either forgot it or discounted it. In the end, Ginger became a Tri Omega because we all loved her. It was impossible not to. She was as gregarious, sweet-natured, and simple as a golden retriever.

"And," Cecie observed thoughtfully, "looks not unlike one."

On the darkening porch that night at Nag's Head, Paul smiled at Ginger and said, "Have you heard the mermaids singing, Ginger?" and the little cold breath on my nape and shoulders strengthened.

"God, no," she said. "It would scare the bejesus out of me. I hope I never do."

"I wish I could," he said, and then he did look at me, and squeezed my hand again. "That would be something to hear. I think that would be worth just about anything."

I actually shivered; it seemed to me as if the very air around us had weight and meaning, and every whirling atom had particularity and portent. But I was so much in love with him by then that everything he said, everything we did, everything that surrounded us, our entire context, had resonance and purpose. Cecie looked at me and then at Paul, and said, "I think I'll go make some tea," and rose and padded into the house. I watched her out of sight, thinking once more how like a small, slender boy she looked in silhouette, wishing that she liked Paul better. For two years Cecie had been the friend of my heart, one of the two real loves of my life, and I wanted her to share this new love with me. I wanted the three of us, I think, to be a unit, a whole. But Cecie, who did not often or easily give her heart, was not about to accord it to Paul Sibley. From the moment she met him she had removed herself from him, physically when she could, emotionally whenever she could not. With another friend I might have thought it was jealousy, but what Cecie and I had went far beyond and deeper than that. I did not know what it was, and somehow could not speak of it with her, and she did not to me. Paul knew that she did not like him, but had been wise enough to simply let it alone. They did not often meet.

That week in September was, in fact, the last time Cecie ever allowed herself to be in his presence, but in the end it did not matter. I lost him that weekend to that old

13

sea and Ginger's new money, but I did not know that until much later.

That winter I studied T. S. Eliot in a Contemporary Poetry class, and when we came to "The Love Song of J. Alfred Prufrock" and the professor read aloud those lines of ineffable beauty and heartbreak,

"I have heard the mermaids singing,
each to each.
I do not think that they will sing to
me."

I began to cry, suddenly and silently, and excused myself from class, and walked across campus to the Tri Omega house blinded by wind and tears, near suffocating with heartbreak and exaltation. I was still crying, intermittently, when Cecie came in from her history lab, and Fig and Ginger stopped by to see if we wanted to go to early supper.

"Who is it? Yeats? Dylan Thomas?" Cecie said, who had had the poetry course the quarter before, and knew my penchant, that winter, for quick, rapt tears. It was mostly the helpless love for Paul that triggered them, a mature and obliterating and sometimes crippling thing, that left me flayed and vulnerable, as if I had no skin. An astounding number of things pierced me and brought tears in those days. But it was partly the poetry, too. Cecie and I often stayed up late into the nights reading poetry to each other, mostly the bitter, beautiful, sharp-edged poetry of the late nineteenth and early twentieth centuries, and if she did not, like me, weep openly, her blue eyes were sometimes liquid with tears. I never saw Cecie cry, but on those nights she often came close.

"Eliot," I snuffled. "About the mermaids singing, but not to him . . . I don't know. It reminded me of that thing Ginger told us up at Nag's Head, about the mermaids and the ships, and then . . . well, I just think that it's such a *sad* line. So sad, so sad . . . it's all of life. It's what ought to happen, but doesn't. It's . . . when you know it isn't going to . . ."

"What is?" Ginger said, her brow furrowed with perplexity. She and Fig shared a suite with us, connected by a bath, and often, in the mornings after Cecie and I had sat up reading poetry, Ginger would stick her shower-wet head into our room and say, "I hear there was a meeting of the Tri Omega Intellectual Society last night," and would grin and put out her tongue and slam the door as Cecie or I threw a book or a stuffed animal at her. Ginger was as slow to study as she was quick to laugh, and her grades,

15

even in her undemanding major of Elementary Education, were in constant jeopardy. It took the entire sisterhood to get her through her pledgeship and maintain a grade average sufficient for initiation, but nobody minded. As I said, everybody loved Ginger.

I read her the lines from Eliot, and she said, "And that's what you're bawling about?"

"I think it's one of the most romantic things I ever heard," Fig breathed adenoidally. Her eyes, swimming myopically behind her thick lenses, looked like those of a rapt bug. She breathed through her mouth, audibly, as she did in times of transport. We hooted her down as we often did, and like a dog that is often threatened but not actually struck, she grinned gummily and tucked her short neck into her heavy shoulders, and looked at us slantwise.

"And sad," she added. "It's really sad." If I had said the poem was the funniest thing I had ever heard, Fig would have laughed heartily. Since we pledged her, Fig had had a kind of suffocating, sexless crush on me that was as obsessive as it was inexplicable. Very few things have made me so uncomfortable. Fig was a triple legacy, and National had threatened to put us on inactive if we did not pledge her. Otherwise, in those days of casual and killing cruelty, there is no doubt that she would have lived her years at Randolph in one of the independent women's dorms.

"If one of us were to hear the mermaids, who should it be?" she said archly. It was the kind of precious, off-balance, idiot thing she was always proposing: "If you were a flower, what would you be?" "If Kate was an animal, what animal would she be?" "If I were a famous woman of history, who do you think I'd be, Kate?"

"Grendel's Mother," Cecie snapped once, and Fig trilled her laughter, by then disconcertingly like mine.

"That's good, Cecie, I'm going to put that in my diary," she said, and Cecie groaned. Fig's diary was infamous at the Tri Omega house. She wrote in it, furtively and ostentatiously, almost constantly. At chapter meetings you would end a heated discussion and look around and Fig would be scribbling in her diary. If you asked what she was writing, or made as if to snatch it away from her, she would pantomime fright and press it to her nonexistent bosom. Often, sitting in our room in one of the endless late night discussions that went on among us, I would feel Fig's eyes on me, and look over and see her staring at me, mouth open, and then she would smile mysteriously and drop her eyes and scribble in the diary. By that winter she had amassed four or five of them, big fake-alligator volumes she ordered from somewhere and filled with her tiny, cribbed hand. She kept them in a locked metal strongbox under her bed, and hinted that they contained enormities. None of us felt anything anymore about the diaries but weariness.

I knew that she knew who Grendel's Mother was, though. Fig was probably, in her own way, as brilliant a student as Randolph had ever had. Her grasp was intuitive and instant, her recall prodigious, and she studied like no one I have ever known before or since. Her point average alone, the sisterhood agreed, was worth the rest of Fig to the Tri Omegas. She was an English major, with a minor in history, and there was not a scholastic honorary she did not belong to. She meant to be a writer, and sometimes, when someone asked her again what she was writing in the diary, she would say, "I'm writing about all of you, and how proud I am to be a Tri Omega." And she would look so humbly, hangdog grateful, and smile so terribly coyly, that the questioner would turn away in embarrassment and distaste. Fig was so thankful to be one of us, and so relentlessly, Pollyanna-cheerful, and effusive in her praise of us, that we soon ceased baiting her and simply avoided her when we could. Most of us could, except Cecie and I and Ginger. Ginger is the only one of us I never heard say an unkind word about Fig. Ginger was, and is, incapable of malice. She came into Tri Omega as a sophomore pledge from Montevallo Women's College, having being sponsored, surprisingly and insistently, by Fig, who had lived her entire life in the shadow of Ginger's father's mill, in Fowler. It was, in fact, the Fowler-Kiwanis scholarship that sent her to Randolph. Fig's people were as spectacularly poor as Ginger's were rich. Ginger roomed with Fig, becoming our second suitemate, and went a long way in making the association bearable to me. I don't think it ever was to Cecie, not really.

Poor Fig. Her name was Georgine Newton, but I think she had probably been called Fig from birth. She was pale, puffy, squatty, spotty, frizzy-haired, sly-eyed behind the quarter-inch glasses, and had the constant, quivering, teeth-baring smile of an abused dog. She had sinus and asthma and snored so terribly that the dean of women made a rare exception and let her live alone. When we pledged her, we drew straws to see who would become her suitemates, and when we pledged Ginger and she moved in with Fig, we had a lottery going to see how long she could bear the fusillade of garglings and snortings. But Ginger was fortuitously deaf in one ear from a stray baseball, and so they simply arranged their beds so that Fig's snores fell on her deaf ear, and remained roommates. It was Cecie and I who heard her, through a plaster wall and a bathroom with two closed doors.

"Oh, *Lord*," Cecie would say, when Fig's name came up, and refused to elaborate. But I knew that she disliked Fig with a pure and fastidious animosity that was, for her, unusual. Cecie was censorious of few people; she simply avoided those she did not like, but she could not avoid Fig. It must have been an uncomfortable three years for her. We never talked much about it, except that once in a while she cautioned me about Fig. I had long since learned to smile and make light of Fig's heavy, cloying adoration and her incessant copying of my voice and gestures and clothes: I was myself a stranger in a strange land, and thought I knew how she must feel, somewhere under all that Fig-ness. But I soon developed a fine-honed skill at mimicking her, and I confess that I often used it in the late nights when Cecie and I lay in our beds with the young moon shining in on us . . . talking, talking.

"Shhhh," Cecie would gasp through her laughter. "She'll hear you. She's got her bed jammed right up against the wall opposite yours."

"How can she hear me through a bathroom and two walls?" I would scoff. "And so what if she does?"

"I wouldn't get on her bad side," Cecie said. "She's not what she seems."

"Lord, Cecie, she's just Fig. What is she, if she's not that?"

"I don't know. But whatever, it's not what you think," Cecie said. "Where's your famous intuition?"

"You're nuts," I said, and went on being polite to the lurking, adoring Fig in her presence, and laughing helplessly at her in the nights.

And Cecie went on bearing her in silence, going away inside her head when Fig was around. It was an astonishing talent; I have seen her do it many times. You would be looking at Cecie, perhaps talking to her, and all of a sudden you realized you were looking at the diminutive, kitten-faced, redhaired outside of Cecelia Rushton Hart from the Virginia tidewater, but that the essential Cecie was simply not in residence at the moment. She could even converse while she was doing it, nodding and murmuring the right things. After a while she would slip back in behind her eyes and Cecie would be there again; I often wondered what inner world she had made for herself that so seduced and comforted her, and what she did there, and with whom. For all our bone-closeness, there was a door very deep inside Cecie through which I could not follow, and I knew it was there she went when Fig stumped too intrusively into her consciousness.

"Who would it be?" Fig insisted with that terrible, lumpen playfulness, on the day I discovered Eliot. "Who would the mermaids sing to? I think it would be you, Kate. You'll be the one who hears the mermaids. I bet you already do."

Cecie snorted.

"Maybe it'll be you, Fig," I said, thinking it would please her. And it did. She blushed an unbecoming magenta and said, "Do you really think so? I'd love that. But I'm sure it would be you. You look like you hear mermaids sometimes . . ."

"No," Ginger said, surprising us. We looked at her.

"It'll be Cecie," she said. "Don't you see? It has to be Cecie."

And I smiled, involuntarily, because of

course she was right. It would be Cecie to whom they sang. Behind her horn-rimmed glasses and dry Virginia drawl, Cecie was smoke and will-o'-the-wisp light, sea spray and flame. It would be Cecie who heard the mermaids singing.

And maybe she did. Maybe they all did, for all I know.

But I know that they never again, after that year, sang to me.

CHAPTER TWO

If I had had a different name and a different nose, I undoubtedly would have had a different life, but I did not realize that until I was very nearly at the end of it. My father, who was the architect of both, was as pleased with his handiwork as if he had plucked both out of a Scott Fitzgerald novel . . . which, in a sense, he did . . . but I spent most of my childhood and adolescence trying to live up to those two icons, and the rest of it trying to live them down.

My nose was and is thin and high-bridged, the type sometimes called aristocratic, a twin to my father's. The Lee nose, as I often heard him say in his careless Virginia drawl when an adult admired mine. Which Lee it was hung, vivid and indisputable, in the very air; I can't remember anyone asking. My name is Katherine Stuart Lee, also the moniker of the aristocrat in the airless Southern society in which my father sought to live, move, and have his being (as it is writ in the *Book of Common Prayer*), that other icon he espoused early on in his life. My father would have shot himself upon hearing that I had added "Abrams" to that distinguished triad when I married Alan, if he had not done so already. By that time he had long and truly forgotten that our Lee name was, if not exactly counterfeit, not precisely real, either.

Daddy was indeed a Lee, and did, indeed, attend the University of Virginia, but he was Charles Horace Lee of Canton, Indiana (pop. 2,456), not Virginia. At the University on a Rotary scholarship in business administration; and the hunt country plantation that was his patrimony existed only in the pages of the florid Southern fiction he perused from childhood, and in his hungry heart. The Stuart he bestowed on his only child did not, in either his or my mother's family, exist at all. Some infatuated idiot from Sweet Briar told my father in his freshman year that he looked just like General Jeb Stuart. And so another branch of my family tree sprouted whole and living.

My mother was not the Mississippi belle Charles Lee represented her to be (and later came to believe she was), but the daughter of a rural grocery store proprietor in Slattery, Mississippi, of such murderous hookworm temper that Lonnie Mae Coolidge ran away from home when she was fifteen with a railroad brakeman, who abruptly detrained her in Lynchburg, Virginia. Charles Lee met her when he took a summer job washing dishes in the cafe where she worked as a waitress. Later he was fond of saying, in that beguiling drawl he had long since perfected, "Well, she hung around Lynchburg so long that I finally married her," and everyone simply assumed that it was Randolph Macon Women's College where she hovered, and not the Virginia Belle Cafe. If asked her class there, pretty May Lee had only to wrinkle her *retrousse* nose, obtained from God knew what long-ago wandering Frenchman who made his way upriver from New Orleans, and murmur, "Well, I never graduated. Charles married me and brought me to Alabama when I was just eighteen. My daddy almost had a fit."

And her audience would smile and nod. In those days few Southern girls made it through college, especially the pretty ones. And tall, slender, slouching Charles Lee did have, in his long gray eyes and wide, sensuous mouth, the kind of banked passion capable of whirling up his love and marrying her and sweeping her away. It was widely agreed in the small society of Kenmore, sixty miles south of Montgomery in the heart of the Black Belt, where he prudently settled as far away from the upper South as possible, that there was a lot of his great-grandfather

Robert E. in young Charles Lee. A few older women, who read, also thought there was a real similarity to the dashing young officer named Fitzgerald who had carried off Judge Sayre's oldest girl up in Montgomery, though it was agreed that May Lee must be much prettier and sweeter than the wild, erratic Zelda.

My father did nothing to discourage either similarity. Indeed, his whole life was dedicated to furthering both. The precarious living he earned from his desultory and inept insurance career went for the renting and meager furnishing of a dilapidated white-columned antebellum mansion on the Santee River west of Kenmore, that stayed, throughout my girlhood, as dilapidated as the day I was born into it. My mother had no bridge or ladies' circle meetings in its splintered, haunted drawing room, my parents had no candelit dinners in the vast, mote-dancing dining room, and in my entire girlhood I never asked a friend home after school to play. The abiding impression I have of it now is dust, dimness, and echoing silence broken by my own tentative footfalls.

"When we get it all fixed up, we'll have a grand housewarming and invite everybody in town. Knock their eyes out," my father would say, as we sat in the thick, wet dusk

27

on the crumbling back porch, which was held together and shielded from prying eyes by vicious, fecund wisteria vines. He and my mother would be fanning and drinking martinis, I would be reading. Or as we huddled around the coal fire in the cracked iron grate in a back room off the kitchen we had adopted as a winter retreat. It was the only room in the house that did not have sixteen-foot ceilings, the only one that could be heated by lump coal bought by the scuttle. I think it had probably been a butler's pantry once. There, too, they drank martinis, and there, too, I read. I read everything, everywhere, whenever I could, making thrice-weekly sorties to the Kenmore Library and coming home tottering under rich piles of spilling books. The reading consumed and saved me; I do not remember, in those early days of my childhood, being unhappy or lonely. That came later, when the world leaked in on me. I am surprised now, when I look back on it, to think that I wondered at the inner world Cecie Hart had fashioned for herself. Mine then was just as total, just as sustaining.

When I was not reading, or in school, my father tutored me. Not from books, but in what he called "the ways of the world." How to speak, and converse, and meet people; how to eat and walk and make small talk;

how to correspond properly and promptly; how to order from an elaborate menu, how to choose and serve wine. How to behave with the president of Kenmore Bank and Trust and with the black woman who came to clean, and why the minute differences were important. "You pay Mr. McClure a compliment when you say you saw his cute daughter in the drugstore, but when you say it to Essie, it's familiar. A lady wouldn't," he would say.

"I'm not a lady," I would say.

"Yes, you are," he would reply. "A born lady, in the bone and blood. I'm not going to let you forget that. It'll serve you well in the world."

And because I was young and loved my handsome mountebank father, I did not ask what world he meant, or see that it existed largely inside his head. He taught. I learned.

Daddy gave it about that all his money was going to buying back his family place in Virginia, which a brother's perfidy had sold to a Yankee businessman. When he was able, he intimated softly, he would take my mother and me back there, rightfully at home at last. All of Kenmore applauded his fineness of spirit, and his patience and gumption, and no one mentioned it when he fell behind in his dues at the country club, or his chit at the grocery, or his tithe to St. Luke's Episcopal Church. Exceptions were quietly made, help quietly given and gracefully accepted. No one remarked upon it when my mother found herself a discreet job as secretary to the principal of the Atwater County High School; no one thought it anything but admirable when, at thirteen, I took modest summer and weekend and after-school jobs clerking about town to help pay for the drifts of clothes and crinolines that saw me through early high school.

"Your little Katie is a sweet girl, and a smart one," the matrons of Kenmore would say to my parents. "All A's at school, and working like a bee after, and never missing a day of Sunday School and Church. And looking like a princess to boot. We're going to hear from her, yes, sir. She'll make a college teacher, no doubt about it."

"I wouldn't be surprised," my father would grin charmingly, modestly, but after a few of the comments about teaching he called me out of my deep Edith Wharton spell one evening, in April of my sophomore year in high school, and set out a new battle plan for me.

"No more drugstore and ten-cent stores for you this summer," he said, swirling the martini glass so that the olive bumped at its sides like a fish in an aquarium. "You're going to work on the Cape, or Nantucket." He studied me with his narrow head cocked to one side, appraising. "And I think we're going to let your hair grow, and put it back and up. We used to call it a French twist. Not one woman in a thousand can really wear it, but you can. It looks like money."

I put a hand up to feel the short, lacquered flip that I and every other teenager in the Deep South wore that year.

"Do they pay you for wearing it?" I said smartly. "Because if they do, I'm all for it. Then I wouldn't have to work on the Cape or anywhere else. I don't want to go away by myself this summer; I'm barely sixteen."

"Eastern girls from the best families fight to be waitresses at the Cape and the Vineyard and Nantucket," my father said. "I've known multimillionaires' daughters who did it every summer. They meet all the Ivy League boys and all the girls from the good schools, from the Seven Sisters. They make contacts that are useful the rest of their lives. A lot of them get into Vassar and Wellesley and Smith because of those summers. They learn the ways of the world they're going to live in. You're a little young for it, but I don't see any point in making you hang around here summers anymore. You'll get to thinking like Kenmore. And you'll have the time of your life. Trust me, you will. You'll have more dates and boyfriends than any girl from Bar Harbor to Rehoboth Beach."

"Why would I there when I don't here!" I said sullenly. "I haven't had a real date ever, except in a bunch, and that was Carolyn Crenshaw's drippy little brother. I look funny, you know I do. I look like an ostrich. And I'm going to look like an ostrich on Cape Cod."

He smiled.

"You're not, you know," he said. "Down here they're all afraid of the way you look; you outclass them by a mile. But up there you're going to look . . . like they do, only better. You have very distinctive looks, Kate. You haven't quite grown into them, that's all. Very Eastern. Very wellborn. Tall, thin, well-shaped head and hands and feet, fine straight features, not too flashy; good teeth . . . and you have a smile that can light a room, when you choose to use it. You want to watch that you don't use it too often; it's the contrast of that smile against all that coolness that's so effective. You have faultless manners, and a nice reserve. I'm glad we started early on that. I want you to watch very carefully and see what the other girls are wearing this summer and that's what

up in a net. I don't want you running around up there with your hair smelling like clam chowder. Harbour House is quiet, but it's old money. Beauchamp Childs takes his family there every summer. His girl Sydney used to work there summers. I think she's at Sweet Briar now. Be sure and look him up. He's the one that got you in there on short notice. I wrote him last month. You need to cultivate the Childs."

"Are they old money?" I said, not sure what that meant. In Kenmore, if anyone had any money at all, it was apt to be old.

"Old enough," my father said. "Champ's family had a string of granite quarries. His father turned it into Southern Cyanamid, and Champ has taken it international. I thought of going in with him once, right after graduation. But I wanted my own business. I don't think he ever forgave me. We used to run relay together at Virginia. He was always the flashiest, but I was better . . ."

He let the sentence trail off, and behind his gray eyes I could see that he had followed the thought back to those gilded long-ago cinder ovals.

"Was he in your fraternity?" I said politely. I knew that would bring him back. The little plain gold Kappa Alpha shield he kept in a velvet box on his dresser was the totem he cherished most. He wore it to church and to parties, but it never left its nest except on those occasions. Often, when he had had two or three martinis, he would tell rambling, sentimental tales of the brothers and he used to say, "Kate, May, remember this: when I die I want to be buried in the Shield. I don't want anybody to forget that. That's a brotherhood that transcends the grave."

I felt something near reverence for the shield. He never let me wear it, but he told me over and over that perhaps I could aspire to it, when I was old enough, for very special occasions.

"It's an honor not given many women, Katie Stuart," he would say in the silken tenor the gin called out. "The girls who walked into the house at Virginia with the Shield on their breasts were princesses, the fairest flower of the South. You have to earn the Shield."

And I would be silent, knowing that of course I had not, and probably never would. I thought of the Kappa Alpha house at the University of Virginia often in those days; my father had described it so often that I could see every polished floorboard and shining stair rail and soaring crown molding, smell lemon wax and Cape Jessamine. In my mind, it was a white-columned palace inhabited by tall, lazy, blond princes, all of whom looked like my father. All wore Confederate gray with gold epaulets.

When he did die, two springs later, he lay in a closed casket because of the damage the bullet had done to his beautiful head. Its lid had already been lowered when I arrived home from school. So I did not know that he had not, after all, been buried wearing the Shield until I found it in the top drawer of his bureau days later. I was cleaning it out, stunned and slowed with emptiness, because my mother asked me to do it. Since the funeral she had sat silently in the dim, near-empty drawing room, having her hands chafed by round-the-clock squadrons of ladies from St. Rhoda's Altar Guild. They must have known the iced tea she kept constantly beside her was half Kentucky Gentleman, but of course, no one remarked upon it.

I taxed her with it that afternoon before the evening shift from St. Rhoda's arrived.

"I can't believe you forgot," I snuffled fiercely. "You know he asked to be buried in it; you know what the Shield meant to him."

She lifted her head, and I saw the face of Lonnie Mae Coolidge, of Slattery, Mississippi, for the first time in my life.

"No, I don't guess I do know what it

meant to him," she said in a flat voice that came through her nose. I had never heard that, either. "The only time your daddy ever went into the famous KA house at the famous University of Virginia was to wash their famous dishes on weekends, and then he went in the back door," she said. "I don't know where he got the pin."

It might have wrecked me, that ugly and resonant little revelation, but by that time I knew about the abyss.

I had no name for it then, but I already knew the awful hollowness under my feet that meant bottomless emptiness, and I knew the smell of it. It was like the cold wet air that coils up from a dead black well. I could smell the breath from my own private pit and I could even smell it about others. There is a fraternity of us, the abyss walkers. In our eyes, the world is divided by it, made up of those who walk frail, careening rope bridges over the abysses and those who do not. We know each other. I do not think it is a conscious thing with us, this knowing, at least not most of the time, or we would flee from each other as from monsters. It is an animal thing. It is only on that wild old neck-prickling level that we meet. It is only in our eyes that we acknowledge that our twin exhalations have touched and mingled.

Sometimes, though not often, one of the others, the non-abyss-people, will know us, too. You may even know the feeling yourself; you may have met someone about whom otherness clings like a miasma; you can feel it on your skin though you can't name it. When that happens, you have met one of us. You may even be one of us, down deep and in secret. As the old women in Kenmore say, it takes one to know one. Being able to feel it is not a good sign. The other half of the world, the solid, golden half, the non-abyssers . . . they feel nothing under their feet but solidity. They inherit the earth. We inherit the wind.

Vladimir Nabokov began *Speak, Memory* with the words, "The cradle rocks above an abyss." When I read it, years later, safe for the time being in a secret garden by the sea on Long Island, I cried. The man who had brought me there looked at me over his own book and smiled.

"Already?" he said. "You just opened it."

They were tears of kinship, and of vindication. It was like hearing the doctor say, "You were right all along, and we were wrong. It isn't in your head. It's a real sickness. We apologize." This Russian, himself an exile, had named the emptiness and shown me it was vividly and certainly there, under all our feet, and always had been. This Russian was a man who knew his way around an abyss. I might walk the abyss again, but from now on this Russian would walk with me, and had given me an entire company of fellow abyss walkers. I wish that I had met him when I first looked down and noticed that beneath me lay . . . nothing.

I did that eight days into my tenure at Harbour House. It's a wonder I made it until the middle of my sixteenth year, given the foundation and fabric of my parents' lives, but I had never been anywhere but Kenmore until then, and Kenmore was, and is, an invincible keeper of dreams. There was nothing in Kenmore to let the light of reality in on me, and conversely, there was nothing on all of Cape Cod to keep it out. I went from dreamwalker to shipwrecked in the space of five minutes.

Up until then it had gone almost as well as my father had said it would. I arrived in a paralysis of self-consciousness and terror and went through my first evening there almost immobile, but no one seemed to notice. The orientation session was full of young women who looked so unlike the girls my age in Kenmore as to be exotic, but since no one seemed to stare unduly at me, it soon dawned on me that maybe my father had been right about this, at least: maybe my plain, pale, blade-thin features and the hated height and thinness were, after all, somehow Eastern and therefore desirable, and here I would, at least on the surface, fit in. Certainly no one else in the dining room listening to the hard-voiced wife of the hotel's owner enumerate our duties looked anything at all like the belles of Kenmore. No one was ripe, no one was vivacious, no one was overtly or consciously cute, or even perky. Everyone was almost determinedly plain. I met a small sea of scrubbed, sun-touched faces and straight, clean hair and cool translucent eyes like mine, over ranks of plain cotton oxford-cloth shirts and faded Bermuda shorts, or shirtwaists unadorned save for circle pins. Weejuns and sneakers underscored everything.

All of them looked, from the neck up, anyway . . . like me. I looked like them. For the first time since the letter of acceptance came, a constricting band around my chest seemed to loosen just a little, and I took a slow, tentative breath.

That night I met the boys at a lobster roast for the staff, and for the first time encountered the careless, lithe-moving, assured young Ivy Leaguers my father had sent me East to meet, and felt the band tighten again. There

41

was not a swagger, a preen, a duck's-ass haircut, a pair of tight jeans, a sneer, or a frogged bicep in the lot of them. No Brylcream. No motorcycle boots. They wore wrinkled khakis and runover topsiders and ancient, shabby school sweatshirts, and brush cuts, and moved as if on balconies before cheering throngs. As little as I had had ken of the young men of Kenmore, I had less of these. But then, after I had introduced myself in my turn, hating my Southern accent, one of them detached himself from a group of his peers and shambled over to me and draped an arm around my shoulders and said, "Hey, theah, Miss Scahlett. Wheah you all from, honey chile?" And some sly taint of my father's in my blood surged to the fore, and I said, "My family is from Virginia, but we live in Alabama now."

"FFV, huh!" he said, and at my blank look, laughed and said, "You know, sweet thang, you jus' bein' modest. FFV as in Fust Fam'ly of Vuhginny. Ah thank I'll call you Effie."

And so Effie I became, that summer, to the boys and girls alike, and though I pretended to hate it, I loved it; it saved me. I kept it, for years. He had given me, in that moment, an identity, a history, and the keys to the kingdom. And a nickname. No one had ever given me a nickname before.

"Oh, okay," I said to my father, when he called that weekend to see how I was getting on. "The work is ghastly, and the food is awful, and the weather has been just horrible, but the other kids are okay. They call me Effie, for FFV; this boy nicknamed me that. We sort of go around together . . ."

"What's his name?" my father asked.

"Uh . . . well, they call him Stick. He's tall and skinny. I'm not sure I remember . . . oh. Peter. Peter Chapin. He goes to Amherst, but I forget where he lives . . ."

"It doesn't matter where he lives," my father said, and there was a hard triumph in his voice. "The Chapin and the Amherst are enough for now. Way to go, Katie. Effie. Effie Lee. You're doing great. You even sound different. Now listen, Kate. Remember what I said about not smiling too often? Don't do that, and for God's sake, don't giggle. And watch the drinking, I know what goes on on those beaches, and I know what they say about the girls who do too much of it. Smoke if you have to, and nurse one or two beers, but no more. And Katie . . . no necking. There'll be a lot of that, and a lot of the other things, too, and you'll get a lot of pressure to do it . . . but don't. You be the one who doesn't. In the first place, you're too young. In the second, you'll be the one they remember next winter when the prom and house party invitations go out. Effie Lee, the cool little gal from Virginia who wouldn't. It's much safer, and it's very provocative. You have a look about you, like a snow queen. Keep the mystery for now. This summer is for learning. Now. Do you need anything? Clothes! Mad money?"

"I could use a little money for clothes," I said. "I don't need much, but nothing I brought is right. I don't have any Bermudas, and I need a couple of oxford-cloth shirts, and some Weejuns. You know. Loafers."

"I know," he said. "Do they still wear pennies in them?"

"God, no," I said, and heard the change in my voice as well as the words. He laughed.

"Doin' good, Punkin," he said. "I'm proud of you. Didn't I tell you that girl didn't belong in Kenmore!"

On the eighth day, there was a new family at my station for breakfast, and their card read Childs, B. and family, Richmond, Va., and I knew that my benefactor had arrived.

When they came into the dining room and had seated themselves, I straightened my apron and went up to the table, smiling.

"Welcome to Harbour House," I said, my

44

heart bucking against my ribs. "I'm Katherine Lee."

They looked at me, a tall gray-blond man in a seersucker jacket and gray flannel pants who did, indeed, look rather like my father, with the eyes of a peregrine falcon; a small woman in a peach linen sundress, skin tanned to leather; an adolescent boy in white shirt and chinos; and a sulky girl a few years older than me, who might have been one of my dormitory mates. This must be the famous Sydney Childs. They looked at me pleasantly, except for Sydney, who pouted, and said nothing. And then the woman said, "Well, hello, Katherine Lee. You're new, aren't you? I'd remember that pretty face if you'd been here before. And is that by any chance a Southern accent I hear?"

She held out her hand to take a menu from me. I thrust one into it. There was another silence. Perhaps they had not gotten my name.

"Katherine Lee, Kate," I said again. "Charles Lee's daughter."

The man and woman looked at each other.

"Charles Lee," the woman murmured. "I'm not sure which Lee . . ."

"He was a KA at Virginia with you, Mr. Childs, and on the relay team," I said, my ears ringing, heat beginning to creep up from the collar of my blouse. "He . . . you . . . I believe you were kind enough to get me my job here this summer. I know he wrote you. I just wanted to thank you for that, we all appreciate it so much . . ."

My voice died. These people did not know who I was. They did not know who my father was.

"I'm sorry, I've been out of the office practically all spring and summer," Beauchamp Childs said, looking at his wife and then at me, and then down at his menu. "My secretary must have . . ."

"Lord, Champ, you'd forget your head if it wasn't glued on," Mrs. Childs chirped, and to me, "Forgive him, sweetie, he means well, but half the time he doesn't remember his own children. You're very welcome, and you tell your daddy we were happy to be able to help. You'll love Harbour House; Sydney worked here one summer when we told her we were throwing her out of the family if she didn't do some honest work, but I'm afraid it didn't take . . ."

The unrepentant Sydney rolled her eyes at her mother. Her perfect skin and nails told me she hadn't worked here or anywhere else one instant longer than she had to.

". . . so she's back to staying out all night and sleeping all day. Your daddy should be proud of you. You give him our regards, will you! I think we'll start with the fresh pineapple. We always do . . ."

I wrote their orders carefully on my pad and walked away, ears roaring, feet seeming to sink spongily into the floor. The surface felt suddenly treacherous, as if it were going to disintegrate. Behind me I heard Beauchamp Childs' slow voice saying querulously, ". . . have the foggiest idea. Helen must have written the letter. I don't remember him around the house or on the relay team, either . . ."

And the earth cracked open under me, and my father and the Kappa Alpha house and the University of Virginia and the sun-flooded cinder track of the athletic field slid into it, and all that I knew of reality and surety slid after them. It wasn't that I thought my father had lied, not then: that was an enormity I did not perceive until a good bit later. What I thought was that he had been there and no one had noticed, no one remembered. It was worse than a lie. It was, somehow, a death. It was as if I had been living for sixteen years with a ghost. With a handsome, vivid dead man who had an entire splendid and complicated life, knowledge, and a history that no one but I could see. No child can bear it that, to other people,

47

its father does not exist, is nothing. It is, for the child, death in the womb.

I went into the kitchen and swapped stations with dim Bopsy Sturtevant from Colby, who had the tables across the room in an ell, much poorer territory. After that I didn't see the family of Beauchamp Childs again, except at a distance. I will never forget that morning. It was, for me, the end of safety.

That night I borrowed Bopsy's Colby sweatshirt and drank five beers and smoked a Pall Mall and let Stick Chapin kiss me under the Harbour House pier. I bought Bermuda shorts and Weejuns and a circle pin that looked like real gold, and learned all the verses to "Lord Jeffrey Amherst," and "Going Back to Old Nassau," and "Roar, Lion, Roar." I learned, with a loathing that never left me, to sail a Beetle Cat, and to play tennis. I learned when to flirt and when to be enigmatic, when to say no and when to say yes. I did say yes, once, near the end of the summer, to Stick, in the back of his father's Mercedes, but God was good and Stick passed out before the Black Act was accomplished. I learned to dance really well and to drop nicknames and place names with an offhand *élan* that would have delighted my father, and I threw away my Revlon and Max Factor and bought Chapstick and sat endless hours in the sun, with lemon juice scalding the silver ash out of my hair. By the end of the summer it was the streaked tow of every other young woman of a certain station on the Eastern Seaboard.

I did all this with a sense of walking on charged black air; I felt like a soldier picking my way across an endless minefield. But it worked. I came home with an address book full of just the sort of contacts my father had envisioned, came home the remote young Easterner he had doubtless besieged Heaven for. At home, my peers in Kenmore took one look at me and shied away like nervous colts with a panther about, snickering their scorn and fear, but books were waiting for me, and I dove gratefully into them. Again, they sustained me.

My father was ecstatic. I could not have pleased him more if he had created me by his own hand, molecule by molecule.

"See how easy it is!" he said, over and over, as postcards arrived from Dartmouth, or the phone rang from Northampton.

And such was his power that I soon remembered only that, in a way, it had been the easiest thing I ever did. How truly terrible, that it is easier to live a total lie, become a lie yourself, than to assimilate a hated truth. But it was so for me, infinitely, and it has

49

been so for many of the people I have been the most drawn to. As I said, we know each other, and we find each other. And for a while, we live wonderfully well with the Big Lie.

It will get you, though. It always does, sooner or later. It bites the hands that feed it most assiduously and gratefully. The Big Lie can kill, and it can maim. Of the people closest to me in my own life, six have been victims of it. It stunted my mother and popped my father's skull like a walnut. It froze Ginger in eternal adolescence and me in an endless, featureless white present, trapped in my poisoned garden like Rappacini's daughter. It made a monster of Fig, and shattered Cecie like an eggshell. Of us, only Cecie was able to reassemble herself and dump the Big Lie for reality, take reality into herself like a lover. Only Cecie won. Yes, she did. Never think Cecie didn't win.

I went back to Harbour House the next summer, and the next, my last summer before I went away to Randolph Macon. By then I was so thoroughly Easternized that I chafed in my new, cool, polite way at not being allowed to consider Wellesley or Vassar or Smith. My father never said, but I think perhaps the tuition for the Seven Sisters proved ultimately beyond him. My grades

50

at James P. Folsom High in Kenmore would have entitled me to a substantial scholarship at any one of them; I had made sure of that. But he would not consider scholarships, or financial aid of any kind.

"That's not for you, Effie," he said. "That's for the hairnet and health shoe crowd. Randolph Macon is a fine school, you'll meet the same kind of girls there you would further north. After all, it's the South where you'll be spending your life; you'll meet the best of the Virginia boys at Macon. And it was your mother's alma mater. Besides, it's time to learn to ride. You can't live in hunt country if you can't at least sit a horse."

And so, after that last summer at Harbour House, where I cemented my Eastern facade irrevocably into place, ignoring the wails of my starved heart, I set off for the old white-columned women's college in Lynchburg. I arrived driving my own ancient, sleekly restored and finely tuned green MG sports car, top down, pink with two days of sun and pride, plain of feature and cool of demeanor and immediately indistinguishable from most other freshmen. I was bid, and pledged, Tri Omega without a hitch; it was, my father had said, the best of the three sororities I was even to consider. God knows whose genteel wife he hustled for the recommendation; I never asked and the Tri Os never told me. But I knew that wherever it came from, it must have been impeccable. I was on the First Preferential list. And I don't think my few expensive, exquisitely plain new clothes and the MG hurt, either. My father considered both investments in my future, and perhaps his. The MG had cost him less, in Kenmore, than a new Chevrolet convertible would have; no Kenmore belle would have thought of leaving for the University or Auburn or Randolph without the latter. And none would have driven the ancient MG to a dogfight. Charlie Culpepper tried to talk my father out of it. But Charles Lee's eye for such things never failed him; the MG was the perfect touch.

God knew what it all cost him, the car and the clothes and that first year's tuition, and the initiation fee for Tri Omega, and the gold and pearl pin, and the house fees, and all the rest. He went deeply and recklessly into debt for them. Joe McClure at Kenmore Bank and Trust made the loan himself.

When I pulled away from the old house on the Santee that September day, my mother cried and kissed me and my father kissed me and did not cry. There was something antic, a kind of capering, crazy glee, in his gray eyes.

52

"Godspeed, Effie Lee," he said exultantly. "Don't you come back here without a Kappa Alpha shield. I've written a few letters to brothers whose boys are at Virginia, you should be getting lots of calls."

My heart contracted with pain and fear at that, but I smiled and waved and said I would do that thing. By the time I reached Lynchburg, I had forgotten it.

It was a good year. The car and the clothes and the sorority were the groundwork, and I worked hard to build on them. I studied prodigiously, and made the freshman honorary. I obediently dated the Virginia KAs who did indeed call, and liked them well enough. I smiled infrequently, and necked never. I got proficient enough on a horse not to embarrass my father; after he saw me riding in the school ring when he and mother visited at Thanksgiving, he sent me a custom-made habit and boots. I still have them, in a trunk in the attic. It amuses Alan no end when I try them on, as I do sometimes. Effie Lee Abrams, sweetheart of the regiment, he calls me.

Randolph Macon was a world that seemed to value my good mind and manners and the Lee nose and name, and did not care if I bubbled or not. I learned some wonderful things and found a grateful and abiding love for learning, and made a few cool, light, seemly friendships, and liked those, and I probably would eventually have married a wellborn young scion who could have made my ravenous, fugitive father secure at last. But in the end, there wasn't time. Late that spring, after receiving no payments at all from him, Joe McClure called my father's loan at the bank, and the country club and the town merchants who had been carrying him for a long time joined the hunt, and on a sweet, cool May evening my father drove his late model Lincoln down to the banks of the Santee, well away from our house, and shot himself in the mouth with a .32 Smith and Wesson. They didn't find him until the next day. The car was a mess; Charlie Culpepper, who had been thinking reluctantly to repossess it, never did manage to sell it.

"Where did he get that gun? He never had any gun. I never saw a gun in this house in all the years we lived here," my mother sobbed, over and over. She was frail and diminished and groping, a pretty mistletoe whose host oak had toppled. "He must have borrowed it; it was all an awful impulse . . ."

Dry-eyed, holding her hands and patting them, my heart stone in my chest, I knew better. I had read the Andrew Turnbull biography of Hemingway in my father's bookcase almost as often as he had. The gun was precisely the same make and model with which Hemingway's father had shot himself and which his monstrous mother had sent him: my father had used Hemingway's gun. He may even have used it for the same reasons that, finally, Hemingway did. It must have been long and carefully planned.

My poor father. Even his death was a lie.

I only cried once during that entire awful time, though my mother and, it seemed, every other woman in Kenmore, wept constantly. The morning after the funeral, J. R. Phipps, the other agent in my father's jury-rigged insurance company, called to say that my father had, the year before, taken out a small policy specifically to benefit my education, and with great care it should see me through one of our state institutions. I did cry then, bitterly and hopelessly and for many hours, cried in my locked room for my father and his sad, malignant foolishness, and for myself, and for Randolph Macon and the vanished East. Cried for the loss of the ersatz accepting life I had found in both, and for all other things forever lost to me. I don't remember crying for my father ever again. For nearly a year I did not even mention his death.

But I cried for Randolph Macon and the East many more times that next year, for at first I was profoundly unhappy at Randolph University. I had chosen it because it sounded most like the school I had loved and left behind, and I entered the School of Interior Design that fall, and moved into the Tri Omega house my second quarter there. But neither school nor sorority made me welcome. The sorority, for all practical purposes, had to take me, since I was a transfer in good standing, but it was plain that they did not know what to do with me. I knew that my new sisters thought me strange, affected, and as exotically odd looking as a giraffe in my height and slenderness, among all the cinch-waisted and diminutive cheerleaders and fraternity sweethearts and beauty queens. My shyness and reserve and heavy, secret, dead grief they thought to be conceit, and my plain, conservative cottons and tweeds made their crinolines and pushup bras seem very faintly trashy. They never said so, but I saw it in their eyes. I did not dare even unpack the habit and boots. I knew Amherst and Yale songs and wrote to girls named Muffy and Smitty at schools like Wellesley and Sarah Lawrence, and I had seen plays in New York and rode horses and had a cocktail shaker with a Hasty Pudding seal on it. I myself heard the rumors that I knew how to make a martini, and the ones that I was rich and blueblooded. I knew that the Tri Os reveled in the patina I lent the chapter, even as they mimicked my slouch and my cool voice and my habit of going completely without makeup. But they did it behind my back.

The Tri O I was assigned to room with was pinned to an ATO and spent every waking moment until curfew with him, and spent the hours after that pointedly studying· in other rooms, coming back to ours only after I had put out the lights, creeping ostentatiously into bed in darkness and silence. She had no classes until eleven in the mornings, and so I dressed in the dark and left the room long before she stirred. If she had not gotten pregnant and dropped out of school to marry her ATO and follow him off on his summer ROTC cruise, I might not have been able to stick the misery, and I truly don't know what would have become of me then.

But she did, and one afternoon toward Thanksgiving, only a few days after she had gone, my door opened and a girl I had never seen before put a copperthatched head around it and grinned a three-cornered dimple-flickering grin, and said in a precise, Tidewater voice, "Is this the dreaded Temple of the Unclean?"

And I answered, on a rush of lightness and deliverance, "It is. Abandon all hope, ye who enter here."

"Consider it abandoned," Cecie said, and tossed a load of clothes into the room and followed them in, and after that everything was all right.

CHAPTER THREE

At noon this past Labor Day Alan came out into the garden, where I was ripping witch grass out of the poppies. Next to dodder it is the seaside weed I hate most; it looks like a delicate green mist, but it can choke an entire bed of the crumpled-silk poppies before they even shake out their petals to the sun. I have them in all colors this year: lilac, crimson, scarlet, rose, white, golden yellow, pure burning orange. I put them out this spring, as bedding plants. Bedding plants are as far ahead as I allow myself to plan. I do not plant perennials anymore, only annuals.

Alan was wearing only his faded old tattersall bathing trunks, that he has had, I believe, since the summer we went to Bermuda when Stephen was two. Twenty-five years ago. Almost impossible to believe; looking at Alan, barefoot on the gray weathered deck, he looked nearer twenty-five himself, instead of the forty-eight he is. I thought again how like a Russian dancer he looked, or an acrobat in the Tsar's circus. That fancy struck me the first time I ever saw him in his undershorts. He was, and is, dark, small, lithe, and perfectly made, with a narrow waist and broad shoulders and slender, sculpted muscles. I still love the feel of his solid body under my hands. I think I would hate the feel of a larger one. He is just as tall as I am when I am not wearing high heels, and his hair and beard are only just now beginning to be threaded with gray. His brown eyes are the brilliant liquid of an adolescent's. Nothing about Alan, bone, tissue, blood, or muscle, has begun to dry out yet. He puts it down to his Eastern European heritage. He is a Jew from Minsk, or his father was, at any rate. Alan grew up in Brooklyn Heights.

"Regular collagen factories, we are," he says, of his blooming skin and moist mouth and eyes and smooth, sliding movements. "My grandfather Moishe, at a hundred and eight, could still kiss his elbow and jerk off at the same time. Grandma Vera was a belly dancer in the court of the Tsar until she was ninety."

He sat down on the flattened chaise longue behind me and did not speak. The silence spun out. It made me restless; it broke the mindless fugue of sun on my back and head and sea in my ears, that I had allowed myself to sink deep into. These hot, late-summer days in our garden behind the dunes of Long Island are the most I know of pure timelessness, and they sustain me like air, like water. Finally, without looking over my shoulder at him, I said, "What's up?"

"You got a letter," he said. "I thought you might want to read it."

"Not right now," I said. "Leave it on the table and I'll read it when I stop for lunch. Crab salad okay with you? And I got some Iron Horse at Silver's."

"I think you ought to read this one now," Alan said, and then I did turn around on my heels and look up at him. He was smiling, though; no cause there for alarm.

"Is there a return address?" I said.

"Yep. It's from Mrs. P. C. Sibley, Croatan Cottage, Nag's Head, North Carolina. Would that be your friend Ginger Fowler, by any chance?"

I turned back to the witch grass.

"You know it is," I said.

I went on with my digging, but he did not go away. Finally I said, "Alan, I really don't want to read it right now. I'll do it later. Make us a Bloody Mary and I'll get lunch, and then I'll read it. If I don't get this damned stuff out of here it's going to murder the last of my poppies."

"The first frost is going to do that anyway," he said. "Come on, Kate. You've hidden from her for twenty-eight years. Him, too.

61

I want to hear what she has to say even if you don't."

"You open it, then, and tell me what it says," I said, aware that my heart had begun to hammer against my ribs, hating the feeling. I have spent the last four and a half years in flight from that awful, breath-sucking fusillade.

"I will," Alan said, and I heard the sound of paper tearing. Then nothing.

"Oh, shit," I said finally, getting up and wiping my hands on the knees of my blue jeans. "Okay, let's have it. I hate this intrigue. What does my dear good friend Virginia Sibley, née Fowler, have to say?"

"She says she wants you to come visit her at their place on the Outer Banks the last week of this month. She says she's asking the others of you who shared the suite at Randolph, that it's just going to be the four of you . . . I gather the divine Paul will not be in residence — and she'd give anything in the world if you'd come. She says it's been more than twenty-five years since she's heard from you, which will not, I gather, be a surprise to you, and she'd have written or called much sooner but nobody knew where you were. That won't surprise you either, I'm sure. She got your address from that new alumni directory Randolph just put out. I sent your name in to it last winter."

I turned back to the witch grass. It has long, exquisite white roots as fine as hair, that make a matted filigree underground that will eventually shut the soil's nutrients away from whatever seeks to live in it. Even though I loathe it, I have been grateful to it this past summer. It has given me a tangible battle in which to engage myself.

After a while Alan said, "You think you might like to go?"

"No," I said.

"You ought to, Kate."

"No. I have too much to do here. Please don't push me on this, Alan. There's nothing of my life left back there. It's all here. It's with you."

He took a deep breath and let it out. Then he said, "No, it isn't. It isn't here with me. It's here with your sickness. We've been living in your sickness like people live under water. We're drowning in it. And we *will* drown, you will, if you don't get out of it. I want you to go. Katie, you loved this gal once . . ."

I did not reply. Please don't, I thought, digging deep into the earth with my fingers. Please shut up. Please stop.

"Cecie's going to be there," Alan said. "Wouldn't you like to see Cecie, after all this time? From what you've told me you'll never have another friend like that."

I rounded on him fiercely, toppling over from my squat to land on the hot planks of the deck. I was very angry. He had broken one of our primary rules. Over my head a flight of gulls wheeled, and I felt on my flaming cheeks the freshening wind that meant the turn of the tide. The flag snapped out full from its pole beside the steps down through the dunes, down to the beach.

"I especially wouldn't like to see Cecie again," I said. "Why should I? She's made it abundantly clear she doesn't want to see me. She didn't even come to my graduation. She's never even written. She's never even called. Not once, in twenty-eight years. Why should I want to see her now?"

"You didn't write either," Alan said. "You haven't called her, either. Maybe she didn't know where you were. Ginger didn't . . ."

"I did call her, once. She never called back. And I wrote; she never answered. Besides, she could have found out where I was," I said. "She knew where my mother lived. She must have known how I was hurting, she must have known why I didn't get in touch . . ."

"How could she know, unless you told her?" he said. "The truth is, Kate, that you ran. You just up and ran, and you never

64

looked back. Maybe she couldn't call you; maybe something went bad for her, too. You've had some terribly hard knocks, but you're not the only one. Nobody ever is. Ginger says in her letter Cecie has had an awfully hard time."

I stared at the mass of whitish-green in my hands, seeing in it, not the roots of the killer of my poppies, but the living copper silk of Cecie Hart's hair, as I struggled to anchor a flimsy crown of white wax candles on it. The candles were burning, and Cecie was yelping with laughter and an occasional drip of candle wax, and I was laughing so hard that I thought I would wet the filmy nylon-curtain pants of my harem outfit. We were dressing for the Beaux Arts Ball in our junior year at Randolph, and I was going as Scheherazade and she as Grimm's Snow Queen.

"Be still, Cecie, or you'll burn yourself up," I heard my young voice gasp, and across the years, heard hers: " 'Oh, life is a glorious cycle of song, a medley of extemporanea,' " she chanted. We were reading Dorothy Parker that year. " 'And love is a thing that can never go wrong . . . *and I am Marie of Rumania,*' " we shouted together.

"That's not all Ginger says," Alan's voice broke in. "She says, 'I want you to come because I want to try to tell you how sorry I am about everything. I've known I was wrong to do what I did for a long time now, and I want to try to find a way to make it up to you. I need to know that you have a happy life. I miss you. I think you were the best one of us.' "

He was quiet, and I knew he was waiting for me to say something. But I did not; other voices filled the silence in my head.

" '. . . and love is a thing that can never go wrong, and *I am Marie of Rumania.*' "

Oh, Cecie . . .

When I first met her, I thought she looked like a garden elf, one of those Disneyesque little plaster figurines designed to peer out from beneath shrubbery or lurk in flower borders. It was not that she was grotesque, it was just that she was so vivid and so tiny. Even on a campus where petite cheerleaders and majorettes were worshiped like pocket Venuses, and taller unfortunates drooped their duck's-ass heads and padded around in soft leather Capezio shells even in January in order to look up sidewise under their Maybellined lashes at stocky, bull-necked, bandy-legged football players, Cecie was small enough to turn heads. Her size was accompanied by a noticeable lack of cuteness; even at four feet ten, Cecie could stalk like a duchess and freeze a fool at forty paces with her round blue stare. The Tri Omegas were always after her to cut her hair, which rioted all over her small head in red ringlets, like a honeysuckle thicket, giving her an antic Orphan-Annie aspect. And her purple-blue eyes were magnified like pansies behind her thick hornrimmed glasses, which completed the Annie look to perfection.

"You'd be so precious if you'd cut your hair and get some harlequins," I remember Sookie Carmichael saying to her once, after a chapter meeting. "Not that you're not cute as pie now; we all know that. But you're hiding your looks under a basket." Sookie never quite got it right. "And those clumpy saddle oxfords and thick tweed skirts don't do a thing for your darling little figure. Why don't you let me and Bitsy fix you up? You'd have to beat the boys off with a stick."

"A firehose would do fine, Sookie," Cecie said in her precise Virginia voice. I loved that voice. "Besides, if I were just like y'all we'd look like a tribe of pygmies around here. No fraternities would dare come around, scared they'd get eaten alive. Not that they aren't, anyway. Besides, y'all need me for dramatic contrast. Makes you look better."

And she smiled, her three-cornered kitten's

smile, that set the dimples flickering.

"Well," Sookie said, not sure if she had been delicately skewered or complimented.

"That was mean," I giggled to Cecie later. "She only wants you to have a date every night. Fit in. Be happy. All that stuff."

"She only wants me not to embarrass the chapter by never being asked out," Cecie snorted. "Lord, she's a fool. Can you imagine me in harlequin glasses with rhinestones?"

I couldn't. Despite her size and her light, sweet voice there was nothing trivial about Cecie Hart. She was smart, she was tough, and she was singleminded in the extreme when it came to her studies. She studied constantly and with relish; she was one of the few people I ever met, besides myself and Fig Newton, who actually liked the process as well as the fruits of it, the A's, the Dean's List, the honoraries. Her clothes were indeed as severe and utilitarian as the chapter thought they were: serviceable tweeds and flannel skirts, plain, good sweater sets, tailored drip-dry shirts and shirtwaists, saddle oxfords. She owned one coat, a venerable camel's hair, and one raincoat, a khaki London Fog. There were few of them, and she took exquisite care of them. She pressed, mended, spot-cleaned, hemmed. She was the only one of us who never sent her laundry home. Sometimes, when she wasn't studying, she sewed for herself, using accomplished small stitches, and there were no cut corners or loose threads.

"I learned to sew in the convent; all of us could sew like demons by the time we got out," she said. "Kept the sisters in altar cloths, we did."

Cecie's parents had died in an automobile wreck when she was very small, along with an older brother; she did not remember them. A grandmother and a trio of spinster aunts had raised her in the big old family homeplace by the water, on the Eastern Shore. They were tiny, cultivated, devout Catholics who taught her music and sewing and what she called Advanced Ladyhood, and sent her to convent school when she was barely nine. They protected and adored her, if at a gentle remove, and the nuns had not been able to outwit or repress her, and it had been a good childhood, if an unworldly and rather lonely one. Her family was rich in culture and affection and antecedents but poor as church mice materially. They could barely send her out of state to school, even with the scholarships and the financial aid. Cecie, who planned to go on to law school after her graduation, knew it was up to her to make their investment work and get herself through Duke Law. Genteel poverty was one reason we knew each other down to the bottoms of our souls when we first met. As money calls out to money, so does the lack of it cry aloud to its own. It was the first of the great bonds between us.

The second was our utter lack of knowledge of what constituted reality. Cecie was pragmatic and tough in her self-discipline, but she was, in her microcosmic world born of loneliness and the company of naive, genteel old women and nuns, a match for me in all respects. Neither of us could have identified "real Life" when we met it, but it was perhaps less a handicap then than it would be today. Few young women of the late Fifties knew much about real life. "Get real" were words most of us had never heard, from our parents or anyone else. Cecie and I devoted the three years left to us at Randolph to the strict avoidance of real life, and succeeded gloriously. Sometimes I think I was the worst thing that could have happened to Cecie Hart. I was running from life, and something deep in her ardent soul was, even then and without her knowledge or permission, running toward it. I have to wonder, now, if I had not been there, whether Cecie might have met it earlier and with happier results. But I was there, and on the November day that she tossed her clothes into my room the great friendship of my life was born, and in a way, though neither of us ever named it, the great love.

They *are* love, those rare, blinding early friendships. Not everyone has them, and almost no one gets more than one. The others, the later ones, are not the same. These first grow in a soil found only in the country of the young, and are possible only there, because their medium is unbroken time and proximity and discovery, and later there is not enough of any of those for the total, ongoing immersions that these friendships are. They are not sexual in nature, or at least most are not; though perhaps, as the Freudians claim, there is no deep relationship that isn't, at bottom. But I do not think mine with Cecie had that dark note in it. We were both, at that time, simply too afraid of physical love. It had, however, much else that an intense love affair has: it charmed us, soothed us, fed us, consumed us. We discovered in each other and ourselves worlds, galaxies, a universe. Discovery, I think, is the hallmark, the one constant. Sadly, most of us are done with that by the time we reach full adulthood. These friendships may continue past first youth, but I don't think they often do. Their primary strength is that fire of exploration and validation. The friend becomes a cicerone, to go with you down to the bottom of your deepest depths, and out to the farthest crannies of your being. All your senses are open, all your reservoirs fill up at a prodigious rate, all your motors hum. A friendship like that is like the start of life, when, they say, a child learns more in a few short months than he ever will again. It was like that with Cecie and me. We could not get enough of each other, and we could not get enough of life, even though it was a life that did not exist except in the bright circle of air in which we moved together.

From the start we were called Mutt and Jeff. It was inevitable, with my lanky height and her childlike slightness, and the air of otherness that hovered around us. We stank of the abyss; of course we did. Neither of us minded. Apart, we might have smarted under the slight, stinging surf of talk that lapped around us; together we simply laughed. It is what I remember most of those three years, the laughter. We did not laugh at everything, of course, but we came near it. It was the laughter of perfect ease and utter delight; it was to us like deep drafts of air, after years of lungs constricted by too-narrow bodies. I don't remember too many days that did not begin with laughter at something, or end with it.

No matter how far apart we had been during

the days, we touched base with each other automatically in the evenings. After classes, we ate together and studied together and visited up and down the hall together and went down for cokes or coffee together, and when we had somewhere to go, we went together. When we were apart during holidays and breaks, we wrote each other every day. Usually we played records and read in our room, reading aloud to each other and laughing, or, less often, sharing the passages that touched subterranean chords and wells in us, and brought the easy, ardent tears of untouched romantics to our eyes. We read all of Dorothy Parker, adoring and adopting that graceful, inch-deep cynicism: " 'Where's the man could ease a heart like a satin gown?' " we would chant to each other. And, " 'The sun's gone dim and the moon's turned black, for I loved him and he didn't love back,' " and " 'Scratch a lover, and find a foe,' " and " 'Guns aren't lawful; Nooses give; Gas smells awful; You might as well live.' " No two young women have ever been so unjaded, or so eager to be.

We read other poetry, too, mostly Irish and English. All touched with the dark romanticism that flourished between the World Wars. I remember that when we first encountered the blood and snot and howling of the

73

postwar poets, her nostrils whitened with disgust and I felt frightened and betrayed, as if I had been lured by Pan's pipes to the mouth of a snake pit. We turned then to Shakespeare or Dickens or Kipling, or each brought out for the other the early loves we had found in pages: I brought Maupassant and Conan Doyle and the Greek and Norse myths and laid them in her lap; she led me to *The Waterbabies,* and *Wind in the Willows,* and Richard Halliburton's *Royal Road to Romance.*

" 'There is nothing half so worthwhile as simply messing about in boats,' " she would paraphrase Rat, talking of her childhood beside the shallow, blood-warm waters of Chesapeake Bay.

" 'Roll on, thou deep and dark blue ocean, roll,' " I would intone, telling her of the great, cold seas off Cape Cod.

And always, over and around and under it all, there was the music.

It was that viscid no-man's-land that followed the prowling sexual exuberance of the Fifties' black rhythm and blues. "Junglebunny stuff," I could hear my father saying. The soprano *weltschmerz* of the teen *ang*sters ruled. Connie Francis whined about everybody being somebody's fool and told us that all we had to do to be happy was to go where the boys were. Brenda Lee was sorry. The

Everly Brothers groveled about being Cathy's clown. The Shirelles wondered cloyingly if someone would love them tomorrow. The hard-grooving Motown sound had not yet caught on, at least not in the Deep South. The lightlessly relevant folk rockers and the acid-drowned San Francisco sound and the cheeky, preening British had not yet come to town. At Randolph, the flipped and brush-cut young twisted and hully-gullied and jitterbugged and dirty-bopped and slow-danced to Dion and the Belmonts, and the Four Seasons and the Drifters and the Everly Brothers and Buddy Holly. Cecie and I could and did twist and bop as well as the next, but neither of us liked the music. To me it remained a kind of body noise, the ceaseless, subterranean pulse of my generation, fore-runner to the white noise of the Seventies. Our music, Cecie's and mine, was music to be listened to and talked or even wept over, music with a dark thread in it, or else the soaring wings of Romance with a capital R. The first thing we did when we walked into our room, after tossing our books on our beds and shucking out of our clothes and into dusters or Bermudas, was to thumb through the stained pile of LPs in the window seat and select a groaning stack and plunk them onto my old gray Webcor portable.

From then on until we finally went to bed, whatever we did was done to music.

One song, a treacly ballad called "While We're Young," was our unofficial anthem. "Songs were made to sing while we're young," we warbled and trilled in our faltering sopranos. "Every day is spring, while we're young . . ."

It wasn't the "young" of the later Sixties that we meant, that megamovement lurking only a few years ahead, that youthquake that wrenched an entire culture apart and spewed up flower children, Woodstock, psychedelics and drugs and love beads and bare feet and fire-blooming hawks and equally savage doves. It was a generic kind of youngness, a lift and swing of heart, a leap of pulse, a thrill of flesh, a cup-brimming brew of joy and yearning and silliness and tenderness and tears and laughter and prickling skin and pure sensation . . . we named it Impulse. Or sometimes, Romance. But it was, purely and simply, the being of young in a time of timelessness. And our music flowed through it like spilled May wine on morning grass.

We would . . . we did . . . go on to other kinds of music, other voices in other rooms, and the music of those brief years seemed, in retrospect, shallow and thin to us, perhaps even trivial. At least it did to me. With a few exceptions, I did not ever choose to play those old albums again. But still, even now, when I hear a snatch of "On the Street Where You Live," or a spilled splash of Tchaikovsky, or a sweet surge of Percy Faith, I am back with Cecie Hart, sitting on our twin beds on the top floor of the Tri Omega house in Randolph, Alabama, late into a May night, with moonlight and the heartbreaking scent of mimosa flooding into our window, talking, talking. Or I hear a sorrowing, searching curl of Mendelssohn's violins, and there we are, same place, same hour of night, but in thick quilted robes now, with sleet ticking against the black, frosted windows and the radiator hissing, sipping cups of thin, vile coffee made from powdered Maxwell House and hot tap water.

"Ugh," Cecie always said, shaking herself all over like a wet dog. "Coffee always smells like it should be thick and wonderful, like hot chocolate, and it always tastes . . . like this. Like pony piss."

And she would fish a dime out of her purse and go padding down to the basement and get a bottle of Coca Cola and a Baby Ruth from the machine, and bring me back a package of barbecued chips, and we would talk some more.

Always, always, like the music, the talking.

We talked about the things that young girls in dormitories and sorority houses all over the country did, in that time: about who was dating who and who wasn't dating at all and who had just broken up and who looked like a sure thing for a pin before the quarter was out. We talked about who we liked and who we loved and who we didn't like and who we hated and about a few who were simply beyond dislike and beneath contempt. Because there were very few things that we could not say to each other, we were able to admit that a few of our Tri O sisters fell into the latter categories.

"You'd think she was proud of that water buffalo ass, the way she prances around here naked. All she needs is a cowbird on her head," Cecie would snort. She was modest in the extreme, no doubt a stigma of the convent. I cannot ever remember seeing her completely naked.

"If she kisses me goodnight one more time to see if I've been drinking I'm going to throw up on her," I would say. Or, "She'd never on earth have passed that sociology exam if she hadn't been a k-ing that old fool all quarter. She was over there typing for him every afternoon last week. That brown stain on her chin ain't nicotine, friends."

We would look at each other, and burst into simultaneous song: "There is a brown ring . . . around her nose . . . and every day it grows and grows . . ."

And collapse into a heap, with weak, eye-watering laughter, laughter that I sometimes sought to keep going for the sheer pleasure of hearing Cecie laugh. It was a chiming, crystal thing, that laugh, that spiraled up and up until it teetered on the edge of affectation, and then it plunged suddenly into a rich, froggy guttiness, and took off upward again. People always laughed along with Cecie, even when they did not know what the joke was, and one of her prolonged late-night spells brought sisters to our door, knuckling their eyes from sleep, mouths twitching with answering laughter, to see what on earth was so funny. It was not often that we could tell them.

We talked of ourselves. Within months of her moving in with me, the dam of stony reticence that had kept the full spate of reality away from my consciousness cracked, and I told Cecie things I had not told a living soul, and would not, again, until much later. I never let the dam crumble entirely; the abyss yawned too blackly, the cold black sea of actuality pounded too savagely. But I did not move to mend the crack, either, and I am sure Cecie extrapolated almost the entire truth about me from the trickle I let through. I think she always saw me much plainer than I did myself, and vice versa. The trust we invested in each other was far more enormous . . . but fragile . . . than we realized.

"I'm not a Virginia Lee," I said abruptly one night, apropos of nothing. "I'm not a Virginian at all. And I don't have any money to speak of. The whole thing was my father's idea."

I could not look at her, and my heart was near to leaping out of my chest. The breath of the abyss blasted furiously up around me.

"Well, I knew that about the Lees," Cecie said mildly, not looking at me, either. "And I didn't much think you were a Virginian. My aunts know every Lee in the Old Dominion, quick or dead. They couldn't place your family. I hope it's not going to bother you that you told me. Lord knows, money is the very least important thing up home, and I don't care about your father. He sounds like an interesting man."

"Was," I said. "He's dead. But you're right, he really was an interesting man."

She did look at me then, briefly and delicately. I could feel the weight of it on my cheek and neck.

"I'm sorry about that," she said. "It's hard

not to have parents. No matter how kind everybody else is, it's still hard."

She had never spoken of her own feelings about the loss of her family; that lay behind the door deep within her, that she did not open for me or anyone else. I was able to look at her then. Something welled up, warm and tremulous, inside me. It was not pity, but a stronger, purer thing altogether. Love, probably, though I was so unaccustomed to it that I did not know it then.

"My father shot himself," I said. "He did it last year, when he lost his money. It's why I'm here. The stuff about Randolph having a better interior design school was crap."

It was a gift to her, to thank her for accepting and containing the proffered truth of me, for giving me a glimpse of her own. And it was a kind of insurance. I sensed rather than knew that to hand someone the secrets of your heart is to bind them to you. I was right about that with Cecie; I did not learn until later that it is not always true. Not even usually.

"I want you to know two things," she said in the same voice that she might say good morning, or remark on the weather. "And then we won't talk about this anymore, because we don't need to. The first is, I will never tell anybody what you've told me. And the second is, I've never really been sorry that my parents and brother died. I've sort of liked it. I don't remember them, and I've gotten attention and love and things that I never would have had if they'd lived; people have always gone out of their way to please me because they've felt sorry for me. I'd never have made it to college if Bobby had lived; there wasn't enough money, and with the Harts it's always the sons who go. Not the daughters. So. Enough. Let's go out to Dairyland and get a limeade. My treat."

We shared, in so far as we could, our provenance. She told me about the strange, lost, primordial water-world of the Tidewater and the great Bay, about the seasons and the tides and the shining, writhing blue crabs that she pulled from the water on the dock in front of her grandmother's house, and the waterfowl and vast, loose Vs of geese that passed over each spring and fall on their way north and south. Once she had been on her way to mass and had stopped to watch the wild geese pass overhead and never made mass at all.

"Grammy found out about it and really let me have it; you'd have thought I was bound for hell that minute. But you know, it seemed as much like church to me as any service I've ever been to," she said.

She told me about the rich, dense ecosystem of the Tidewater, and about the stars and the clouds and the wild things of the Chesapeake. Cecie's curiosity about and love for the natural world was a living thing. She told me about her garden at home in the cove. She was passionate about that. Our room swam perpetually in a fetid green miasma of hanging and potted plants, and she is the only person I have ever known who really could root and grow splendid, shining plants from avocado pits. She talked to them all, sometimes in light, rapid convent French.

In return, I told her about sailing and tennis and horses and the East. I did not think it was a fair trade even then. I never thought to tell her about my life in Kenmore. To me it was no more real by then than something I had read in a book, long ago.

The one thing that Cecie and I did not talk about, except obliquely and with an ersatz veneer of weary sophistication, was sex. Here we were, I am convinced, unique, at least within the perimeters of Randolph University. All around us, in dormitory and sorority rooms, in parked cars and on blankets out at the lake and in fraternity party rooms, everyone talked of It and a good many did It. Despite the fact that pregnancy loomed like a glittering killer iceberg, and every quarter a few girls dropped out of school and disappeared from view, or married in haste and pretended it was a matter of glorious Impulse, sex was the universal obsession and the motive power behind all our music and dancing, the market impulse behind the sales of Fire and Ice lipstick and Tonis and Peter Pans and Listerine — the reason many of us were in college at all.

Looking back, it seems to me that on any given night the very campus rocked, quietly and cosmically, like Emma Bovary's carriage. I don't think the advent of The Pill, a few years later, resulted in many more instances of the Black Act and the Dirty Deed. I just think it wiped out a great deal of the monthly breath-held terror. It was not always possible to tell who was Doing It; if you were, you did not admit it, and the raw evidence of beard burn and hickies and ravenously smeared lipstick could just as well mean HP . . . heavy petting, an amenity permissible and even expected of pinned and engaged girls. There were no sanctions at all against the boys at Randolph. It was simply assumed that every boy who wanted to, did, whenever the urge struck. Since most of the girls denied it, I suppose we assumed that the guys were getting it from the same small group of rosy roundheels, but somehow the subject never came up. Guys did, we didn't . . . or did and said we didn't. *Simplis in extremis.*

But Cecie and I simply never talked of it. Oh, we learned and sang the raunchy songs with relish, and made the right noises when we were part of a group who was talking about it. Sooner or later every group did; where there were three or more of us gathered together in Its name, there It was also. Cecie would blow twin plumes of Pall Mall smoke through her nostrils, something it had taken her months of choking and coughing to master, when Ginger came crashing exuberantly into our room smeared from forehead to knee with lipstick caroling, "Yum, that SAE Bets fixed me up with is hot to trot."

"You've really got both feet in the trough tonight, Fowler," Cecie would drawl, and Ginger would burble with laughter. She relished physical touching the way a puppy did romping, and sought it, I expect, in the same happy-go-lucky spirit. We never knew just how far she went, but it was impossible to censure her for it. As well to censure a golden setter joyfully romping out of the water, shaking himself.

And I was able to say, world-wearily and through half-lowered lids, "It's even better with a little Bailey's Beach sand thrown in," when someone spoke slyly of an evening of making out. And everyone would laugh, and the looks that were thrown at me under Maybellined lashes told me that I was considered sophisticated in the extreme, undoubtedly a veteran of who knew what Kama Sutric Eastern excesses.

Even Fig Newton sometimes got into the act, with the grace of a charging rhino. One night she wiggled her toes in our faces and sang out, "Look, I shaved them. Makes them fun to suck."

"Ugh, Fig, YUCK," we shouted her down.

"Well, Sister does it," she said defensively.

"I'd as soon suck a rotten persimmon," Cecie said later that night, when we were alone. "Do you think Sister really does shave her toes?"

"She says she does," I said.

"Does Franklin really . . . you know, suck them?"

"I guess he does," I said. "Why on earth else would you shave them?"

Cecie gave the small all-over shiver that meant, with her, disgust and annoyance.

"The convent looks better and better," she said.

I think she more than half meant it. It's hard to say what a convent education does to young women on the deepest level; later I would meet many who seemed much the wilder and more wanton for theirs, as if each overtly physical act had a double meaning, the one that informed it in the moment and the one that said to the sisters, many long dead, *"That* to you, and *that,* and *that!"* But there was not much doubt what it had done to Cecie. About sex, as about other things to a lesser degree, she was chaste and remote. And it somehow annoyed her. After we read *Lady Chatterley's Lover* and *The Tropic of Cancer,* this time not aloud, she said, "I don't think it would be half so bad if you weren't expected to make those noises . . . during it. And if you could just do it in utter darkness and privacy, and not talk endlessly about it. But it just sounds messy and loud and somehow public, and there's no way it can be graceful. What a shame there's no other way to get children."

"You don't have to be loud or public about it," I said, amused. "Who says you do? Lord, Cecie, for all we know it's as graceful as *Swan Lake.* How do you know what it looks like?"

"Because I do," she said. "Somehow I know it looks just like that what's-her-name in

Henry Miller's book, who pulled up her dress and did it to herself in the middle of the Tottenham Court Road. *God!* Not me, no thank you."

And I think she did mean that. Marriage and children were not in any of our talk at night, not even an alliance of any sort. Sometimes we made vague talk about Great Loves, and the suffering they entailed, but if we got more specific than that, we set foot on a heavily mined path that led inevitably to It, and we fled from it. She shied away, I am certain, out of a deep fastidiousness of soul. I shied out of embarrassment and fear of the ensuing entanglement. In my mind, It meant, inevitably, marriage, and that meant that strange, duplicitous, abyss-dance that had linked my father and mother.

And so I was able to say, when she said, "No thank you," "Amen." But I wondered about sex, endlessly and sometimes near obsessively. I would lie in bed at night, after we had turned off our lights, and move around two anonymous, androgynous figures in my head like cutout paper dolls, trying this position and that, and I still could not quite figure out what you actually did. Who gets on top of who? If it's him, does he mash the breath out of her? If it's her, how does it get up in her? I had seen male genitalia only in paintings and statues, cozy, chunky bundles that dangled straight down. Even if he lay on top, how would he get it inside her? And then what? Does that stuff come right out into her, or do you have to wait for it; is it like pushing the button on a can of shaving cream? Do they move? Does he? Does she? How do you know when it's over?

And the questions at the heart of it all: Does it hurt, and will I want to?

It did not seem likely to me, on those nights, that I would ever learn the answers, though common sense told me that one day even I would cross that damp chasm between those who had done It and those who had not. But my heart didn't believe it. Meanwhile, there was Romance and Impulse, and songs to be sung . . . while we were young . . .

And so we talked, if we talked of the future at all, about careers, and what we would do after school. I planned to go straight to New York and plunge myself into the esoteric world of Eames and Bertoia and Saarinen furniture and rich, thick textiles and bright, explosive abstract paintings and cool, sculpted white houses by the sea. Cecie meant to go through Duke Law, pass the Virginia bar, and then take off for a couple of years and roam the world before settling down to practice some nebulous, unnamed branch of law in an old house on the shore where water light danced on walls and ceilings and the tide slapped hollowly under a silver-gray dock. Neither of us thought how we would get from graduation day to those distant, shining futures, but neither of us doubted that the worlds of international design and law would welcome us with open arms. Our grades, after all, were exemplary.

"Come with me to Europe before we start to work," she would say. "It won't cost anything; we'll backpack and get jobs along the way if we need to."

"You come to New York with me," I replied. "You can practice out on Long Island if you have to have water and gray shingles, and I can come out on weekends, and we can earn enough to go to Europe in style."

"You're going to be perfectly happy to find somewhere wonderful and stay, Kate," she said. "But I'm always going to want to see what's around the next turn."

It was a simplistic prophecy, but I thought at the time it probably had a grain of truth in it. I also thought that somehow, when all was said and done, Cecie and I would stay close to each other through our lives. It was what you do think, in the middle of those devouring early friendships. That it is simply ludicrous to think that anything, even marriage, even death, can broach them, such is their power and sweetness.

Cecie was always the one of us who had doubts about that.

"You're going to meet somebody and get pinned and then married," she would say. "You've just got that look about you, no matter what you say. It's not that you don't date. You just haven't found anybody with any sense yet. Wait till you do."

"Not now," I said. "Not yet. I date just for fun now. There isn't anybody at Randolph I'm interested in. Besides, you date, too."

She did; and in spite — or perhaps because of — the Lee nose and the so-called Eastern la-di-da, so did I. They were, for the most part, as I had said: light, easy, spindrift alliances, borne up on gusts of laughter and music and the elaborately, ostentatiously romantic things we devised to do. We danced one night on the lawn of the president's formal rose garden to the music of "Moonglow" on the car radio, and fell in love, not with the boys who had brought us there, but with the idea of it all. We drank Lancer's and Mateuse and Rhine wine on blankets by the star-pricked water of Lake Randolph, and went to fraternity formals in clouds of net and tulle bellied out over clanking plastic hoops, and we got huge, bulbous yellow chrysanthemums on football weekends, with fraternity letters tricked out in scattered glitter on them, and purple and white orchids for our wrists on formal weekends, and went to Destin and Panama City for house parties, and we laughed light laughter and sang and danced, and kissed light kisses. And none of it touched us to our cores; all of it blew about us like feathers in a summer zephyr.

A few times I got fairly serious about someone, most likely a brooding loner in the school of architecture on the G.I. Bill. Once I dated, for a quarter or so, the president-elect of the student body, and was so flown with myself that I went about mooing about first ladies, and bought a hideous lipstick called First Lady Pink. It took only one snort from Cecie to bring me out of that. I threw the lipstick away.

But when the affair ended, as it was predestined to do, I was briefly and badly hurt, and took to walking the campus at night in the November cold, alone, my hands jammed in my raincoat pockets. Cecie may have wanted to snort, but she did not, then. On the night that the fever of sorrow snapped I prowled for hours in a downpour and Cecie walked beside me, hands jammed into the pockets of *her* yellow slicker. She did not snort and she did not speak. She simply matched me, stride for stride, which, considering her short legs, took some doing. Neither of us was unaware of the drama of it all. Finally I turned to her, water running down my face, and said, "This is really stupid, isn't it?"

"It really is," she said. "But it's better than cancer."

I looked down at her, her face shadowed under the dripping rainhat, and then burst into laughter. She did too. We laughed until we had to hold each other up, and then we walked in the rain to Pennington's Drugstore and had hot chocolates. We had to stop several times on the way, doubled up once more with laughter, and we were still laughing when we crawled, sodden and chilled, into our beds. It became the talisman we invoked whenever sorrow struck, or the abyss stirred and howled beneath our feet.

"Well, it's better than cancer."

Oh, Cecie. It is. It is.

CHAPTER FOUR

After Alan went back into the studio I stayed in the garden for another hour. It is a secret one now, walled away from the beach, the houses on either side of us, and the road in front by dunes and a weathered fence and tall shrubs and whatever else I could coax into life in the constant rush of salt off the Atlantic. I began the garden when we moved into the house in Sagaponack, the year after we married. It was just a small beach shack then, a weathered gray cube among far grander houses around it, and it sported not a petal or a leaf that was not wild. But it had a magnificent view of the entire sweep of the South Shore from the upstairs crow's nest we added, and the dunes that shielded the first story from the sea were the tallest and wildest on all that coast. I started the garden before we even moved in.

At first I had a rich sweep of perennials in the border behind the dunes and beach plum, and I built up a tier of weathered wooden boxes and tubs so that passersby on the beach below could see them far above, like pennons on a rampart. We planted black pines, sedum, juniper and glossy privet to shield the deck and garden from the punishing torrents of salt wind, but I kept them shaped and clipped. Outside, on the dunes, were beach grass and sea oats, beach morning glory and sea rocket and dune spurge and panic grass . . . a subtle palette of wild gray-green that set off to perfection my carefully nurtured perennials. I hauled black soil and compost and fertilizer all one summer, and the next I had yarrow and bellflowers and delphiniums and lilies and iris and geraniums and fever-few and a full spectrum of the gaudy poppies. I loved the flowers and loved showing them off; we began our series of deck parties even before the house had a proper kitchen. I hauled food and liquor and ice out to Sagaponack from Bridgehampton and some-times Manhattan for three summers, and everyone we knew and some we didn't came to have drinks in my twilight garden by the sea. I always loved my flowers best when the pearl-gray evening light ignited their colors to radiance. Stephen was just-born then, and the garden was a celebration, a desti-nation. I was not even aware when it became a fortress.

When I had my first miscarriage I stopped some of the parties and let the shrubs grow wild, for I could not seem to get my strength back that summer. Two years later, when our daughter was stillborn, I enclosed the side approaches from the road to the garden in privet hedges. After that you could get to it only from the house, but you could still see the flames of the perennials from the beach, and I worked as assiduously to cultivate the garden for just the three of us as I had when passersby regularly saw it. We still had an occasional party, and our guests still loved my garden.

When Stephen died I let the black pines grow tall and wild and the juniper overrun the side yards, and we did not have the parties anymore. When they found the ovarian cancer and I came home from that first surgery, and the chemo that followed, I took down the tiers of tubs and pots that were visible from the beach, and put up the fence, and concentrated on my borders. It was about that time that I tired of perennials, and began replacing them with the annuals I have now. There were two exploratory surgeries after that, both with negative results, and the acute fear I had felt at first slid into chronic anxiety and then over into a kind of level white peace that was most pronounced when I was in the garden. Soon I was spending most of my daylight hours there. In winter I spent them at my desk in the alcove off the living room, that looked directly onto the sleeping garden. That was nearly five years ago, and all the perennials are gone now except the poppies. Now I have blanket flower, annual phlox, gazania, lantana, gerberer daisies, purslane, larkspur, statice, zinnias, marigolds, black-eyed susans, and a glorious rank of sunflowers, like sentinels, like Swiss guards at the Vatican. Each autumn I rip them out. Each spring I replant them.

"Don't you think it's okay now to plan further ahead than three months?" Alan said last spring, when I came home from the nursery with the bedding plants. "It's been four and a half years. In October you'll be officially cured. You can afford to look ahead now. I miss the iris and the lilies, and I miss seeing the colors from the beach. Now, when you're down there, it's like there's nothing at all up here behind the dunes. Those flowers always had a nice, go-to-hell look about them: look, world, Kate and Alan Abrams are up here."

"Is that what you think I'm doing?" I said. "Refusing to look ahead?"

"I know you are," he said. "You've been doing it for almost five years. I could understand it for a while, even if I didn't think it was exactly healthy, but there's just not any reason to do it now. You're virtually well. You need to get on with your life.

We need to make some plans. We need to get you out of this fortress back here. It's beautiful, but it doesn't make a life, Kate."

A little cold wind breathed up out of the abyss, that I had buried deep these past months in a grave of flowers and solitude.

"Don't push me, Alan," I said. "I want to wait a little while. It hasn't been five years yet."

"Katie, dear love. It's been okay for four and a half years. It's going to be okay this time. Why is it that you can accept bad news so much more easily than you can good?"

"Let's just see what happens," I said, and he left it at that. Alan is one of the other half, the ones who have never walked the bridge over the abyss. He listens with fierce sympathy when I talk of it, and tries with all his good, bright being to impart to me his innate feelings of safety and optimism, but he simply does not know what I know, what the abyss-walkers know.

One thing I have always known, since they found the cancer, is that the Pacmen were ultimately going to get me, and I am fairly sure now that it will be sooner rather than later. It's how I always pictured the cancer cells inside me, like those maniacally teeming, ravenous little round heads in the witless electronic game, all blind gobbling mouths. In the beginning I actually thought I could feel them there, darting and shooting about like terrible reverse sperm, bearing death rather than life, gobbling, gobbling. Even after the surgeries and the rounds of chemo, I fancied that they were still at it in there, down in that fertile red darkness. Then, gradually, I simply stopped feeling them or much of anything else; as the years and the exploratories and the checkups passed and the results came back negative, the garden and the still, suspended white peace claimed me and I had no sense of them at their busywork.

But one morning this July I woke and thought, simply, They're back, and by nightfall I was convinced of it, and I have known it ever since. There are no other symptoms, but it is my body and my abyss, and I know what I know. The Pacmen are on the march, and I do not think I can go through it again. Not another surgery, not another of the terrible, wracking rounds of chemotherapy, not another siege of baldness, not another night spent staring into thick, dead darkness, not another day swinging from hope to despair a hundred times between sunup and nightfall. I can't and I won't.

I have not told Alan. He would not believe me, anyway.

"You have no way of knowing that without seeing McCracken," he would say, and he would have me there, in that airy, elegant office on Madison that still stinks, to me, of that first terror, before I knew what had hit me. So I will not tell him. This way, there are almost two months left before my checkup. Two months of the autumn light that is so magical out here, the clear golds and blues, the high, honey sun and nights literally swarming with stars, and the great sweeps of space and emptiness without the summer crowds. Two months of just the darkening blue of the sea and the bright, hot tan of the sand and the great autumn skies, with the last butterflies teeming in the sun and the migratory birds sweeping over on their way south. Two months of the garden. It will be wonderful; it will be enough.

I finished with the witch grass and started in on the dodder that threatens always to choke the daisies and zinnias. The sun beat down on my head and the tops of my shoulders; from the angle I knew it was long past noon, and I ought to go inside and shower and make lunch. But I lingered, listening for the roar of the sea that always increases when the tide turns. But it was very still, and I could not hear the ocean, only that great diffuse hum you sometimes hear out here at the end of Long Island when the crowds are gone, that has always seemed to me the voice of the earth itself.

And over it, unbidden, unwanted, unheard for many years, other voices out of another time. I shook my head, but they would not go away. Finally I sat back on my heels and let them come: Cecie's voice, and Ginger's, and Fig's. And Paul's . . .

I almost killed Fig Newton the day I first saw her. I came very near to running over her in the MG. I had been down to the little Victorian Randolph train station to pick up Cecie, who had just come in from Virginia, and we were late for the last chapter meeting before rush started. It promised to be irredeemably awful; everybody was tired from two weeks of non-stop rehearsing skits and songs and polishing silver and cleaning the house until it shone, and we were drained and white-bled from the heat. It was the worst early fall I could remember. The temperatures were still grinding into the very high nineties, and the humidity on Randolph's fecund plain was nearly that. But it did not rain; day after day dawned white and set gray from heat, and water was restricted, and electric fans droned themselves into smoking, screeching suicide. Nothing on campus was air conditioned then, except the drugstore and the movie house and the Student Union. Those of us who had come back early for pre-rush had slept, if we slept at all, under towels wrung out in tap water, in the tepid rush of the fans. Every other one of us had a summer cold.

I was thick-nosed and miserable and running sweat in stockings and high heels and a tight-belted cotton dress. Traditionally, the last chapter meeting before rush was a "dress" meeting with the Tri Os; nobody remembered why, since its sole purpose was to review the bids that had gone out and wade through the incendiary matter of legacies, those "must-takes" of whom it was usually said, by the insisting alumna, "She's a legacy, and a lovely girl, and loves Tri Omega better than life itself." We would end up bidding all our legacies of course, and in the end would come to accept, if not cherish, most of them. But it never happened without a floor fight that went on until all hours, and the reasons for dressing for that feline fray were lost in the mists of history. It virtually assured that everyone would be miserable and mean, thus prolonging what was at best a bad business. I was in a vicious mood, and jerked the MG squalling around corners. Beside me, Cecie grabbed the seat and grimaced.

"Look, if you think you can do it better, you're welcome to it," I snapped. "We're going to miss the stupid prayer and the stupid roll call because your stupid train was late, and Trish is going to say something sweet and shitty, and I really may kill her this time. God, Cecie, I wish you'd learn to drive."

She was silent, and remorse flooded me. Cecie did not have a car, of course; the aunts were far too poor for that. Many girls at Randolph did not, but Cecie was the only one I had ever met who did not know how to drive, and did not want to learn.

"I'd kill everybody in a ten-mile radius," she said lightly, when one or another of us offered to teach her. "Y'all drive and I'll pay for the gas."

And she did try to do that, though most of us wouldn't let her. It was a subject of mild annoyance to the chapter and to me, until one day when I was battling a wasp and cried, "Take the wheel, Cecie," and she did, and when I had ousted the intruder and took it from her again and looked over at her, she was paper-white and shaking all over and wet with sweat. Her hair and clothes were sopping with it.

"It's always been that way," she said, not looking at me. "I guess it has something to do with the accident. I don't know why; I can't remember it. But it's the only explanation I can think of."

After that I did not tax her with it. The fear had been a terrible thing to see.

"Sorry," I said, on that blistering day. "It's just been so damned hot, and it won't let up, and I think dressing for this meeting is the silliest . . ."

"Look out!" Cecie cried, and I wrenched the car to the left and a short, thick figure scuttled back onto the curb. I slammed on brakes and pulled up at the first of Randolph's two traffic lights and glared at my victim. My heart was pounding, and my ears rang.

"Sorry," the girl sang out, and smiled gaily. "That's a pretty car. I wouldn't mind being hit by that car."

Cecie and I simply stared at her. The street corner was momentarily empty. In the merciless white light of afternoon she was grotesque, there was no other word for it. She was very short, almost as short as Cecie, but massive and square. Her head was large and appeared larger because of an appalling permanent that looked as though she had fashioned for herself a helmet of well-worn Brillo; it slid into her shoulders with only a passing nod to a neck. Her face was large and her eyes, behind quarter-inch-thick pink harlequin glasses, swam like a bug's. All her features sat in the middle of her face as though drawn there by a first-grader. Her nose was pugged far past pertness, and her eyebrows almost met over her eyes. She wore, incredibly, a ruffled, off-the-shoulder red peasant blouse and a flowered, ankle-length skirt over many crinolines, and her non-waist was cinched in with a red elastic belt. She wore red high-heeled pumps on feet that, Cecie said later, looked like Alley Oop's, and red earrings that dangled from her lobes to her shoulders. She resembled nothing so much as a dwarf peering out of a heap of clothing tossed on the sidewalk by a Gypsy. Her voice was an affected trill. Looking at her was like looking at something both comic and sad, as clowns have always seemed to me. I wanted to avert my eyes.

"I'm sorry," I muttered. "I was going too fast."

"No, it was all my fault, really," she shrilled merrily. "I'm such a silly. It would serve me right if you *had* hit me."

I could think of nothing to say to that, and felt my heart swell with gratitude when the light changed. I gunned the MG away from there.

"Bye," I heard the crystal tinkle. "I hope we run into each other again!"

Her hooting laughter followed us like a demented terrier.

"Lordy, I hope not," Cecie breathed. "Did you *see* that outfit? With my luck she's probably going to be in every class I have from here on out."

"Not a chance," I said, looking uneasily in the mirror. The squat heap of red flowers was still there on the curb, looking after us. "It's predestined that she'll be my lab partner."

"Don't let the sun set on yuh head in Randolph, pahdnuh," Cecie drawled. "This here town ain't big enough for all of us."

The chapter meeting was just as bad as it had promised to be, and lasted just as long. Heat and fatigue and pre-rush jitters made us all whiny and picky and contentious, and we fought over every bid we tendered, and over the costumes for most of the skits, and the refreshments for all the parties, and the allotment of duties. We finished with the preferred bids and started on the legacies. Fortunately there were not many that season; our president, Trish Farr, had only a handful of recommendations and photographs to pass around, and discussion of each was perfunctory. Even the objectors could not work up a full head of outrage. The heat was doing its work. And it seemed that each legacy had some fortuitous asset attached, that would, in the end, benefit the chapter more than her presence would harm it. The extremely fat girl from Bessemer had a voice like an angel and had placed first in the Met's Junior Regional competitions that summer; Step Sing would be a shoo-in with her for a soloist. The one who looked like James Dean, complete with duck's-ass haircut and biceps, was rich as Croesus. A chapter endowment was hinted at when we pledged her. The one with the ghost of a mustache and the coronet of Heidi braids had the only Jaguar XKE any of us had ever seen.

"Shoot, I'll cut that hair and yank those whiskers out myself," Rosemary Bates said.

"I'm glad I'll never know what you all said about me," I said wearily. I meant it, too.

"Not much, really," Rosemary said, matter-of-factly. "You looked pretty classy in your picture, and you had the MG."

Beside me Cecie snorted.

Trish held the last photo up, its back to us.

"Y'all aren't going to like this," she said. "But before you scream and jump all over me, let me tell you that she's a triple . . . grandmother, mother, and aunt . . . and that her grades are higher than any we've ever had, and that even if she was an idiot, we wouldn't have any choice, because this rec came straight from Mrs. Claiborne herself, and she says if we don't take her we can do some serious thinking about our charter."

Annabelle Claiborne was our Grand National President, an autocratic bison of a woman who could indeed lift our charter on her discretion alone, and she was already angry with us because we had refused to bid the last unspeakable legacy she had sent us. The girl's father had, unfortunately, been chairman of the board of directors of Mrs. Claiborne's husband's firm, and he had not been at all pleased. By the time we had been persuaded to see the error of our ways he had sent his distraught daughter to a finishing school in Switzerland, and we had been unable to make amends, either to her or Annabelle Claiborne. The jig, for us, was up. We looked apprehensively at Trish.

She made a little wordless sound, and turned the photograph around. There was a collective gasp from the chapter. I gave an involuntary squeak of recognition, and Cecie choked on a mouthful of Pall Mall smoke, and coughed violently. It was the girl from the street corner that afternoon. Even with the soft lighting and fluid black drape of the studio, the camera had been unable to help her in any way.

"NO-O-O-O-O-O!"

A collective roar went up from the chapter,

except for Cecie and me.

"Maybe you should have hit her after all," Cecie said, and then, "Oh, shit. Forget I said that. It can't be easy for her."

"No," I said. Under the profound distaste and dismay I felt at the sight of that Toltec face, something else was uncurling. It was the breath of the abyss; I knew with absolute certainty that the grotesque girl in the photograph felt it, as I had until I met Cecie, every day of her life. Too, I hated my sisters' careless venom even as I echoed it. Under it all, pity leaped like a lick of flame.

I waited until the shouting had stopped and the chapter sat staring sullenly at Trish, bested and knowing it, and then I said, "A — we're going to take her and we know we are. So let's do it and save time. B — if we're going to, we ought to do it as well as we can. None of us is so perfect that we can afford to be mean to her. How would you all like to be this girl?"

It was a prissy little speech, and gave them the target they sought. They hooted me down hotly, and when the jeering had stopped, Trish said snippily, "You're right, Kate, and since you were so kind as to point it out to us, I think you ought to be her big sister and take her through rush."

The room exploded with cheers, and my

heart tumbled into my stomach. Sponsoring a little sister meant many hours in her company, drilling her on her pledge tests and initiation material, and initiation itself meant six hours of, among other things, embraces and a kiss.

"Of course," I said crisply, in my best Seven Sisters' voice. "Glad to."

"No good deed goes unpunished," Cecie whispered to me.

"Maybe she'll pledge somewhere else," Bird Stanley said. Bird was optimistic to the point of simplemindedness. We simply looked at her.

"Does she have a name?" Carolanne Gladney said. Trish looked into the folder and then back at us.

"It's Helen Georgine Newton," she said. "But everybody calls her Fig."

The chapter howled and screamed and chortled itself, finally, up to bed. As Cecie and I trudged the stairs to our room, she shook her head.

"Fig Newton," she said wonderingly. "Wouldn't she just."

And so Fig came into our lives, that first quarter of our junior year and the first quarter of her freshman, and was moved, in part for expediency and in part for spite's sake, into the vacant room that formed the second

110

one of our suite. Cecie and I had been storing things there.

"It'll make it easier for you to teach her, Kate," Trish Farr said, grinning. I grinned back, fiercely. Trish and I had detested each other on sight, and spent the rest of our years at Randolph pretending we didn't. It was as purely a chemical thing as I have ever seen.

"Good idea," I said.

From the instant we met at the first rush party, when she burbled, "I just knew that day on the corner was fate," Fig attached herself to me like a limpet to a rock. I still don't know precisely why. It may have been the faint breath of otherness, the issue of the abyss, that drew her to me: as I have said, we know each other. But Cecie was an abyss-walker, too, and Fig never clung to her as she did to me. Indeed, if she could be said to avoid any of us, she rather avoided Cecie. But no matter what I said or did, I was to Fig Newton as catnip to kitten. If she had had a roommate things might have been mitigated a little, but five days into her tenure, the new pledge who had been quartered with her went to Dean Parker in hollow-eyed despair, and the beleaguered dean had Fig's snoring monitored at the college infirmary, and after that no one slept in the other twin bed in Fig's room. She did not seem to care.

"It's my adenoids and tonsils," she said complacently to Cecie and me. "Everybody in my family has bad ones. They hold fluid like sponges. It's a Newton family characteristic."

She said it as smugly as if she had said, "Naturally curly hair and blue eyes." I grimaced at the sponge analogy in spite of myself.

"Did you ever consider surgery?" Cecie murmured sweetly. "They're doing wonders these days."

"Oh, no, none of us have ever had surgery," Fig said reprovingly.

"Obviously not," Cecie said that night, when we lay in bed listening to the fusillade of snores that emanated through the two closed bathroom doors. "Or somebody would have had her mother sterilized long before the fabulous Fig appeared."

Fig was the youngest of five children, all the others boys, all of whom, according to the terrifying photograph she kept on her bureau, looked like her.

"I'm the baby of the bunch," she said. "Mama finally decided to quit when she got her little girl."

"To paraphrase what Dorothy Parker said

when they told her Calvin Coolidge had died," Cecie said delicately, " 'How could they tell?' "

And we laughed, Cecie and I, until we choked, and pulled the covers over our heads, and then laughed some more. We did not stop for a long time. It was the start of a pattern that stayed with us as long as Fig did: muffled, explosive laughter in the late nights, endless and self-perpetuating laughter, laughter tinged with guilt and despair and the louder for that, probably not as well concealed as it could have been. I think we even knew that at the time. But we could not stop laughing. Fig was simply too dreadful for anything else.

"It's better than being unkind to her," I said more than once. "I think we're the only two in the whole chapter who aren't out and out nasty to her, at least part of the time."

"It's probably just as bad, but there's no way you can be mean to her," Cecie said. "It really would kill her. She's absolutely gone on you. Have you noticed that she's making herself over into you?"

"That's not a bit funny," I said. But in the weeks that followed, I saw that it was true. All that fall, bit by bit and as inexorably as a glacier's movement, Fig Newton appropriated unto herself her version of my looks and mannerisms and clothes.

At first she just watched me. She watched me as I put on makeup in the morning, and watched as I dressed for dates, and watched as I took the makeup off and got ready for bed. Cecie and I took turns dressing and undressing in the bathroom, doors closed; she did not seem to notice. When we came out again, there she was, nestled cozily on my bed like a toad in sunshine. She usually had the diary with her, though by that time both of us would have died rather than ask her what she was writing. We knew that we would get either the sly innuendo or an excruciating speech of gratitude at being one of us. Sometimes she asked questions.

"What kind of shampoo is that?" she would say, and when I told her, she would write it down in the diary. Or, "Can you recommend a good mascara?" Or, "What kind of lipstick do you think would be right with my skin tone?"

"Mud," Cecie said under her breath at the latter. She was vastly exasperated with Fig; it only served to make her politer, and more remote. She watched coolly with her blue eyes as Fig catechized me, and dutifully recorded in her diary what she called her "beauty secrets."

She went after my clothes next. There was no way she could have worn mine, but she did her best to copy them. The ruffles and crinolines and high heels disappeared, and she emerged in the mornings in fuzzy skin-tight tweed skirts that came down to her ankles, skirts with slits that showed coy, dismaying inches of waffled blue-white leg and thigh. Pencil skirts, she called them. She topped them with sweater sets and crew necks that on her neckless barrel torso looked like strait-jackets. They were not the creamy cashmeres and hearty shetlands that I had bought under my father's tutelage when I began Randolph Macon, but nylon and wool so flimsy that they pilled dismally after the first washing. She bought thick Fruit of the Loom crew socks and rolled them atop clunking penny loafers, and a few men's oxford-cloth shirts and sweatshirts appeared. Instead of Yale and Princeton and Amherst, the sweatshirts said Randolph and Georgia Tech and Roll Tide.

"I know they're not as good as those Ivy League ones you have," she said. "I'll get some of those, if you'll tell me where you got them."

"I didn't buy them," I said. "They were gifts."

"Oh, sure," she said. "I should have known that."

I don't know where she found the sad clothes, and how she paid for them; she said her parents had sent her the money but I did not think that was true. Most of us knew Fig was on full scholarship from the Rotary Club back in Fowler, Alabama, and that her parents had virtually no money at all. Her mother had disgraced her own family, it was said, by running off and marrying a virile bricklayer, who, after presenting her with five children, threw his back out hauling hods and never worked another day in his life. There could not have been any money from home. Cecie and I, who both knew about scrimping and saving, tried to talk to her tactfully about the clothes she bought. It was the closest I ever saw Cecie come to overt pity for Fig.

"Listen, Fig, I'm poor as a church mouse myself, so it's no disgrace," Cecie said. "I couldn't for the life of me afford a whole new wardrobe, and I don't think you can, either, and it hurts me to see you waste all that money. Your clothes are perfectly fine. You don't need to buy new ones."

"Mine don't have any style," Fig said, looking down at the floor. "I thought they did, until I saw Kate's. Kate's have real style. Yours do, too," she added, looking up at Cecie and smiling her ingratiating smile.

"Yes, but Kate's clothes are Kate's style, not yours," Cecie said kindly. "I'd look just as silly in Kate's clothes as . . . anybody else. What she wears is right for her, but not for me and you. We're too short. Us shorties have a whole different look."

"I want to have a style like Kate's," Fig said simply. "Kate is a real aristocrat. Anybody can see that. My mother always says blood will tell. Kate looks like an aristocrat, and she walks and talks like one, and she even laughs like one. I'd love to be like that."

Fig had a way of saying terrible, naked, self-deprecatory things that none of the rest of us would have said to save our immortal souls, and making them sound ingenuous and somehow poignant. My heart squeezed with pity for her.

"Oh, Fig, you don't want to copy me," I said. "Truly, you don't. I'm too tall and too skinny and I slouch this way because I'm always trying to look shorter, and I talk this way because I spent a lot of summers up in the East, and I have these clothes because I bought them then and can't afford new ones now. I laugh like that because I'm self-conscious about my laugh; my father always told me it sounded like a hyena. And I'm not an aristocrat. I'm really not. I don't have any money, and I'm just an Alabama girl like you are. People will like you much better if you'll just be yourself."

"No, they won't," she said. "They never have."

"I promise they will," I said.

"No. They won't. And I don't believe you about the other. You're just being nice to me because you're that way; on top of everything else you're good and kind. Mother says a real lady is never consciously unkind, and you never are."

I looked at her in despair.

"Your mother was right," Cecie said, grinning. "Of course, Oscar Wilde also said a gentleman is never *un*consciously unkind, so you can take your pick. But ol' Kate here is an aristocrat, no doubt about it. Did you know they call her Effie, because she's so FFV? That," she added at Fig's thick look, "stands for First Family of Virginia. Yep, ol' Effie Lee."

"Oh, shut up, Cecie," I said crossly.

"You're modest, too. I noticed that about you right away," Fig went galloping on through her litany of my virtues. I thought I would scream with frustration and annoyance. "I think Effie is cute. I didn't know about that. I do know your whole name, though, I wrote it down from the chapter list the first night, in my diary. Katherine Stewart Lee. I noticed it because of the Stewart. My mother has some Stewarts from Virginia in her family; we're probably related. They almost named me that." She thumbed through the diary and held the page up for us to see. My name, misspelled, leaped out at me. It gave me a chilly, unpleasant twist in my stomach.

"Kate is one of the 'U' Stuarts," Cecie said blandly. "You know, as in General Jeb Stuart. Those are another matter altogether."

"Well, we could still be related," Fig said stubbornly, looking down at her great loafered feet. Dull magenta stained her neck and face. "Mother told me we changed the spelling somewhere along the line."

I raised my hands and dropped them in surrender.

"Well, maybe we are," I said. "So be a good little fifth cousin thrice removed or whatever and stop drooping around and talking like Katharine Hepburn. And stop craning your neck back like that when you laugh. You'll choke to death. I like you just the way you are, and I don't want you to change."

"Okay, if you really feel like that," Fig said submissively. And then looked up slyly at me under her lashes and added, "Effie."

And nothing could dissuade her from that.

She did stop the ridiculous attempts to slouch and talk and laugh like I did, but until the day I left Randolph Fig Newton never failed to call me, elaborately and with much mock cringing and many little winks, Effie Lee. It drove me nearly mad. Cecie adored it. For an entire quarter she herself called me Effie Lee, and then, unlike Fig, tired of it. Ultimately I was able to laugh about it in the nights; it became a part of the great body of what Cecie called Figiana, that we sorted over nightly for each other's delectation.

I resolutely spent an hour or so each week, in the afternoons with Fig in her room, drilling her from the Tri O pledge manual and preparing her for initiation that winter. She was an awesomely quick study, but she made a tedious business of it, pretending not to understand so I would have to repeat things over and over, and writing everything I said down laboriously in the by-then-hated diary, her tongue out in concentration, breathing wetly through her nose, giving me conspiratorial little looks.

"Come on, Fig," I said finally. "You know this stuff backward and forward, better than I do. There's no sense in making me repeat all this."

She smiled at me, twinkling her bug's eyes.

"I know," she said. "I just like to hear

the sound of your voice."

There was something intimate in her voice, a damp and familiar emanation, that I shrank away from. Distaste and a vague alarm stirred in me. After that I dropped the lessons. There was nothing, by then, about Tri Omega that she did not know.

I began spending all afternoon until six o'clock in McCandless Hall with the permanent legion of architecture and interior design students who kept drafting tables and did their work there. I found an empty table by the great bank of windows that overlooked the street and a coffee shop and coin laundry and rooming house, and set up my stuff, and found that I liked working in the new, light-flooded white building. In the daytime it was among the coolest spots on campus, and at night the building was like a great aquarium swarming with friendly fish, and the coffee shop was full until very late of students talking design and materials and construction methods. Many were men, older than the norm for Randolph, back in school on the G.I. Bill, worldly and cool-eyed and faintly scornful of the scurry of collegiate life around them. Most were considered by the fraternity and sorority contingent to be "bohemian, arty," and "funny," and therefore beyond the social pale. I found myself drawn to them, and they seemed to like and accept me, seeing, no doubt, below my Tri Omega pin, the outsider that I was at heart. Often I did interiors and renderings for the budding architects, and just as often they straightened out my faulty perspectives and took me for coffee. It was a soothing and pleasant interval for me. Cecie was in late labs of her own that fall, and Fig could hardly pursue me into my very laboratories. I think I first began to take Interior Design seriously that quarter.

But then Fig began to shadow me like a comic-strip detective.

"Don't look now, but one of the Seven Dwarfs is staking you out," the married architect at the table next to mine said one day in November. I followed his glance out of the window and saw Fig, swathed in a raw new yellow polo coat and swaddling scarves down to her ankles, standing on the sidewalk outside, looking in at me. She looked, in her wrappings and layers, like a squat, burlap-wrapped pipe that had been readied for a freeze. She gave me a bright smile and a little waggling wave. I waved back, and waited for her to move on, but she did not. My face and neck began to burn. I bent close over my work.

"Okay, she's gone," my table neighbor

said presently. "Who in God's name is she?"

"One of our new pledges," I said, not looking at him.

"Christ, she must be worth a fortune," he said. "Or is Tri O into good works now?"

"She's a very nice girl," I said stiffly, cursing her silently.

"Sure she is," he said equably. "How could she be anything else?"

The next day Fig was back at the same time. And the next, and the next. We would go through the same routine: the little finger wiggle and the vivid smile, the ducked head, the silent waiting it out. On the fifth day she came into the building and stood in the open door of my lab, fidgeting and looking for all the world like a pit bull expecting to be kicked, until someone said, "You got company, Kate," and I looked up and saw her. I went to the door and drew her out into the hall.

"What can I do for you, Fig?" I said crisply, aware that everybody in the room was listening.

"Well, I was just over this way and saw you through the window and thought we might go get some coffee," she said. "I know you go over there to Harry's in the afternoons. I've seen you. So I thought since I was here anyway . . ."

"My break isn't for another hour, and I can't let you stand around in the cold waiting for me," I said. "Dr. McGee is funny about outsiders . . . you know, people who aren't his students . . . being in his lab. But thanks anyway. By the way, what are you doing over here? I thought you had P.E. afternoons."

"Well, I dropped it," she said, not meeting my eyes. "I get these awful cramps, you know, and they wrote me an excuse at the infirmary. I switched to Music Appreciation right over there in Smythe."

"Well, anyway, I've got to get back to work," I said. "See you tonight."

"Are you coming back for dinner?"

"I . . . don't know," I said. "I've got to have this project finished by Thanksgiving holidays. I'll probably be working every night until then . . . ."

"I'll help you," she said brightly.

"Fig . . ."

"Okay, okay," she said, putting her hands up as if to ward off a blow, and chortling merrily. And went scurrying off, not looking back.

After that she stopped appearing on the sidewalk outside McCandless, but then one afternoon, as I sat in a booth at Harry's drinking coffee and laughing with a group of architecture students, I felt, distinctly, eyes on my face, and turned, and there she was, alone in a booth across the room. Even through the still strata of cigarette smoke and the steam from many cups of coffee, I could see that she was staring fixedly at me. But when she caught my glance, she looked down at the book she was reading, and did not look up again. She was there, off and on, for the remainder of that quarter, and she never acknowledged that she saw me, and never spoke of it afterward. I was so outdone that I was determined not to mention it to her, either. So we rocked along, stalker and quarry, neither admitting by so much as a gesture that she was aware of the other. I was tense and jittery and always faintly angry at her, but so long as she kept up her airy pretense of ignoring me, I could not seem to broach it with her. The campus was, after all, open territory.

And then she showed up in my weekly History of Architecture class, still pointedly not seeing me, seeming to be enraptured with the slides and the mumbled droning of the old German professor, and began to talk glibly at meals of Mies van der Rohe and Florence Knoll and Barcelona chairs and Dudok's City Hall in Hilversum, and I snapped at her one night in utter exasperation.

"Look, Fig," I said, following her into her lair. "Cut out that silly stuff. You don't know an Eames chair from a toilet, and you couldn't care less. You're an English major, and the best one I ever saw. Interior Design shouldn't matter to you. I don't understand why you're bothering with that stupid class; everybody hates it. And everybody's talking about the way you follow me around. Do you want that?"

"I wasn't aware that I was," she said prissily. "My goodness, it's a free country, isn't it? If I want to audit a course that isn't in my major, I don't see why anybody should care. Who said I was following you around?"

"Everybody. People," I said. "Listen. There's something Kahlil Gibran said in *The Prophet*, that I always thought was true and wonderful. He said, 'Let there be spaces in your togetherness.' So let's do it, Fig. Let's let there be spaces in our togetherness."

"That's beautiful," she breathed. "It really is. I'm going to put that in my diary. And" — she looked meltingly at me — "that you quoted it to me. I'll never forget it."

I stamped out of her room, bested. I was damned if she would goad me into one of these discussions again; it was like Br'er Rabbit and the Tarbaby. To touch Fig was to be ensnared by her.

During the whole insane siege, Cecie, oddly, said very little. I related each of Fig's atrocities to her, indignantly, waiting either for her dry, crisp perspective or her whooping, healing laughter, but she offered neither. It was about that time she began to warn me about Fig, to caution me not to laugh so loudly, to keep my voice down when I spoke of her. Instead of defusing the whole affair with her delicate satire, she cautioned me that Fig was not what she seemed. "I simply can't believe you can't see . . . how she is," she snapped once, exasperated. "You act like a horse with blinders on."

But she would not speak of it further. I felt vaguely betrayed, and bereft, as if deprived of both my audience and my co-conspirator in laughter. For a while, we did not laugh much at night, Cecie and I, and I realized only then how much of our easy mirth had had its source in Fig Newton.

And then Fig began to leave me poems, on my pillow or under the windshield of my car or on my drafting table in McCandless, and they were so obscure and flowery and exalted and altogether dreadful that I could only laugh helplessly when I read them to Cecie in the nights. This time she did laugh with me. It simply was not possible to do otherwise. I began to read them aloud in

Fig's voice, and discovered an arrow-true facility for mimicking her voice and inflections, and used it shamelessly and often. I never failed to reduce Cecie to utter, breathless helplessness with the sorry little imitations, and I gloried in this new power. She was so often the one who had made me laugh until I thought, literally, that I would die.

"Oh, hush, oh, hush," she would gasp. "Oh, stop! I can't stand it! She'll hear you! Stop, Kate . . ."

And on I would go, flinging Fig's poor, awful words into the air on a careless flood of laughter and mockery.

And then one morning Cecie came out of the bathroom with a wet snippet of paper in her hand, and passed it to me. She did not look at me.

"It was pinned to the shower curtain," she said. "You're going to have to do something about this, Kate."

I read the poem Fig had left for me and reddened, painfully and profoundly. I could actually feel the air beating at my face and hands, as if a silent detonation had taken place. I was giddy and breathless and almost physically sick. The poem was graphic in the extreme, and spoke of physical love in terms that I had never even imagined before.

There was nothing in it of normalcy or grace. I was sure Fig had not composed it herself, but the fact that she had dared to even think about me in those terms left me weak and trembling with anger.

I slammed into her room and snatched the covers off her. She pantomimed waking, stretching and smiling languidly. Without her glasses her face looked weak and naked.

"Morning, Effie," she said.

"Don't you ever, ever, leave anything like this lying around where I can see it again," I shouted. "Don't write me any more poems, don't follow me around anymore, and don't pretend you don't know what I'm talking about, because you damned well do!"

She looked at me in exaggerated surprise and injury.

"Well, I don't," she said piteously. "I don't have any idea what you're talking about. Why are you so mad?"

"This," I said, waving it in her face. "This. This is . . . filthy! This is a whole other thing than those silly things you've been sneaking into my room, and on the car . . ."

"I only wanted to please you," she whispered, tears starting in her naked eyes. "I thought you loved poetry. You quoted *The Prophet* to me . . . I thought you cared about it, and about me . . . I didn't know

129

that stuff was dirty. I just . . . copied it out of that book of Cecie's, I thought you all read it to each other, like you do that other stuff . . . I didn't know what it meant . . ."

She broke into loud sobs, looking up through her fingers to see my reaction. I knew she meant the *Kama Sutra;* Cecie and I had, indeed, been reading it, though not to each other, and had found it both shocking and titillating. I thought, also, that she did indeed know what it meant, but I was past caring whether she did or not. The book was one Cecie had gotten from an Oriental friend in one of her classes, and had been in her desk, and the only way Fig could have found it was to go through her things.

"Don't do any of this stuff anymore, Fig," I said coldly. "I've had it with you. Stop it or I'll get you moved out of this suite. I can and I will. I mean it."

"I can't stand for you to be mad at meeee!" Fig wailed as I turned to leave. "You're my big sister! You have to love me! That's what being a big sister means . . . but now you hate me-e-e-e . . ."

The rage went out of me abruptly, and I sat down limply on the vacant twin bed that faced hers. She had rooted under the covers, sobbing and snuffling, and I spoke to the lump she made under them.

"Fig, listen," I said. "Listen, because I'm only going to say this once. I don't hate you. I just want you to stop . . . dogging me. I know I'm your big sister, and I always will be, but that doesn't mean I automatically . . . you know, *love* you. I'll try to be a good sorority sister, but you just can't legislate love, it isn't a policy, something you decide. It's a feeling, and it's given to you. It just comes. A real friendship is a light thing. A real friend holds you loosely. Look at Cecie; she the best friend I have in the world, but she doesn't crowd me, or follow me around, or try to imitate me . . ."

She pulled her swollen red face out of the bundle of covers and looked at me. I have never seen such desolation in a pair of eyes.

"I know I can never be to you what Cecie is!" she said, and began to weep again, nasally and hopelessly.

I looked at her, and then walked out of her room. It had probably been the wrong thing to say, but I was past caring. I thought that at least she would stop now.

"I feel like a heel yelling at her like that," I said to Cecie a couple of weeks later, "but it really does look like the Reign of Terror is over."

"Mmmmm," Cecie said. She had been quiet the past few days, and we did not laugh so

131

much in the nights.

"Well, don't you think?" I said.

"Sure looks like it," Cecie said, and went off to class.

And it did. Fig no longer haunted Harry's or my History of Architecture classes, and the unsought poetry stopped cold. She did not come into our room at night either, as she always had. It was not that she was pouting, or seemed particularly chastened by my outburst. She was cheerful and open, or at least as much as Fig could be, when we met in the halls and at meals, and went home to Fowler for Thanksgiving calling bright goodbyes to us all. When we returned she was still the changed Fig.

"She's really working out okay," the chapter said. "Maybe it's not going to be as bad as we thought. You've done wonders with her, Kate."

"Boy, if they only knew," I said to Cecie. I did not think they did. There had been some good-natured teasing about Fig's copying my clothes, and leaving poems about for me, but it seemed forgotten now. I was sure no one but Cecie and I and Fig knew the extent of the aberration. I was equally sure that none of the three of us would ever speak of it. And we didn't. Fig did not apologize, but I thought perhaps her new,

132

exemplary behavior served, in a way, as her apology. I was still not eager to share her company, but there was no doubt about it: the new Fig was vastly preferable to the old one. If she would only stop calling me "Effie."

A week before our Christmas break, Cecie and I came home from seeing *The King and I* for the third time at the Tiger Theatre to find the campus fire department just leaving the Tri O house, and the slippered and robed sisterhood just filing back into the living room, chattering like parakeets. No smoke was visible, but we could smell it, faintly, coiling down from upstairs.

"Oh, thank God you're back," Carolanne Gladney shrieked, darting at us. A throng of twittering Tri Os followed her. "There's been a fire in your room, but it's out now and no damage except some smoke. Fig smelled it and called the fire department and rang the alarm, and went in and pulled all y'all's clothes out of your closets. She's a hero, Kate, she got her hands and arms burned a little bit. She's in the infirmary until tomorrow, but she'll be all right . . ."

My head spun with alarm and contusion, and beside me, Cecie stood on her toes, giving little jumps, trying to see over the crowd and up the stairs.

"My God," I said in shock. "How did it

133

start? We've been gone over three hours . . ."

"They're not sure," Trish Farr said solemnly, but I thought there was a certain chord of relish in her voice. "But they think somebody might have left a cigarette burning . . ."

Cecie went white. I actually saw the color drain from her face. I saw, also, the veiled, avid looks the chapter bent on her. Cecie was the only one of us in that suite who smoked. Everyone knew that.

"I didn't leave a cigarette burning," she said, precisely and remotely. "I never have, and I didn't this time."

"I know you didn't," I said, fiercely protective. "I'd have seen it if you had. It had to be something else."

"Well, I said they weren't sure about that," Trish said piously. "It could easily have been something else. Nobody's accusing you of anything, Cecie."

"I should hope not," I said in a bright, hard voice. "I'd really hate to hear anything like that. I think it would be tacky in the extreme if that got around campus. Everyone would know it was one of us who started it."

"Well, talk to Fig," Trish huffed. "She's not saying, but I have an idea she knows."

But Fig professed not to. She came home from the infirmary the next morning, pale and somehow apologetic, pointedly not meeting

Cecie's or my eyes, her hands and arms swathed in white bandages.

"I really don't know how it started," she murmured, when we went in to thank her and see how she was. "Nobody could say for sure. The room was already pretty smoky when I got there. It probably wasn't a cigarette at all. Listen, Effie, Cecie, I'm sorry if I got your clothes dirty. I just threw them out the door on the floor; I didn't think . . ."

"Oh, Fig, don't even think about that," I said. "You saved the house and probably some lives as well as our clothes. None of us will ever be able to thank you."

I knew I was right, but somehow the words did not come easily. I felt, instead of gratitude, the old annoyance. Except to murmur, "Thanks, Fig," Cecie hardly spoke at all.

I have to give Fig credit. She could have made much of her role as wounded heroine, but she did not. She did not speak of the fire at all. But the sisters did. Perversely, they lionized the heretofore plague-ridden Fig, petting and cosseting her, bringing her tidbits of food and even seeing that a small article about her role in averting tragedy appeared in the *Randolph Senator*. It must have been a time of triumph for her, but she was still modest to near-obsequiousness. No one mentioned the origins of the fire

135

again, but there were some oblique glances thrown at Cecie before the looming holidays claimed our attention. Cecie herself was quiet and remote, staying long in the library and often going down to the chapter room late at night to study. I knew that she had gone through the door deep inside herself and shut it behind her. I could not lure her out.

"You know I don't think you caused that fire," I said once, desperate to penetrate the white shell around her. I missed her good sense, and our late-night camaraderie, and her charming, drypoint foolishness. I missed all of her.

"I know you don't," she said. "The problem is, I've been wondering lately if maybe I did after all. I don't remember it, but I guess it isn't impossible . . ."

"No," I said. "It *is* impossible. I know. I really do know. I wish you could forget it. I need somebody to laugh with. Fig as St. Joan isn't very funny."

"No," Cecie said. "She isn't."

After that she seemed to make an effort to be herself again, and we occasionally sat late into the nights once more, listening to music and sharing poems and books, and finding, with only a little forcing, new things to laugh about. But the laughter rang a bit hollow, and didn't last long. Cecie took to sleeping a great deal, and I spent more and more evenings over at McCandless. In the other room, Fig received a modest stream of visitors and enjoyed with becoming modesty her small vogue. She still wore the white bandages. No one mentioned the fire.

On the day we finished our finals I loaded the MG and stopped on my way home to Kenmore to drop Cecie at the train station. Neither of us wanted to go home; my mother was seeing a pious, stupid deacon in the Baptist Church whose idea of a proper Christmas celebration was to attend church three times a day and participate in the Living Nativity on the brown church lawn. I did not like him nor he me; I knew that the scent of the abyss below me was strong in his nostrils. Cecie was, she said, simply not in the mood for the gentle blithering of the grandmother and the aunts.

"I wish we could spend this Christmas somewhere like Monte Carlo or Gstaad," she said, humping her duffle bag out of the MG.

"Well, let's make a note to do it, the first year we're in Europe," I said. "Meanwhile, cheer up. Things will be better after Christmas."

She didn't answer. She bumped the duffle up the wooden steps to the platform and turned to wave at me. I waved back, and slid the MG into gear. Somehow, I did not like to drive away and leave her there.

"Kate . . ." she called after me.

"What?"

"I didn't leave that cigarette burning."

"I know it," I said. "Merry Christmas, ol' Cece."

"Bah, humbug," she said.

CHAPTER FIVE

We did not sit down to lunch until two, and I never did eat the crab salad I made. Instead, I did something I have not done since the night I met Alan, close to twenty-eight years ago. I got very, very drunk.

He brought a pitcher of Bloody Marys to the umbrella table on the deck, and put two glasses full of shaved ice and a saucer of kosher salt and sticks of fresh celery, and tilted the umbrella to shield us from the high sun and the salt wind streaming over the dunes, and said, "Booze is the answer. But what is the question?"

And I laughed, because it was precisely the same thing he had said to me that long-ago night when he had found me at my drawing board overlooking Third Avenue, crying. The rich red Bloody Marys looked, suddenly, like the best things I had ever seen, and I drank half of my first one without stopping.

"Since you mention it, I guess there's nothing for it but to repeat history and get knee-walking smashed," I said. "These are wonderful. What's that, horseradish?"

"Sorrel," he said. "There wasn't any dill. What's with you, Tondelayo? You've got that look about you."

I actually blushed. Tondelayo is what he always called me when I wanted to make love; he claims that I had a kind of languid, loose-jointed, half-lidded playfulness about me then that I never had at other times. Pure progesterone, he called it. I had not heard the nickname in a long time. We had not made love in a long time. Somehow it seemed to me a kind of desecration to have Alan inside me along with the Pacmen.

"I'm thirsty is all, you satyr," I said. I drank the rest of the Bloody Mary and held out my glass. "Hit me again, Sam."

I think I had four in all. I never could drink well, and I am still very thin from the long siege of chemo. I was not one of the ones who sailed through it with just a modicum of easily controlled nausea. I retched and gagged and vomited for the entire four days each course ran, and lost all the flesh that middle age had settled on me, and have not managed to gain it back. So the four drinks literally carried me into a kind of walking oblivion. I remember dimly the passing of time and the gradual lessening of the heat on my face and body, as the sun swung around to the west, and I remember laughing a great deal, and I have a white-lit, frozen flash in my memory of a precise moment, when I stood up and came around the table to Alan and sat in his lap and put my arms around him, and drew his head and face into my breasts.

"Come inside now," I heard my voice saying, fogged and thick with languor and liquor. "I want you to love me."

The next memory I have is lying in his arms in the tumbled bed of the guest room, my sweat-damp body shivering in the wash of the ceiling fan and the wind off the sea that billowed the sheet muslin curtains, crying as I had not cried since Stephen died, crying the sour, endless, breath-sucking tears of loss. He held me silently and loosely, his breathing still ragged, and I could literally feel the heat ebbing out of his body against me. I was clutching him as a drowning person might clutch a floating log, my arms and legs locked around him. His small, hard body was cool and slippery with sweat. I remember feeling a great, simple desire to press myself through his skin and into his flesh, to become him. To become . . . not me. Loss flattened me like the corpse of an animal in the road. It was so strong and terrible that for a moment I thought I was back in those first anguished hours after we heard about Stephen. I must have called Stephen's name, because Alan was murmuring into my wet hair, over and over, "It's all right now, Katie. It was a long time ago, and it's over now."

I think I slept a little then, because my next clear memory is sitting up in the guest bed to take the cup of scalding hot coffee he brought. The sun was off the deck and the light in the room had cooled from the shadowed red of mid-afternoon to the gray-blue of nearing dusk. I shivered, and he saw it and switched off the overhead fan. It thumped and shuddered to a stop, and the silence was very loud. Even the sea had cooled, with approaching evening, to the gentle husshhhhh that meant the dropping of the wind. In the silence I could hear, as well as feel, the dimly-remembered throbbing in my temples and throat that meant hangover. I sipped the coffee with one hand and scrubbed at my aching temple with the other.

"The wages of sin," Alan said, sitting down on the bed next to me. He reached over and brushed my tangled hair off my face.

"You feeling better?"

"No," I said miserably. "I feel just like I should. I feel awful. I don't know what got into me . . . besides vodka. Did I pick a fight with you, or what? I remember waking up feeling like I'd lost you forever."

"Not me. You were back with Stephen,

I think. Don't worry about it. I still cry for him sometimes."

"Do you?" I said in surprise, looking at him. His face was just the same as it had been for twenty-eight years: wry and sweet and faintly simian, and so somehow redolent of health and balance and youth that I used to tease him about having made a deal with the devil. I had not heard him speak of Stephen in a long time, not since the cancer, and it surprised me profoundly to think that he still cried for him. I had not myself, not for a very long time.

"Sure I do," he said. "It doesn't mean I'm desolate, or that what I have isn't enough, but I do. I love him and I miss him."

I felt the tears come back into my eyes and throat, and I leaned my head against him.

"It's been awful for you, too, hasn't it? I keep forgetting," I said against his bare chest. He wore shorts now, but no shirt or shoes, and his skin was cool and sweet-smelling, from the French-milled soap I kept in the guest bath. His hair and beard had droplets in them.

"Not, I imagine, as bad as it has for you," he said, and there was such a universe of rational perspective in the sentence that some of the pain in my chest eased, and I had a sense of the world shifting forward into another gear, and flowing on. It has always been his best gift to me, that all-healing clarity of vision, that unshakable grounding in the earth. I feel sure it was why I married him, under all the other reasons. For all these years he has been, as well as my friend and my lover, my anchor. No one was ever that before, not even Cecie. It was only then that I had a brief glimmer of what the role has cost him. I had taken it for granted, his constancy, his never-flagging willingness to be present at my pain, but I saw in that moment that it must have been a heavy load to shoulder and carry. He had lost a son, too. He had just missed having two other children, too. His wife had had cancer; his wife had hung for five years over an abyss that was open for him, too.

"I cannot imagine what I would do on this earth without you," I said.

"Me, neither," he said, and kissed the top of my head. I wriggled across the bed to come nearer to him, and felt a large patch of sticky wetness. Like the hangover, it had been a long time since I had felt it.

"Whoa," I said, grinning up at him. "I must have jumped your bones. I think I remember mentioning something about it, around the tenth drink. Well, what do you know. Did we . . . was it okay?"

The few times we had tried to make love, after the last chemo series was over, I had not been able to finish. I would want to, and his hands and body would bring me just up to the brink of that long, red fall that I so loved, and I would be crying out and clutching him like a small monkey, as I always had, but then, when he slid into me, a smothering white panic would rise up in my throat and over my head, and I would literally feel inside me the Pacmen boiling up out of my flesh, where they had lain vanquished, and swarming at him as he entered me, mouths gobbling. It was as if, with the act of love, he released death inside me, death both to me and to him. I felt both poisoned and a poisoner. I would wrench away violently and cry, shivering and nauseated, unable to go on and unable to help him finish. I know that he understood, and that he did not blame me, but it had been a very long time since he had approached me, and I had had the soaring thought, when I touched the sheet where he had spilled out, that this time we had done it, and I was healed.

He did not answer for a moment and I knew that it had not been okay.

"Oh, God," I said hopelessly.

"Don't," he said, holding me and rocking. "It was a lot closer this time. We got a lot further. We got so close this time that I couldn't . . . I didn't stop. Sorry about that. We'll make it next time. We really were almost there."

I started to cry again.

"It's my fault," I said. "I just plain seduced you, and then I . . . God. It's not bad enough to be frigid. Now I'm a drunk cock-teaser and still frigid . . ."

He laughed.

"And a pederast and a closet Klansman and didn't vote in the past four elections. Come on, Katie, it isn't your fault. We'll get it next time. We could probably get it now, if you're still interested . . ."

"No," I wept. "No. Not now. Soon, I promise, but not now, Alan. I'm sorry, I'm so ashamed . . ."

"Well, make it soon," he said mildly, into my hair. "I want to screw you sometime again before we're both dead."

Before I even thought the words I heard myself saying them.

"It's back, Alan."

He went perfectly still. I felt him draw a deep breath.

"No it isn't," he said.

"Yes. This summer. I've known for a while."

146

"How?" he said fiercely. "Do you have pain? Are you bleeding? What?"

"No, none of that. I just know . . ."

"You don't know!" He almost shouted. "You don't know! How can you know if there's no pain and no blood, nothing? How on earth can you know?"

He had pulled away from me and we sat looking at each other in the dim, underwater light. His eyes were very white in his tan, and there was a ridge of white around the base of his nose. He looked scared to death, and angrier than I have ever seen him.

"I just know," I whispered. "Alan, I just know."

He pulled me to him again and began to rock me once more. He rocked me back and forth, back and forth, on the bed.

"No, it isn't back, Katie," he said softly. "No, love. You're upset, and you've got this last checkup coming up, and it's natural for you to be apprehensive. I've known all along you were sweating it out. But you're okay. I'm going to prove to you that you are. I'm going to call John McCracken tonight and get him to see you tomorrow, and then we'll be past and done with this, you'll see . . ."

I shook my head against him. I must, *must* have the rest of the summer. If he insisted on taking me to the doctor, I did not know what I would do. I would run away . . .

"I'm sorry," I said, as reasonably as I could. "I'm being silly. I knew I was even when I said that. Don't make me humiliate myself in front of John. He already thinks I'm a world-class hysteric. It was just the booze talking. And I guess the letter did upset me a little."

I felt his chin move and knew he was smiling.

"Did you know that you called me Paul this afternoon?" he said. There was no pain in his voice, only mild amusement. I thought the pain was there, though. I thought I could feel it moving through him in the very conduit of his blood.

"Oh, Alan, oh I never . . ." I said, appalled. "Oh, shit. I can't believe it. Alan, you *know* I don't think of him anymore. You know I don't, and I haven't, in all these years . . . it was just Ginger's letter, and the thought of going back to that house after all this time . . ."

"I know," he said. His face was calm, his eyes clear again. Alan is certainly not incapable of jealousy, but he would know in an instant when it was warranted and when not.

"I really do know all that, Kate. Of course, it doesn't mean that I shouldn't have killed the bastard back when he first needed it."

"You didn't have to," I said. "I killed him myself. Her, too. Dead and buried and out of my life for good and all. That's a promise."

"I know," he said again, and kissed me. "Now why don't you finish your nap and then maybe we'll go get a hamburger at Bobby Van's, or something. I'll call you about six."

I did sleep then, with the sound of the ocean fizzing on the tan sand far below the dunes in my ears, and the cool, fresh-fish smell of the incoming tide in my nostrils. Just before I slid down into it, I thought, I did kill them. I really did.

But the dead do walk.

Three days before that winter quarter began, Tri Omega initiated its pledges in a formal candlelight ceremony in the Chapter Room of the house, and Fig Newton became, officially and for all time, one of us. My sister in Omega Omega Omega.

The Fig who had left Randolph a heroine came back considerably diminished. At our ages, memory, even of heroism, was short, and most of us had forgotten our canonization of her in the flurry of the holidays, and preparations for Initiation. Few of us made a fuss over her anymore, and, understandably reluctant to relinquish the only glimmer of limelight she had ever had, she found ways to remind us.

"Did I tell you all that my church asked me to make a little speech at Youth Appreciation Sunday?" she said to us at our first dinner the first night we were back, modestly looking down at her meatloaf and batting her lashes. The effect, Cecie pointed out *sotto voce*, was that of two centipedes trapped behind portholes.

"No," I said dutifully. "That's great. What about?"

"Well . . . about the . . . you know. About the little fire. And my getting your stuff out . . ."

"Heroism travels far and fast," Cecie said.

"The minister's daughter went to Randolph. She gets the *Senator*," Fig said primly. No one else spoke.

"I haven't seen you wear the blue cashmere," she said to me in the company of most of the chapter, after breakfast. "Is it ruined? It was at the back of the closet; I couldn't get to it very fast. I think that's how I burned my hands."

"No, it's fine," I said, though in fact the sweater smelled horribly of smoke and always would, and I had left it in Kenmore. "I just haven't worn it yet."

"I wonder if my lashes will come back dark and long?" she said, peering into the hall console mirror as we gathered one evening for a pledge swap. "I read somewhere that they usually do when they've been burned off."

"Oh, Fig, enough about that stupid fire," Jeanine Sefton said irritably. "Your eyelashes don't look any different. You didn't burn a one of them."

"Well, I did, too," Fig said indignantly. "Right off. This is just mascara."

But we could not be wooed back, and she soon became as fully and dismally Fig as she had ever been.

"The reason I know there's a God is that it's you who have to take her through initiation and kiss her, and not me," Cecie said. She had come back seemingly herself, and a weight had slipped off my heart. The Cecie who had left for Virginia before Christmas had haunted my days at home.

"I lie awake at night thinking about it," I said. "I'd kill myself now, but I figure it's going to be my good deed for the century. Who else is ever going to kiss her?"

"I bet she's been practicing on her arm for weeks," Cecie said. "Did you used to do that? Kiss your forearm passionately, with your eyes closed like they did it in the movies, so you'd know how when the time came? Every one of us in the convent had big red hickeys on our arms. The sisters thought it was impetigo."

"Oh, God, yes . . . I'd forgotten," I cried, convulsed with laughter. "All over America at any given time you can hear the piggy, snorty little sounds of ten-year-old girls kissing their arms."

We were off into one of the late-night gales of glee, laughing until we could not speak and clutching our sides, keeping it going out of sheer relief and joy at having each other back.

"Listen!" Cecie hissed. "Hear that? She's in there now, getting ready for the one she's going to lay on you. Listen!"

And she made a hideous noise with her mouth on the back of her forearm.

"Oh, stop, I'll throw up in her face, I'll be sick on her shoes!" I cried. "I'd rather kiss a frog!"

"And you will," Cecie howled. "When you kiss Fig that's what she turns into!"

"Shhhh! She'll hear us!" I gasped.

But it was a long time before we could stop the laughter.

Three nights later we stood in a semicircle in the darkened chapter room, dressed in white robes over white formal gowns, the air dense and funereal with the smell of banked pine boughs and carnations, our twenty-seven new pledges in a semicircle before us. They wore white formals like us, but not the robes, and all were blindfolded. The room was silent except for the sound of a triangle being struck softly and monotonously in the back of the room by our Music Master, and the quick, shallow breathing of the pledges. The room was darkened by thick, heavy drapes and hot from the sucking tongues of many white candles, and our waists were all girt into breathlessness by Merry Widow waist cinches. I knew that before the five hours were over at least one of the pledges would have fainted. A pledge always did, at a Tri O initiation. It was as much a matter of exaltation as airlessness. Tri Omega brought you into its body on a tide of mystery bordering on the Eleusinian. Even though I had been through it twice now on the other side, I could remember vividly my own initiation far away in Virginia.

I cannot remember now a single secret and holy vow that I took, but I knew them all then, and I could recall in stark lunar detail the terror, exaltation, and sense of life-changing import I had felt when I became a sister. I had a craven, fleshly urge to go to the bathroom, but over that was the tremulous conviction that when the blindfold was removed and "the scales fell from my eyes," as the ritual had it, my life would forevermore be changed. I would be enhanced, enfolded, accepted; I would be given substance and purpose and definition.

I would know who I was, and what.

It had not happened so far, but I knew that our pledges felt the same. The developing hyperventilation told me, and the tears that slipped from behind several blindfolds. I felt a great surge of sisterly love, looking at them. I had wept, too. Even Fig, whose nose rattled with mucus, seemed at that moment vulnerable and dear, blood of my blood. They were all roughly eighteen years old, and as featureless and malleable as tablets of clay. That night began the process of their formation. We, the full members, were the sculptors. We loved them, in that moment, as the artist does the dream of creation before the actuality of it has sullied his canvas.

"This is going to be fine," I thought to myself. "I'm not going to have a bit of trouble kissing her." Beside me, Cecie cut her eyes over at me and grinned slightly.

"Piece of cake," I mouthed silently at her.

The ceremony began; candles were lit and extinguished, bells and the triangle rung, chimes chimed and songs sung. Solemn, binding Greek phrases, rendered doubly exotic by our Southern accents, were chanted and our pledges parroted responses like young cockatoos. The room heated and seemed to shimmer in the wash of candlelight and the miasma of nervous young bodies; the droning and the bells and chimes were both hypnotic and faintly nauseating, like the onset of seasickness. I saw a couple of pledges start to sway.

We were nearing the end of the fifth hour when the first one went over and was neatly and quickly dragged out to the anteroom. We habitually had a second, shortened ceremony for those who fainted and missed the entirety of the first one, but it was matter-of-fact and sparse, somehow shameful. A moment later another pale white form was ushered out, head bobbling. The sound of sobbing rose over the chanting, and I could hear Fig in full cry, blubbering like a giant toddler. I hoped wearily that she could get herself in hand before kissing time came round.

It was time then for the vows, and the pinning on of the golden pins, that lay in a row on a length of velvet at the altar. Each pledge was led forward by her big sister, and together the two repeated the vows of Tri Omega, and the Big Sister pinned the pin on her pledge and gave her the secret handshake and whispered in her ear the most holy Greek words of all, words that must never be said aloud. And then we untied the blindfold and kissed our new sisters, and the service was over. For reasons known only to our original founders, three pallid, bookish young women at Temple University circa 1894, this kiss was bestowed on the mouth. Many jokes were made about the founders' proclivities and the extracurricular activities at Temple but the kiss was really not a laughing matter. In those days of passionate homophobia, everyone dreaded it as if it were an act of Babylonian perversion.

I felt the first coil of nausea when the pledge just ahead of Fig was drawn forward from the semicircle by her big sister and placed before the altar. The tuna casserole we had had for dinner gave a greasy wallow in my stomach, and rose up into my throat. It stung in my nose. I shook my head, hard. I had never been sick at my stomach before in my life, or fainted. Panic rose behind the tuna fish.

I looked at Fig, and another wave broke. She was holding her arms out before her, her fingers grasping and ungrasping air, and her thick lips were working as if she were trying not to spit, or perhaps mumbling to herself. Tears spurted out below her blindfold; it was totally sodden, and the top of her skimpy white formal was as wet as if it had been rained upon. Her chest and shoulders were wet with tears, too. Her tongue flicked out and claimed one, like a lizard's a fly. She gave a great, rattling sniff. I shut my eyes and half turned away.

"Dearest God, just get me through this," I prayed. "Just do this one thing."

Somehow I found myself standing in front of Trish Farr at the altar, my hands on Fig's shoulders as she stood in front of me halfway through the vows of sisterhood. Rote took me through them. Nausea and dizziness howled around me like a storm. Fig cried loudly and openly, but she managed to repeat her vows, and I pinned the pin on her flat chest and gripped her icy hand in my icier one, and whispered the unspeakable words into her ear, and fairly jerked the blindfold off her. One more obstacle, just one, and then I could escape to the kitchen, where there was light and cold water and cool air. One more . . .

I shut my eyes and leaned in for the kiss, and then opened them. It was fatal. Fig's face was truly hideous: mottled and wet and mucus-tracked, her eyes screwed shut until they almost disappeared behind the scummed glasses. Her nose was completely sealed, and bubbled. But her mouth was slightly open, lips parted so that she could breathe through them. I could see the veining of blue on the underside of her lower lip. And I could see her pink tongue as it slipped in and out of her mouth after a stray tear, like a humming-bird darting, like a snake's. Ecstasy played around her face like heat lightning. I thought, suddenly, that when I put my mouth to hers she was going to put her tongue into it.

"I can't," I whispered. "Oh, I can't." And I turned and ran past Trish into the kitchen and slammed the door and was sick in the aluminum sink. I was still there, retching miserably, a cold dishcloth on my forehead, when the service ended and Cecie came into the kitchen to see what was the matter with me. Fig was behind her, her face blind and rapt.

"I'm so sorry," I said weakly. "I've never done that before. It was just so hot, and I felt sick . . ."

"Please don't apologize," Fig said, putting her arms around me and hugging me. I stiffened, afraid that I would vomit on her. She stepped back.

"I was deeply touched and honored," she said, her voice trembling. "I felt it, too. It was the most wonderful and powerful emotion I have ever felt. We're sisters forever, now."

Cecie and I looked wordlessly after her as she scuttled out of the room, fresh tears starting behind the thick glasses.

"Dear Jesus, God and Holy Mary," Cecie said.

I was sick in the sink once more.

Fig lost no time in exercising her powers as a Tri Omega in good standing. She was entitled to, of course, but tacit chapter etiquette held that new initiates eased into it gradually, observing a kind of seemly apprenticeship, keeping silent in meetings until opinions were invited, voting with the majority, volunteering for the most onerous tasks, like kitchen detail and pouring for coffees and teas. By the second quarter of full membership they might begin to voice opinions, and by the second year had full shouting, disagreeing, and policy-setting privileges. But Fig, being Fig, waded right in at her first chapter meeting, the one held to discuss winter rush.

This rush was far less elaborate than the big fall one, and far less favored. It was widely agreed among the Greeks that the best pledges had been snatched off in fall rush, and pickings in winter were dreary, but we went through the motions neverthe-less. The dean of women had long since decreed that winter rush be held to "give those thoughtful girls who had held back in the fall a chance to make their decision." We all knew what that meant, but there was no circumventing this small official stab at humanity. We held the rush, gracelessly and flatfootedly. As Trish Farr said grumpily, "Nothing good ever came out of winter rush."

But that year Ginger Fowler did, and it was Fig who brought her to us.

At first, we simply stared at her when she rose at the end of the meeting and said, "I've found a really super way to pay you all back for letting me be a Tri Omega. I've got us a new pledge you're all going to just love, and she's already said she'd pledge the second we bid her. She's already left Montevallo and she gets in tomorrow."

She flashed her gummy grin around the circle of sisters. Her new gold pin rode astride an astonishing left breast wrought by a new, fiercely stitched Peter Pan bra, and her eyes, behind the harlequins, shed benevolence on us like the morning sun.

I am absolutely sure that the same thought ricocheted in ninety-four other minds as it did in mine in that moment: any candidate

160

Fig Newton might bring us would be a disaster of irremediable proportions. I could not even imagine who or what this phantom rushee might be. As far as I knew, Fig had no friends outside Tri Omega, and had never given any indication that she had them at home in Fowler. I did not dare look at Cecie.

"Let me get this straight, Fig," Trish said levelly. "You've already told this . . . person . . . that we'd pledge her, and she's dropped out of Montevallo to come to Randolph and join right up. Is that right?"

Fig could read the tone, if not the words.

"Well, I guess so," she said, cutting her eyes around the room. If she had been a puppy she would have wriggled and wet the rug. "I know it was a sort of a big step to take, but you know what an impulsive old silly I am. And there's just not any doubt you're going to love her. I knew there wouldn't be. This saves us a lot of time. We could just have her over some night and give her the pledge pin then . . ."

"She will come through rush like everybody else," Trish said icily, "and we will pledge her if, and only if, this full chapter decides that she's Tri O material. If she's not, you're going to have to be the one to tell her we can't take her. What you did is against every rule we have. We could lift your pin for that."

Fig's hand flew to her pin. Her face flushed the dull magenta that, with her, meant overweening emotion.

"Well, you don't have to snap at me," she said, tears trembling in her voice. "I was only trying to do Tri O a favor. I love you all so much. And I'm right, I know I am. She's awfully rich. My home town is named for her family."

"My home town is named for a family who's given the world nine generations of albino idiots," Cecie said sweetly. "Rich doesn't always follow."

Fig looked stubbornly down at the rug. She would not meet our eyes.

"Everybody loves Ginger," she said. "And she really is rich. Her family owns all kinds of textile mills. She's got a trust fund of her own worth five million dollars. Everybody in Fowler knows that. Everybody loves her."

"Fig, she better be good as well as rich, because let me tell you, there's not enough money in the world to buy a . . . drip . . . into this chapter," Trish said righteously. I knew that she had barely restrained herself from saying, "another drip," and I knew from the deepening of the magenta flood on her neck and face that Fig knew it, too.

"She is good," she said sullenly. "You'll see."

162

And surprisingly we did, and she was. Ginger Fowler came to our first party that rush with a hot pink Jackie Kennedy pillbox on her cropped, tow-white head and pink cuban heeled pumps on her big, clumsy feet and burned a hole in our white sofa with a Menthol Kent and fell out of her pumps and over an end table, and said "Oh, shit," in such obvious anguish that laughter exploded, spontaneous and healing, and by the time we stopped we were hugging her and assuring her that we had hated the sofa anyway.

"Y'all were lucky," she said in her rich molasses voice, that always sounded as though she was just about to break into laughter. "I spilled scalding hot coffee on the Tri Delts' housemother. And one of my fingernails fell off in the ADPis' punch. At least I think it was the ADPis. They passed me through there so fast I didn't get a good look at their pins."

Her blue eyes were crinkled to slits with laughter. There were faint white lines at their corners, in the still-tanned skin. But her round, freckled cheeks were scarlet with embarrassment, and behind the white lashes I caught a glimmer of tears. I did not think she was kidding about the housemother and the fingernail.

"Your fingernail fell off?" Cecie said, her

voice bright with enchantment.

Ginger Fowler peeled off the white gloves she wore, that gave her something of the look of a traffic policeman in a dress, and held up a freckled hand. Four of the big fingers ended in perfect, gleaming, ruby-red ovals. The fifth, the middle finger, had ragged cuticles and a nail bitten down to the quick.

"It would have to be that finger, wouldn't it?" she said mournfully. The room exploded in laughter again. I knew then that rich or not, she would be one of us. Ginger Fowler remains the single most lovable and endearing person I have ever known.

The chapter spent a lot of time that winter, after we had pledged her and she toiled away in Fig's room trying desperately to make her grades for initiation, attempting to lay fingers on just what it was that made Ginger so irresistible. The closest most of us could come was "cute." "She's just so cute," one or the other of us would say helplessly, knowing it was not the right word. And it wasn't; cute, in that time and place, meant fragile, perky, fluffy, helpless, adorable, chaste as a baby chick. Ginger was none of those things. She was both tall and large-boned, with big hands and feet and the shoulders and calves of an athlete, and deep, full breasts. She had, she said, played intramural softball at

Montevallo State Teacher's College, where she had started the fall before, and been on the swim team. She was square and solid instead of fragile, clumsy instead of perky, slapdash and plainly dressed instead of fluffy (the pink pillbox and pumps disappeared after rush, never to be seen again), and about as helpless as a mechanic in a small-town garage. Instead of adorable she was profoundly and naturally funny, as opposed to clever or witty or flirtatious, and instead of being dainty and chaste she was as overflowing physical as anyone I have ever known. She touched, patted, hugged, romped, ruffled hair, slapped rumps. And she loved being touched. She had an enormous warm vitality that was like catnip to the boys: from the first night she spent under the Tri Omega roof the telephones rang off the hook for her, and she dated every night her faltering grades would allow, and never failed to come back into the house arm in arm with some rumpled, happy suitor, disheveled and smeared and grinning her exuberant white grin. It was simply not possible not to grin back at Ginger when that smile lit her chipmunk face, even when you were lecturing her despairingly about her behavior on dates, or her teetering grades.

"You just can't *do* that with everybody you

go out with," I heard Trish or Sister or someone whose business it was to keep the chapter's reputation lustrous admonish her, time after time. "You come in looking like you've been in a motel. What if you got pregnant?"

"If I got pregnant a star would rise in the East," Ginger laughed. "What do you think I could possibly be doing with an eight o'clock curfew?"

And she would come in again the next evening with another boy, laughing and rumpled and chapped with beard burn.

"Oh, Ginger, you're such a child," Trish snapped once.

"I know. I never pretended to be anything else," Ginger said contritely.

"That's just what she is, you know," Cecie said to me later that night. "A child. A big, simple child in love with the world, just delighted with it, who hasn't learned yet that the world can hurt you. That's the attraction, that innocence. It's as sweet and plain and appetizing as pancakes."

"I wouldn't call her simple, exactly," I said, looking at her in surprise. "She's quick and smart as a whip, and she's awfully intuitive. She knows what you mean without your having to spell it out. She's really got a lot of sensitivity. I don't think her grades have much to do with how she really is."

"I didn't mean simpleminded," Cecie said impatiently. "I meant . . . direct. Uncomplicated. Head on. She says whatever comes into her head and does whatever feels good. You know, she plays when she wants to and drinks beer when she thinks it will taste good and necks when she likes the guy and laughs at whatever tickles her. She'd give you the shirt off her back; you don't dare admire anything she's got, or she'll give it to you. And there isn't a female-mean bone in her body. She's like a man that way. She's even good to Fig. But she isn't mannish; in a way she's one of the most feminine people I've ever known. She's like . . . she's like . . . some kind of Mayan fertility goddess in gym shorts, or something . . ."

"Wow. I gather you approve."

"Oh, yes. I really like her an awful lot. Something about her scares me a little, though," Cecie said.

"Lord, what on earth about Ginger could possibly scare you?" I said. "She's one of the most . . . oh, vulnerable . . . people I've ever known. Like a big puppy."

"That's what," said Cecie.

She was right about Ginger's sweet nature. Ginger was the only one of us I never heard say a single malevolent thing about Fig, even though I know that Fig's cloying, Uriah-Heep obsequiousness often irritated and puzzled her. Ginger's directness could find no ken in Fig's oblique affections, and I have seen her, time after time, look at Fig in a kind of uncomprehending dismay. All that was missing, at those times, was the cocked head; she would have looked, then, uncannily like Nana in *Peter Pan*.

But she was devoted to Fig. Even when one of Fig's excesses prompted the rest of us to groan or snap with annoyance, Ginger would only smile indulgently at her, like an adult at an obstreperous child. The gargantuan, gargling snores that erupted from their room did not seem to bother her; we knew about her deaf ear, and assumed that she simply did not hear them. But she must have, for she heard other things. She heard Cecie and me laughing in the nights, and she often put her head into our room in the mornings to tease us about the late night meetings of the Randolph Intellectual Society. If she heard what we said, what we laughed at, she never said. I think she would have spoken of it, if she had. She would not have stood by and let us slander Fig.

Her patience was monumental. Fig told the story of how she brought Ginger into the bosom of Tri Omega so often that the rest of us stuck our fingers into our ears when she began it again, but Ginger heard it out every time, with only a hint of wryness in her smile.

"She was in the congregation the day I spoke at the Youth Appreciation Day service," Fig would say, "and I noticed her face looking up at me, with this kind of yearning look on it, and I knew then that rich or not, this was a lonely girl who needed friends, because you know, money doesn't always mean you'll have lots of friends, and so after the speech I went down and talked to her and told her about Randolph and Tri Omega, and before that day was over I knew she would be one of us . . ."

"Hallelujah, praise the Lord," someone would shout. "Another sinner brought into the fold!"

"Well, if it hadn't been for me you'd never have had her for a sister," Fig would say sullenly, and even though this was true, we could not seem to stop jeering at the self-serving little story. And she could not seem to stop telling it.

Finally she did, and I could not resist remarking upon it to Ginger.

"I haven't heard the story of your conversion on the road to Damascus lately," I smiled at her one night, after dinner. Fig was not about.

"My . . . ? Oh. No. I finally just told her to stop it," Ginger said.

"We are eternally grateful," I said. "I think somebody would have throttled her the next time she trotted it out."

"Well, I don't care if she tells it every day," Ginger said. "She's right. If it hadn't been for her, I wouldn't be in Tri O. But I didn't want y'all mad at her. She really doesn't know how she sounds sometimes."

I went back to my room, chastened.

"Ginger Fowler really is too nice for the likes of us. I'm glad to be back with catty, comfy old you," I said to Cecie. She looked up over the horn-rims, which had slipped down on her nose.

"Glad to hear it," she said. "Fig is foiled once more."

"What?" I looked at her.

"Haven't you caught on yet that Fig lured Ginger to Randolph to be the friend of your bosom?" Cecie said. "What do you think all that business about compatibility is? Why do you think she pushes Ginger down your throat every time you turn around?"

"Cecie, what on earth is the matter with you?" I said, honestly puzzled.

"Think about it," Cecie said, and went back to her paper on Disraeli.

I lay in bed that night staring at the pattern

170

of light from the outside floods on our ceiling, and I did think about it. And I saw what she meant. Or at least, I saw what might have brought her to say it. I did not, then, see that it was true. For the longest time I thought, simply, that Cecie might be the slightest bit jealous of Ginger Fowler. Later I apologized to her for the thought when I came to see that she was right, but it put, that quarter, a tiny distance between Cecie and me, and I can only speculate what that cost her. She did not speak of it again.

From the night Ginger pledged, Fig had told me over and over that I was going to love her.

"You're going to be just so compatible, you two," she would say. "You're so alike, and you have so much in common . . . you know, your background and all." She did not say money, but I knew what she meant. No matter what I said, I could not disabuse Fig of the notion that I was rich and attempting to appear not to be.

"She's just like you, you'd never know she was . . . you know, special. She's just as everyday and down to earth as you are, Effie. But you can tell, oh, yes. Blood will tell. My mother says that. Blood will tell."

"Let's spill a little and see," Cecie said once. Fig did not hear her.

As the days went on, it was apparent that Ginger was as unlike me as it was possible to be; she was all the things I was not: open, direct, earthy, uncomplicated, unlettered and uninterested in being so. The affection between us was warm and real, but it never was grounded in likeness. But Fig went on all that quarter, in full cry about our compatibility.

"Did you ever see two people as compatible as Effie and Ginger?" she would say to whoever was around us in a group. "Just as alike as two peas in a pod. They might be twins."

The others would look at Ginger and me in puzzlement, and politely let it drop. But it began to bother me, especially in light of what Cecie had said. I think it did Ginger, too. Sometimes she gave Fig a long, unreadable look.

Fig did not stop with her observations of compatibility. She pressed us together as if she had been a professional Jewish matchmaker.

"Are you going to the drugstore?" she would say, as I left the house jingling my car keys. "Wait a minute and let me tell Ginger. She needs some Tampax."

"Let's go to Bernie's and get some hot chocolate," she would say. "I heard Ginger say she wanted some."

And: "If you're taking your car over to McCandless, would you drop Ginger off at the library? She's got a cold, and it's starting to sleet out."

And: "Come in our room and listen to Ginger do 'Streets of Laredo.' Her daddy sent her a guitar for her birthday."

For a while I went or did not go as the spirit moved me; I noticed nothing odd about the invitations until Cecie's calm statement that night. And then I noticed their deviousness and frequency, and became so self-conscious and annoyed with Fig for issuing them and even Cecie for remarking on them that I stopped going into Ginger's presence altogether for a time. And then one night at supper Ginger herself said, in as much annoyance as I had ever heard in her voice, "Fig, I don't want to go to the drugstore with Kate and she doesn't want to hear me do 'Streets of Laredo' again, and nobody gives a shit who's compatible with who. Will you please lay off it? What's the matter with you?"

After that Fig stopped her Kate-Ginger campaign. But I knew then that Cecie had been right, and I told her so.

"I'm sorry," I said. "She's such a toad, she even had me thinking you might be jealous of Ginger. What do you think she thought, that Ginger and I would be queer for each other?"

"I rather think she thought that you and I already were," Cecie said dryly. "And she couldn't abide that. Poor old Ginger got brought in as a stalking horse."

"God," I said, my cheeks burning. "Sometimes I think I'm going to spend the rest of my life in the shadow of Fig Newton."

"Don't even say it," Cecie said.

All during that winter, Ginger toiled valiantly to get her grades up so that she could be initiated at the beginning of spring quarter. She gave up her nightly dates and her bridge games and stayed doggedly at the library or in her room, buried in books. Her major was elementary education and there was nothing in the textbooks on basic English, civics and sociology that demanded much of her, but her attention span was short, and sustained concentration was agony for her. We would find her in tears of frustration and hopelessness often, her freckled face red and screwed up like a child's, her cottony thatch of hair wet with sweat. It was a sight to wring the heart, for she was making a heroic effort, and so Cecie and I and Fig took turns drilling and tutoring her, from the time our last class was over until far into the nights.

On the day of her last final that quarter she came into our room with her broad face suffused with joy.

"I think I did it," she said. "There haven't been more than three or four questions on any exam that I haven't known. I think I made my grades, and it's because of y'all, and we are all going to get drunk as skunks tonight."

Fig's mouth dropped open, but Cecie and I looked at each other with speculation as well as apprehension. On the one hand, drinking at Randolph was, for women students, an offense punishable by dismissal; but on the other, I knew very few women students who had not at least had a covert beer or two on a fraternity houseparty weekend. Cecie and I did not drink much, and I knew Fig had never even tasted what she called, piously, spirits. But abstinence was not a policy with Cecie and me, and we could see, in each other's eyes, speculation winning out over apprehension. It was unusually hot for March, and we were exhausted, and finals were over. Ginger's success was a real triumph.

"Oh, why not?" Cecie said.

"Why, indeed?" I said.

"I'm not going to do anything that would get me thrown out of Tri O," Fig mewled.

"Y'all can if you want to. I won't tell. But *I'm* not."

That clinched it.

"Let the good times roll," Cecie chanted. Then she stopped. "Where are we going to get the booze?"

"Already got it," Ginger grinned. "It's in the bottom of my laundry bag. A fifth of gin and a fifth of bourbon. I got Snake Clinkscales to get it for me at the ABC store over in Montgomery. I thought tonight could either be a celebration or a wake. Thank God and y'all it's not the latter."

"When?" I said.

"After last curfew. And I have another surprise. I got the key to the roof door. We can take pillows up there and get cold drinks for mixers and nobody on earth can hear us."

"How did you get the key?" Fig asked, clearly horrified. The door that led up a short stairway to the flat, Greek revival roof of the Tri Omega house had only one known key, and that was kept on a peg in our housemother's suite. Too many sisters, over the years, had had the same idea Ginger had.

"I got it off her peg last week when she went to get me an aspirin," Ginger said, wrinkling her nose. "I told her I had awful cramps. I got a copy made at the hardware store and put it back when she went to Montgomery last Sunday. She never missed it."

We burst into laughter. She was so clearly and ingenuously pleased with herself, and so blithely unconcerned with the morality of the thing, that any lingering doubts we had faded like smoke. There could be no more serious repercussions to our night of sin than to a child's prank, for Ginger's authorship of it made it just that.

"You have a great career in crime ahead of you," I told her. "You could be a cold-blooded murderer and you'd still look like Huckleberry Finn stealing apples. No jury on earth would find you guilty."

Fig abruptly abandoned temperance.

"You talked me into it," she chortled, though no one had. "I can't wait to see Effie Lee drunk. That'll be something to tell my grandchildren." And she rolled her eyes at me.

"Please don't be swayed on my account," I said acidly. "I wouldn't corrupt you for the world."

"Oh, no. I know if you do it, it's okay," she said. "I'm looking forward to it. You all will have to show me how, though. I'm really an awful square."

"You could have fooled me," Cecie said.

That night, after all the other lights on

the top floor of the house had darkened, we took pillows and towels and sweating bottles of Coca Cola and Seven Up and Ginger's clinking laundry bag and stole up the stairs to the roof. We were already laughing so hard, and shushing each other so loudly, that I am sure we would have been apprehended except that most others in the house were sleeping the dead sleep of post-exam exhaustion. We may have been seen anyway; if so, nothing ever came of it. But I can imagine what we must have looked like: four furtive shapes in shortie pajamas and pin curls, with Noxema dots shining fluorescently in the dark, bent over with laughter, legs crossed to keep from wetting our pants, gasping with fright and glee. It makes me smile even now, to think of it. Even with Alan, one of the world's great, gifted laughers, I have not laughed as we did that night.

We did get drunk. It did not take long. We lay on our towels and pillows on the gritty, cinder-strewn roof, with only a fretted white wooden railing around us, and resolutely drank our foul-tasting, warm drinks, and reveled in the wash of air on our near-naked bodies. The outside air was not much cooler than that inside, but it seemed so; there was such an amplitude of empty space around us, three stories up, looking down into the lacy treetops. Over us stars swam, and fireflies made a storm of tiny lights below us. There was an enchantment abroad that night, star-silvered and airborne, that was not entirely the work of the liquor. Below us, the dark campus slept.

I think we sang a little, in low, cracking voices, to the faulty strain of Ginger's birthday guitar. We did not dare raise our voices high. I know that we laughed a great deal, but softly, holding our hands over our mouths and snuffling. Fig snorted and gargled through her poor, afflicted nose, and giggled so hysterically that we fell to shushing her fiercely, which only spurred her on. Finally the laughter feathered out, and we lay back and watched the skies wheel over us, the liquor seeming to bear us up to meet the very swimming stars.

We talked a little about what we would do after graduation, or rather, Cecie and I did. By this time of night and level of the two bottles our already splendid careers in design and law bloomed into singular magnificence. I would be designing rooms and houses and furniture that defined and named decades; she would structure and defend legislation that would ensure prosperity and justice for those same decades. Medals, prizes, international honors rolled around the Tri Omega roof like fireballs. Glory burst in the heavens and spilled down on us. Tears of exaltation and humility stood in our eyes.

"It's important to use your gifts for mankind," I remember saying carefully, unaware that I was slurring very slightly.

"Oh, it is," Fig said, tears husking her voice. "You're so right, Effie. I'm going to remember that when I'm a famous author. I'm only going to write profound, uplifting, beautiful things. And I'm going to start with what you said tonight. I'm going to put it in my diary right now."

And she reached for the diary, which lay under her towel.

"If you write one word in that thing I'm going to throw it off this roof," Ginger said. But she was smiling. She had been lying back listening to us, her head pillowed on her crossed arms, chugging steadily on her Bourbon-spiked Coke. Her white-blond hair gleamed eerily in the dark. She had not joined our talk of the future.

"What will you do when you graduate, Ginger?" Cecie said.

"Go back to Fowler and teach school, I guess," she said comfortably. "Get married. Have children. You know."

"Well, sure, eventually, but I mean right

180

after?" Cecie pursued. "You could do anything in the world you want to. Go to New York with Kate. Come to Europe with us and bum around for a year. Join the Peace Corps, if you want to teach. But you really ought to live a little before you settle down. Set the world on fire."

"Oh, I couldn't," Ginger said. "I'm not smart like you and Kate and Fig. I'm not exactly stupid, but I know I ain't much in the brains department. My dad has always told me that. He laughs and says I'll need a keeper all my life. And I guess he's right; I couldn't even make my grades without you all."

"That's ridiculous," I said. "Next time you'll do it by yourself. Who does he think is going to be your keeper when you're out and on your own?"

"I don't think he thinks I ever will be," Ginger said. "He'll have somebody picked out for me, when the time comes. There are lots of boys my age in Fowler. Not bad ones, either. I don't think it'll be a problem. I'll inherit the mills, you know."

There was no hint of boasting or rancor in the words, not even of resignation. Her voice was light and level and rich, as always. The appalling scenario seemed not to bother her.

181

"That's awful," Cecie said heatedly. "You deserve better than that, Ginger. You can't just let somebody else decide your whole future for you. What about what you want?"

"Well, see, there's not anything I really want, except what I have now," Ginger said, and suddenly there was something in her voice. Sadness lay under it, and something that I thought was fear.

I looked over at her, and she smiled at me. There was a gleam of wetness in her eyes.

"Sometimes I think I can't stand for all this to end," she said. "Sometimes I think school and singing and laughing and you all are the best there is in the world. I really can't bear to think about graduating."

"Well, you have a way to go yet," I said, unable to think of anything else that might comfort her. I could not imagine thinking of school that way. To me, the best that there ever was was always around the next bend.

We lay silent for a while, looking at the night. On the hill above the Tri Omega house the edge of the national forest that housed Lake Randolph rose up against the sky. It was black and deep, and above it the sky was milky with stars. Behind the trees, a late moon climbed, and as we looked, it rode out and above them into the sky, like a galleon on fire. I felt tears of liquor and profound exaltation fill my eyes. My heart felt as if it would burst out of my chest at the sheer beauty of the night around me. It is easy, these years later, to appreciate how much of the drama and profundity of that night, that time, was melodrama and sentimentality. But I would still give much to recapture the totality of those feelings.

"That's the very bulk of God," I said lugubriously, pointing at the line of the trees. "That makes me believe in all of it. Everything."

"Well, not me," Fig said. Her voice was, suddenly, very faraway and cold, and her words were singsong and as precise as flint. I had never heard that voice before. We all looked over at her.

"It makes me believe nothing," she said. "It makes me see it's all a lie. There isn't going to be anything for us when we die. Look at those stars. Do you realize that those stars are going to be burning up there in that empty sky long after we and everybody else are dead and in the ground? There we'll be, just lost in blackness, and those stupid stars will shine on, and on . . . and for us it will be . . . black. Nothing. Black nothing. Black forever and ever and ever . . ."

We were silent. Cold crept along my spine and into my blood. Cold and emptiness. The abyss whispered below me like a snake. Beside me, I felt Cecie stir uneasily.

"Just black," Fig said.

Suddenly Ginger was weeping. She cried like a child, her mouth open and square, her fist scrubbing her eyes.

"I don't want to die," she sobbed. "I don't. Oh, God, I don't . . ."

"Well, you will," Fig said in the new, eerie voice. "You will. All your money won't stop you from dying, and you know it."

"I don't know it," Ginger wailed. "I don't have to know it, and I won't. I won't."

"You do have to. You do and you will. You can't ever not know it again."

"Shut up, Fig," Cecie hissed suddenly, furiously. "Shut up or I'll shut you up . . ."

Fig lay still for a moment, breathing hard and wetly, her eyes screwed shut behind the glasses. Then she rolled over and was sick over the roof railing. We could hear it hit the brick walkway far below.

We slept late the next morning, all of us, and when we woke, it was to rueful laughter, and much ceremony about the taking of aspirin for our aching heads. We seemed, in our sleep, to have come to some agreement not to speak of the sad, sorry end to the evening, and no one did. Fig was fully back to herself, and so was Ginger. But I knew something new about Ginger now. I knew that she was, like me, like Cecie, a walker over the abyss, and that she would never allow herself to acknowledge it. I knew, without being able to articulate it, that she would die, literally die, in order to remain a good child, one who would always be shielded by others from that waiting emptiness. It was not a knowledge that I could bear, and so I put it away from me. But after that, it was always there.

Grades were posted the next day and Ginger passed all her exams, though admittedly in some instances by a hair. That night at dinner we gave her a standing ovation, and she cried and went around the table, hugging us one by one.

"I don't think there'll ever be a happier night in my life," she said mistily. "Not even my wedding night."

"Oh, how can you say that?" trilled Francine Powers, who had recently become ostentatiously engaged to her porcine SAE, Grunt. We all groaned. Everyone was getting a little tired of Francine's exalted carryings on.

"Well, see, I've *done* the Black Act," Ginger

grinned at her. "I've never made my grades before."

"Do you think she really has?" I said to Cecie that night.

"Probably," Cecie said. "I have a feeling it's no bigger thing to Ginger than sleeping late or dancing or eating pizza. It all feels good and makes her happy, so why not?"

"Do you ever wish it was that simple?"

"I've always thought it probably was going to be that simple, when I got right down to it," Cecie said equably. "It's just a matter of finding the person it'll be simple with. That's the one requirement. Can you imagine doing it with Grunt?"

"Well, it would be simple with Grunt, all right," I said. "Wham bam, thank you ma'am. The thing is, I can't really imagine doing it with anybody."

"You will," she said.

School closed that Friday for spring break, and the night before, Ginger put her head into our room and said, "I just talked to my folks, and they're going to open the house at Nag's Head this weekend. Daddy said if y'all would like to come up with me he'd send Robert for us with the car and he'd drive us up, and bring us back next week in time for classes. Please come. I want to show Daddy what kind of friends I have.

He won't believe it."

We said yes before the words were out of her mouth. I had been dreading going home to the crumbling house on the Santee where my mother entertained, prissily, the disapproving deacon, and the prospect of adventure was always manna to Cecie. Fig was beside herself. She prattled about suntan lotion and Rose Marie Reid swimsuits and summer houses until Ginger told her, good-naturedly, to shut up. I felt an unexpected pang of pity for her, watching her put dreadful and inappropriate things into an aqua plastic Samsonite suitcase. This trip must be, to her, akin to a street urchin's being invited to the palace. It was something she had never even aspired to. A kind of irritated protectiveness flooded me. I could already feel the cool eyes of Ginger's rich mother on her.

"Robert and the car" proved, astoundingly, to be an enormous Cadillac Coupe de Ville with a jump seat in back, driven by an impassive middle-aged white man in a dark sack suit and a peaked chauffeur's cap. Cecie and Fig simply stared, mouths open, as he loaded our luggage into the trunk and held the doors for us. Even I stared. I had seen chauffeured automobiles before, but not at Randolph. The rest of the chapter stood on the steps and hung out windows, goggling frankly. Ginger stomped about cheerfully, but her neck and cheeks were dull red under the freckles. We had long known that there was money behind Fowler Mills, of course, but none of us had much concept of wealth, and Ginger went to elaborate pains to conceal her provenance. Her clothes were plain and disheveled to the near-edge of shabbiness, and she had brought no car to school with her. We forgot, for long stretches of time, that the cold, fast Warrior River pumped money into C. D. "Buck" Fowler's pockets as steadily as it powered his mills. But we would not forget now.

Robert acknowledged Ginger's introduction with a nod so scant and a brow so thunderous that we were intimidated. But Ginger giggled as she watched him toss our luggage into the vast trunk.

"He's mad," she whispered. "Daddy's regular driver is Woodrow and Robert feels like driving a bunch of giggling college girls is beneath him. Usually he works in the mill."

"Where's Woodrow?" Cecie said.

"Well, you know," Ginger said. "Woodrow is a Negro. We're going to have to stop overnight in Charlotte or somewhere, and . . . it's just better if Robert drives. But he feels like he's been demoted. I'll bet you he doesn't say five words between here and the Outer Banks."

And he didn't. The new green of the advancing spring streamed across Alabama and Georgia and into North Carolina, and we chattered and giggled and slept and woke again, and Robert drove stoically, stopping only when Ginger pleaded, "Robert, I don't think we can wait till you get low on gas. And we're hungry. Please stop the next place you see."

And he would, silently. He would be waiting in the car, eyes straight ahead, when we came gratefully out of the rest room, and we ate our candy bars and potato chips and drank our Cokes on the road. I never saw Robert eat, and I never saw him go into a men's room.

The next afternoon, after a straight, seemingly endless, grind across North Carolina's fertile black flatlands, we crossed the Albemarle River and then Roanoke Sound, at Manteo, and turned left onto a narrow, pitted blacktop road that paralleled the coast. It was lined with small, unpainted beach shacks on stilts, and bait and souvenir shops, and an occasional fish restaurant; on the left, on the land side, great dunes lifted their heads into the paling sky, larger dunes than any I had ever seen, even on the Cape. They were small sand mountains; they were awesome, out of humanity's scale. They were covered with low, scrubby vegetation, but there were no houses on them, and no roads seemed to lead up to them. On the right, more unpretentious beach houses lifted their second and third stories above another, lowered line of dunes that fringed the ocean. But the ocean itself was out of sight. It was both a wild landscape and an entirely banal one. I was obscurely disappointed. The Outer Banks had always been in my mind the very epitome of wildness and romance.

Then Robert turned the big car off the blacktop onto a narrow sandtrack that led through the secondary dune line, straight toward the hidden sea, and I saw them for the first time, the grand old Unpainted Aristocracy of Nag's Head. A line of perhaps thirty or forty huge old beach houses, side by side at the crest of the primary dune line, alone against the pearled evening sky like a congregation of crouching witches looking out to sea. They were enormous, tall, black-weathered, stark against the horizon, unsoftened by trees or plantings or much of anything else. Just the great, shifting, breastlike curves of the sand and the houses and the empty sky. They stood, all of them, on great stilts, like massive old crones on

190

reed-thin legs, and they soared three and sometimes, with widow's walks and crows' nests, four stories into the sweet, streaming salt air. I felt something old and slow and heretofore undiscovered turn over in my chest, as if a sleeping homunculus had wakened.

Robert pulled the car up into the soft sand yard of one of the last houses in the line, and we got out, stretching and sniffing and staring, silent. The house was a beetling, shingled Victorian pile, weathered dark gray to near-black, its turrets and towers roofed with lighter gray cedar shake, its seemingly countless deep-shuttered windows open to the sea wind. It had portholes and millwork and chimney pots and cupolas and porches and gray steps connecting many levels of decking; it sat in a feathery nest of beach grass, and had a border of old wax myrtle, yaupon, bayberry, and Spanish bayonet. A line of stunted black-green Norfolk pines made a windbreak that, with the line of the dunes' crown, shut the sea from sight. But we could hear it, booming hollowly on the beach below and beyond us. Ginger ran up the wooden steps to greet her parents, who were standing on the deck, waving their welcome. Fig trailed her like a puppy. Cecie and I, without a word and with one accord, went straight through the pines and over the dunes as if sung to the sea by a water witch.

We stood on the high green crown and looked down at the sea. A wooden walkway led from the porch down through the low, scrubby vegetation to the tan sand itself. The walkway was weathered to near-black like the house, and it snaked its way through drifts of sea oats, beach grass, and a dense, low matting of little running plants and flowers I could not name. The sand itself was powdery and soft, drifting like whipped cream and then melting into damp, packed flatness and finally a shining mirror where earth met water. The combers marched in stately and perfect, unhurried and unimpeded in their progress straight from Spain. The water, except for where it broke white on the beach, was the deep, true blue of gentians, or lapis lazuli. No one was on the beach below, and no sails broke the great, tossing blueness, and no sound but the hollow boom . . . hushhhh of the water and the bronze calling of gulls reached our ears. The wind was straight off the sea and fresh and nearly chilly, blowing our hair straight back, but the sun on the backs of our necks and shoulders was still hot.

We stood for a while, not speaking. When we heard Ginger calling out to us, we turned toward the house. We stopped once more. On the sea side it was all glass, one entire wall a great arched window that came to a point up under the eaves, framed in gray Victorian millwork and unimpeded by panes. The half-oval of glass must have been two full stories tall; inside we could see, dimly, a great stone wall dominated by a huge fireplace and shining bare floors and oversized furniture set about, and an enormous refectory dining table and chairs. It was simple, but the total effect was breath-stopping. Its impact was, I saw, all in its scale, and in the uninterrupted mingling of living space and sea and sky. The architect who had envisioned this window had known what true enchantment was.

"Oh, Lord," Cecie murmured. I thought it was a prayer. "Amen," I said. And we turned from the sea and went in to meet Ginger's parents.

Fig told me later that she had been a little disappointed with the house.

"I mean, they hadn't even painted it," she said. "It was big and all, but with all that money, you'd have thought they might get something, you know, a little grander. It just doesn't look like rich."

But I had seen the austere, sprawling old summer enclaves of the truly wealthy on the islands and beaches of the Northeast, and I knew what this house said. I was unalterably and forever lost to it by the time I set foot on the first step leading up to the deck; I could feel my very bones softening with love and yearning for this crazy, wind-borne old house, and my heart aching fiercely with the wanting of it. To this day, long gone to earth in my own much-loved house by the sea some eight hundred miles north of it, I still dream of Ginger Fowler's house on the Outer Banks of North Carolina. Everything about it, and the fierce old coast around it, had the ring and taste and feel of utter rightness to me. Its peace and loneliness crept into my veins and ran there, its wildness called out to the deep-buried wildness in my heart. I, who had never found earth beneath my feet that called "home" up to me, here found home raging through my entire body like an ague.

"If I ever get married I want to spend my honeymoon here," I said, smiling at Ginger's mother and taking her outstretched hands in mine.

"You can have it for as long as you want it, if you'll let me be your bridesmaid," Ginger said, wriggling with the happiness of showing this treasure to us.

"Me, too," Fig chimed.

"Well, why not just have the wedding here, then?" Mrs. Fowler smiled, and "It's a deal," I said, and we went into the house where Ginger's father waited to impale steaks on skewers and immolate them, and the week flowed forward.

Late that night a storm broke over the house. Ginger's father had told us he thought one was likely; it was, he said, the season for the great spring thunderstorms, and he had seen the vast sweeps of the feathery mare's-tail clouds riding in off the sea earlier in the day.

"Outer Banks are the storm capital of the world," he said, with the genial, savage authority with which he said everything. He was a giant blond copy of Ginger, with a blunt red face, white eyebrows and lashes, narrow blue eyes, and a perennial shout that made even his frequent sallies into humor threatening. I could see why Ginger had remained the sweet-tempered child that she was; it was clear that that was how Buck Fowler wanted her, and it would have taken a daughter of far rarer complexity, toughness, and guile to circumvent him than Ginger. I doubted that I could have. Cecie might have.

"Right down the coast yonder, at Hatteras, the Gulf Stream and the Labrador Current come together, and it kicks up such a fuss that they call it the graveyard of the Atlantic," Buck Fowler said. "More than five hundred ships have gone aground there. Up here at Nag's Head, too. Way it got its name, the old-time Bankers used to hang lanterns on the heads and tails of their horses and lead 'em along the dunes down the beach, and the ships would think they were heading into safe harbor and go aground on the shoals right out there. Bankers would come out and plunder 'em."

And he laughed hugely. I shivered. In my mind's eye I could see it, the black raging seas, and the splintered ships sliding slowly under the surf, and the screams in the darkness, and the silent rowboats coming on inexorably, like a flock of poisonous water insects. . . . When we were lying in the twin beds in the room Mrs. Fowler had given us that night, that faced the Porch and the sea, and had turned off the light so that the faint silver line of the surf shone like ghost water, I said to Cecie, "What do you think of them?"

"She's nice," Cecie's voice came through the darkness. "But he's . . . he's something else again. I think he'd have loved to be right out there with those pirates, carrying off the spoils from dead men. He makes my blood run cold."

"Mine, too," I said. "Poor Ginger. But this place. Cecie . . . what about this place?"

"It's better than cancer," Cecie said drowsily, and we laughed, and slid into that thick black sleep that the sea sends.

When the lightning and thunder and the great, booming surf woke me hours later, I could see instantly, from the malign white flashes of the lightning bolts, that Cecie's bed was empty, and she was not in the room. Alarm had me on my feet and at the door of our room before I consciously thought of getting up. I did not know why I was uneasy; it was likely that she was in the bathroom, down the hall. I padded barefoot out into the hall and looked, but the door was ajar and the room dark and empty. I went silently through the sleeping house in my shorty pajamas, and out onto the porch. Cold rain blew almost horizontally onto the porch, so furiously that I could not see into and through it. I peered along the walkway through the dunes down to the beach. It, too, was black, and roared with the fury of the storm. I was suddenly terribly, terribly frightened.

I put my hands to my mouth to call her, and then a great bolt of lightning split the teeming sky and I saw her. She was far below me on the beach, at the very edge of the water; had, in fact, waded in as far as her knees. Lightning bloomed again and I saw that she was naked, her small body silver-white and perfect against all that shouting, heaving blackness, her arms lifted to the sky, her head thrown back as if to receive in her face the full fury of wind and rain. As I watched, in the flickering light of the now near-constant lightning, she began to dance, an exultant, splashing little dance, turning round and round in the water and flinging her arms over her head. She stooped and scooped black water up and flung it about her, and then she dived into the sea and disappeared.

My heart stopped absolutely still, and jolted forward only when I saw her dark head break the water a few yards out. She was swimming strongly, parallel to the beach, and every now and then she turned over on her back and let the rain pound into her face. I watched for another moment, and then I turned and went back through the house and crawled into my bed and pulled the covers over my head. My heart was pounding, great, slow, dragging beats, and the picture of her, pagan-naked and alone in that terrible storm, in that black sea, seemed literally burned into my retinas. I still see it; when I think of Cecie Rushton Hart, that image from the beach at Nag's Head is what comes to me first.

I had my back to her and was feigning sleep when she came into the room. I heard her slide under the covers, and it seemed a very long time until I heard the familiar sound of her breathing in sleep. I knew that I would never speak of it to her. I would as soon have asked someone about their wedding night, or their conversion to faith. But I hoped she would speak to me about it. It seemed to hang in the air between us, an enormity.

But, the next morning, when Mrs. Fowler said, "I thought I heard somebody out on the porch in the middle of that storm last night," Cecie said only, mildly, "It was me. I went out to bring in my bathing suit. I left it on the railing last night. I hope I didn't disturb you."

"Oh, no," Regina Fowler said. "But it was quite a storm, wasn't it? I'd love to have seen it over the ocean. Did anybody wake up and look?"

"Not me," Fig and Ginger said together. Cecie turned and looked at me, an unreadable look. And I knew then that she knew I had seen her, dancing her little dance of rapture and abandon on that wild beach, swimming in her pearly nakedness in that wild sea.

"I woke up but it was too dark to see anything," I said.

She never did speak of it to me. From that moment, I think, we began, in grief and helplessness, to part from each other. I still do not know why. She always was a creature of secrets and intuitions; perhaps she sensed him waiting ahead for me, felt and smelled Paul Sibley like an animal or an Indian, and knew him for what he was, and would be to me. And began to leave me before I could leave her.

When I got back to Randolph for the last quarter of my junior year he was there, and after that nothing was ever the same.

CHAPTER SIX

I saw him days before I met him. He walked into Louis Cooney's dreaded, mandatory Survey of World Design class on the first day of the spring quarter, fifteen minutes late and obviously unrepentant. The soft inhalation that went up from perhaps eighty throats was as much for his audacity as his physical presence. Both were formidable.

Nobody was late for Louis Cooney's class with impunity, and no one was ever late twice. Cooney was a slight, shudderingly homely, snake-tongued homosexual who punished male students for being not-so-covertly repelled by him, and female students for being competition for the males. No one escaped his tongue and few of us escaped his punitive grading system. He seemed to dislike me more than the norm for the women students, and to spew over me more than his automatic spray of sarcasm and spittle; it had become, last quarter in his Industrial Design course, a kind of grim joke. Since I could not escape his classes if I wished to graduate and it was clear that to call attention to myself was suicide, I sat far in the back and kept as quiet as I could. When the newcomer strolled in fifteen minutes late without even the coating of sweat that meant an earnest attempt at promptness, I cringed for him, and waited for the inevitable.

"Ah, well. And what have we here, dragging in like the cat's dinner? Sitting Bull, I presume?" Louis Cooney drawled.

The class gasped again. The young man did indeed look like an Indian, though perhaps an idealized Frederic Remington Indian. He was tall, and appeared taller because he held himself very straight, and his high-planed, narrow face was dark with what seemed more than sun. He had a high-bridged hawk's nose and dark eyes set very deeply under level brows, and a lock of thick, absolutely straight black hair fell over his forehead. Somehow the sheer, physical fact of him smote the air, and a kind of stillness radiated from him like an odor. He stopped in the door and stood looking mildly at Louis Cooney. His hands hung loosely and easily at his sides, and he seemed to me very like a wild animal at rest in its habitat, relaxed but alert. He did not speak.

"Do you have a name or shall we call you Tonto?" Louis Cooney said. He was flushed, and I could see that something about the young man made him very angry. He did not usually resort to clumsiness.

"Paul Sibley." The man — for he was that — was, I thought, a good five years older than the rest of us. "But Tonto will be fine. And I'll call you White Eyes, shall I?"

He smiled lazily at Louis Cooney. His voice was deep and slow, with nothing of boyhood in it. There was a faint something there, the edge of an accent of some kind. His teeth were very white. I felt my chest tighten, and realized that I was holding my breath. I let it out, and inhaled.

"Sit down, Mr. Sibley. You have just had a point taken off your final grade for this course. You will be silent in my class and you will not behave like a *cochon* here."

Louis Cooney had studied in France, and let no one forget it for long.

Paul Sibley smiled.

"Tout les hommes sont des cochons, non?" he said in rapid, fluid French.

There was a furtive ripple of laughter from the class. Not one in twenty of us understood French, but we all understood the tone.

"That's one point off the grades of every person in this room," Cooney spat, and the laughter stopped. But glee lingered in the eyes that followed Paul Sibley as he found a seat near the front and folded himself loosely into it. Eyes swung to him from time to time throughout that entire first lecture. Mine hardly left him. I could not seem to will them away, and I could not stop the pounding of my heart. I had never seen anything remotely like this dark hawk of a man.

"Who is that?" I said to Janellen French, who worked in the admissions office, after class. Janellen would know, if anyone would.

I did not have to tell her whom I meant. Several other students were clustered around her, obviously having asked the same thing. Janellen was pursed with importance.

"He's a transfer from North Carolina State, in architecture," she said. "He must be good; I've never seen grades like that. He lives off campus, over on Scofield. He's here on the G.I. Bill and the McCandless scholarship. He lists North Miami as his place of birth, but he's lived all over, and he was in France in the army for four years before he started at N.C. State. No living close relatives. He qualified for room and board in one of the dorms, but he refused it. He's paying for his own apartment. It must be the pits, if it's on Scofield; I think he's probably very poor."

"Lord, Janellen, no shoe size? No color preference?" I said. I did not know why her smug litany of information about Paul Sibley annoyed me. I had asked, too, after all.

"Well, don't pretend you wouldn't have

204

read his folder after you'd gotten a look at him," she said, smirking. "You're only the fifth girl who's asked me about him, and this is the first day of classes. And look at your face; you're red as a beet!"

I knew from the heat in my chest and cheeks that it was true. I left hastily for my next class. The image of that dark face and ripe voice went with me through the day, and was there when I awoke on the next.

I thought that I might meet him naturally in the course of the design class, but it was soon obvious that he was not interested in meeting any of us. He was not rude, only remote. He was usually in his seat when I got there, intent on his notes, and left without speaking or nodding to anyone when the class was over. He went purposefully, with a long, padding stride that seemed to start in his hips, like a big cat's. Cooney didn't speak to him again after that first day, and did not call on him in class.

I saw him frequently after class that first week, but he never saw me. I could have sworn to that. I saw him twice in Harry's in the afternoons, drinking coffee and reading alone in a booth, but though I haunted Harry's in the afternoons after that, his visits had no discernible pattern. Both times he was in what had become, to me, his uniform:

sharply creased cotton chinos, a blue oxford-cloth shirt with the sleeves rolled up his dark forearms, white tennis shoes with no socks. Both times he seemed oblivious to the eyes that turned to him. I was not the only one who felt the magnet of his presence.

I saw him sometimes at the drawing board in his permanent lab on the third floor of McCandless, but since the Interior Design department was on the first, I had no real reason to be there, and was embarrassed to be spotted lolling about the halls. Once I saw him going into the coin laundry across from McCandless, his laundry bag over his shoulder, and felt a flush of intimate heat all over my body at the thought of his clothes, that had been next to that dark body, crumpled softly in the bag. I was so discomfited at the thought that I blushed even darker. Charlie Boyd, who had the board beside mine, said, "You okay?"

"Yeah," I said. "Hot in here, though."

I found excuses to drive down Scofield at least once a day. Cecie remarked on it.

"What are you going this way for?" she said, when I drove that way en route to Dairyland for a limeade one warm afternoon that first week.

"Why not? We never come this way," I said casually.

"Nobody does, who doesn't have to," she said. Scofield was an unlovely street of sagging small frame houses with garages behind them, melting into the earth and supported by honeysuckle and kudzu thickets. Many of these garages had been converted into student apartments; I knew that Paul Sibley lived in one.

"I just get tired of College Street," I said.

"You're the driver," Cecie said.

On Thursday of that week I saw him coming out of one of the garage apartments, and my heart gave a lizardlike leap in my chest, as if I had seen a wild animal or a fire raging. I stepped on the gas and swept by, eyes ahead. The number was 43 Scofield. I did not drive that way again. I was acutely embarrassed by my own behavior, and besides, now I had a context for him.

Talk about him was rife in McCandless Hall. He had captured our collective imagination as surely as if he wore a dark cloak and a slouch hat. I heard that he had made the best grades in architecture anyone ever had at North Carolina State, and that two of his student projects had been built. He had, it was said, won an international design competition while he was in Paris and, on the strength of it, had a job waiting for him in New York with the legendary McKim,

Mead and White when he graduated from architecture school, providing that school was an American one. He had transferred to Randolph because it had a superb reputation for engineering and building technology and he wanted to learn that; he was purported to have said, at his application interview, that he did not think his own innate design ability needed much in the way of instruction. He was, indeed, very poor. He was half Seminole Indian. He had won regional races on a Harley Davidson in his youth, and had been a cycle racer of some note in France.

He was a widower. He had married a French girl, from Orléans, early in his stay there with the army, and she had been killed in a fall from the back of his cycle. He never spoke of her, and he did not race anymore. They had had no children.

No one knew the real truth of the talk, nor where it had its genesis. College students are inveterate and creative gossips. Their world is small and their imaginations still unsullied. But somehow I believed all of it. It was all of a piece with him. I had read *The Fountainhead* early on; all the design students had. When I looked at Paul Sibley, I saw Howard Roark. I think that I was utterly lost to him the day I heard about his young French wife, and the motorcycle.

Once a week, on Wednesdays, because his was the largest class held in McCandless that quarter, Louis Cooney grudgingly allowed announcements of general interest to design students to be made at the end of class. I was chairman that quarter of the special events committee for the school of art and architecture, and it fell to my lot, the second week of classes, to announce a film on Mussorgsky's *Pictures at an Exhibition,* to be held in McCandless's small gallery. I began to dread the announcement days in advance. There was little chance of avoiding humiliation from Louis Cooney's tongue, and this time it would be before the dark Seminole eyes of Paul Sibley.

But at least he would see me; would have to. Could not avoid it. The Tuesday night before announcement day, I washed my hair and did my nails and gave myself a raw-egg facial. The next morning I got up early and put my hair up into the French knot that Cecie said looked so much like Old Money it ought to be dirty green, and applied more makeup more carefully than I ever used except for dates, and put on my treasured black cashmere sweater and good gray Irish tweed skirt from Jaeger, that was my last Christmas present from my father. I hesitated, looking under my lashes at Cecie's sleeping form, and then pulled out the string of pearls he had given me for my high school graduation and fastened them around my neck, and fled from our room. I did not want Cecie to wake and see me, I could not have said why. But as I closed the door softly and went down the hall, I felt the first pangs of guilt I had ever felt in connection with her.

My heart hammered and my mouth dried to parchment during the class, and I mentally rehearsed my short announcement over and over. When the time came and Louis Cooney said, "I believe our own incomparable Miss Lee has a tidbit of culture to offer us," I stood up, head light, eyes blind, and mispronounced Mussorgsky. I did not even get close. I heard it myself . . . *Moosursky* . . . and stood stricken dumb and mindless, unable to remember the correct pronunciation.

"Anyway, you all come," I blurted. "It's a good program and you'll like it."

There was general laughter, and even though I knew it was affectionate, I shrank into my seat and dropped my eyes to my notebook in utter humiliation. My body burnt in the fires of mortification from my waist to my hairline. I could feel tears of shame rising behind my lowered lashes. I waited dumbly to hear what Louis Cooney would say. He said it with swift, savage joy.

"Well, Miss Lee," he said. "*Moo*sursky indeed. Oh, no, no, no. Not from one of your obvious distinction and cultivation, not to mention your splendid family pearls. Who'd have thought it? Might I just suggest that you invest some of your filthy lucre in a good dictionary?"

The class roared with uneasy laughter, and I laughed too, a blind idiot's bray, and went directly to the women's room and locked myself in a stall and flushed the toilet over and over, and cried. Then I dropped the pearls in my purse, took down my hair, washed my face, and slunk over to Harry's. I cut my next class. The next period was a lab, and everybody would be working; Harry's would be safe. I bought a cup of coffee and took it to a back booth and put a dime in the jukebox by the table and pressed "Unchained Melody," and buried my nose in my steaming cup. I tried very hard to will my mind blank and cool, and succeeded. I don't know how long I sat there.

I heard no sound, but I looked up and he was there, in the seat across from me. He was not smiling, and then he did. I had never seen him smile before. It transformed the dark face entirely. I felt my mouth curve into an answering smile of its own volition.

"I told Harry you were buying," he said, gesturing at his coffee. "Since you're so rich, I thought you'd spring this time."

"I'm not rich," I said. I found it hard to make my voice work. "I could kill Cooney for that."

"Forget him. He's a turd, and a queer one at that," he said. "He wishes he looked like you, and since he can't, he's going to punish you for it. He can't, you know, if you don't let him."

"How can you stop him?"

"By not caring," he said. "By not giving a flying fuck."

I used the word myself, to Cecie, mainly, but I was not accustomed to hearing it from men. I felt the hated red crawl up into my neck and face again. His grin deepened.

"S'cuse me," he said. "I forgot. You poor little rich girls aren't accustomed to such functional things. I like the blush, though. Do they pass it along with the family pearls?"

"The pearls are fake," I muttered. Under the embarrassment I felt an aching disappointment. Please don't be like this, I said silently to him.

"Uh huh," he said. "Look, I don't care if you have money. It's nice. You can buy the coffee all the time. You can even pay for the movies and the pizzas. I have, to my entire name, two pairs of khakis and three shirts and one pair of tennis shoes and a G.I. Bill check every month, and that's it. But I didn't pick you out because of it."

"Have you picked me out?" I said. I could scarcely breathe over the pounding of my heart. I was terrified that he would hear it.

"Yep."

"Why?"

"Because I like the way you look," Paul Sibley said. "And I like the way you talk — or don't — and I like it that you don't giggle. And you're talented; I went in and looked at your board. And you're smart. I know you can pronounce Mussorgsky, no matter what that asshole says. And you're not like the others."

"How do you mean?" I said faintly. I watched him steadily, hypnotized like a bird by a snake. It struck me suddenly that his nose had been broken.

"You're just different. You must know by now that you are. So am I. I thought we might as well be different together."

"Do you always come on like this with girls?" I said. I could not think of anything clever, profound, or even basically intelligent to say.

"No," he said. "Only one time before."

I knew he meant the girl who had been

his wife, and was silent. I could not think of anything to say. The silence between us spun out, and finally, I said, "I have to go now," and rose. He watched me without speaking, and I turned and walked away.

"See you tomorrow," he called after me. I nodded without looking back. Joy started up; I knew it would soon flood me.

"Hey, Kate?" he called after me once more. This time I did turn.

"Don't forget to pay Harry for my coffee," he grinned.

I paid for the coffee and left Harry's, laughing and near tears with the rising of the joy. I do not remember driving the MG back across campus to the Tri O house.

I was sitting in the twilight looking out my window when Cecie came in from her lab.

"What's the matter?" she said, her radar instantly alert.

I did not turn to look at her. I could not. I was profoundly and viscerally reluctant to speak; I actually dreaded the words. But I said them.

"I've met somebody," I said.

She was quiet for what seemed a very long time.

"Oh, Katie," she said then. "Oh, Kate."

And so it began, that spring that took all

my deep aches and diffused yearnings, all my subterranean fires and storms and tears and laughter, all my buried hungers and thirsts and terrors, and focused them on the dark face and body of Paul Sibley. The spring of becoming. Not everyone has such a season; I had not thought it would come to me. If I looked far ahead at all, I saw myself, Kate the child, only older, and in a different place. But now I looked and saw a woman I did not know, and I was both tremulously grateful for her, and terrified. She was all appetite and response, and she had no boundaries.

From the very beginning I wanted him physically, fiercely and sometimes even savagely; I would sit across from him at Harry's, or beside him at his board, and I would be weak and almost sick with the longing for him to touch me. I felt every inch of warm, thick air on my skin, wherever my clothes were not, and so wanted to feel his hands there on me that I grew dizzy from it, and blushed. In the secret places beneath my clothes, the longing was so particular and piercing that I was frightened and appalled, and wondered in shame if people around us could read the stigmata of it on my face. I had never felt anything like it before.

I remembered my voice, not so long ago, to Cecie: "I can't imagine wanting to do it with anybody," and her cool one, to me: "I can if it's the right somebody. That's everything." So here it was, that imagining, that somebody. This was it then. I would like to have told her she was right, but I would have died before I would have spoken of it to anyone, even Cecie. Especially airborne Cecie. This feeling was in every way of earth and flesh. Every day after that first one, in Harry's, I sat beside Paul and laughed lightly and talked glibly and listened in cool amusement, and came near to shuddering apart with this thing that I could not control, and could not abjure. I think, if he had touched me, even on the arm, even on the hand, I would have bolted like a spooked horse.

But he didn't. He did not so much as indicate that he might like to. He smiled, and teased me, and sometimes laughed aloud at me, and asked me questions about myself, and listened while I answered, and he talked. Mostly, he talked. He talked, and I listened. I would have listened to him forever. He talked, in those early days, about architecture, and what it meant to him, and what he wanted to give it, and what he wanted it to give him. I could not imagine that all of it would not come true. He was awesomely, slashingly talented, almost savagely disci-

216

plined, in love with architecture as he would be with a woman, with a dark and obsessive joy. The sketches and elevations and designs that piled up on and around his board were soaring things, seemingly formed of earth and air and steel and stone, and they were where he put his passion and his touch. I was envious of his work that spring. I wanted that wholeness for myself.

He wanted to do residential architecture. Just that.

"I don't want to do habitats for cat food and potato chips, or for places where people hurt and die, or for assholes who make rules for other assholes," he said. "I want to do places where people live, and where there are no rules but mine and the house's, and the site's."

"What about the people who live in the houses?" I said.

"Their rules will be the same as mine, or they wouldn't hire me, and I wouldn't work for them," he said.

"You really do sound like Howard Roark," I said. I knew that he had read the book.

"He was an asshole, too," Paul said.

"No, he wasn't! Why?" I cried. This was heresy. I had never heard an architecture student say this.

"Because he blew up his own work," he

said. "No real architect would do that."

"It was to keep it from being . . . sullied . . . by idiots," I said.

"Better just to shoot the idiots," Paul said.

"Well, you're going to have a hard time at McKim, Mead and White, then," I said. "They're not going to take it kindly when you refuse to build cat food plants or call your residential clients assholes, much less shoot them."

"I know it," he said soberly. "I don't know how I'm going to handle that. I don't know if I *can* handle that. If there was any way on earth to just start out with my own practice, I'd do it, but there isn't. I don't have any money and there's no way to get any. Not even any family to steal it from. McKim was the best I could do, and I'm going to do it for the very minimum amount of time I have to, to build a practice. But Jesus, it's going to take years . . ."

"Paul, it's one of the best firms in the world," I said. "Everybody I know would kill to work for them. I would."

"You could," he said. "You're good enough. They have an interiors department, one of the biggest in the country. Maybe I'll take you along when I go. Make it a condition of employment. It's not a bad idea, come to think of it. Might make the slave labor easier to take."

I was faintly stung, that he seemed to think I would need the entree of his auspices for a job with such a firm as McKim, Mead and White, but I knew that he was probably right. The firm would be flooded each year with newly graduated applicants. Talent would not be enough.

"You think a word from you would do it?" I said tartly. Under the acid my heart sang. He was talking in terms of the far future.

He looked at me gravely.

"Yes," he said.

"Well, for your information, I was going to New York anyway, after graduation," I said. "And a lot sooner than you are. If I go to summer school this summer I can double up, and do my thesis in the fall, and graduate at Christmas. I'll be there a good two years before you will."

"Good. Then you can stake out the territory and find a loft or something. Pay for it, too, since you'll be a career woman."

I did not know if he meant for myself or for both of us, but my heart began a pounding that made speech impossible.

"Hah," I managed, idiotically.

He laughed.

"Don't knock me down accepting my offer,"

he said. "Thank God for you, Kate. If you hung on to me I don't think I could stand it."

And he bent back over the drawing that was sprouting like a flower or a tree on his board, and I leaned back on my stool to try and slow my runaway heart. What was he doing to me? He spoke of apartments in New York together, of a future that included me, and then of my not hanging on to him. Was the dichotomy purposeful? Did he even know he was doing it? In addition to being hopelessly in love that spring, I was painfully and permanently off-balance. It would have helped, I think, if I could have talked to someone about him. But I did not think that I could. He was in another country from anyone I knew at Randolph.

I did not see him at night; he did not make any effort to see me then, and I could not bring myself to mention it. I knew that he worked at his board far into the nights, and in any case, I did not know where we could have met. I was loath to hang around his lab; men habitually worked late at their boards in McCandless, but women normally did not. I could not even imagine him on the brocade sofas in the Tri Omega drawing room, and could imagine myself even less in the shabby little garage apartment on Scofield. In any case, women students were not permitted in men's rooms and apartments, on campus or off. And I knew without knowing how that it would simply never occur to him to take me to a movie or to get a hamburger. I supposed, bleakly, that I was doomed to see him in an endless succession of afternoon booths at Harry's. And so I spent my nights as I always had, with Cecie, or studying at the library, or dating this fraternity boy or that, all the while the fact of Paul Sibley roaring in my blood like a fever, unseen and consuming.

Only once did Cecie mention him.

"What happened to that somebody you met?" she said casually, not looking up from her history textbook. Her head was bent beneath the desk lamp for better light, and her copper curls flamed in it. She was wearing an oxford-cloth shirt, an outsized one, and she looked in it like a little boy dressed up in his father's clothing. She looked, suddenly, very thin; her neck in the drooping collar of the shirt seemed as fragile as a lily's stem, and her collarbones stood out in sharp relief. It seemed a very long time since I had really seen Cecie.

"Oh, he's around," I said. "I have coffee with him sometimes in the afternoons. Probably nothing will come of it. He's even poorer than you and me and Fig, and he works all the time. He's going to be one of the architects we'll remember out of this century."

She looked up and smiled. There were lavender smudges in the thin skin under her eyes, and the faint stain of golden copper that usually lay just beneath the skin of her cheeks was gone. Her pointed face was pale.

"He sounds nice," she said. "Does he have a name, or shall we just call him Louie?"

"Paul Sibley," I said, feeling my cheeks flame at the sound and taste of his name on my lips. "Are you not feeling good, Cece? You don't look like you are."

"I'm tired, is all," she said. "I can't seem to get my ass in gear, as Ginger says. I've got this research thing on English Common Law coming up next quarter, that's going to take two whole damn quarters to finish; I won't be done with it till Christmas, and I'm trying to double up in history this quarter to clear some time for it. But it's awfully hard, for some reason. I feel like I'm wading through molasses."

"Why don't we drop a hint to Ginger that the Outer Banks might not be amiss between quarters?" I said.

"Can't," she said, taking off her glasses and rubbing her eyes. "Aunt Eugenia wants to go to the Holy Land with her Circle, and there won't be anybody with Grammy.

I need to read Keynes, anyway."

"God, I wish school was over, that I was out of here, that we were. I wish we were already in New York, or Europe," I said, suddenly restless and uneasy. I longed suddenly and with all my heart for the days before Paul Sibley, when the future meant endless days, bright past imagining, in the quicksilver company of Cecie Hart. I missed her, acutely and painfully, as if she did not sit here in the room with me.

"You're wishing your life away," she said lightly. "That's what the sisters always told us when we wanted time to pass."

She did not comment on New York or Europe. Presently I put out my light, and slid into an unquiet sleep. Her light was still burning when I finally drifted off.

On the last day of classes I loaded the MG and dropped Cecie off at the train station. We were not going to be apart long . . . both of us would be back in three weeks, for summer school. But I felt suddenly chilly and peculiarly vulnerable, as if I stood on a plain ringed with forests, and in those forests eyes were watching. I felt as if someone, either Cecie or I, were not coming back.

"Well . . . see you in June," I said, still not moving away in the car.

"Yep," she said. "*Toujours*. Tomorrow is

another day, Katie Scarlett."

"Oh . . . bye!" I called out, laughing, and put the car into gear.

"Bye," floated back to me from the closing door of the station. I stepped on the gas and drove a block or so toward the south-bound highway that would take me to Kenmore and the dank, peeling house and the light-eyed deacon and the prim-mouthed stranger who was my mother now, and then I swung into the driveway of the post office and turned the car around and drove back up College Street and turned left on the street that ran past McCandless Hall. It was twilight, and a few lights bloomed in the big bay of windows, but most of the boards were empty.

Across the street, Harry's glowed bright with supper lights, and the marquee on the Tiger Theatre advertised *La Strada*. In the coin laundry I saw a few figures, the faceless shadow band, none of whom I knew, who did not go home between quarters. It was a desolate and banal little street scene; but suddenly as dear and precious and full of splendor and nuance as any I had ever seen. This was home. That other place, on the Santee River, was . . . anathema. I felt a surge of simple longing that hurt my heart and brought tears scalding to my eyes. They ran over and down my face, and I tasted the salt of them. I could feel my mouth working. I pulled the MG into a parking place in front of Harry's and got out and ran across the street to McCandless, and up the dark, echoing concrete stairs to the third floor where the architecture lab was. At first I thought it was empty, but then I saw his dark head bent over his board, far in the back of the room. The only light came from the drafting light clamped to its edge.

He raised his head and looked at me. We had said our carefully casual goodbyes earlier, over coffee, but somehow I did not think he was surprised to see me. He stared at me levelly. I stood in the doorway feeling as foolish as it was possible to feel, trying not to cry.

He grinned then, and gestured me to him with his T square, and before I knew it I was sitting in my accustomed place on the stool next to his, and he was leaning on his board and grinning the white grin at me. His hands were in his pockets, and his head was cocked to one side. The comma of hair fell into his eyebrows. I did not think I had ever seen so wonderful-looking a man. I grinned back, feeling the color rise from my collar.

"Forget something?" he said.

"Nope. Remembered something," I said, trying to match his tone. "I remembered you'd never seen *La Strada* and it's on over at the Tiger, and I came to take you to the movies."

He did not move, and the grin did not fade.

"Want to go over to Harry's and call home first?" he said.

"They aren't expecting me till . . . later," I said, face beginning to burn like fire. "I can be home by midnight."

In truth, I did not think they were expecting me at all. I had not talked to my mother in weeks. She probably did not even know the date of school's closing. Before I had always called and told her when I was coming home; this time I had not. I did not want to examine my reasons for that.

"Sure?"

"Yes."

"Let's go, then," he said, and switched off his desk lamp and followed me out of the dark lab. He did not touch me, but I could feel his presence behind me as palpably as if he had both hands on my shoulders. He was so close that I could feel his breath on my hair.

I think *La Strada* is my favorite movie of all time; I had seen it twice then, and I try to see it whenever there is a revival in Manhattan. But that night I sat in the darkened, near-empty theater next to Paul Sibley and saw almost nothing but flickering idiot images. He did not talk to me, or even move often; he seemed totally absorbed in the drama unfolding on the screen. But his physical presence consumed me. My flesh seemed to pull toward him of its own accord; my head inclined toward the dark bulk of his shoulder; my very blood seemed to flow toward him. Every atom in my body whirled toward the answering atoms in his flesh; I became aware, about the middle of the movie, that I was breathing in unison with him.

Toward the end of the movie he took my hand. Fire seemed to leap from his fingers to mine. I would not have been surprised to see a spark arc through the darkness, as from the end of God's finger to Moses' on the ceiling of the Sistine Chapel. All sensation left my body and flew to dwell in the hand that his held. For the rest of the movie I sat breathing lightly and quietly, my hand in his as hot and heavy as if it had been fresh cast of lead . . . seeing nothing, hearing nothing.

When it ended and the house lights came up, he dropped my hand and we walked silently out of the movie house and into the fragrant, mothy dark of late May. Honeysuckle poured its scent like a river from the banks of privet hedge behind the parking lot, and over that the light, heart-shaking smell of mimosa swam from somewhere near. Katydids called off in the thick, warm darkness. Otherwise there was little noise. The campus seemed suspended at the bottom of a dark, still sea. We reached the MG before he spoke.

"That's the saddest movie I ever saw in my life," he said quietly, and I looked up and saw the silver tracks of tears on his dark face. I thought of the movie: loss and poignancy, innocence shattered and dead, remorse and heartbreak on the shores of a dark ocean. I thought of his dead young wife. I did not think I could bear, for him, whatever brought the tears to those dark Indian eyes.

I reached up with both hands and took his face in them, and kissed him. It was, in the beginning, a soft kiss, but it turned to fire and thunder under my mouth, pure, tearing need. I was totally without wits or breath when he finally let me go. We looked at each other silently, and then he said, softly, "Oh, shit. Let's go."

"Where?" I whispered. I hadn't enough breath for anything else.

"To my place. I'm going to cook dinner for you. You can call your folks from there."

"Okay," I said. But I knew that I would not.

I fished the car keys out of my purse and handed them to him. My hands were trembling; I knew I would drive badly.

"Would you mind driving?" I said. "I don't know where you live."

In the darkness he laughed softly.

"Yes, you do," he said. "I've seen your car go by about a million times. I thought you were looking to buy the place."

"It's a shortcut to Dairyland," I muttered.

"One thing you don't ever have to do with me, Kate, is lie," Paul said. "I'm not going to lie to you and I don't want you to do it to me. You don't need to. God, what a grand little car. I haven't driven anything like it since France. I had a wonderful old Citroën touring car, about a thousand years old. We . . . I drove it all over Europe before it finally died on me, in Grenoble."

I thought of him in the big car, top down, the black hair blowing in the high, pure sunlight of the French Alps, laughing down at a dark, vivid girl beside him. Somehow I could see her plain: small, sharp-featured, doe-eyed, graceful as a new fawn. It was only later that I realized the ghost wife in

229

the car beside Paul was Audrey Hepburn. Cecie and I had both agreed that she was the one woman in the world we'd most like to resemble. I said nothing on the drive over to Scofield Street. Audrey sat in the space between Paul and me.

Paul cut the motor of the MG when we reached the driveway and coasted down it to the backyard, where the forlorn little two-story garage peered out of its thicket of kudzu and honeysuckle.

"We'll have to be quiet," he said. "My landlady has suffered keenly all summer because she hasn't been able to catch me with a woman back here. Once we're in, it's okay, though. She's used to lights and music at all hours."

"I'm signed out for home, anyway," I said, and then wished I could have bitten out my tongue. Now he would think I had planned this night, even if he had not before.

He laughed again, and opened the door for me very quietly, and motioned for me to go ahead of him up the perilous-looking wooden stairs. The night around us was very black, and the smell from the honeysuckle thicket was overpowering; it was like breathing wine or honey.

"I can feel you blushing in the dark," he said. "You put out heat."

"I'm really not accustomed to going home with boys late at night," I whispered, wishing someone, something, would stop my idiot mouth. He was light years, millenniums, away from being a boy.

He stopped on the little porch and turned me to face him. I could see only his outline, and the gleam of his eyes in the warm dark.

"When I said I was going to cook dinner for you, I meant just that," he said gently. "I'm not going to seduce you. I'm not going to put the make on you. Later, almost certainly, but not until you're ready for it. My self-control is legendary. You're going to have to ask."

The sucking, shimmering apprehension died in my chest, but under it flickered a feeling that I recognized as loss.

"What if I don't?" I said.

He pushed the hair off my forehead very gently, and smiled. His teeth flashed white in the dark.

"You already have," he said.

I said nothing. We stood silent as he fumbled for his key.

"It ain't much, but it's home," he said, and ushered me into his apartment and closed the door. I stood still as he went around pulling shades. Then the room bloomed into light, and I gasped in surprise and delight.

The little room was exquisite, as compact and jeweled as a pomegranate, as exotic as a miniature seraglio. At first glance it was overwhelming; pure, deep colors flashed and swam in patterns like a kaleidoscope, and fabric and texture shimmered so richly that I could not take it in. I simply stood and stared. It was a small room, low-ceilinged and beamed, and he had stuccoed the walls and painted everything structural . . . walls, beams, ceiling . . . a pure and shadowless white. But floors and walls and furniture teemed with color.

The floor was completely covered with as magnificent an Oriental rug as I had ever seen, even in the homes of my friends from Randolph Macon and Cape Cod. Its stained-glass colors actually pulsed in the light: deep crimson, azure blue, jewel green, cream, and gold. There was a daybed covered with another rug in softer colors, those of the desert; a tall Gothic armchair of black wood, covered in lovely, faded old green damask. A magnificent black leather Eames chair and ottoman sat beneath one of the room's two windows, with a rough white wool robe thrown over it. Beneath the other window, a white built-in desk and shelves held books and models and pottery in the same jewel tones as the rug, and a table board and drafting lamp. Enormous patterned pillows littered the floors, and the white walls burned with prints and paintings with the stark, sun-smitten look of Italy, Mexico, and Spain about them. The windows were covered only with pleated white parchment-paper blinds, and hanging white pleated paper lamps provided the only other illumination besides the drafting lamp. But the room was not dark. It seemed to swim in pure, concentrated light and color. At the far end, a massive painted screen depicting a medieval hunting scene half hid a rudimentary kitchen. I saw bits of an ancient gas stove, a sink, an oilcloth-covered table on which sat a laboring pint-sized refrigerator, and a lone shelf that held plates and cups and a great, trailing fern. Other plants rioted in the room from ceiling brackets, tables, the bookcase, the desk; a growing tree of some sort dominated one corner, behind the Eames chair. I did not see a separate sleeping alcove. I supposed that he slept on the daybed. A great, dark armoire, by far the largest piece in the room, undoubtedly housed his clothing. It, too, looked Mediterranean, and very old.

He turned to me, smiling, and I said, "It's absolutely beautiful. I never saw anything like it. It's like finding a Fabergé egg in a garbage can . . ." and then I stopped, and reddened again. I could scarcely have found a more insulting analogy.

But he laughed.

"I may not have a pot to piss in, but I refuse to live like an animal or a fraternity boy," he said. "I'm glad you like it. I do, too. This stuff needs a room at least twice this size, but I could barely afford this dump, and I'm sure not going to store it or give it away. Not after dragging it all over Europe and the southern United States."

"Oh," I said. Of course; this was the furniture of his marriage, his and the French girl's; I kept forgetting that he had had another life, another context entirely, than that of impoverished student. His sophistication was real, acquired by living his way into it. I thought, bleakly, that I could not hold a candle to the cultivated ghost who had chosen these beautiful things, lived among them with him.

"Did you buy it all abroad?" I said, as much to break the silence as from a desire to know.

"No. I was as poor there as I am here. I can't remember a time I wasn't in school of some kind, except the Army. All this stuff was my wife's. Her family's, that is. They had money. I should have given it back to them when she . . . died, but by that time they hated my ass and I theirs, and it gave me no end of pleasure to abscond, as M. Foucald put it, with this stuff. It was wasted on them, anyway. They didn't pick it out; some designer did. It came from their place in Marrakesh."

The fabled name swam in the air between us.

"It must be a great comfort to you, to have these things to remember her by," I said. It sounded like a line out of a bad movie. Even Deborah Kerr couldn't have done it well.

He laughed again, wearily.

"It's a great comfort to have these things, period," he said. "She didn't like me a damn bit better than her family by that time; she had already filed for divorce when we had the accident. I'm sorry she's dead, but I'm not a bit sorry she isn't in my life anymore. We were both stupidly young when we married; I was a skinny, arrogant kid and she was a fat, spoiled one. By the time we'd grown up another year it was apparent to everybody that it was a marriage made in hell. I consider these things payment in full for some very bad years. She was just as impossible to live with as I was."

Again, I could think of nothing to say. We were quiet for another space of time.

"I just don't want there to be any false sentiment between us," he said presently. "It was a bad marriage. She wanted a husband to take care of her and show off in Orléans, and her family wanted the same thing, and about that time I discovered Mies van der Rohe and Le Corbusier and decided to be an architect, and it all went to hell about then. She never would have come to America, and McKim made it plain I had to come back if I wanted the job. They won't hire foreign-educated architects. But it would have unraveled sooner or later, anyway. Berthe was about as unlike Leslie Caron as anybody you ever saw."

I put my face into my hands and shook my head. Helpless laughter bubbled through my fingers. My heart soared.

"I was thinking Audrey Hepburn," I whispered.

"Not on her best day." He laughed, too. "And the worst thing was, she never cooked a meal the entire time we were married. At least I can thank her for being probably the best cook you've met in your young life. Wait until you taste my *cuisine française*."

He disappeared behind the carved screen and I heard the creak of an oven door. A rich, deep, winy smell curled out and into my nostrils, and I felt saliva start. It was past nine, and I had not eaten since lunch at Dairyland with Cecie. That seemed, as Hemingway said, long ago and in another country.

"That smells heavenly," I said, looking into the wretched little kitchen. "What is it? When on earth did you start cooking it?"

"It's coq au vin," he said, lifting out an earthenware casserole and slamming the oven door. He was as deft as a cat in the kitchen. "Otherwise known as chicken in wine. It's got chicken, ham, little white onions and garlic, seven herbs, mushrooms, and a slosh of red wine. Chambertin is best, but I can't get that here, so this is plain old Taylor's table. You flame it with a little cognac and then stick it in the oven for as long as you feel like it. I put this on about five this afternoon."

"How on earth did you know . . ." I began, and stopped in confusion. Of course he could not have known I would appear in his lab.

"I eat well," he grinned. "And I can do it cheaper than eating at a dining hall or boarding house. If you can call it eating. I make this, or some other kind of stew, once a week and eat on it for days. The only real expense is the cognac, and I've had this bottle for six months. The temptation to scarf it down by itself is great, but I'm only a so-so drinker, and I am a devoted, fanatical eater."

"I've never even tasted cognac," I said.

He looked at me and lifted a dark eyebrow.

"What? A rich little girl like you?"

I started to protest, and then did not. All of a sudden, in the midst of all this rich, careless beauty and exotica and worldliness, my phony wealth seemed almost all I had going for me.

"My father was a martini man," I said lightly.

"Was?" he said.

"He died," I said neutrally. "At the end of my first year at Randolph Macon."

"And you came back to be closer to your mother. I wondered what you were doing at Randolph."

"You're here," I said carelessly, hoping he would drop it.

"I have to be. You don't," he said. "Well. I'm sorry about your father. Shouldn't you call your mother, then? I don't want to get on her bad side before I've even met her."

"She really isn't expecting me until tomorrow," I said, not looking at him. "I'm going to go back and sleep at the house tonight. I don't have to sign in, and there's a basement door that's always open."

He laughed.

"Always leave yourself an escape hatch," he said. "Well, in that case, let's eat."

It was an enchanted meal. Probably as near a perfect one as I have ever had. I have never forgotten it, and I know that I never will. Partly it was the strange and wonderful food; strange at least to me. Besides the coq au vin he produced a crusty loaf of walloping chewy bread that he said he had made himself, and a platter of apples and grapes and an odd, soft, nutlike cheese for afterward, and kept our stemmed glasses filled with the tart, dry red wine. We ate on lacquered trays in the living room, I in the armchair and he in the Eames. He put a stack of records on the hi fi set he had assembled in the bookcase, and soft, sensuous music with the sun and sea in it swam through the room. A candle burned in a beautiful pottery candlestick on the bookcase, and he lowered the lamplight with a rheostat. After dinner he brought us each a tiny, jewel-like glass of the cognac, and made bitter, smoky espresso on a battered copper machine he pulled out from under the kitchen counter. I was more than slightly drunk on the wine and music and strangeness and his physical presence, and felt both serene and detached, and reckless and clever and worldly. I laughed a great deal, and tossed my head to feel my hair swing against my cheek, and felt about thirty-five years old and incomparably chic in the sun of his lazy grin.

He got up to clear the dishes, flicking on an Edith Piaf record as he went. The dusky lament overflowed the room. I got unsteadily to my feet, almost losing my balance.

"Whoops," I mouthed silently, balancing against the rough white wall. I peered in to see if he had noticed; he had not. Laughter welled up in my chest. I remember thinking, if this is what it is to be drunk, I see why people do it.

My eye fell on a framed sketch, and I leaned closer to look at it. All senses opened and heightened by the liquor and the man, I stared at it, widening my eyes to focus it. It swam into sharp focus and I drew in my breath, as I had when I had first seen the room. It was a watercolor sketch of a low, carved white building spilling down a rock ledge over a burning blue sea. One graceful, gull-roofed wing of it soared out over the rock and hung over the sea itself; its seaward wall was a long curve of glass, and its roofline made a sweeping, carved overhang, so that the sea light would flood in, but not the fierce, remorseless sun. It was purely, absolutely beautiful; it looked like a seabird just lit on the cliff. I knew with certainty that

240

he had designed it.

I felt him behind me and turned. He was looking at it impassively.

"It's incredible," I said. "It's yours, isn't it?"

"It's my design," he said. "It never got built. It was going to be a house in Morocco. The cantilevered wing is a studio."

Light dawned. It was to have been his house, his and the dead Berthe's.

"I'm sorry you never got to live in it," I said. I was. The simple sadness of it brought tears to my eyes.

"I will," he said. "I may be eighty years old, and I may have to rob or commit murder, but I will live in that house. It's a condition of living at all, that house."

He laughed then, and I looked over my shoulder at him again. It was not a laugh I had heard before.

"It was a condition from the very beginning," he said. "It was a condition of staying in France and being a good little bourgeois husband and son-in-law. I would stick around Orléans with Berthe half the year and my prince of a father-in-law would finance this house for us, and we could spend the other half in it. I can't tell you how close I came to accepting that condition. To paying that price. I might have done it, if the thing with McKim hadn't come up."

"You'll build it, on an American beach," I said around the lump in my throat.

"Yeah, I will," Paul said. "But when I think how long it's going to take to be able to afford it, I get a little crazy. So I just try not to."

"Could you . . . can you, you know, scale it down a little? Build it somewhere else, build it cheaper?" I said, "Not so big, and so *avant garde?* Almost every inch of that house would have to be custom . . ."

"No, I can't," he said. "I'm surprised you don't understand that I can't."

His voice was cold and flat, as if he stood a far distance from me. I felt the tears slide over the rim of my lids and start down my cheeks. I shut my eyes and prayed that I would not cry with the hurt.

I heard him sigh, and he took me by the shoulders and led me to the daybed and pulled me down on it, beside him. He held my hand loosely in his, and looked off into the middle distance, while I struggled not to yield to the tears.

"I want to tell you something, so you'll understand, and then we won't have to talk about it again," he said. "I don't tell people this because it sounds like I'm trying for sympathy, and there's nothing I hate more

242

than that. But I need for you to understand about the architecture and about that house, because until you do you won't understand me. And nothing at all can work for us until you do."

He looked at me and made a half-exasperated, half-amused sound and reached over and thumbed the tears off my face.

"Shit, Kate, don't turn into a cryer on me," he said. "I'm sorry if I hurt your feelings. I'll try not to snarl if you'll try not to cry. Deal?"

I nodded, unable to look at him.

"Okay. My mother was a Seminole Indian from the Everglades outside Miami. She was born in them and she died in them. I don't know if you've ever seen the Everglades, but it isn't fit country for anything but rattlesnakes and alligators and, of course, Seminoles. There was a settlement of 'Noles back in there, in tarpaper shacks on stilts, so far back that the water was always black and the air was always gray and the sun never got through the moss and trees. The mud stank and the misquitos never stopped and the heat never let up. Some of the old people had spent their whole lives there. I was born there, and lived there for the first seven years of my life . . ." He paused, and then laughed the tight, bad laugh I had heard before.

"You know, people are always pissing and moaning about the fires in the Everglades, and the droughts, and the poaching, and how they're a national treasure and we've got to save them for future generations. But I tell you, if mine could be the hand that lit the fire that burned that fucking murdering swamp to hell I'd die a happy man.

"Anyway, my mother was a squatty, dark little lady with no schooling and no skills and no maternal instincts to speak of. She lived to drink, and to drink she had to hook, and she did hook, whenever she ran out of booze. She'd bring her gentlemen friends back to the shack, or they'd show up sniffing around it, and they'd go at it with me on my little pallet in the corner. I had standing orders to turn my head to the wall when she brought a date home. That's what she called them, dates. Until I married, I thought you couldn't fuck without yelling like a wildcat or a Seminole. I never knew who my father was because my mother didn't. It could have been one of those guys who came to the 'Glades, for all I know. Most of them were crackers. I know I've got a lot of white blood in me."

I made a small sound of horror and he waved me quiet.

"It wasn't all bad," he said. "I had an uncle, Uncle Jimmy, her older brother, and he was good to me. After she got to drinking so bad he used to take me to work with him sometimes. He was a framer for construction companies, and a good one. He always had work. He was little and dark and catlike, like her, and there wasn't anywhere he couldn't go, hand over hand, like a monkey. I'd sit on the ground under a tree being real quiet and watch him. He worked for Sibley Construction the year I was born, and that's how I got my last name. My mother just told them that at the county hospital and they put it down. Hell, who cared about one more skinny, squalling little 'Nole?

"The year I was six Uncle Jimmy was working on a big house out on the ocean, one of those fifty-room jobs with the big stone fence and the iron gates and the pools and the fountains and tennis courts. He took me out to see it on a Sunday, when there wasn't anybody else around. We walked all through it, and my eyes were just getting bigger and bigger, and something was happening to my heart, and I could smell the wet concrete and the plaster dust and the sand and black earth in the sun, and see the ocean beyond, cool and clean and free, and it just came to me that I was going to build those babies, too. Design and build them, I mean. I think I can remember having this distinct sense even then about how you would do it. And then he took me out back to this kind of white tower that stood all by itself in a grove of palms, and we climbed up the outside steps and at the top there was this round white room with glass on all sides, looking straight out to sea over the top of the palms. All you could see was clean blue sky and clean blue sea and gulls, and way off in the sea, little white sails. Christ, it was so *clean* up there. That was the thing that got me. I'd never seen clean like that before, or light, or space. And the wind flowed through singing like a river. The floor was white tile, and the walls white stucco, and the ceiling . . . white. White and empty and cool and clean. And beyond it more clean blue, clear to the end of the world.

"I remember that I said to him, 'I can do this.' And he just looked at me and said, 'Yes, you can, and you do it, Paulie. You get out of there and you do it.' "

He was quiet for so long that I thought that was the end of the story. I felt that my heart would burst with sorrow for him.

"And you did do it," I whispered.

"Yeah, sort of," he said, smiling down at me. "At least I got out. He fell off a scaffolding the next winter and crushed his spine and went on disability, and she died of cirrhosis the next spring, and the county came and got me and put me in foster homes, and I did okay. Hell, I would have gladly become a Filipino houseboy if it would have gotten me out of the 'Glades. I worked hard and minded and studied and got good grades and joined the army when I was eighteen, and the army sent me to France, and I toured around Europe looking at buildings until I got out, and then I took what I'd saved and started at the École and met Berthe and . . . the rest, as they say, is history. So, yeah. I did do part of it. But I missed on the house. I missed out on the house."

I looked up at him. The tears overflowed, and through them I saw both the tall man who sat beside me in a garage apartment in Randolph, Alabama, and a dark-eyed, thin little boy in a white tower by the sea, his heart bursting with an epiphany of light and air and cleanliness and blue water. I wanted nothing on the earth at that moment but to give it to him, to hand him with both hands his house by the sea. And then I thought, in simple joy, I can do that. I can.

I turned to face him squarely. I put my hands on him; I touched his face and his hair, and his mouth, and I wept, and I laughed, and I fell over my own words as you do, sometimes, your feet.

"Listen," I cried. "Listen! Let me help you! Let me do it. I want it too, I always have . . . a house by the ocean, by the dunes, I can just see it, I want that house, I want to live there with you . . ."

He took my hands in his and held them, and I could see him smiling in distress, and shaking his head, no, no, and trying to calm me, but he could not. I would not be stopped.

"Yes," I said. "You were going to New York anyway, you know you were, you know you said you'd get me on at McKim . . . well, do it, Paul, and I'll work for them and you start your own firm and we'll build the house wherever you like . . . Long Island, or New England, or anywhere, any ocean, anywhere . . . let me help you and live there with you. I have a little money, it will be enough, we can do it . . ."

"Katie," he whispered, "Kate, Kate listen . . . I can't take your money, I can't let you support me . . ."

"I don't see why, when it's what I want more than anything in the world," I said, beginning to weep in earnest. "I don't see what difference it makes who earns it if we're together . . ."

He did not answer, and he did not look at me. I turned away. The enormity of my words and actions beat dimly at the bell of liquor and exaltation and love and pity that enclosed me. I could literally hear again my father's voice: "That coolness of yours, that dignity and distance . . . it's one of the best things you've got going, Effie Lee. You use that." I shut my eyes tight. As I could hear the voice, so could I see myself, a drunk and disheveled college girl, weeping lugubrious tears and begging love and allegiance from a man a universe beyond her in experience and heart.

"Oh, God," I whispered, putting my hands over my face. "I'm so ashamed of myself."

"No," he said. "No, don't be. You're wonderful. You're not like anybody else, you don't have anything to be ashamed of. But Kate, what kind of a man would I be if I let you do that? You'd come to hate me after a while . . ."

"No," I whispered. "No. I wouldn't."

I turned around again on the sofa, so that I was facing him. I put both arms around his neck and locked my hands there. I took a long, deep breath. My ears rang and my head spun.

"You said I'd have to ask," I said. "You know, tonight, out on the steps? Well, I'm asking."

"Kate . . ."

"Will you make love to me, Paul?"

"Jesus, Katie . . ."

"Yes or no. If it's no, that's fine. But if it is I'll want you to run me back over to the house."

"Think about what you're saying, Kate . . ." he said.

"No. I don't have to. You think about it. Was that just hot air, then? Did you not mean it?"

"I meant it. I did and I do. Christ yes, I meant it," he said. His voice was low and ragged. "You think I don't want you? I want you so much I take cold showers in the middle of the night . . ."

"Well, then, for God's sake, do it," I said, teeth chattering in fear and wanting and inevitability. "Only promise me no fancy French stuff. I just don't think I'm able to do that."

He laughed and moved over and put his arms around me, and put his mouth to the side of my neck and made a rude noise, like a Bronx cheer.

"Miss Otis regrets she's unable to fuck today," he said into my neck.

So that whatever I came to think of him after that, I will always remember that when he led me out of my damaged girlhood, through fear and pain and then, incredibly,

250

flowering, secret warmth and finally pleasure so intense I cried aloud with it, across the whistling abyss and beyond it into the company of women, it was to the sound of laughter, his and my own.

Much later, around three, he got up to bring coffee and came back spinning my white cotton panties on one finger.

"Pretty tame stuff for a rich girl," he said. "I figured you for different colors and days of the week, at least."

I should have told him then, of course. It was the time for it. I knew it, and lay there smiling at him in his dark nakedness, my heart still galloping, my body still sheened with sweat, and did nothing of the kind.

"I was raised to think that anything but plain white cotton is ostentatious," I said.

"Christ," he said, tossing the panties aside. "There's absolutely nothing more boring than a rich puritan. I'd rather you didn't wear panties at all."

"Your wish is my command," I said, giddy with joy and transformation and the suspected sensuality I had found within myself. Or rather, that he had found, and set free.

I held out my arms to him, and he came into them. After that, of course, it was too late.

CHAPTER SEVEN

In the middle of summer, when we had been together almost six weeks, I gathered my courage and said to Paul, "I want you to meet Cecie now."

He lifted his head from the model he was working on and looked at me, frowning. I knew that it was not my words that he frowned at, but the interruption. When he worked, Paul was a drowned man; it took him minutes to surface.

"I thought we'd agreed about that," he said mildly. But his eyes were opaque with patience. He had a temper but it never flared at me; nevertheless, I knew when he was irritated. He looked more like an Indian than ever then, closed and turned completely inward.

"I know. We did," I said. "But I'd like to change my mind about this one thing, if I can. She's the most important person in my life, next to you. I want you all to know each other."

He got up from the desk and walked into the little kitchen and came back with two glasses of wine. I took mine and he slumped bonelessly on the daybed beside me and sipped his, looking at me over the rim. I thought again what a flawless, all-of-a-piece kind of beauty he had; rough-hewn and completely masculine. I never tired of simply looking at him.

"Ah, Katie, give me a break," he said. "I just can't go over to the Tri Omega house and meet the girls. I can't do pledge swaps. I can't sing to you under the balcony and get thrown in the fish pond. I couldn't when I was the right age for it and I can't now. You know that."

"I'm not asking you to do that," I said. "I'm just asking you to meet Cecie. She could meet us for coffee. Or we could have her over here. She'd love this place; it would just enchant her. I want her to know that I . . . have something like you and this in my life. Paul, it's like I have this whole other life, my real one, and nobody knows about it. It makes me feel . . . unreal."

"I don't see why you need anybody else to make your life real," he said. "I'd hoped that by now I was enough."

I felt unreasoning tears start in my eyes, and blinked rapidly. Being so much in love did that to me: I felt as if some vital, protective emotional connective tissue had simply melted. Everything . . . tears, laughter, joy, fear . . . was so close to the surface that summer that it seeped out at the slightest pressure, like an underground spring. It made me feel as if I had no skin, I was absurdly and totally vulnerable.

"You are enough," I said. "I just don't see why it has to be either or. Either you or Cecie. It's not as if there's only enough of me to go around once."

"Well, maybe there's only enough of me," he said. "I've never been able to handle many people at one time."

I thought of his terrible, blasted childhood, the feckless, faithless dead mother, a grotesque Circe; the smashed uncle, the stinking mangrove swamp, the foster homes. And of the prim, sucking marriage. My heart twisted. Later then, I thought. Later, after he's used to the fact of us. After he feels safe.

I did not come often to his apartment. The need for darkness and drawn curtains and lowered voices was just too oppressive; it angered him too much. When I did, I sneaked in up the dark stairs as I had the first time, heart pounding, feeling like a paid strumpet. Perhaps, as he said, the love we made on the daybed or the floor on these nights was the wilder and sweeter for that element of stealth, but I never got used to it. I wanted to shout aloud my rapture and completion, to laugh, to yell, as he had said he sometimes did, like a panther or a Seminole. It was such an alien need for me, the compleat fabricated woman, that I longed to indulge it, but he was teaching me control, he said, along with some delicate and dexterous French tricks. Or at least, I assumed they were French. Whatever they were, they made me burn and ache and itch at the very center of my being, my dark and secret core, and nothing would assuage them but more of him and his swift, skilled, driving love. It was, almost completely, a summer of sensation.

But far more often we would meet at Harry's for coffee, or sit in one another's labs while we worked. He never faltered a beat with his work, or his awesome, still, white concentration.

"I want you in my world," he said once. "But this *is* my world. You need to know that right off the bat. If you're not in it, there won't be anybody else. But this will be it. And the more I can learn, and the better and the quicker, the closer the house by the ocean comes. We have the rest of our lives to be together and play and screw, and we will, in that house. But first, let's get the house built."

Somewhere in those summer weeks we had tacitly agreed that after my graduation I would go to New York and begin work, and he would follow when he finished, after his fifth year, and would begin his practice and the house by the sea.

"I'll let you work and support us for a little while because you're half of me, and you were going to, anyway. But I'm not going to take any of your family's money," he said.

"Well, actually, everything is mother's until, you know, she's gone," I said, not looking at him. It was not precisely a lie.

"Yeah, and she's going to want to subsidize us; all good little Southern belles' mamas do. Don't trust their sorry men. Hell, she'd probably be right not to. But I'm putting you on notice now. We're not taking a penny of it."

"Well, all right," I said with deep-hidden alacrity. This was a fine way out; by the time the truth of my patrimony came to light we would not need it anymore, and the whole thing could dissipate as naturally and unnoticeably as ground fog. As for his going home with me to Kenmore and meeting my mother, I did not plan to allow that to happen. Given the scope of my mother's placid indifference, it would not be hard to circumvent. I thought, if I could arrange that they meet away from the house, she might carry off the FFV business to perfection; she had, after all, been doing it all her adult life. So she would come to Randolph, or we would meet in Montgomery. But we would not go home. The thought of Paul in that squalid, melting house, in the bull-necked presence of the deacon, made my blood run cold.

We did not talk much of the future, and I don't recall that he had actually mentioned marriage, not then, anyway, but it was there, under everything, a solid, shining bridge over the abyss.

Often I would laugh aloud with the sheer joy of it all, of this miraculous love and my liberation into pure flesh, and the fact of a life with him in his white house by the sea. And burn with the wanting of him so that to reach out and touch his arm with one finger would set off a violent, silent, interior explosion. And settle back once more to wait and be silent, even while my raucous heart nearly burst to tell of all this . . . to tell, to tell.

I could have spoken of him, of course, at least to Cecie. He had not asked me not to. He had said merely, one of the first times we had made love and were lying half-asleep in each other's arms in his apartment, "The thought of anyone else knowing about this makes me almost physically sick."

And rapt and humbled with this new love, I had vowed an unspoken vow that it would remain perfect and secret, ours alone. But it was proving a hard vow to keep. I was beginning to realize that it was the sharing of a love, at least a young one, that kept it vivid. Like fire, it needed oxygen. I looked at Cecie sometimes, studying on the bed or at the desk opposite me, and she would lift her red head and smile, and I would almost cry aloud with the pain of my own joy withheld. We were not talking nearly so much in those days. I missed the simple fact of Cecie. I was annoyed with myself that my heart could not seem to stretch to encompass two. And irrationally, I was sometimes annoyed with her.

I realized much later that I had wanted her, in those first days, to storm my barricades and have it out of me, to topple walls, to take my hidden happiness by force. Being Cecie, of course, she did not. Her fastidious delicacy of heart would permit no such thing. She retreated into her unassailable inner world, leaving me with a love affair that was somehow not complete and an aching loneliness for Cecie Hart. I did not thank her for it.

It was no secret at the Tri Omega house that I had a boyfriend. It would have simply been too much to expect that such intelligence would go undetected on a small summer campus. I had always been too bizarrely different, too visible, to escape notice, and Paul was simply too spectacular. People saw us in Harry's or in McCandless Hall, if not at the apartment, and of course they talked, and of course the talk drifted back to the Tri O house. I had been dodging, not very successfully, smiles and talk and teasing and questions all summer. Remarks about Kate's mystery man and the ice queen and the Indian chief flew like gnats at those summer suppers, and there was much hilarity at Ginger's proposal that the sisters form spying parties and track us to our lair. But I was sure they did not know a lair existed, and I would simply smile and pretend the talk did not bother me, and if it did not die, at least it did not flame into wildfire. I knew that the others pumped Cecie, but I knew also that she would not tell them what little she knew. At that point, his name and the fact of his Seminole blood were the only things she did.

Paul and I looked up from my desk by the window in McCandless one July afternoon to see Fig and Ginger waving elaborately from the sidewalk and pantomiming the drinking of coffee, and I knew then that the game was up as far as secrecy went, and sighed.

"Who in God's name is that, Brünhilde and Loki?" Paul said irritably. He was fond of Wagner, and played *The Ring* frequently on the hi fi. He was teaching me as much about opera as about love, although I was enjoying it considerably less.

"It's my suitemates," I said. "Ginger Fowler and Fig Newton. Fig is the little one; she has a kind of history of spying on me. Lord, I'd like to kill them. They'll break their necks getting back to the house to tell all about you. I better go have some coffee with them at Harry's and see if I can short-circuit this. I gather you don't want to join us?"

"God, no," he said, mock-shuddering. "I thought the Tri Os were into cheerleaders and majorettes."

"They're nice girls," I said, defensive, suddenly, even of the goggling Fig. "They're good friends. You can't blame them for being curious. I'm the only one in the whole house who doesn't bring her boyfriend around, or talk about him."

"I'm sorry," he said, bending his head back over his board. "You go on. I'll meet them another time. This is due tomorrow."

He was alone with the wood and glass and stone structure growing under his hand before I left the room. I looked back at the window as I reached the sidewalk where they stood, staring, and saw what they saw, and smiled in spite of my annoyance. He was utterly beautiful in his dark aloneness and his oblivion, and he was mine. Now I could share at least the fact of him, and that fact was enough to make Fig's mouth hang open and her breath honk adenoidally through her nose, and Ginger's blue eyes round with appetite and awe.

"Holy cow, Kate, no wonder you hide him," she said, grinning. "You ought to put a chastity belt on him."

"Heathcliff," Fig breathed. "Effie, he's Heathcliff. He is! I always thought of you as Catherine; I put it in the diary when I first met you, but this is just too perfect! Oh, wait till I . . ."

"Shut up, Fig," Ginger and I shouted together, and she clapped her hand over her mouth and pantomimed guilt, and we crossed the street and went into Harry's. When we came out again, Paul was gone from the window of my lab.

After that the talk at supper took on fresh life, and one by one the Tri Omegas began to appear on the sidewalk outside McCandless on this urgent errand or that, and Paul took refuge in his own third-floor lab.

"I feel like some kind of rare specimen

of swamp bird being stalked by the Audubons," he grumbled. "Can't you call them off?"

"Nope," I said. "They're only doing it because you won't meet them. Let it go and they'll stop; you know how it is summer quarter. Everybody gets silly. I do wish you'd at least let me bring Cecie up, or come and meet her, though. She's my best friend, Paul. I miss her."

"Then spend more time with her," he said. "I'm going to be over my head with the hospital thing for another couple of weeks. I'm not going to be able to be with you much. McGee said today they might build the winning design. That would mean a little money for Operation White House."

"Well, would you maybe meet her after it's in?" I persisted. "Just have coffee with us at Harry's? She's the only one of them who isn't going to come parading past your window. And she means more to me than any of the rest of them put together."

He smiled.

"Tell you what," he said. "After the competition's over I'll cook dinner for her. For the dwarf and the valkyrie, too, if that's what you want."

"Oh, it is," I said, hugging him. "Oh, it is. And you'll see, you're going to like them.

Well, Cecie and Ginger, anyway. Fig is . . . Fig is our collective punishment for being sorority snobs in the first place. The fact of Fig Newton will keep you humble, I'm here to tell you."

That night I stayed in my room at the Tri O house for the first time in weeks and settled in for one of mine and Cecie's marathon talks. I brought cokes and Baby Ruths from the machine in the basement, and put a stack of June Christy and Jeri Southern on the Webcor, and took a shower and got into my nylon shorties. Cecie was at the library, and I was alone in the room for the first time since the end of the previous quarter. I looked around it; for a moment it might have been the room of strangers. In the few weeks that I had been with Paul it had lost the spoor of me, of Kate Lee, and in the hot twilight it seemed to have lost more, too: lost the rich particularity and the little resonances that made it mine and Cecie's and no other room on earth. Cecie's plants looked leggy and frail and some had browning tips and yellowing leaves, and my books, that had always lain scattered on my side of the desk, had been neatly stacked in the corner beside my dresser. Cecie's alone littered the top of the desk and her bed now, and on my bare side of the desk a coffee cup that I recognized as Molly Sloan's, from down the hall, rested, half-full of scummed liquid. My Dorothy Parker anthology lay on the desk beside the cup. I wondered if Cecie and Molly had been reading it together, and felt something akin to panic flutter briefly in my stomach. I looked at the page that was marked with a pencil; it was Cecie's favorite, *Testament*. I picked the book up, and read:

"Oh, let it be a night of lyric rain
And singing breezes when my bell
   is tolled.
I have so loved the rain that I
   would hold
Last in my ears its friendly, dim
   refrain. . . ."

I felt a curl of sullen anger.

"That nitwit Molly Sloan isn't going to have the slightest idea what Dorothy Parker's talking about," I thought.

"Well, hey," Cecie's voice said from behind me. I turned. She stood in the twilight, with the light from the hall behind her, and I drew in my breath sharply at her silhouette. She was as frail now as a starved child, and her red hair, that had burnt like living fire with health and vitality, was dull and lay in damp tendrils against her skull and her cheeks.

I snapped on the overhead light and looked at her.

"Cecie, what on earth is wrong with you?" I whispered. "You look absolutely sick."

"I think I might be," she said, and I noticed then that her voice was husked and forced. She was white, too, and soaked with perspiration. It was hot outside, but it was not that hot. I reached over and felt her forehead. It was dry, and burned as if flames roared behind it. I let my hand trail down the side of her neck. There were spongy lumps under and behind her ear. I jerked my hand away.

"They've been there for a week or two," she said in the new froggy voice. "And my throat's been on fire, and I can hardly drag myself out of bed. I . . . Kate, I'm really scared."

"You've got a high fever," I said. "Oh, Cecie, why on earth didn't you tell me?"

"You haven't been around much," she smiled. It was as if a skeleton smiled; I grimaced in pain and fear.

"Or somebody, anyway," I said. "Come on. We're going to take you over to the infirmary right now. Tonight."

"Tomorrow, maybe," she said, looking around. "Look at you, you've brought the cokes and everything. Let's have an old fashioned Hart-Lee gabfest tonight, and you can run me over there in the morning. It's been so long since we've talked . . ."

"Absolutely not," I said. "We're going now. Sit down and I'll get a nightgown and toothbrush for you. You probably just have a bug of some sort and they'll pump you full of penicillin and you'll be back in a day or two, and we'll talk then. But not now. Cecie, how long have you felt this way?"

"I don't know," she said vaguely. "A long time, I think. Not as bad as this, not with the sore throat and the lumps and stuff, but I've been tired an awfully long time. I was tired when I went home between quarters."

I remembered that indeed, she had been. Why had I not paid more attention? But I knew why. Guilt spread a flush of anger along my veins. She was surely old enough to get herself to the infirmary without waiting for me to take her.

"It was really dumb of you to wait this long," I said crisply.

She was silent a moment.

"I've been afraid it was cancer," she whispered, and I turned and took her in my arms and hugged her. It was like hugging a bird, all light bones and damp, feathery hair. She hugged me back, briefly, and then pulled away.

"You don't have cancer," I said. "People our age don't get cancer. But we need to go tonight and find out what you do have."

"Okay," she said. "I guess you're right. I just can't go any further like this."

On the way over to the infirmary in the MG, with the hot, sweet air rushing past us, she said, dreamily, her head back against the seat, eyes closed, "You were going to tell me about Paul Sibley tonight, weren't you?"

"Yes," I said. "And I still am, when you're feeling better. And what's more, you're going to meet him, because he wants to cook dinner for you, and maybe Ginger and Fig. We'll do it when you get out."

"That's nice," she said. "And I'm glad you were going to tell me about him. I wanted to hear it from you, not from that idiot Fig, who's got him kind of a combination of Rupert Brooke and Laurence Olivier now. She's devoted a whole chapter to him in the famous diary."

"I was never not going to tell you," I said. "I just . . . it hasn't seemed to me that I knew quite what to say about him yet."

"He's the biggie, isn't he?" Cecie said.

"Oh, yes. He's it, Cece."

"Well, tell, then," she smiled, her eyes

still closed. "For starters, what does he look like? Can he possibly look like Ginger and Fig say he does?"

"This time they're right," I said. "He's . . . oh, Cecie, he's beautiful. He's very dark, and his eyes kind of tilt up, and his hair is as black as a crow's wing, and falls in his eyebrows . . ."

" 'Because your eyes are slant and slow,
Because your hair is sweet to touch,
My heart is high again, but oh,
I doubt if this will get me much.' "

Cecie murmured it drowsily.

"This time it got me everything," I said.

"Really everything?" Cecie said. I could barely hear her; her voice was fading in and out.

"Really everything," I said. "Cecie, what's the matter with you? You sound like you're passing out or something."

"Nothing. Just sleepy," she slurred. "Oh, Kate. Remember that other one we liked? *Sanctuary?* 'My land is bare of chattering folk; the clouds are low along the ridges. And sweet's the air with curly smoke, From all my burning bridges . . .' Have you burned your bridges, old Effie Lee?"

I knew what she was asking me.

"Yes," I said, and when she did not reply, I looked over at her. She lay still and white, her head had slumped against the door. I stepped on the accelerator and took the corner on two wheels into the street where the infirmary was. When I reached it, Cecie was unconscious, and they carried her in on a stretcher. I sat in the bleak, antiseptic-smelling waiting room until nearly eleven, when I had to be signed in, and then sat, silent and frightened, in our room until Mrs. Frederick, our housemother, came up at midnight to tell me that Cecie had mononucleosis, and would have to spend at least two weeks in the infirmary.

"But she'll be all right?" I said, my voice quivering.

"Oh, yes, she'll be fine," she said. "But I wish to goodness she'd come and told me earlier, or you had. She's let it go far too long. She's going to miss a lot of classes. Really, you girls act like children more often than not . . ."

She clopped back along the hall in her backless slippers and I shut the door to my room and crawled into my bed and cried. I cried for more than the fact of Cecie's illness; I knew that, but I did not know for what, and for the moment I did not wish to know. I turned my face into my pillow so that the weight of the great white moon hanging level with my window did not press on it, and I cried silently for a long time. And finally, without knowing when I did it, I slid into sleep.

The next few days were strange for me. I felt disoriented and divided: incomplete. Cecie, virulently contagious, was as effectively shut away from me as if in a cloister. Paul was utterly sunk in his hospital competition; except for a quick cup of coffee here and there, and once a brief, hard kiss in the stairwell in McCandless, I saw almost nothing of him. He looked sallow and haggard when I spied him in passing, and his white smile was perfunctory. I knew he probably was eating little and sleeping less, but knew, too, that there was virtually nothing I could do about that. I had the odd and vivid impression that despite the stress of the charette, he was happier than he had been since I had known him, and I know he was more alive. He hummed with excitement like a telephone wire. Not for the first time, I felt a craven coil of jealousy for the drawings that he was shaping with his dark hands. They were, I suspected, more seductive to him than my body.

But that was as futile as being jealous of the dead wife, and I knew it. If there was a living woman for him, it was me, and I could and would be content with that. And I was content in those long summer days, despite my loneliness for Cecie and my wanting of him. It was as if the world was in suspension; had ground to a stop. Soon a great gear would slip forward and the world would flow on, but for now, it was permissible simply to float on the surface of it, at rest, rocking gently in the sun, fitting everything that had happened to me into the grid of experience. I slept a lot, and read voraciously, and visited back and forth with girls I had scarcely seen for three months, and cleaned our room until it shone, and washed and ironed my clothes, and listened to every one of my records in a nonstop marathon of music. I think of those days, now, as perhaps the most peaceful I have ever known, although the strange sense of mutilation, the emptiness where Paul and Cecie had been, was never far from me. For the first time in years I was alone with myself, and for the first time ever, found the company fulfilling. There was no conflict in my heart, or for it. The abyss was silent. That sense of myself, alone and sufficient, has never come to me so completely again. I floated, and was happy.

Looking back, it seems incredible to me

that I did not worry about sleeping with Paul. Or rather, worry about the consequences of it: pregnancy and ostracism. No child of those times was ever more primed for worry. But I didn't, not for a moment. Perhaps it was because I had already known and bested the latter, and the former seemed to have nothing whatsoever to do with the wild, sweet, joyous things we did in the nights. My mind knew we were running risks; but my heart basked in safety. Paul used condoms with wry resignation and efficiency, never failing to observe that he felt like an SAE at a houseparty, with that little round intaglio in his wallet.

"Why bother, then?" I said once, when his disgust at the devices became apparent. "You're going to marry me anyway. You could just make an honest woman of me at a JP someplace and I could move in here and it would be a whole lot simpler."

"You know what a kid would do to our future right now?" he said, and I saw that he was absolutely serious, grimly so. "It would be the end of everything. We'd be living in Levittown and I'd be working at McKim for the rest of my life. Right now the whole ball game is riding on you, Katie. When we're in the white house you can have ten, if you like. But for now, it's Trojans or nothing. The first thing I want you to do when you get to New York, though, is get fitted for a diaphragm. As it is, we're taking chances with these things."

"I could go to Montgomery or somewhere and do it now," I said, obscurely hurt at his insistence. Somewhere deep within me, the thought of a child of his had lain like an actual embryo, warm and safe and secret.

"Too easy for talk to get back here," he said. "My landlady knows every doctor in a five-hundred-mile radius. Your house-mother probably does, too. The whole campus would have it in an hour."

"God, Paul, you think they don't talk about us now?" I said.

"Yeah, but they don't *know* now," he said. "We'll just have to be careful until New York."

"Okay," I said obediently. But I never could, that enchanted summer, make myself worry about the specter of pregnancy. It seemed, like all other perils and dangers, simply outside the charmed circle in which we moved.

Cecie came back from the infirmary near the end of July, having been adjudged no longer contagious, but still too weak to attend her classes. I went and picked her up, and Ginger and Fig and I installed her in her

273

bed, and heaped books around her, and dragged the Webcor and the pile of LPs close to the bed so she could change them without getting up, and trained the laboring fan on her. Ginger called home and the mute and thunderous Robert arrived with a new compact refrigerator and enough Coca Colas and fruit juices to stock it for the rest of the summer, and we plugged it in and set it up on the desk. Fig went down to the big dim kitchen and produced, from various boxes of mix, a sagging, sprawling chocolate cake that lay on its plate like a clubbed animal, and bore it proudly into our room.

"It sort of split in the middle, but I filled the crack up with icing, and it really tastes fine," she said, hanging her head and smiling at Cecie. "I thought double chocolate might be good. This is Duncan Hines; it's the one Mama always makes."

"It looks wonderful," Cecie said in her still-husky voice, smiling valiantly at her. "Why don't you cut it and give us all some?"

Fig did, bustling about like a Vermeer dwarf. The cake, in fact, tasted as dreadful as it looked, of stale cardboard and grainy, unmixed frosting. But we all ate it. Fig's power in some matters was awesome.

Later, when Cecie and I were alone, we looked at each other and burst into laughter.

We were, I think, so relieved to be laughing together once more that we carried the laughter further and louder than we would have ordinarily. Her laugh was the same, with perhaps a rasped edge to it now, but still the rich, skating, fluting, careening thing that drew people like Pan's pipes.

"It looks like a scale model of a medieval fort," she snorted, and I fell backward across my bed, clutching my sides.

"Or a sacked and pillaged Greek city-state," I gasped. " 'This is Duncan Hines; it's the one Mama always makes.' God, I'll bet Mama makes Libby's English peas and mushrooms for Christmas dinner, too, and lime sherbet and ginger ale punch."

"And jello with those shitty little marshmallows in it," Cecie howled, tears running down her face.

"And Spam with cloves stuck in it," I choked, rolling back and forth on the bed, my hands over my face.

And for the space of minutes we could not speak for the laughter, which trailed to a stop and broke forth again whenever we looked at each other. Several people came and stuck their heads into our room to see what was going on.

"It sounds like old times in here," Trish said. "I could hear you all the way downstairs.

You must be feeling better, Cecie."

"I am," Cecie said. "If I don't die laughing."

In fact she was not feeling all that much better. She was still very thin and shadowed beneath her eyes. The horn-rimmed glasses would not stay up on her nose, and her red hair was wispy and ragged. She was no longer flushed and glassy-eyed with fever, but she was pale, and the laughing fit so drained her that she fell asleep in mid-sentence, and I drew the shades and tiptoed out. When I came back from McCandless late that evening, having done some work on my own summer design project and had a quick cup of coffee with Paul, she was propped up in bed reading Dorothy Parker and drinking Coca Cola.

"Have you had supper?" I said. "I'll go get you something from the kitchen if you haven't."

"I'm not hungry," she said. "I did try to go down, but my legs just gave out on the stairs and I came back. I guess it's going to take longer than I thought. And I don't see how on earth I'm going to finish classes this summer. I'll bet you anything I lose this entire quarter."

"So what?" I said. "You'll catch up. It's better than making yourself sick again."

"Well, you know, with you graduating a quarter early and me a quarter late, you'll

276

be gone half a year before I will. What's that going to do to Europe?"

I had not thought about our plans to tour Europe after graduation since I met Paul; not seriously, anyway. The plans had been comfortably nebulous. I looked at her, and looked away.

"Actually, I may be going straight to work," I said. "Paul is pretty sure he can get me on in the Interiors department at McKim, Mead and White. I just couldn't turn that down. I'd never do it on my own."

"That's terrific," she said quickly. "Could he really do that?"

"Well, he has a job waiting there for him, and they want him awfully badly. He thinks he can," I said.

"Ah," she said in her light, sweet voice. It was the tone she used when something had touched her in some way and she wished to conceal the fact. I had heard it often, but never directed at me.

"But listen," I said hurriedly. "He's got another year or two here, and I'll be by myself in the apartment . . . if I can even find one. Why don't you come share until he gets there? Oh, Cecie, think about it . . . New York, and all the plays and the museums and things; maybe we could even meet Dorothy Parker. She reviews books for *Esquire* . . . and Long

Island for you, if you want the water . . ."

"It's certainly an idea," she said, and I knew then that it would not happen.

"Cecie . . ." I began.

"Oh, Katie, of course you have to do it," she said warmly. "Lordy, McKim, Mead . . . you'll be lunching at the Algonquin with Parker inside a year. You go on and I'll come visit. You'll get so sick of me you'll start locking the door in my face."

"We could all go to Europe, you know," I said. "Paul knows it like the back of his hand. We were going to go sometime during his first year up there, anyway. You couldn't have a better tour guide than him."

She smiled at me.

"I gather Paul is going to be permanent," she said.

"I guess . . . yes. He is," I said. For some reason I blushed furiously.

"Then don't you think it's time you told me about him?" she said. "One might almost think you were ashamed of him."

And so I did, that night. We sat up late with Dave Brubeck spilling out "Lullaby of Birdland" into the hot night, with the tepid wash of the fan on us, and I told her what I could about Paul Sibley. I found the words frustratingly flat and short of the reality of him, but all of a sudden I wanted Cecie to know him intimately, in all his contexts and aspects, almost as I knew him. I fairly stammered with the effort to make him live in the air between us.

I told her about his childhood, and his mother and uncle and the foster homes, and about what he wanted to do as an architect, and what I believed he was capable of doing. I told her about what he wore and ate and drank and listened to and thought about and laughed at. I told her, finally, about the French marriage and the dead wife.

"She sounds awful," Cecie said. "Does she haunt you?"

"Not for a minute," I said.

She grinned, and parroted:

" 'Let another hail him dear —
Little chance that he'll forget me!
Only need I curse and fear
Her he loved before he met me.' "

"Nuts to that and nuts to her," I grinned back. "I don't think he ever did really love her, and there wasn't a single thing he wanted out of life that she liked or approved of. Not to speak ill of the dead. But oh, Cecie, everything he loves, I love! Everything he wants is what I want! Listen, let me tell you about his white house . . ."

And I did. When I had finished, she was still smiling, but the essential Cecie-ness had gone out of it. I stopped talking and looked at her.

"Don't you think it sounds too perfect for words?"

"I sure do," she said. "I also think it's at least as much your white house as it is his. You're going to be the one supporting him while he makes his dream come true."

I could not think of anything to say. Did she not see?

"Well . . . one of us will have to work full time, and he can't do it and build a house and a practice at the same time," I said. "And I was going to try for a job in New York, anyway. What's the difference? Now I'm working at a dream job years before I could expect to, and for a house and a man I never even dared to dream about . . ."

"No difference, really," she said in her precise voice. "It's just that he's an extremely lucky guy, and I want him to realize it. And you should realize it, too. At least call it 'our white house.'"

" 'Our white house,' then," I said. "Oh, this is useless; I can't describe him. You're just going to have to meet him. You'll see, then. We're about one week away from that dinner party."

"Good," Cecie said. "I look forward to it."

On the first Friday evening in August Cecie and I and Fig and Ginger tiptoed up the stairs to Paul's apartment in the thick, leafy dark. There was not so much need for silence; the landlady was at the Passion Play in Oberammergau. But Paul had asked us to wait until dark fell.

"I think she's put her neighbors on red alert," he said.

And so we groped our way, trying not to fall and not to giggle. There was a white half-moon rising behind the trees, but it had not broken clear yet. I thought suddenly how much earlier dark was coming now. Off in the distance, at the edge of the trees, cicadas called and winter waited, crouching. I felt a wing-brush of melancholy. The coming fall would be my last one at Randolph, my last one with Cecie. After that, I would be in another country entirely.

He opened the door to us in tight white pants and a striped French sailor's jersey. On his dark head was the little round *matelot's* cap, and he wore, astoundingly, well-worn rope-soled espadrilles. Behind us, Edith Piaf wailed of pain and degeneration and late nights and cigarettes, and something smelling powerfully of raw red wine and herbs bubbled audibly behind the painted screen. I stared at him as if I had never seen him before, and indeed, I had not, not this Paul. He looked absurdly, theatrically, indescribably wonderful, and as remote from Randolph, Alabama, or even New York, not to mention Kate Stuart Lee, as it was possible for a human being to look. This man was the very essence of the word exotic. It struck me, standing there dumbly and hearing the little, indrawn breaths behind me, that he might be mocking us with the costume, but then he grinned, easily and charmingly, and I saw that he was not. He was parodying himself for us. He had surely known that I would make much of his years in France to my friends. This was his way of defusing the formidability which he well knew clung to him, of laughing at himself so that we might laugh, too.

And at his grin we did, all of us, even Fig. Even as they gaped around at the apartment, even as they sniffed the air and heard the Piaf and the accordions, even as they stared at Paul Sibley whenever his eyes were not on them, Cecie and Ginger and Fig laughed with delight and a kind of relief, and with capitulation. I had seen him do it before; topple walls and barriers with one brief, wry smile. He had done it to me. But it never failed to amaze me. I loved him so much in that instant that I closed my eyes with it; so the room swam.

"Thank you," I said to him silently. "Oh, thank you."

Aloud I said, "Where on earth did you get that costume? You look like Gene Kelly in *An American in Paris.*"

"Actually, I look a lot better," he grinned. "Kelly is a dwarf. This is not a costume, my dear; I actually wore these astounding garments during my first days in Paris. I even carried a baguette around with me under my arm. I thought I was wonderful. But I had to give it up; none of my French friends would be seen in public with me."

Cecie's laugh burbled.

"What did they wear?" she said.

"Blue jeans and Brooks Brothers shirts," he said. "Come on in. I'm making tripes à la mode de Caen. It's as authentic a peasant dish as I could think of."

"Smells heavenly," Ginger said, wrinkling her freckled nose at him in appreciation. It included, I knew, Paul as well as the food.

"It sure does," Fig echoed, faintly. Something was wrong with Fig's voice. She sounded as if she had been hit in the midriff with a baseball. I looked at her. She was very pale, and two vermilion spots stood out on her cheeks. Behind the thick glasses, her eyes looked stunned and stupid. She seemed to be breathing hard through her nose, as if an asthma attack were imminent. I opened my mouth to speak to her, and then it dawned on me. Fig had, in that instant, fallen in love with Paul.

"Oh, shit," I whispered, and saw Cecie's mouth quirk.

"I'll say it does," I said briskly, to cover the "shit." "What is it?"

Cecie snorted. Paul grinned at her, the dark eyes dancing.

"Actually, it's tripe," he said. "The first and second sections of the stomach of a ruminant such as a sheep, or a goat. The guy at the grocery store gave it to me free; I think he called it a gut. Of what animal I dared not ask. I do it the classic way, with pigs' feet and carrots and onions and leeks and all kinds of herbs and wine, and pastry. Plus enough Calvados to make you forget what it is. Or at least not care. It's the acid test. If somebody I've just met eats my tripe without throwing up, or at least tries, I know I've got a friend for life."

"Maybe it would be easier to try a little Russian roulette," Cecie murmured, and he laughed outright.

"It may be the same thing," he said.

"The only way you're going to get me to

eat that stuff is pour scotch down me from now till dinner time," Ginger said.

"I love tripe. We have it all the time at home," Fig said. Her voice sounded so frail and bruised that I thought she might burst into tears.

"Then," said Paul, "there's no help for it. I will simply have to marry you. Kate here has said she'd as soon eat dog."

"I've said nothing of the kind," I said in mock indignation, loving him and his foolishness and his kindness to poor Fig, loving them for admiring him, loving the place and the night and the world and everything in it, stars and bugs and elephants and shoes and pins and needles. I felt ready to burst, in that instant, with pure joy.

"Ha, I accept, then," Fig brayed, in a savage attempt at sophistication. He smiled at her and ruffled her wiry, impossible hair, and she turned fuchsia and clamped her jaw shut. I saw that it was working as though she were chewing something.

"Drinks coming up," he said, and led us into the room, and the night flowed on.

We drank a great deal of wine before he finally served dinner, and somehow he even had scotch for Ginger, though I did not remember having told him she drank it, and he told wry, deadpan stories of his adventures and misadventures in France, omitting any mention of the dead Berthe. She was there, though, hovering in the air above us like a thwarted demon, and I thought how very attractive it was of him, how becoming, not to at least allude to her. The sympathy for him was palpable in the room, though he obviously did not seek it. We laughed, and he played the velvety music of the Mediterranean, and taught us a few simple French songs, including some that made Cecie blush to the roots of her hair through her laughter, and before the night was over he had out of each of them at least the bare bones of their lives and experiences, and their plans for the future.

"What about your future?" Ginger said as we waded into the tripe. By that time the wine had done its work, both on the meat and us; the dish, served with more Calvados and tiny boiled potatoes and a simple green salad, was sublime, and we ate it all. We were on Stilton and dry red wine when Ginger asked her question.

"I don't have to ask if it includes old Kate here, do I?" she grinned. "She's been mooning around lovestruck for weeks and weeks."

"*Ginger,*" I hissed at her, and she put out her tongue.

"Oh, yes, it sure does," Paul said, reaching over to touch my cheek. I heard Fig make a small, strangled sound. I did not look at her.

"At least, long range, it does," he said. "Although I'm not going to have one, if I don't do something about that goddamned English 401. I think I flunked another test today, Kate. One more and my point average is going to be in more trouble than I care to think about."

I looked at him blankly. I had not even known he was having trouble with his English course. I knew that he did not often read; when he had spare time he spent it at his board. But I could not imagine that he would not pass his courses.

"Welcome to the club," Ginger said comfortably. "Don't worry, though. Kate'll get you through. She and Fig and Cecie carried me bodily through my English classes when I was a pledge. Hell, get Fig to tutor you. She's the best there is at Randolph. She's going to be a writer. She's written at least five books since I've known her."

Paul looked over at Fig.

She ducked her head.

"I'm really not very good," she mumbled.

Suddenly I wanted to shake her.

"Fig has the highest grades anybody has

ever made in English at Randolph," I said. "I can't imagine why she's acting so coy. There isn't nothing she doesn't know about it, and I'll bet she'd love to tutor you, if you asked her nicely. And if you won't I will. You can't afford to let your point average slide, Paul."

He shook his head.

"I wouldn't wish tutoring me on anybody," he said. "I'm impatient and downright bad-tempered when I'm not interested in some-thing, and I just can't manage to get interested in the Elizabethan poets. Fig would hate me in two days."

"No, I wouldn't," she said, looking at him with such naked adoration in the swimming bug's eyes that I turned my head. Oh, don't, I said silently to him. Can't you see how she feels about you?

"I'd be very honored if you wanted me to help you," Fig said formally. "If Kate doesn't care, I mean."

And she looked at me with such abject obsequiousness that I felt amusement and annoyance spurt up. "Of course I don't care," I said crisply. "Did you think I was afraid you were going to run off with him behind my back?"

"No," Fig said in a low voice, looking down. My heart smote me with remorse at my careless words, followed by fresh irritation.

"Well, I think it's a great idea," I said.

And so it was arranged that Fig would work with Paul on Monday, Tuesday, and Thursday evenings, from seven to nine.

"Will you mind coming here?" Paul said to her. "I'll have to sneak you past the old dragon, but I can promise you a glass of wine and some supper, and you can kick me in the ass if I snap at you."

"I don't mind," Fig whispered, and I did not know if she meant she did not mind coming to the apartment, or being snapped at. Both, probably.

On the way home, crammed into the MG, Fig was uncharacteristically silent, and had the rapt look of a heroin addict or a charmed snake on her big face. Ginger was overflowing with talk of Paul.

"He's fantastic," she said. "He's incredible. Can I date him?"

"No."

"Well, then, can I screw him?"

"Ginger, *really* . . ."

"Are y'all doing the Black Act?" she said.

"Will you stop it?" I cried, my face flaming in the dark.

"Well, if you're not, you're crazy," she said. "I bet Cecie knows. What about it, Cece?"

"I certainly don't know," Cecie said. "But he sure is handsome, isn't he?"

I knew in that instant, though I will never know how, that she did not like him. I knew that, even though I was never able to get her to admit it.

"Why don't you like him?" I said that night, as we got into our beds.

"Who says I don't?" Cecie said, and it was all she would say.

When I thanked Paul again the next day for the evening, he said, casually, "And how about Cecie? Did I pass the famous Cecie Hart test?" And I knew that he did not like her, either.

"Oh, lord," I said. "Why don't you like her?"

"Who says I don't?" Paul said.

"This is ridiculous," I snapped. "That's what she says, about you. What's the *matter* with you all? I thought things went so well . . ."

"I did, too," he said. "I tried. But I'm really not surprised. She's jealous of me, Kate. It makes me uncomfortable."

"I don't know what you mean," I said irritably. "Why should she be jealous of you? She's not jealous . . ."

He studied his coffee cup.

"I've seen it before, in France," he said, not looking up.

I stared at him. A chilly stillness seemed to spread up over me from somewhere in my center.

"Are you implying that Cecie is . . . queer or something?" I said. "Because if you are . . ."

"No. I'm not. Forget it," he said. "It wouldn't be the first time I was mistaken. I'll do better, I promise."

And he did try. He always asked after her, and he cooked dinner for just the three of us one night, and he took my car and picked her up at the library each night for a week so that she would not have to walk home to the house; she was still weak, and though she struggled not to, was falling farther and farther behind in her work. When we were together, the three of us, he went out of his way to make her laugh, and she did, always.

But I took to closing the bathroom door when I showered. I had never done that before. If she noticed, she did not comment on it.

CHAPTER EIGHT

"We had navarin d'agneau," Fig said, mispronouncing it so badly that Cecie winced. "That's lamb stew with a lot of French things in it. And lots and lots of wine. It was quite exquisite, really."

You could tell she had had wine. Her eyes, behind the thick lenses, looked poached, and her pug nose burned fiercely. She was just home from her first tutoring session at Paul's apartment, and her manner was that of a demi-mondaine Parisienne visiting the provinces under duress. She had been home less than ten minutes and she had said "Paul said," and "Paul thinks" and "as I told Paul" so many times that Cecie and Ginger and I were mouthing it silently with her whenever his name came up again. I wanted to strangle her.

In the days that followed, we heard that he was teaching her about contemporary European architecture ("Corbu and Mies"), opera, and the cuisine of the French provinces. With each ponderously dropped disclosure, she became more officious and more obviously smitten. Most of the chapter gathered to hear her recitals when she came in from a tutoring session now. I could hear them laughing all the way down the hall. I managed to laugh, too, sensing that to show my annoyance would be fatal. The nearest I came to it was to inquire acidly, after hearing that he was instructing her in French abstract impressionistic art, "I do suppose that you're getting a few licks of Edmund Spenser and George Herbert in between taste treats and artistic thrills?"

"Oh, yes," she said seriously. "He's really doing awfully well. I just don't think he's ever had the right teacher."

"Ah," Cecie said. "That's undoubtedly it."

The next evening she came into our room, diary in hand.

"I want you to tell me everything about him, Effie," she said in the low, rapt tones of one of Gandhi's handmaidens. "I've started the story of you and Paul. It's the perfect love story. I know about you, but I need to know about him, and he won't tell me anything at all. You know how modest he is. It would make a wonderful novel. I'm going to write it one day. But I'll let you read what I write in the diary when I've finished."

"Thanks," I said. "But if Paul doesn't want to talk about himself, I don't think I ought to, either."

"Well, he probably just needs to get so he trusts me a little more," she said. "He's opening up, bit by bit. Tonight he told me about the white house, and showed me the drawing. I think it's the most wonderful and romantic thing I ever saw, that he's going to build that house for you. It's like you were a princess, in a castle. He's the most wonderful man I've ever known. If you weren't my big sister and my best friend I'd steal him."

And she gave me a dreadful, slantwise grimace that I supposed was meant to be a leer.

"Well, please don't," I said as evenly as I could.

"Why on earth did you tell her about the house?" I said to Paul at coffee the next day. "I think she thinks you're building it for her now."

"Oh, I don't know," he said. "She saw the painting and asked. It was a relief to have something to talk to her about. Most of the time she seems like she's about to jump out of her skin. Like she thinks I'm going to put the make on her, God forbid. It would be like humping Dopey or Sneezy. Or sometimes she acts like I'm some kind of deity, and she ought to take her shoes off before approaching me. She's not so bad, really; and she's a damned good English teacher. She's helping me a lot."

"She's bloody awful and you know it," I said. "You mean you aren't teaching her about opera and French art and food, and architecture?"

"Hell, no," he said. "I can barely get her to talk about Edmund Spenser. I give her supper, usually, and tell her what's in it, and ply her with wine so we can get some work done, and I guess she listens to what I have on the hi fi and sees what's on my walls, but we don't talk about it. The house is the only thing she's ever asked about."

"You ought to hear her when she gets back from a session with you," I said, annoyed and amused. "She's so full of French culture and so la-di-da that the whole house is laughing at her. It would be sad if it wasn't just so awful."

"Well, she's not that way with me," he said.

Late one night toward the end of the quarter I told Cecie what Paul had said about the nights of tutoring, and she grinned. It was her old grin, whole and light-spilling and full of Cecie. I had not seen it often that summer.

"Did it ever occur to you that maybe they're not doing what either one of them says?" she said. "That maybe he rips her clothes off the minute she walks in and they make mad, passionate love *à la française* for three hours? That he calls her Emma and she calls him Gaston and the whole apartment rocks with the force of their passion?"

I stared at her for a moment, and then the mental image of it forced its way into my mind and I gave a shriek of purely involuntary laughter and collapsed onto my bed. Cecie began to laugh, too.

"I can just see it," I cried. "First he pulls her exotic French silk underwear down and nibbles at her navel, and then he covers her with kisses from her neck to her waist . . ."

"Oh, Jesus, stop!" Cecie howled. "I'm going to have a heart attack and die. What navel? What neck? What waist? It would be like kissing a totem pole!"

"And then," I gasped, rolling from side to side, "he sinks to his knees and kisses *her* knees, and then, one by one, her toes . . ."

"Stop," Cecie choked. "Oh, stop! I'll throw up. *He'd* throw up! Oh, my God, her toes! Fig's toes!"

I put my arms over my face and twisted myself into a knot of hysterical, unstoppable laughter. We were in the midst of finals, and everybody was tense and fatigued, and much of the laughter was about that. But the image of Paul with his mouth pressed to Fig's toes while she writhed in ecstasy was too grotesque for my mind to contain.

"He said," I shrieked in a transport of joy, "that it would be like humping one of the Seven Dwarfs!"

And we howled and shrieked and hooted and yodeled our glee and release until Ginger beat on the wall and the girls next door yelled at us to shut up.

"It's enough," Cecie murmured after our lights were out and we were drifting toward sleep, "to give the Dirty Deed a bad name."

I lay awake for a time, thinking about that. It struck me that to Cecie, the act of love still meant words: the slang of lasciviously innocent college girls, or a line in a dirty fraternity limerick, or words on a page of Flaubert or Henry Miller, or even the Song of Solomon. But to me, now, it was flesh and blood, my own and Paul Sibley's. I *knew*, and she did not. It must have occurred to her; of course it had. But I knew that she would not speak of it to me. I was in another place from Cecie; I had crossed a border. I could not go back for her. It was a great gulf, one of the primal ones. I felt the isolation of it that night as keenly as if I were in a foreign city, completely alone.

I think of that night often. I remember

the laughter. It was the last time that we laughed together, Cecie and I.

We had planned to go back to the Outer Banks to Ginger's parents' cottage between quarters. She had asked us weeks before. I was torn; that old black house by the sea called me like a siren. But Paul's dark flesh called me to stay in Randolph. On the night before we were to leave in the car sent by her father and driven by the unhappy Robert, Ginger came into our room grinning. Cecie was tossing clothes into a suitcase. I had not yet made a move to pack. I felt drowned in lethargy.

"I have a surprise," Ginger bubbled. "I just called Paul and asked him to come with us, and he said he thought I'd never ask, and now you can stop mooning and start packing, Kate."

"Oh, Ginger, that's a wonderful idea," I cried. "Oh, bless you for thinking of it! I've told him so much about that house . . ."

"Thank Fig," Ginger said. "It was her idea. I guess she can't bear to be parted from him. Of course I had to be begged, but in the long run she talked me into it."

"Lord," I said. "I hope you don't mind . . ."

"Mind?" she grinned. "Two days in a closed car with Paul Sibley? Five days on the beach looking at him in a bathing suit? Mind?"

I laughed and hugged her. I thought, as I did, how solid and warm her flesh was, how comfortable and comforting.

"I love you, Ginger," I said.

"Me, too," she said.

It was a far better trip this time than the first. Paul kept us laughing with scurrilous lies and half-truths about the French and himself among them, and taught us French sailors' ditties, and even sang an accomplished two-part duet of a particularly odious one with Cecie. I knew it was odious because she was red from chest to hairline even as she sang and laughed. He and Ginger swapped what he called bawdy songs and backroom ballads until he wrung a reluctant grin out of even the dour Robert. By the end of the trip he was riding in front with Robert, telling him jokes in low tones that had him chuckling outright, and I think, from the smug masculine tone of Paul's laughter, that Robert even contributed a few himself. I could just imagine the tenor of those. When we stopped overnight in Charlotte Paul bunked in with Robert, and when we stopped for food and bathrooms he ate with him, or accompanied him to the men's room, or sat in the Cadillac with him. By the time we reached the Warren Bridge over Croatan Sound they were friends of the bosom, as Paul put it later.

"I figured it was him or Fig," he told me. "And of the two, I'd a hell of a lot sooner sleep and eat and pee with Robert. And, I suspect, he with me."

"Well, you got the best of it," I said. "I got to sit in back and watch her make love to the back of your neck with those eyes, and breathe like a guppy out of water. Cecie said it was like riding eight hundred miles with a pygmy in heat."

"For a convent virgin, Cecie knows a lot about the darker passions," Paul said, grinning.

Once past Manteo he fell silent, and as we crossed the Umstead bridge over Roanoke Sound to Nag's Head, he leaned slightly forward and crossed his arms on the dashboard. At a low word from Paul, Robert cut off the air conditioner and lowered the right-hand front window, and the wild, sweet, salt-fresh wind off the sea poured into the car. I took a deep breath, and saw that Paul did, too. To me there has never been anything more evocative of summer and wildness and bittersweet joy than a sea wind.

When we came bumping up into the back-yard of Ginger's house he sat still for a moment, staring up at it, while the rest of us tumbled out yelping with joy and freedom. He got slowly out of the car, and hung back, hands in pockets, while Robert trailed Cecie and Fig and Ginger up the steps with the luggage. This time Mr. and Mrs. Fowler were nowhere in sight.

I took his hand.

"Come on," I said. "I want to show you something before we go in."

And I led him around the house through the pine and juniper windbreak and across the open deck and up to the crest of the dunes.

As it was on that day the spring before, when I had first seen it, the wide, tawny beach was empty. The dunes still soared high and lonely against the evening sky, and the sea oats flattened themselves backward in the steady stream of wind off the Atlantic. The tide was high today, and the white surf creamed at the feet of the first low dunes. The water was very dark blue, and the pale light was so clear that you could see the rippled herringbone pattern of the sand in the shallows of the tidepools, and the bankerly patrols of strutting gulls that must have been two miles away. The air was warmer around us than I remembered from the spring, like warmed honey. But the wind was cool and fresh and tart as wine. We both inhaled deeply at precisely the same instant, and looked at each other. We smiled, but neither of us spoke.

He turned then, and looked back and up at Ginger's great house, dreaming above us in the September sun. I felt his hand tighten almost convulsively on mine, and a tiny, hard tremor go through him, that I felt sometimes at the moment of his orgasm. His face did not change, but I saw the muscles in his jaw clench.

"Didn't I tell you?" I said, loving him for that silent interior explosion.

He did not answer. He continued to stare up at the house, and then along the line of the dunes that fronted it on both sides.

"I'd put it right there," he said finally. "On that highest dune, off the left end, where it would look straight out to sea. That way it wouldn't break the roof line of the house, but you'd have a sense of connectedness. Inside, you'd see water on three sides, all the way to Spain or wherever. I don't know if you could cantilever in sand, though; there are probably ordinances . . ."

He fell silent. I knew what he spoke of.

"How would it look, all that white concrete connected to that weathered old black?" I said. The words were pedantic and tiresome;

I did not know where they had come from.

"I'd use the weathered wood on the outside. It doesn't matter about that; that old sable black is wonderful. Strong, for a strong, cold sea. Inside it would be white. In spirit it would be white . . ."

"It would be beautiful there, wouldn't it?" I said. "I knew you'd love the Outer Banks, and this house. Of all the people I know, it seems the most like you. It's definitely not contemporary, though."

"No," he said. "I thought that would matter, but it doesn't."

At dinner that night, at the big refectory table overlooking the deck and the moonlit sea, he charmed the Fowlers just as he had Robert. It was a side of him I had not seen before; I was as proud of him as a mother with a precocious child. He said just the right thing to the right Fowler, and I beamed fatuously.

But there was a strangeness, too. The laughing man who knew how to make small talk with a new-rich mill owner and his pretty, fluttering wife was such a different persona from the intense, consumed builder and wildly inventive lover that I had the feeling of sitting in the presence of someone I was supposed to know, and did not. I waited restlessly for the time when we could sit alone in the dark of the porch or walk on the night beach, and the lover would come back to me. I was weary, suddenly, with sharing him.

As Regina Fowler brought in dessert, she cocked her head at us, birdlike, and said, "I gather there'll be a honeymoon here sooner, rather than later."

I felt myself flush, and Ginger said, "As soon as Kate can get him to propose. She won't marry him unless he gets down on his knees."

Fig laughed loudly, and Paul smiled at her, and then, questioningly, at Regina Fowler.

"Kate said last spring she'd like to spend her honeymoon here," she explained. "And of course we said we'd love that. She must have been psychic; I don't think she'd even met you yet."

Paul's smile widened. "That would be as near heaven as I'm apt to get in my lifetime," he said.

"Why not get married here?" Fig blurted. Her face was flushed with wine and something that approached religious rapture. She had changed into a strange garment of flower-printed chiffon, or perhaps polyester, that brushed the floor and tied at her thick waist. I could not imagine where she had gotten it. She looked like a character in a grade B 1930s movie, the comic lead in an all-wrong peignoir.

"Why don't we just ask the Fowlers to deed the house over to us?" I said, embarrassed.

But Regina Fowler took up the cry.

"Oh, wouldn't that be sweet?" she fluted. "I've always thought a summer wedding on that lovely old porch, or maybe at the edge of the dunes . . . you know, with a little arbor, and simple, old-fashioned flowers, and maybe a little string quartet . . ."

"Yards and yards of aqua tulle, and big picture hats for the attendants," Fig leaped in. "Me and Ginger, of course, and all the sisters could come . . . oh, Effie, our first Tri O wedding!"

"Well, I always thought it would be Ginger's, but the way she's going I'll probably be in a wheelchair and we'll have it at the nursing home. So you children have yours here in the meantime," Regina said.

"It's at least a year and a half away," Paul said.

"Well, don't you forget. The offer stands."

"I won't forget," he said.

The Banks and the sea and the September weather seemed in conspiracy to soothe and seduce us. We had arrived planning to sleep until noon each day, but the lambent morning light and the soft sigh of the sea below the dunes sang us out of bed early, and the extravagant show of stars, both fixed and falling, in the great black autumn sky kept us up late, lying in deck chairs under blankets and sweaters, silent with the weight of all that beauty. During the day we lay under the high golden sun, its warmth red on closed eyelids, boneless and near-mindless with the peculiar contentment that comes only beside the sea. It was that September that I discovered the powerful and particular timelessness that is the ocean's best gift. Time stops; it literally does. Beside the sea, hovering at the edge of sleep, its great breath surging in and out with the very rhythm of the blood in your body, the sea will smooth away all but the essences of things, so that you are very near the creatures that crept out of those warm new seas and began life on earth, all those millions of years ago, under that strange, terrible young sun. I knew from that first day on the beach at Nag's Head with Paul that I could not live for long away from the sea.

We did not touch each other in those first days at the cottage, except to join hands as we lay in the sun or climbed the dunes or ran into the surf. It was a kind of delicious postponement; I would look at him, and he at me, and our eyes would grow heavy, and my wrists and knees would buckle with the sweet weight of desire for him. I would look at his strong brown hands and think where they would touch me and what they would do, and I came near to fainting. Once I reached out and traced the line of dark hair that ran from his navel down his hard, flat stomach, down to where it disappeared into his damp trunks. He rolled over on his stomach and smiled at me without opening his eyes.

"Do that again and I'm going to give Fig something to write about in her diary," he said.

"What are you going to do?" I said, my voice soft and thick.

"Do it again and see."

I heard my laugh, low and throaty and feral in my throat.

"Turn over so I can get to it," I said.

"Are you kidding? The lifeguards would come with hoses and water trucks and spray me. Little children would cry out in wonder. Fig would wriggle out of that incredible garment and jump my bones."

Fig had bought, for the trip, a fiercely boned and padded Rose Marie Reid confection with much draping and ruching and puffing of leg, in violent shades of pink and magenta. She had a bathing cap with pink rubber fronds all over it.

"It's a water lily," she said, showing it to us.

"Fig, neck deep in the water looks like a Portuguese man o' war," Cecie said.

"Fig neck deep in the water looks better than Fig out of it," I said. Paul shook his head at me.

"Jesus, that poor girl. With friends like you all, she doesn't need enemies. I'm going to take her swimming."

And he did, towing her far out beyond the line of the breakers, holding her in his arms because she could not swim. Even from the shore we could see that her eyes were shut and her face was still and bone-white.

"Oh, Lord, she's terrified," I said. "He shouldn't have done that."

"She's not terrified, she's having her first and probably only Big O, right there in the Atlantic Ocean," Ginger chortled. "I'd know that look anywhere."

"Ginger!" Cecie and I shouted together. But we laughed.

Paul was as easy to be with on the beach as he was in the car and at the dinner table. He not only swam with Fig, he and Ginger went out beyond the surf line and raced, and porpoise-dived, and rode the combers into the beach. Both of them were wonderful in the water, he like a dark, sleek, lightning-fast otter, she like a sturdy bronze seal. He walked the dune lines with Cecie, quizzing her about the ocean and dune plants, learning what grew where and why. He was intent and interested; she was courteous and pleasant. But I knew, and Paul must have, that she still did not like him. It was the only small, hot point of wrongness in the entire week.

Sometimes Paul and Ginger's father surf-cast, at evening when the blues were running, and Ginger's mother pan-fried them for dinner. Or we went out to eat fish and oysters and clams and endless hush puppies at weathered, screened little seafood shacks up and down the coast highway. Once we toiled to the top of Jockey's Ridge, the highest dune on the East Coast, and watched the kite-flying at sundown; it was an hour woven entirely of wind and sea and space. We were drunk on it. We visited the Wright Memorial atop Big Kill Devil Hill, and all of a sudden the fact of flight seemed simply miraculous, impossible to me, standing there in the teeth of that vast, streaming wind, looking out at the empty, endless sea; to think that two men had hurled their bodies, borne up only by a spidery web of wings, into all that wildness.

We planned, lazily and formlessly, to make side trips: over to Roanoke Island, to see the scruffy little fishing port of Wanchese and eat fresh-caught tuna; up to pretty little Manteo to see the Elizabethan Gardens and Sir Walter Raleigh's stubby, gallant little *Elizabeth II*. But in the end, for most of the week, we simply stayed on the beach. Ahead of me lay three months of endings: school, the great friendship of my life, my uneasy turn in the South itself. No matter how I looked forward to it — and I did, hungrily — the future was a heavy weight on my heart. The unknown had always frightened me in a profound and atavistic way. I could not control what I did not know. And so I was content, in those last days of summer, to lie in the blue and gold stasis of the sea with all the elements of my life, past and present, close at hand. Time enough for Life to start. Time enough. . . .

On our last full day we took the big Cadillac and rode down Highway 12, that threads the narrow ribbon of the Banks from just below Nag's Head to the Hatteras Ferry over to Ocracoke Island, eighty-odd miles to the south. It was a day so blue and vivid that there were gentian edges to everything, and the ocean was a dazzle of restless light. Ginger's father told us, as we set off, that on the Banks they called such a day a weather-breeder.

"Get a day like this and a storm is sure to follow," he said. "Probably a good thing you all are going back. This time of year the storms tend to be hurricanes."

"I'd love to ride out one of those babies in that house," Paul said. "I've seen what the big winds can do to the 'Glades, but you're on high ground here, and solid as a mountain. It really ought to be something."

"You just think you would," Mr. Fowler said. "Fella told me this summer that in the big blow of '38 the water came up so high a couple guys down the beach there found a porpoise stranded in their living room."

"Oh," I said softly, involuntarily. "Oh, poor thing . . ."

"Oh, it was all right," he said, grinning his fierce grin. "They were weight-lifters, or something. They just rolled him onto a door and walked him back into the surf. Probably lived a long and happy life right off their beach."

We smiled, charmed with the story.

"This place is under a spell of some kind, no doubt about it," I said. "Everything here has a happy ending."

"Seems like it, doesn't it?" he said, and slapped the fender, and we rolled out onto the coast highway.

Below Nag's Head, past the fishing pier, you come to Bodie Island, and the sea and beach turn wild. The wreck of the *Laura Barnes*, the last ocean-going schooner ever built in the United States, lies off Coquina Beach, driven aground there in one of the great spring storms in 1918. Across Oregon Inlet, National Seashore land begins, and the wildness deepens and thickens, until it is palpable on the skin, thick on the tongue and in the nose and ears. No houses break the towering lines of the front dunes, not even the ubiquitous fish shack; the sea, glimpsed between breaks in the solid, sunless maritime forests of yaupon, red cedar, live oak, sweet bay, and beech olive, seems fiercer here, and bluer, and somehow colder. The long beaches are wind-scoured and high-duned and absolutely empty. It is an impersonal landscape; nothing there speaks to the heart of man. I was aware, as we bore steadily south, that we were talking in hushed tones. I looked at Cecie and then at Paul; both had looks of distance and otherness in their eyes. I thought that this place of storms and emptiness and magical light was uniquely their place. I remembered, suddenly, the night of the storm that first trip, back in the spring, and Cecie's naked figure far below me in the line of the angry white surf, and how she dove into that black devil water and swam straight out into the storm. It seemed so much something Paul would do that I wondered again why they could not like each other; they seemed, in many ways, the most alike of any two people I have ever known.

Below the vast Pea Island Migratory Waterfowl Refuge we flashed past a few perfunctory little towns; mostly matters of gift and tackle shops and a tarpaper, stilted beach shack or two. They had names with music in them . . . North and South Rodanthe, Waves, Salvo. They looked like places few people lived and fewer stopped; I wondered how they sustained life, and what a life there would be like. The thought was somehow attractive to me; light years removed from New York and the Northeast Coast that I knew, but steeped in the timelessness of the sea that so beguiled me. If you came to one of these places in the fullness of happiness, surely you would keep that happiness forever, be frozen in it . . .

Far down the highway, nearly to Cape Hatteras itself, just past the tiny hamlet of Avon, we passed a cluster of buildings on the seaward side that made Paul slam on the brakes and back the Cadillac up, to look. We all did, and burst into simultaneous delighted laughter. It was a semi-circle of tiny, narrow, black-weathered houses like dollhouses or even fanciful outhouses, with peaked cedar shake roofs and much scrollwork and fake diamond panes and ornate shutters and faded red doors. On each door, and in each shutter, half-moons had been cut. Tiny window boxes filled with straggling geraniums and clumsy stone chimneys completed the look of a demented child's playhouse colony. Each postage stamp yard was encircled with white-painted rocks, and a birdbath adorned the precise center of each.

"Jesus, it's Snow White and the Seven Outhouses," Paul crowed. It was plain he was delighted. We all were. The little structures were the quintessence of all an architect and a designer should have deemed irredeemably tacky, yet somehow they lifted the heart and tickled the funny bone. The fact that they badly needed paint and shingles and repairs did nothing to dim their crazy joie de vivre.

"Whatever it is, I want it," Cecie gurgled in pleasure.

"There's not a sign," Paul said.

"Yes, there is; it's fallen. It's back there

314

on the ground," Ginger said. "I was waiting to show y'all this."

Paul backed the car up further and we saw the sign then: Carolina Moon Motel. Daily — Weekly — Hourly. Magic Fingers.

"What are Magic Fingers?" Fig said, her brow knit.

"It means you put a quarter in the bed and it diddles you," Ginger grinned. "This is the local who' house. It's been here forever."

We got out and looked at the little cottages. All were dark and seemed unoccupied. The slightly larger one that was the office had a sign on the door that said GONE TO LUNCH. BACK 1:00.

"Guess that's tough luck for the nooners," Paul grinned. "God, what an absolutely perfect, glorious, wonderful place. Katie me love, if we do have our honeymoon here, I'm going to bring you here for the wedding night itself. Those magic fingers will make a crazy woman of you."

"I can hardly wait," I said acidly, thinking that I really couldn't.

"Ha, that's rich," Fig shouted nervously. "That's one for the diary."

This time no one even shouted at her. We went on past the Carolina Moon to the great Hatteras Light House and then into

Hatteras itself, and had a late lunch of steamed blue crabs and beer, and were back on the road home by four. The Carolina Moon sat as it had that morning, shuttered and promising Magic Fingers to all takers. There had been none since we passed the first time.

"Now that's the place to ride out a storm," I said. "Light your little fireplace and take a bottle of wine and keep feeding the bed quarters. Wow."

Ginger laughed.

"You'd have to be a good swimmer to do that," she said. "If it's a bad enough storm the bridges are under water. Nobody comes down here in a blow. Not even for Magic Fingers."

"Pity," I said. "It would be the perfect aphrodisiac. Oh, Lord, y'all, has this been a perfect day, or what?"

That last night we sat late on the deck after supper. The first of the wispy mare's-tail clouds that preceded the storm Mr. Fowler had promised trailed milky skeins across the clouds of stars, and the ocean seemed stiller than I had ever seen it. It was then that Ginger told us the story of the mermaids that sang the sailors to their fate on the shoals.

"What kind of mermaids would those be?" Fig said earnestly. "The only kind I ever read about were Greek, like the sirens, or German, like the Rhine Maidens. I guess these would be Indians. They'd probably be singing Indian songs."

We were all elaborately silent. None of us dared look at the others. I knew we were struggling, in the dark, not to laugh. We had simply laughed too much at Fig this trip; we all sensed it. But the image her words called up was almost too much for us to handle.

From the open kitchen window, where she had gone to make tea, Cecie's voice trailed sweetly out into the still night.

"When I'm calling you — ooo-ooo," she warbled, "will you answer tru uuu-uuue . . . ?"

And the laughter exploded out of our mouths and noses into the night. Even Paul laughed. It went on and on, and every time it drifted to a stop a snort from one of us would set it off again.

"Well, I wanted to get it right," Fig said primly. "Y'all are always telling me to get it right."

After everyone had straggled off to bed, Paul and I lingered on the deck, moving finally to the big new hammock Mr. Fowler had hung at the far end, tucked under the overhang of the great roof. We climbed carefully into it, so as not to fall out, and lay as still as we could, and as quietly.

"We really should go in," I said. "We've got to get an early start tomorrow. I haven't packed yet."

"Stay a minute," he said. "I haven't had any time at all alone with you. I've been looking at that body practically naked for five days, and I've hardly touched it."

"Well, don't touch it now," I said, only half-teasing. "If you do, we'll end up doing it in this hammock and everybody will hear us and know what we're doing . . ."

"They already do," he said, and put his hand on my breast.

I drew in my breath sharply. Fire leaped in my groin.

"Don't," I whispered. "Oh, don't . . ."

"Then what about this?" he said, and slid his hand down my body and under the waistband of my shorts, and finally to the secret warmth between my legs. I arched my back and opened them for him. I knew as I turned my body and face into his that we were lost.

He was nearly inside me, murmuring, moaning a little, I was blind and fully opened with pure sensation, when it happened. I shifted my weight and the hammock tossed us onto the deck with a hollow thud that sounded as if it might be heard to the mainland. We froze in a tangle of arms and legs and naked skin, hardly breathing, laughter beginning deep inside us, skirling relentlessly up. At the end of the dark house a light went on.

We righted ourselves and our clothing and sat demurely side by side on the steps down to the sand, feeling it snake-cold on our bare feet, shaking with suppressed laughter and the release of tension. Presently the light went off again.

"I guess that was an omen," he said. "But I promise you one thing, Katherine Stuart Lee. The minute I get you here again I'm going to bang you in that hammock. Before we even unpack. Before we even go in the house. I'll drive all night to do it, if I have to."

"You know, if we got married here, you wouldn't have to drive all night," I said. "You wouldn't have to unpack. You'd just have to wait till the last guest left and unzip your fly. It's the best argument for a Nag's Head wedding I ever heard."

"Don't tempt me," he said. "But I'm sure your mother would never stand for that. It's bad enough I'm dragging you away to the Yankees. I know Southern mamas. It's got to be the big deal with the twelve bridesmaids and champagne fountain and an orchestra and a tent and God knows what else. I'll be lucky to get you into that hammock for a week after we're married."

I told him then. I sat in the darkness beside him and told him about my father, and the summers of servitude on the Cape, and the careful, unceasing tutelage, and the money that was not, and the Lee that was not *that* Lee, and the sad squalor of the old house on the Santee River. And I told him about my father's suicide on its banks.

"I should have told you before, but I didn't really think it mattered," I said. "And I know it doesn't, not to you. But I can't go on letting you think I'm rich. I'm an awful long way from that. It doesn't change anything; I'll still be going to New York and working, and you'll be starting the house and your practice . . .

I let my voice trail off so that he could speak. He did not. He sat beside me on the steps of Ginger's big house and stared out to sea, where the clouds had finally eaten the thin moon, and said nothing. I could not see his face.

"It does matter, doesn't it?" I said finally, my voice breaking. "You're mad at me."

"The only thing that matters is that you thought you couldn't tell me right off," he said in a remote voice. "The only thing that matters is that you thought it would matter to me. You must have, or you'd have told me. Did you really think I'd care about that?"

"I guess I didn't think at all," I said despairingly. "Somehow it just never seemed the time for it. I'm sorry. Please don't shut me out."

He was silent again, and I began to cry, quietly and in absolute anguish at what I had wrought. I could not bear his silence.

"Ah, Kate, don't cry," he said finally. "It doesn't matter. Nothing has changed. You've told me now, and that's the end of it. Come here and give me a hug."

And he pulled me to him and kissed the top of my head. Gradually I stopped crying. We sat so for a long time, I listening to his breathing and feeling the warmth of him in the cooling night. Finally, with the sharpening of the wind that meant the turn of the tide, we got up and went inside. In the other bed in our room, Cecie slept quietly, her face turned to the window on the sea. But it was a long time before I slept.

We were almost across the Lindsay Warren Bridge to the mainland the next morning before anyone spoke.

"Well," Ginger said to Paul, turning around in the front seat so she could see him. "Wasn't it everything I said it was?"

"Oh, yes, Gingerrooney," he said. "It was all that and more."

It was upon me then, the time of urgency and endings: there was nothing, now, between me and December graduation. No break existed so that I could say "after vacation." Nor could I say "this time next quarter." There would not, for me, be a next quarter. The sense of imploding time was terrifying.

Paul said more than once that I reminded him of an overtuned violin. I wept more often, and more easily, that fall than I ever have since, even in the days after Stephen's death, even after they found the cancer. Those two horrors were beyond weeping. But in that last autumn at Randolph, everything touched me like an electrical charge, and everything brought quick, tremulous tears. I would walk across the campus in the grape-colored early dusk of October and smell the smoke from the Friday night pep rally bonfires, and I would think, "This is the last time I'll ever smell that smell, or see this light." The Saturday thunder of the drums from the stadium, on bronze afternoons, made my heart hurt. I would walk into the steamy clatter of Harry's out of a nippy November wind and the dreary, banal little scene would move me to blindness with its sweetness and beauty. The light from my drawing board lamp on a night of blowing rain, seen through the bank of windows in McCandless, struck me to the quick. Next quarter another head would lean over into its white pool. Even the midge-whine of chapter meetings, and the fretful scramble of rush, made me nostalgic. Ginger's white grin made me want to run across the room and hug her, and I often did. Once or twice I even did it to Fig, who colored and simpered.

I found that I could hardly bear to look at Cecie. Whenever I did, and saw her red head bent over her books, or received her full, sweet kitten's smile, loss nearly drowned me. I had to turn my head away frequently, lest she see the tears in my eyes. I had the sense, at those times, that it was Cecie's ghost I saw; that the essential Cecie had moved on somewhere else, somewhere I could not follow. I found that I was starting a great many sentences to her with "Do you remember?"

"Of course I remember, it was only a year ago," she said to me once. "What's the matter with you? You'd think you were going to Inner Mongolia for the rest of your life."

"I'm afraid I'm going to forget it," I said.

"I want to keep all of it, everything we said and did and laughed at, everything we read. And I want you to remember it, too."

"I'm not going to forget it, ol' Kate," she said seriously. "And I'm not going to die, either, and you're not. Stop acting like December was the end of everything. We'll see each other. I'll come to New York next summer, if you still want me to, and we're all going to meet at Ginger's in March, remember."

"I know. It's just that there's something so . . . bittersweet about everything this fall. Everything I see or hear . . ."

She smiled.

" 'The look of a laurel tree birthed for May
Or a sycamore bared for a new November
Is as old and as sad as my furtherest day —
What is it, what is it, I almost remember?' "

she quoted.

"I know I'll never forget the Dorothy Parker," I grinned mistily. "It's the first thing I'm going to unpack in New York. I'm going to read it every night, like the Bible."

"So will I," she said. "And I'll read aloud to you in my head, and you to me, and we'll be able to laugh just as hard as if we were in the same room."

"Oh, Cecie . . ." I began, my eyes flooding with tears.

"Don't you dare," she said fiercely. "I don't have time to cry. I'm doomed as it is. We'll cry later." And she left for the library, and I for McCandless.

I was finally into my senior design thesis, and was spending virtually every waking hour in labs or with my adviser. I felt a keen pressure to make the project as good as it could be. Paul had, indeed, written Carl Seaborn, his mentor at McKim, Mead and White, about employment for me, and Carl had called the next day to say that they'd found both a place for me as a junior draftsman in their interiors department and a tiny apartment on First Avenue in the 80s, that had just been vacated by an employee who was joining the Peace Corps. The job was a foregone conclusion, he said, but they'd want to see my thesis, just as a formality. And so I poured heart and soul and hundreds of hours into it, and Paul photographed it in progress and sent it to Carl Seaborn, and the word came back that they thought it very good indeed, and were proud to have me on the team. I thought they probably were. The project was good; even I knew that. I had, inevitably, chosen to do interiors for the house by the sea, and the clean, low lines of the massive furniture and the sea-and-wind-cool blues and greens and vibrant whites and gull grays flowed from my fingers as if fountains had been tapped.

"We're going to do these rooms just this way," Paul said, looking at it. "It's perfect. I won't want to change anything. The house is a real partnership now."

And happiness flooded me, bringing, inevitably, tears.

Urgency infected everyone that autumn, it seemed. Paul's entire quarter was devoted to a design competition for a bus station in Tuskegee, and his hours at the board were even worse than mine. We made silent, urgent love in haste, gulped coffee in haste, met in dark stairwells and parking lots and kissed and broke apart, sweat-damped, and dashed on our different ways. He continued to work three nights a week with Fig, at the English, but mercifully she ceased making so much of it, and he simply forgot to mention it unless I remembered to ask. I seldom did. His summer English grade had been a B. The tutoring was obviously a success.

Ginger was away much of that quarter, doing a stint of elementary school practice teaching in nearby Montgomery. She stayed with elderly relatives in a dim, enormous old house during the week and streaked for

Randolph like a homing pigeon when her classes were over on Friday afternoons.

"She has shingles and the UDC at her house every Wednesday, and he doesn't do anything but talk about Martin Luther King," she said in disgust. "And they as much as said they thought Daddy was trashy. I said in North Alabama we called it rich. They'll be as glad as I am when this quarter's over."

I saw less of Fig that quarter than I ever had. Perhaps it was because I was so distracted and overflowing with work and angst. But often days went by before I was aware of seeing her, and when at last I put my head into hers and Ginger's room, she was usually curled up on her bed writing in the diary. She was still as secretive about that as ever, shielding it elaborately from my eyes.

"I've started my novel," she said one evening. "I'm going to make you and Paul famous, like Cathy and Heathcliff. But you can't read it till I'm finished."

"Well, I hope we come to better ends than they did," I said, smiling to hide my annoyance at her fatuousness. "Does Paul know you're immortalizing him?"

"Yes, but he can't see it, either. He's already said he was going to break my neck if I tried to publish it."

And she smirked.

I went back into our room, thinking she would be lucky indeed if he didn't. I was tired and edgy and lonely for Paul, for Cecie. But one was in the lab and the other the library. Presently I crawled into bed and put out the light. It was much later when I finally heard Cecie come in.

She was carrying a double course load that quarter, trying to make up for the classes she had lost when she was sick in the summer, and it was soon clear to me, if not her, that she was not going to be able to sustain the pace. She looked as bad to me by the middle of November as she had when I had finally taken her to the infirmary, thin and white and glittering with fever, and soaked often with sweat that matted and darkened the copper curls. There was a pinched look at the base of her nose, and I knew that her throat hurt her, because she stopped going to meals and began living on soup and colas and tea and things that would slip down easily, and lost even more weight. She would not even talk about going back to the infirmary.

"I've just got four more weeks and I'll be caught up and I can go home and crash over Christmas," she said hoarsely. "Don't touch me or drink after me and you ought to be okay. I scald out the sink after I wash. And don't nag me, Kate; I can't afford to lose any more time. I'm going to start going to bed earlier and sleeping later. That will help."

And she did, and after that, the most I saw of Cecie Hart was the diminished mound of her little body, as still as death under the covers, or the tip of her nose, or the lustreless tangle of her hair. It was like, I told her once, when I found her awake, living with the dead man in Yossarian's tent, in *Catch 22*. She laughed, but it was not her old, full laugh.

I did not go home to Kenmore for Thanksgiving. When I called my mother to say that I'd like to bring a friend home to meet her, she said, fretfully, that Mr. Jessup, the deacon, had asked her to share the holiday with him and his married daughter and her family in Selma, and she didn't like to impose two extra people on them.

She sounded like someone I had never even met, determinedly middle class and deliberately banal, and I knew that she had, in her inimitable way, assumed the coloration of the world in which she found herself. My mother became a Methodist deacon's wife before the deacon ever got around to asking her; just as she had been a Virginia belle long before my father plucked her out of her waitress's uniform to bring her South.

I thought that she could probably survive so on Saturn.

"Well, maybe we'll come the Friday after, then," I said. "I want you to meet Paul. You'll have to, sooner or later. I'm probably going to marry him, mother."

There was a silence.

"Paul who?" she said finally.

"Sibley," I said. "From Miami."

"We never knew anybody from Miami," my mother said suspiciously. "Who are his people?"

I thought of her own provenance, in the blasted little roadside store in rural Mississippi. Anger leaped bright and clean in my chest.

"A Seminole Indian princess and a Negro preacher from the Everglades," I said sweetly. "Boy, when he speaks in tongues, he speaks in *tongues*. He's so full of the Spirit you can't even understand him. Of course, you never know if it's the Holy Spirit or the Great Spirit."

"If you can't speak nicely to me, don't bother to come at all," my mother said righteously.

"I guess I won't, then," I said. "Because I probably can't speak any nicer than that."

And so we did not go, and I found to my surprise that I did not at all regret it.

I suspected that Paul might simply never meet my mother at all; that did not bother me, either. She seemed no part of me; she had not, for a long time. We stayed at his apartment for the long weekend, while his landlady was visiting her son in Texas, and made love and listened to music and worked on our boards and ate the roast duck à l'orange that he made, and drank a great deal of wine. And made more love. And drank more wine.

"Do you care if you don't meet her?" I said once.

"Only if you do," he said. "I can meet her now or later; it isn't going to change anything. I hate to think you've fallen out with your mother over me, though."

"I think I must have separated from her a long time ago, and just not realized it," I said. "Probably when my father died. It was like that line in that Frost poem, 'The Hill Wife': 'Sudden and swift and light as that, . . . the ties gave.' I didn't feel anything when I talked to her and I don't now. I think the main connection for me was always my father, as sad as that was."

"Well, then, that's two of us," he said. "Travel light and travel fast. And far. Right now let's travel over there to that bed."

And we did.

The second week in December I had my thesis hearing, and after waiting an interminable afternoon, head ringing and heart pounding, while Paul left his lab all those precious hours and sat in Harry's with me, went to the McCandless bulletin board where the grades were posted and found that I had made an A.

My thesis adviser, a rangy, immensely talented young designer with the look and manner of an Alabama farm boy, kissed me on the cheek and said if I ever got tired of New York and the big time and Paul, I could come and teach at Randolph.

"Hell, I'll marry you and you can design *my* white house by the Randolph water works," he said.

He hugged me again and shook Paul's hand, and I cried, and Paul went back to his lab, and I went back over to Harry's and sat and drank more coffee and got my bearings. Fall graduation was three days away; until this morning there had been the great, glittering iceberg of the thesis between it and me, but now that was gone, melted into the swirl of Randolph that was vanishing as rapidly as water down a drain, and I was face to face with it. I was suddenly terrified, as frightened as I have ever been in my life, immobile and weak with panic. I sat still in the booth, trying to breathe normally, trying not to look as though I were going to die in a spasm of terror, and gradually the vise loosened. I was limp and wet with sweat and very, very tired. I got up and got into the MG and drove back to the Tri Omega house. I had done nothing; everything remained to be sorted, packed, loaded, stowed away. It would take me the entire three days to arrange my erasure from this room and this house and this campus. Instead, I lay down on my bed and went to sleep. Cecie, as usual, was not there. This time I did not hear her come in.

The night before graduation Ginger sneaked three iced bottles of Mumm's into our room and locked the doors and had a farewell party for me. Driven by the stinging cloud of endings hanging like furies in the air about us, we drank down the first bottle as if it had been cola, and by the time we started on the second the constraint and prickling strangeness of my leaving were gone, and we laughed and sang and riffled through all the memories we had forged in those two dark little rooms and that one dingy bath, and we all cried except Cecie.

"I'll do my crying after you're gone, Kate," she said, swigging champagne. "I don't want you to remember me weeping like a willow.

Toujours gai, by God, is what I say!" And she waved the bottle aloft.

"Toujours gai," we all shouted. Fig burst into howls of wet woe and launched herself at me.

"I can't stand for you to leave, Effie," she sobbed. "I just know I'm never going to see you again!"

"You're going to see me in March, at Nag's Head," I said, disentangling myself from her short, solid arms. "And lots of times after that. Don't make me start crying now, Fig. And don't say goodbye, just get up in the morning and go on home and pretend it's between quarters. You're really going to undo me if you carry on like this."

And so we drank the rest of the champagne and I went back to their room with them and hugged and kissed them, and Fig cried some more, and Ginger sniffled, and I did, and I came back through the bathroom to take a shower. When I went back into our room, Cecie was asleep, covers over her head. I was obscurely glad. I knew that we would have to say goodbye at some point, and I did not want to do it yet.

She was still asleep the next morning when I left the room to go and get my things from McCandless Hall, and when I got back that night, there was a note on my bed that said she had felt so ill that Trish had run her over to the infirmary for some penicillin and that she'd see me at graduation the next day. Fig and Ginger were gone, their room neater than I had ever seen it, and as empty of them as if there had been two deaths. I could not believe I would not see them again for three months. I knew that when I did, everything would have changed for good and all. I had, in effect, said goodbye to them forever last night. A great emptiness settled over me. I packed my bags and signed out for the last time, unable, suddenly, to bear the room where Cecie was not, and drove over to Paul's apartment and stole softly up the stairs. I rapped on his door and presently he let me in.

"I want to be with you," I said. "I don't want to be by myself anymore."

We made love many times that night; it seemed to me that we did not sleep at all. Sometimes I wept, and once I thought that he did. But mostly he was silent; it was hard, urgent, voiceless, scouring love, and all through the last time he kept whispering, until he was almost shouting it aloud into my ear: "Hurry! Hurry! Hurry!"

We finished in an explosion of breath and heat and tears, and when I awoke the next morning, my graduation day . . . a soft one, and gray . . . the tracks of my tears were still damp on my face. He was sitting by the window in the Eames chair, in pants and a tee shirt, drinking coffee and staring out at the thick morning.

" 'This is the way the world ends,' " I said from the bed. " 'Not with a bang, but a whimper.' "

"This is the way it begins," he said, getting up and coming over to kiss me. "Not with a whimper, but a bang."

I do not remember much of my graduation. It was a small one in the ballroom of the Student Union, not nearly so large and festive as the big one, in spring. Most people had left for the Christmas holidays, and the applause for the seniors who rose and went up to receive their diplomas and shake hands with the president and pass their tassels to the other side of their mortarboards was sparse. I graduated with the Magna Cums, but there was little applause for me: my mother had not come, and Ginger and Fig had left early the morning before. I looked for Cecie's red head in the audience, but did not see it. It did not matter; in my heart I was, at last, gone from there. I had done that sometime in the December darkness, before dawn.

Back at the Tri O house, Paul came up

to our room with me to carry my bags down to the MG while I said goodbye to Cecie. We found the bags stacked in the hall and the door closed. Pain seared me, and tears started once more in my eyes. Did she mean, then, simply not to see me again at all?

"Come on," Paul said softly. "Some people just can't say goodbye; I can't. You'll see her in March when we're in Nag's Head. Give both of you a break."

I started to pick up a bag and follow him down the stairs, and then I went back and opened the door, softly, and looked into the room. It was darkened, and Cecie lay asleep as I had seen her so often the past two quarters, very still, head under the covers, back to me. For a sudden, awful moment I thought she was not breathing, and then saw that she was, lightly. I started to go across and wake her, and then I did not. I closed the door and picked up my train case and went down the stairs. Paul was right. Time enough at Nag's Head.

Outside the train station, we sat in the MG not looking at each other. He would keep it while I was in New York; it would save me garaging fees and endless trouble. We had agreed earlier not to try to spend Christmas together; Carl Seaborn had asked me to spend Christmas Day with him and his family out in Bridgehampton, at the end of Long Island, and Ginger's mother had written and asked if Paul would like to come and have Christmas dinner with them at their home in Fowler. He did not think he would go.

"I wish you would," I said. "I hate to think of you here by yourself while I'm scarfing up whatever they scarf up in the Hamptons on Christmas Day."

"Lox and bagels, most likely," he said. "Well, I might. It would be sort of fun to see the birthplace of the famous Fig Newton while I'm at it. Unless you think she sprang full blown from the head of Zeus."

Down the track we could see the Crescent Limited — New Orleans to New York by way of Montgomery and Atlanta and Washington, with stops in between — crawl into view like a weary mastodon. I felt a sob start in my throat, and swallowed hard. Paul closed his eyes.

"Oh, Kate," he said, and pulled me to him. He did not kiss me; he held me against him, hard, and put his hands on my breasts, and ran them up under my sweater and over my shoulders and back, as it to memorize my flesh.

"Go on now, and don't say anything," he whispered against my hair. "Go on and hurry

338

back to Nag's Head. I love you. Call me when you get in."

"Paul . . ."

"Go," he said. His voice was thick and rough. I got out of the car and ran up the steps and into the station where my luggage waited to be put aboard. I handed some money to the porter, blindly, and when I turned back to look, the MG was gone. I could hear it, burring away like a toy auto, its engine muffled in the raw silver fog that was beginning to settle over Randolph. The train was moving out slowly when I found my seat and sank into it. Tears scalded my throat and nose, but we were almost to the Georgia-Alabama state line before I began to cry.

From the minute I set foot on its mica-speckled sidewalks, New York embraced me. The fatigue of the overnight trip, the misery of leaving Paul, the pain of Cecie . . . all of it evaporated into the raw evening air of 43rd Street when I came up out of the pandemonium of Grand Central. My heart gave a great, unexpected swoop of joy. I had expected to be lonely and afraid, at least at first, but I had told myself over and over that I had had, by that time, sufficient practice in bluffing my way into new worlds so that at least the clumsiness and self-consciousness of the newcomer would not show. But from the beginning I was good at being a New Yorker. As my heart had found its home by the sea, so my mind and body found their counterpart in the bruising, smart-ass, exhilarating maw of Manhattan.

It seemed to me that the city did all its tricks for me that first night. Carl Seaborn sent a slim, elegant young man from the firm to meet my train, wearing a bored, polite smile with a bunch of hothouse violets in hand, and he tucked me and my luggage into a waiting limousine. It was a small, hired one, and the driver did not wear a livery, but it was a limousine, nevertheless.

"Good Lord, what an introduction to New York," I smiled at the captive minion.

"Well, I hear your boyfriend is practically a partner before he even gets here," the young man said. "Of course, we're glad to have you, too."

"Of course," I said dryly, and turned my attention to the city flashing by. It was raining that night, a soft, fine, icy rain, and lights wore halos, and hissing tires left iridescent snails' tracks on the streets. Horns blatted and street corner Santas rang bells and crowds jostled on the sidewalks and lights climbed into the skies and vanished into the clouds and the very air seemed charged with particles of diamonds, like the sidewalks.

I said something about the diamond sidewalks to the young man.

"Manhattan is built on mica schist," he said, lighting a cigarette and leaning back against the seat. "It's a pain in the ass to build on."

I fell silent, determined to stay that way, but just then the car flashed past Rockefeller Center at the precise second that the great tree bloomed into light, and I gave a small cry of pure pleasure.

"Don't you dare tell me how much lighting that tree sets New Yorkers back every year," I said to my companion.

He laughed. "Don't worry, I wouldn't even try," he said. "You're a goner. I know that look."

He brought my bags up to the apartment for me, through a dim, tiny lobby and past a dozing doorman, and unlocked the door and saw me in, and made a perfunctory sweep of it before surrendering the key. The apartment was about the size of mine and Cecie's room at the Tri Omega house, with a thin, flaccid bed that pulled out of the wall, a kitchen even smaller than Paul's behind a screen, and a bathroom in which it did not seem possible even for midgets to ablute themselves in any comfort. It had scarred parquet flooring and a growling radiator and a liver-colored, metallic-threaded couch and a formica table and two aluminum dining chairs in front of its lone window and an enormous leather Morris chair, patched with tape a shade darker than the burgundy leather. A long-dead, copper-brown palm tree in a plastic pot sat in a corner. Someone had tossed Christmas tinsel over it.

"I love it," I said. "It's wonderful."

"Better you than me," he said, turning to leave. "First month's rent is free; they should pay you to live here. Welcome and enjoy."

And he was out the steel door and gone to wherever elegant young men went in New York on icy evenings just before Christmas, and I was alone with the city.

I walked to the window and rubbed the steam off it and looked out. I saw an alley with garbage cans far below, and other pale cubes of buildings, and jumbled rooftops, and, in a gap between two of them, far away and luminous, the top of the Empire State Building. Tears came into my eyes again.

"I am in New York," I whispered to the black window. And then, turning to the room, hugging myself, eyes closed and head thrown back, I shouted as loud as I could, "I AM IN NEW YORK!"

"AND I WISH YOU WAS IN CANARSIE," a voice yowled thinly through the wall, and I sat down in the Morris chair and laughed until I was out of breath and my sides hurt. I was still laughing, off and on, when I finished unpacking late that night and heaved the bed out of the wall and crept beneath the lone nylon blanket. At least, I thought, I would not need more covers. No matter how I tugged and banged on it, the radiator continued to pump steam into the apartment like a fire-breathing dragon. When I awoke in the middle of the night, somehow absolutely certain of where I was, I was soaked in sweat.

It was a good job, or at least I knew that it was going to be. I had an anonymous drawing board in an anonymous big room full of bright, serious young men and women bent over similar boards, all in smocks over the chic wine and eggplant and gray clothing that all New Yorkers seemed to wear. The entire office had an air of forward motion, involvement, muted excitement. From the beginning everyone was nice to me, and Carl Seaborn was warm and courtly and downright fatherly. He had a long, pale Medici face and thinning white hair, and might have been

343

formidable, but wasn't. He sent a car and driver for me on Christmas morning to bring me out to the big, gray-shingled house in Bridgehampton, and I fell in love with the serene little green and white towns, all clapboard and drifted snow, that we passed. Wainscott, Southampton, Water Mill . . . they looked like the substantial, insular towns and suburbs I had visited with my friends from the Cape, all those summers ago; I would be all right here. And I was. The drill came back to me, word and gesture and inflection: perfect. In Carl Seaborn's big Colonial, I was surrounded by his picturebook family: smiling, ash-haired, tanned wife, identical daughter home from Wellesley, two well-mannered young sons home from Choate, beaming, white-aproned retainer in the fragrant kitchen, capering sheepdog on the hearth rug in the library where the big, radiant tree stood. We had roast beef and Yorkshire pudding for dinner, and carols played softly on the hi fi set, and we had toasts to the New Year and my new job and Paul's imminent joining of the firm with lovely, silken, dry champagne, and I thought, gratefully, that even if the whole thing was almost ridiculously redolent of an upperclass Norman Rockwell painting, it was still as seductive a scene as my starved heart had ever beheld. I determined then and there that somehow Paul and I would surround ourselves with family at our Christmases by the sea, even if they were someone else's.

"It was like something in an English country house play from the Thirties," I said to Paul the next night, when I phoned. "I kept expecting the vicar and his wife to come by for brandy after dinner."

"Neat trick, considering that they're Jewish," Paul said, and I could hear the smile in his voice across the night miles. "What about the apartment?"

"It's perfect. Of course, it's awfully small, and it has no furniture to speak of, and the bed comes out of the wall," I said. "I thought I was going to be able to pick up a few things for it, but even at second-hand shops things are so expensive up here. And do you know what a junior draftsman makes? We're going to have to be very, very frugal for a long time . . ."

"You won't be a draftsman long," he said. "By the time I get there you'll be a full-fledged designer, and you can get discounts. And I'll hit 'em up for new furniture just before I come."

"Well, you can hardly do that, seeing as how you're not going to be going with them," I said. "They'll probably fire me, as it is, when you don't."

"How will they know I'm not, until the stuff's bought and in?" he said. "And you're too good to fire. All's fair, Katie. All's fair."

"How was your dinner at the Fowlers?" I said. "Did you get roast turkey and Grandma's stuffing and all that? What's the house like?"

"The house is sort of like the Boston Public Library," Paul said. "I kept wanting to check out Proust. Everything in its place and the flowers and plants are artificial. The bed in the room I slept in had red silk hangings, for God's sake. And we had an all brand-name Christmas dinner, served, by God, by a Negro butler."

"Lord," I said. "You'd never know it from Ginger, would you? Was it just you all?"

"No," he said. "Fig was there, too."

"Fig? Why wasn't Fig at her own house for Christmas dinner?" I said.

"I don't know. I didn't want to ask, and she didn't say. I didn't see much of her," he said. "I took her and Ginger to the movies the last night there, but mostly I was with Ginger's father. We went duck hunting up the Warrior, and played some poker. I like him, I think. He's a pirate, of course, but not a bad kind of pirate. And I think he liked me. It's plain he wishes he had a son;

346

he tried hard with Ginger, but it's pretty clear she's afraid of him."

I did not say anything for a moment, and then I said, "How long did you stay? I thought you were just going up for the day . . ."

"Well, I was, but then the heat went off in the apartment, and the Gorgon was in Texas, and so I went for three or four. It was okay. They're pretty loose people, and I was able to give them a little design advice on a pool and pool house they want to put in this summer. It paid my way, I think."

"I miss you so much," I said, suddenly desolate.

"I miss you, too, my dear, lovely Kate," he said. "You just don't know. I guess I'm just going to stay in a cold shower from now until Nag's Head."

"I know. I don't think I can wait," I said. Tears were beginning to thicken in my throat.'

"Work hard," he said. "Work very hard; work night and day so you don't think about it and you won't have time to go out with slick New York guys. The time will pass before you know it, and we'll be there."

It didn't, though. I did work prodigiously, as much to advance myself to the rank of designer so I could afford some things for the apartment as to keep busy, but the time

347

still crept by on sticky small fly's feet. Nag's Head and the big house and the beach seemed stuck in amber, far in the future. I did little else besides work; somehow I kept putting off the trips to the museums and galleries and the theaters, and the concerts and the plays that I had planned. For one thing, they cost a great deal. For another, always, in the back of my mind was, "I'll wait for that until Paul comes. I'll save it until he's here." I walked about the city a great deal, and I read enormously, and I worked. I wrote him every night. I read and reread his letters, that came twice a week; I could not realistically expect him to write as often as I did. I called him as arranged every Wednesday night and every Sunday, after the rates went down. And I waited.

In the first week of February, his Monday letter did not come. When I called that Wednesday night, I said, "Is anything wrong? I missed your letter."

"Oh, Christ," he said. "No, nothing's wrong. I just flat forgot. I'm sorry, Katie. I've been in the lab every second I wasn't asleep; there's a competition from Raytheon with a three thousand dollar prize, and I'm trying for that . . ."

"Oh, good," I said. "What are you doing for it?"

"Actually," he said, "I'm doing the pool and pool house for the Fowlers. The project is for a residential leisure facility."

"Oh," I said. "Well, that's great. Bring some sketches to Nag's Head, will you?"

"Sure will," he said.

"It's only five weeks now," I said.

"Don't I know it," he said.

On Sunday when I called he was not there. It had never happened before. I was worried, and sounded it when I finally got him, at midnight.

"The library," he said. He sounded distracted and tired. "I'm sorry again, sugar. This is really a bad quarter for me. You mustn't worry when you don't get me."

"No, I won't. It's just that we decided on these nights . . ."

"I know. I'll do better," he said.

There was no Monday letter; and he did not answer his telephone on Wednesday or Sunday. The letter the Monday after that was scribbled and brief and noncommittal, and the alarm that I had steadfastly banished to the back of my mind surfaced. He was sick; something had happened with his grades; he had been evicted . . . I called. He was not at home. He was not there the next night, either, or the next.

That night I swallowed my wounded pride

349

and called Cecie, to see if she had heard anything from him. The phone rang and rang, and finally it was Fig who answered it, not Cecie.

"Oh, Effie, it's you," she caroled. "I thought you'd deserted us. I was just telling Cecie the other night that you'd probably gotten so New Yorky that . . ."

"Is she in? Cecie?" I said. I could barely hear myself over the pounding of my heart.

"No, I think she's at the library," Fig said. "Won't I do?"

"Well actually, I was trying to reach Paul, and I thought maybe . . ."

"You mean he hasn't called or written you?" she said. Her voice was intimate and horrified, as if I had confessed I had a venereal disease. "How thoughtless! I'll get on him tomorrow night, I have a tutoring session with him. He's fine, Effie; he's working awfully hard is all. I fuss at him all the time about it. Boy, am I going to read him the riot act about not calling you . . ."

"No, don't," I said numbly. "Just ask him to call when he has a minute."

And I hung up.

He did not call.

I spent two days and nights in dumb, sleepless misery, and then I called Cecie again. Again, I got Fig.

"I'm afraid she's in the infirmary," Fig said solemnly. "She should have been a long time ago. All she ever does is sleep. She doesn't go to classes anymore. I'm sure she's flunking. Did Paul call? He said he would."

"Yes," I said.

I called again two nights later, dulled and sapped with fear and despair. This time, after many rings, it was picked up by Lucy Davenport, who lived two doors down.

"She went home yesterday," Lucy said. "I think somebody was sick, or maybe it was her. Listen, how's New York? We envy you to death; we were all talking about it at dinner last night."

"Fine," I said.

"Maybe we'll all come see you, *en masse*," she giggled. "Do you want to talk to Fig?"

"No," I said.

The next day, when I got in from work, as ill and detached as a person with one of the great, depleting tropical malaises, there was a letter from him in my box. It was a thin one. I did not wait for the elevator, but ran all the way up four flights of stairs, and dashed into the apartment, leaving the door open, and sat down to read it. Everything would be all right now, there would be a perfectly simple explanation, I would laugh at myself and sleep that night, the frail spring would come on in a rush, in two weeks we would be together by the sea at Nag's Head . . .

The letter said that he was marrying Ginger Fowler the day after her spring graduation, at the house on the Outer Banks. They would be moving there; her father was giving them the house for a wedding present, and he had already designed the studio addition. It would begin rising on the dunes in April. He was desperately, terribly, miserably sorry. There was no excuse for any of this. He was a complete rat and he knew it. He had loved me, truly. But he loved Ginger, too, and she him, and quite frankly he needed the kind of money she had, and she knew that, and was willing to take him on those terms, and he thought they could have a good life. I was not to blame her. It had all been his idea. I must forget him forthwith. He knew, with my gifts and a promising career with a great design house, that I would do wonderfully well. Better by far than I might have with him. At least he had been able to give me my start.

"I would have hurt you sooner or later," he said. "It seems to be what I do best. At least it won't be when there's no turning back for either of us."

He signed it, simply, Paul.

Sometime in the middle of the night, when I was struggling to keep on breathing through the white-hot anguish, when I was thinking in terms of living just one more hour, and then just one more minute, ". . . surely I can do that, surely I can get through one more hour, one more minute, and then it will be day . . ." I thought of Cecie. The thought was like cool water, like night, like sleep. I rose and stumbled to the telephone and lifted the receiver to dial, and then I remembered that she was not there; that she had gone home. I could, I knew, get the number of the old house on the Tidewater cove from Information, but I did not. Cecie had not even come to my graduation. She had not even said goodbye. And she had not liked Paul; had almost, at times, seemed to fear him. I knew that I would get sympathy and succor from Cecie; I knew that as certainly as I knew she still lived on the earth. But I knew, too, that under it there would be relief. I did not call.

Sometime later even than that, my eye fell on the dog-eared little chartreuse and rust copy of the Viking Portable Dorothy Parker that I had brought from Randolph. "I'll read it every night before I go to bed, Cece. Like the Bible. And you do, too, and we can laugh together." I picked it up and it opened itself to a page near the beginning of "Enough Rope." There was a red-violet blot on the page; raspberry turnovers, I remembered, one night in the winter, saved from supper. I read:

"Oh, sad are winter nights, and slow;
And sad's a song that's dumb;
And sad it is to lie and know
Another dawn will come."

I took the book to the window and cranked the dingy casement open and flung it out into the night. There was the faintest thinning of the dark in the east, toward the hidden river, and a fresh, small wind smelling of earth and new green, somewhere far out on Long Island, came teasing by, and was gone. I waited until I heard the book land in the alley four flights below.

And then I sat down to wait for morning.

CHAPTER NINE

Alan woke me at seven, as the pink was beginning to go out of the flat sheen at the tide line, and I got out of bed and showered and put on clean slacks and a shirt, and pulled my wild hair up into its French knot. How long had I been wearing it like that? So long that my fingers could and did gather up the heavy mass and form the knot of their own volition. I had not paid a great deal of attention to my appearance in a long time. It seemed somehow to be thumbing my nose at fate to do so.

I was as stiff and sluggish as if I had slept off a hangover, and then I remembered that indeed I had. I grimaced. The few times I have ever waked after drinking too much, it has taken me days to make peace with myself. Control is still too important.

Alan was sitting at the umbrella table on the deck drinking coffee. The cool sea-light picked out the gray threads in his beard and hair, and threw the lines at the corners of his dark eyes into sharp relief. At first he did not see me, and sat slumped on his spine, legs stretched out before him, head resting on his chest as if he were sleeping.

But I knew he was not. Tension was clear in the muscles of his neck and shoulders and arms, although people who did not know him well probably would not have seen it. But I knew. I knew that worry about me lay like sinew just below his skin. Remorse at the sorry little scene in the bedroom, and at my blurted words about the Pacmen's return, flamed through me and I ran across the deck and put my arms around him from behind and kissed the top of his head. His hair was thick and springy, slightly wiry, under my mouth.

"I hate what I did to you this afternoon," I said. "It doesn't do for me to drink, and it doesn't do to go back into all that. I should have known better even than to open that damned letter. Forgive me and feed me, in that order."

"I will, both," he said without turning around to me. "Forgive you now, and feed you forthwith. But I want to talk to you first. Sit down for a minute."

"Uh-oh," I said, going around the table and sitting opposite him. "This sounds like a capital T talk."

"I guess it is," he said. "I hope it won't be, but I guess it is, at that. Kate . . ."

And he fell silent and looked at me. My stomach plummeted as in a runaway elevator, and sweat broke out at my hairline. I knew the look. It was a look that said that something greatly different from the way I was accustomed to things happening was about to be asked. Perhaps even commanded. Alan could, sometimes, command; he did it rarely, but enough of the blood of those iron Minsk patriarchs still ran in his veins so that he did it easily when he thought he had no other recourse. I thought that we were at one of those places now. I damned myself silently; I had gotten us here myself.

"Tell me," I said. "Nothing could be as bad as The Look."

"I called Ginger Sibley while you were asleep and told her you were coming," he said, calmly and reasonably. But the pulse in his throat said that he was not calm.

"No," I said, just as calmly. My own galloping heart showed me the lie of it.

"I'm going down to Bucks County at the end of the month on the Conroy project," he said. "I called them, too. It's set now and I can't back out of it. And I can't leave you alone the way you are. You're not fooling me; I know you've got it in your head the stuff's back. I'll lay off taking you to McCracken now, but in return you're going to have to go to Nag's Head while I'm gone. You just can't ask me to give up my work on top of everything else."

I was very angry with him; this was not fair. He had promised to put off the Bucks County project until the fall, after my last checkup, and now he had gone back on his word. And he had come very close to betraying me by calling Ginger when he knew that I did not want to go. It was blackmail, and his closed, stubborn face told me that he knew it.

"You know what I think of both those things, I suppose," I said coldly.

"I do, and you're right to think it, and I'm sorry I had to do them. But I'm not going to apologize to you. I have a life to lead, too. It can't stop because you've put yours on hold."

"Alan, I don't mind being by myself," I began. "I like it, I'll be perfectly happy here while you . . ."

He rose.

"Then I'm calling McCracken and putting you into the hospital in the morning and getting the tests done now," he said.

"No, don't," I cried softly, and he sat back down. He stared levelly at me. I knew that I could do or say nothing to change his mind. Under his easy sweetness, Alan is as stubborn a man as walks upon the earth. And he seldom doubts the rightness of his decisions, though he comes to them very slowly and carefully.

"What are you doing to me?" I whispered.

"Trying to save your life," he said. "Trying to give it back to you. Trying to save . . . us. I don't think the lovely thing that we are can stand another month of this death in life. We may stay together but the thing that we are won't be here anymore. I can't stand that, Katie. I'd rather leave you. I'd rather you left me. If you don't care about yourself, can't you care enough about me just to go down to Nag's Head and see your oldest friends for a week? Is that so hard? Don't you care about me, Kate?"

I began to cry again, drearily, tiredly, dully. It seemed in that moment that there were more tears in my body than blood or bone or tissue. Just tears and the Pacmen.

"More than anything," I said. "I just don't know if it's enough."

"Well, decide," he said. "And let me know."

He turned and went into the house, and in a minute or so I heard the sound of the Volvo's engine start up, and heard it wind out onto Potato Road and finally vanish down it toward Bridgehampton. I sat on the deck as the dark fell down around me and thought, very clearly, just exactly what would my life be like if Alan were not in it, and never had been?

And the answer was, nothing at all.

I met him at almost the exact instant that Ginger Fowler was marrying Paul Sibley beside the sea at Nag's Head, and we went out and got drunk together, and were seldom apart after that. Years later a friend of ours got a contract to do a book called *Meeting Cute*, and wanted to use ours in it.

"It's got everything," she said. "Sex, romance, revenge, urban interest, and a happy ending."

But I would not allow it. There was nothing cute about that time in my life; when I met Alan I had not yet decided if I would live, and though I did not see it until much later, he was one of the factors that tipped the scales toward life. When he touched his gin and tonic to mine that night and said, "L'chaim," he spoke a greater truth than he could possibly have known. I was far too superstitious to let that meeting be put into a book for the momentary titillation of stockbrokers on the 9:20 from Larchmont.

The unique legacy of the suicide to his children is possibility. Death as an option. Even while the thought of it appalls and angers and devastates, suicide remains one of the things the suicide's child may consider with impunity as an answer, because it has been done successfully by his parent. It is not that he wants to die by his own hand; it is simply that it can never be something of which he can say, "I would never do that." His creator has done it; ergo, so might he. As a possibility it has probably saved as many lives as the actuality has taken. It is only when it is acted upon that it kills. I know that many of the nights after the letter came from Paul I was able, finally, to sleep enough to sustain life because the thought would come stealing into my mind, cool and whole, "I can always die. If it gets too bad, I can always do that."

And knowing it, could go on for one more day.

It is how I got through those first cold spring days: one hour at a time. One twilight at a time. One evening. One midnight. I went to work at dawn and stayed late; I walked home slowly and turned on my second-hand television the instant I entered the apartment. I could not watch dramas, and it was nearly a year before I could listen to my records, but the idiot noise of game shows and comedy half-hours got me through many nights, and books of a certain type got me through the others. I don't remember crying much; I was terribly afraid that if I began the tears would sweep me swiftly into the abyss. I don't remember very much of what I actually did in those early months; that period of time to me now seems like time spent in a long illness, an illness with fever. I have some impressions, and a general sense of desperate and primitive pain that did not end, but over it all there is a kind of still nothingness. Alan calls it my First Ice Age.

I do remember that about the second month, in April, I devised a way to get through the pain. Or rather, I resurrected it. I simply sat down and thought, "How would a woman who was not about to die of pain live in New York?" and I acted like that. It was how I had gotten through long stretches of childhood and adolescence, and it served me remarkably well again, for a time. I don't know why I did not think of it sooner.

A young woman in New York with a job like mine would be happy and energetic and committed, so I smiled and made friends and worked prodigiously and volunteered for more. I went to lunch with this young man or woman or that; I read the *Times* Arts & Leisure section conscientiously every Sunday, so that I would be able to join in the repartee about books and movies and plays. No one asked me on formal dates; it was widely known that I was the property of the paragon who was coming from France, like Lancelot, to be the King's favorite, and that was respected. But I know that I was liked for myself — or for the self I presented — and I was grateful for the easy conversation that wrapped me from morning till night. Often I could not put a name to the face from which it was issuing. But I was still grateful. When the sound stopped, ah, that was when danger lurked. That was when the abyss howled.

"How's Paul?" Carl Seaborn would say frequently, stopping by my board.

"He's fine," I would say, smiling brilliantly.

"Haven't heard from him in ages."

"He's awfully busy. He's got some kind of monster project going."

"And boy, would you be surprised at what it was," I did not say. Maniac laughter leaped inside me. I bit my lips. Destruction by sheer craziness was never far from me in those days.

Despite the success of my Kate-Career-Girl role, I began having panic attacks in early May. I would be walking home up Third Avenue in the sweet, green spring twilight and suddenly terror of such magnitude that my heart nearly stopped and my legs buckled and sagged and I was drenched in an instant with sweat would sweep over me. I would clutch a lightpost or a store window and presently it would ebb, and I would creep home and shower and turn on the TV and lie watching it, limp as a dishcloth. But it would come again in a day or two, or a week, perhaps at work, and once in the middle of the night. It was indescribable, awful, close to unbearable, but I bore it. I told myself that the attacks were fear of being totally alone, and of losing my job when Carl Seaborn found out about Paul; but somehow, on a deeper level, I knew them for what they were, though we would not have a name for them for many years. Abysswalker that I was, I knew that they were the price I paid for success in my daytime persona. I had learned that truth early: suppress pain, abandon reality, and you will pay the price in another anguish. Never think that you won't. I handled this monstrous fear the same way I had every other pain: I acted my way through it like Bernhardt.

I went that spring to see the movie of *To Kill a Mockingbird*. I went right after work, with a girl from my office; I do not remember her name. I am willing to bet, though, that she will never forget mine. Minutes into that ineffably tender, heartbreaking, and evocative little movie I began to cry, and by the time Atticus Finch walked out of the courtroom

364

and the Negroes in the balcony stood silently to salute his passing, I was crying so hard that I had to excuse myself and leave. I mopped my face in the washroom and tried twice to go back into the theater, but it was no good. Gregory Peck's good face on the screen drove me back like the Cross of Jesus would a vampire. Finally I simply went home, without telling my friend I was going, and sat on my sofa and cried for all truths fought for and lost, and all fathers gone, and all strength and goodness never experienced at all. When at last I stopped, I called the girl from work and apologized. She was polite and cool; I did not blame her. I would, I thought, take her to lunch the next day by way of atonement.

Then I called Cecie Hart. This time I did not call the Tri O house but the old house in the Tidewater; I did not dare risk hearing Ginger's voice, or even Fig's. I did not know why I was calling; it had more to do with the movie than with Paul, I thought, but I was simply not clear on that. I knew only that I wanted Cecie.

A very frail, old voice, crazed like an egg-shell, answered and said that Cecie was in Boston, and might she take a message?

"This is her friend Kate Lee, from Randolph," I said. "Her roommate. When will she be back?"

"Lee?" the old voice quavered. "Does Cecilia have your number, Miss Lee? What Lee is that? Are you one of our Lees? We have a great many, you know . . ."

I gave her the number, shouting; I realized that she was quite deaf, and that it was probably useless to try to gain any information about Cecie from her. But Boston? Why Boston, in the middle of a school term?

"Will she be in Boston long?" I tried again.

"Just a little social visit; we have people there, you know," the old lady said. I gave up.

"Please have her call me," I shouted.

"Oh, I will," she said.

But Cecie never did. And I did not call back.

Much later I wrote; she did not answer.

I sat down then and thought about the fear, and the aloneness, and the truth. I saw that I always had been alone, as alone as I felt now that, without Paul's metaphorical and lethal presence behind me, I was in New York. I had just not known that I was. It was all perception; always had been. The truth of the thing changed nothing but the way I felt, but it was enough. The next morning I went into Carl Seaborn's office and told him about Paul and me, and that he would not be coming to work for McKim,

Mead and White.

"I know that you might want to think twice now about keeping me on," I said. "And I wanted you to know I would understand if you did."

He looked at me for a long moment, and then he smiled.

"Did you think that I was going to fire you, Kate?" he said.

"Well," I said, "I know that he was the reason you took me. A favor to him. And I know how valuable he was to you. Would have been . . ."

"What I know mainly is how valuable you are to us," he said. "You have talent and grace and wit and sweetness, and you work harder than any young person I have ever seen. No, I do not want to think twice about having hired you. I am, however, going to move you over into the design department, as a junior associate. I should have done it long before now. We'll do it as soon as I can find the right project for you. Let me look and see what's coming in and I'll be in touch. And Kate . . . I'm sorry about Paul."

"Thank you," I said. This time I did not cry until I had reached the women's room on the executive floor. When I had finished, and repaired my makeup, I went back over

367

into the drafting department, to make peace with my friend from the movie. I thought then that perhaps I would, after all, live. I just did not know yet how.

One of the odd things about intense loss and pain is that it comes close to blinding you physically. For more than three months I did not see faces. I made friends, or acquaintances, rather; went out with them, lunched with them, laughed and talked with them, spent an evening or two with this girl or that. But I found that two minutes after leaving them I could not have described their faces. Paul's was as vivid and close to me as if he stood two feet away; Paul, whom I would never see again, lived with me permanently, burned into my retinas. But the people with whom I was attempting to make a new life eluded me altogether. It did not worry me, particularly, but it was odd, and gave everything I did in those days an air of even greater impermanence and unreality. I was, I thought, as ready as I would ever be to resume some sort of life, but there simply did not seem any imperative to do so. I paddled in circles in the pain, like a duck, but at least by then I had come to the surface of it.

On the Saturday after Randolph's graduation I went to my office at eight A.M. and stayed there until after eight that evening. I knew that if I did not, I would spend the day in a hell of images: Ginger getting out of her bed for the last time as a single girl, breakfasting with her parents at the big table by the sea; Paul walking alone along the tide line, or perhaps driving far down the National Seashore by himself, trying to avoid seeing his bride until the wedding; the bustle of caterers' trucks and bridesmaids and chairs being aligned on the deck over the dunes; armfuls of white wild flowers and beach grasses being set about in baskets; the little liquid skirl of the string quartet spilling out into the fresh salt air. And the guests arriving, and Paul coming out into the sunset with his best man . . . who? . . . from the great house, and finally Ginger, her plain face aflame with love and happiness and the last of the sun, walking to meet him above that eternal old sea. . . .

I worked as steadily as an engine, and as mindlessly, all that day, but the images came anyway. And always, in my mind, it was I who walked to meet him. At eight o'clock, when the twilight that washed Third Avenue was bathing Paul and Ginger in its benediction a scant three hundred miles to the South, I put my pen down and cradled my head in my arms on my board and began to cry. I had meant only to rest a moment, but the tears flooded up and out as though an inexhaustible underground spring had been tapped. I let them come. I was simply too tired to battle them. I had been alone in the great, dim room since mid-afternoon; there was no one to hear me. It did not occur to me to be afraid there, as it might have normally. Bodily harm had been far from my thoughts for months. I had some idea, as I cried, that these tears would be the last; that when the moment of his marriage passed so would some of the pain. I cried and cried and waited for relief, but found only more pain below the first, and more tears.

When a dry voice with the rasp of Brooklyn in it said, "Booze is the answer, but what is the question?" I flung my head up and saw, for the first time since March, clear and whole, a human face. It was sharp and clever and somehow simian, with bright, opaque dark eyes and a long, humorous upper lip and sharply slanted cheekbones. He was smiling through a clipped, short beard, and his teeth were small and white, like a clever carnivore's. He was small and slender and well-muscled, and wore a close-fitting black tee shirt and black jeans and tennis shoes. His face was the peculiar pale olive of the

Eastern urban male: very slightly greenish, probably impervious to suntan and sunburn alike. His hair was black and curled closely. I remember thinking two things, sharply and instantly: he could only be Jewish, and his hair under my fingers would feel rough and springy, like the coat of a well-tended terrier.

The third thing I thought, even before he spoke again, or I did, was that I was alone with him on the floor and perhaps in the building and I did not know who he was. He did not look like anyone who would work for McKim, Mead and White. It was not that they did not have Jewish employees, but that all their employees wore the carefully careless khakis and Oxford-cloth shirts of the Ivy League, and all looked as if they would go to Brooklyn only to catch a plane at LaGuardia or a train for the Hamptons. This man wore sinister black like a foreigner, and talked like a mobster from Flatbush, and moved like a cat burglar. Sudden fear made me angry.

"If you aren't out of here in one second flat I'm calling the police," I said, reaching for the telephone on the windowsill beside my board.

"For what, felonious possession of a T-square?" he said, and grinned again. "Take it easy, lady. I've only come to carry you off to Long Island. I can just as well make it another day . . ."

I stared at him stupidly, aware that my eyes were swollen nearly shut, and my nose ran.

"Aren't you Kate Lee?" he said.

"Yes . . ."

"I'm Alan Abrams. I work for McKim; I'm an architect. I'm doing the beach house you're starting the interiors for next week; I was in the office and saw that you'd signed in, and took a chance that you might be free to run out to Sagaponack with me and look at the site tomorrow. I could have you back in town by four. But this is obviously a bad time for you . . ."

"Am I doing a beach house?" I said numbly.

"Carl told me yesterday he was assigning this one to you. Has he not gotten to you yet?"

"No," I said. "He hasn't. I didn't . . . maybe he's changed his mind. I've never done a design project before, except at school . . ."

"He hasn't changed his mind," Alan Abrams said. "He told me he'd seen interiors you did for a beach house that knocked him out. He said he thought you'd work well with me and for me to see if you'd like to drive out to the site before we did any actual work. He'll probably tell you himself Monday. I was going to call you tonight, but then I saw your name on the board downstairs . . ."

"A beach house . . ." I said again.

"Yeah," he said dryly. "Like a house at the edge of the ocean. Lots of people around here have them. See, there's this ocean . . . shit, I'm sorry. I come across as sarcastic when I don't mean to. Something's upset you; I'll let you alone till Monday, why don't I? We can have some coffee or something and talk then."

He turned to go, padding silently out in the sneakers. He walked like a dancer. I looked after him. At the door he turned and came back.

"Look, I can't leave you up here in the dark crying," he said. "Go wash your face and I'll buy you a drink and some dinner. Like I said, booze is the answer. I won't even ask the question."

"You don't have to buy me dinner," I said in a small voice.

"I don't *have* to do much of anything," he said. "I *want* to buy you dinner. I'm going to be spending a lot of time with you. I want to see what you look like when you're not crying. You will stop crying, won't you?"

"Yes . . ."

"And you would eat some dinner if somebody put it down in front of you, wouldn't you?"

I realized I had not eaten since a slice of cold toast at breakfast.

"Yes," I said. I managed a small smile. It made my lips tremble, but no more tears overflowed my bottom lashes.

"Come on, then," Alan Abrams said. "P. J. Clarke's for drinks and a hamburger, and then we'll go down to the Village Vanguard and listen to Gerry Mulligan. You like jazz?"

"I love jazz," I said. "But I don't look like going anywhere."

"Are you kidding? You look great. A little wet, is all. Like Ondine. Just the thing for a beach house."

When I came out of the ladies' room he was sitting at my board, doodling on tracing paper. He looked up and smiled at me. It was a singularly sweet smile. You could not help but smile back at him.

"Better and better," he said. "Like Grace Kelly playing Ondine. My goose is cooked. I'll probably propose to you by the time we eat dessert. I never could resist cool blond shiksas. It's the bane of my mother's existence."

"She wouldn't approve of me, I gather," I said, following him out into the warm twilight. The lights were just coming on along

Third Avenue; it struck me suddenly as very beautiful. *L'heure bleue,* the French call it. The term might have been invented for New York. It had been a long time since I had noticed it.

"Are you kidding? She'd hire an assassin to dispatch you," he said, holding up a finger for a cab. One cut out of the river of lights and came sliding over to the curb. "She's already hired a matchmaker to fix me up with a nice Orthodox girl. Spent a fortune, she has."

"So has she found you somebody?"

"Nah," he said. "The last one had a mustache."

At P. J. Clarke's we sat on stools at the little bar and ordered gin and tonics. When they came, he lifted his glass and touched it to the rim of mine.

"L'chaim," he said.

"L'chaim, indeed," I said, and took a long swallow. The drink was wonderful, clean and icy. I drank it down and ate my lime, making him wince. He ordered us another, and again I drank deeply, and sighed and put it down on the counter and leaned back on my stool. The edge of the pain was blunted and the wires that had bound my chest for all those months eased a bit.

"You're right," I said. "Booze is the answer.

I wish I'd thought of it sooner."

"Then do I get to ask what the question is?" he said.

"Not yet. But one more of these and you can ask me anything."

My head was spinning and my ears rang slightly, but I was not dizzy. I felt more focused and clear than I had in many days; as if a miasma of some sort, a fog, had lifted from around me. The clarity felt delicious.

"Actually," he said, looking at me obliquely, "I know what the question is. Or at least, I think I know what the matter is. I don't want to start things off between us under false pretenses. Carl told me about your chickenshit boyfriend, the man with the golden arm, as it were."

"He had no right to do that," I said, the gin-induced well being vanishing. "That was a very private thing."

"He had every right, even a responsibility, to tell his architects that Mies Junior wasn't coming on board after all," Alan said mildly. "We've all been living under that sword of Damocles for two years now. A cheer went up you could have heard in Newark. Most of us met him when he came up for his interview with Carl. Captain Tightass, we called him."

"You didn't have a chance to get to know

him," I said in a low voice. And then I stopped. Why was I defending Paul Sibley?

"Chance enough to tell that he'd have screwed Carl and the firm and taken off with as many clients as he could, as soon as he could," he said. "I have an infallible radar for assholes. I know I'm right, too. Carl told me what he was doing instead. Marrying your rich buddy, I mean. He didn't tell anybody else, but he thought I needed to know it, since we were going to be working together. Don't worry, I'm not going to tell anybody else. For one thing, they'd be all over your bones the minute it got out. This gives me a leg up, you should pardon the expression."

"Well, we don't have to talk about it any-more, then, do we?" I said. Far down, I could feel the tears gathering once more.

"Nope," he said. Then he looked more closely into my face.

"The wedding was sometime this weekend, wasn't it?" he said.

"Just about an hour ago," I said, trying for an ironic smile. I didn't do too badly. "About the time you were saying booze was the answer, he was saying I do. That's all, now. I'm not going to talk about it anymore. It's done."

He was silent for a while, sipping his drink,

and then he reached down and took my
hand and held it lightly in his, in my lap.
His hand was small and hard and warm.

"Tough," he said. "Tough."

We drank a great deal that night. I don't
remember how many we had. P. J. Clarke's
gradually filled with the kind of crowd a
summer Saturday night brought out in those
gentle years: well and casually dressed, handsome, young, laughing, laughing. I remember
that mostly, from that warm, long night:
the succession of clean white drinks and the
laughter. I laughed as I had not since I
laughed in the nights with Cecie, and I
laughed at the same kinds of things. Alan
had a sharp, clever, and self-deprecating
tongue; sheer kindness saved it from malice,
and sheer intelligence gave it wit and focus.
He had read the same writers Cecie and I
read, and liked much the same music and
art and drama and architecture and furniture,
and most important of all, disliked the same
things. We talked of them all that night,
and laughed at most of them. I knew by
the time my hamburger came that I was
very drunk, but it was not the kind of slurring, stumbling drunkenness that shames and
incapacitates. Everything sharpened, glowed,
was enhanced. I did not see how he could
have escaped being drunk, too; he had had

even more than I, but he did not seem so. His hand under my arm, as we got into a cab to go down to the village to the Vanguard, was light and steady, and his step was still lithe and quick and sure.

"Are you a dancer?" I said to him, getting out in front of the Vanguard, watching him climb out behind me. "You walk like a dancer. You have a dancer's nice, tight little behind. Whoops. You didn't hear that. I don't say things like that."

"I'm a boxer," he grinned. "Welterweight at NYU. Golden Gloves welterweight in the Army, in France."

"Ah, France," I said. "Very popular with architects, France is. Must be something in the wine."

"That's right," he said. "That's where Carl first got Captain Tightass, isn't it? Well, never mind, he couldn't have gotten his fingerprints on all of it. Enough left for us common folk to enjoy."

Soon after we sat down in the smoke-blued dark of the big, subterranean room, and Mulligan swung into his first skittering, dissonant set, I began to black out, and from that point on, remember only chiaroscuric flashes and snatches of sight and sound. I remember standing on my feet clapping and yelling, with everybody else in the room, as the trio, with Mulligan on baritone sax, romped coolly and fluently through his classic "Walking Shoes." I remember a bit later, standing on the sidewalk outside the Vanguard, holding hands with Alan and singing, loudly, "On the Street Where You Live." Even later we were in a car, humming along a dark, deserted, seemingly endless highway, the light from the dashboard radio glowing green and throwing his slightly Oriental face into Mongol relief, and I was quoting Dorothy Parker to him. I have the impression that he quoted a lot of it with me; at any rate, he told me later that I must have parroted, fairly accurately, almost everything she ever wrote.

"I'd like to meet this Cecie of yours, that you keep talking about," he said at the time. "From what you said about her, I fully expect holy miracle rays to shoot out of her ears."

But I did not remember, that night, speaking of Cecie at all. There was a long, dark space in which I remembered nothing more at all, and then a very clear and somehow delicate memory of waking up on an empty beach at dawn, the sand cold under my legs and feet, the sea silver-pink and perfectly flat and still. I lay on my side, curled up fetally on a beach towel, and a man's tweed jacket was spread over me. The first thing I saw was the flat silver sea, and then a flock of small, stilted seabirds skimming the creaming shallows, and then, beside me, Alan Abrams, sitting with his arms around his knees, looking straight out to sea. I heard the soft, sibilant husshhhh of the tiny surf, and the rattle, in it, of shells and pebbles, and the cry of gulls, and far away, on the horizon, the muffled chug of a fishing boat heading out. I heard Alan's soft, even breathing. I felt the wet cool of dawn sea air and tasted salt on my parched lips and felt the pounding in my sinuses that signals, as soon as sensation hits fully, the hammer of hangover. I struggled to sit up, tangled in tweed. I did not know where I was, on what beach. But I never for a moment did not know who Alan was.

He turned to me and smiled. Incredibly, he looked as fresh and clear-eyed as when I had first seen him, the night before.

"But soft, what light from yonder window breaks?" he said. "It is the East, and Juliet is the sun."

"Where are we?" I said. "What time is it?"

"We're on the beach at Sagaponack," he said. "It's five fifty A.M. Before you say another word, let me assure you that the whole thing has been as excruciatingly proper as dancing school. You insisted on coming out to see the sun rise and looking at our site, and you went to sleep the minute we hit the beach, and that's where we've been ever since. Except to cover you with my coat, I have not laid a finger on you. I have, however, had three hours worth of improper and unclean thoughts, watching you sleep."

"If I don't get a cup of coffee and some aspirin, and go to the bathroom, I'm going to die," I said. "And I think, in a minute, when I remember everything, I'm going to wish I would die. I sang, didn't I?"

"You did," he said. "Well and loudly. Thousands cheered."

"Oh, God," I said.

We found an all-night diner on the Sunrise Highway outside Bridgehampton and I washed my face and scrubbed my teeth and we got paper cups of coffee and carried them in the car back to the beach. I remembered the town from Christmas at the Seaborns', but it had been closed and silent with snow then. Now it was green and fresh and vibrant with full summer, and the flat black and green potato fields and gray barns and small, still ponds and straight little roads that led toward the beach charmed me, reminding me as they did of the country outside Nag's Head. When we came out to Sagaponack and turned onto Potato Road, and I saw the high, ragged, grass-crowned line of the dunes

382

against the pale sky, my heart contracted painfully. So like the Outer Banks, it was, so like. . . .

We parked the car beside the road and walked through the shifting sand and the thickets of sea oats, beach grass, primrose, sea spurge and beach pea to the top of the dune line. I drew in my breath. Below the high dunes beach grass and sea oats ran thick and wild down the steep slopes to the tawny sand, and beyond it the flat beach disappeared into a sheet of vivid pink fire. The sun, at that precise moment, broke over the sea, and set the earth aflame with dawn. I closed my eyes against it, and felt tears start behind the lids. In its wild aloneness and its great and timeless peace, it was Nag's Head all over again. Its beauty pierced me like an arrow.

Beside me, Alan said, "Do you know that poem of Eliot's? 'I have heard the mermaids singing, each to each. I do not think that they will sing to me.' Prufrock, I think it is. This reminds me of that."

I turned and looked at him. Who was this man?

"I know it," I said. "I hate it."

We were silent for a bit, sipping our coffee, and then I said, "Why did you bring me out here? Really?"

"Because I wanted to see how you felt

about the ocean," he said seriously. "This beach house is very important to me. Any house by the ocean is. I love the sea better than just about anything on earth, and I don't think I could work on a seaside project with someone who didn't."

"And what do you think about me?" I said.

"I think you do, too," he said. "You can't fake much of anything when you first wake up with a hangover. I saw your eyes light up."

We walked down the beach a way, the cool water lapping at our ankles. The sand was like that of the Outer Banks, too; almost too soft to walk in, so that you had to walk at the tide line. He pointed to a tall white silolike shape in the distance.

"Our site is next to that abomination," he said. "Of all the unspoiled coast along here, the Friedmans had to buy right next to the Maginot Line there. Maybe they felt it was appropriate; they fight all the time. He gets mad and flies the private plane home to Sneden's Landing, or she gets mad and calls the pilot to come get her and fly her home. At this rate we'll never get the house done, but at least they're pretty good about letting me do what I want to. They'll probably let you have free rein, too. We ought to break ground this week."

We walked on in silence, comfortably, companionably. I thought only once of Paul and Ginger, waking up in a tumbled white bed that faced that other beach, on this same sea, and shoved it far down inside me. As well to begin now to bury them.

"Want to buy me some breakfast?" I said.

"In a minute. I want to show you something first," he said.

Down the beach the shoreline curved back into a small bay, and as we reached the curve and came around it, I saw that the tallest dunes of all crowned the beach here, soaring to a height that dwarfed the others around them. Sea oats waved gently against the deepening blue of the morning sky to the east, and behind them a thicket of wax myrtle, bayberry, yaupon, cottonbush, catbrier and beach plum stood dense and green and untouched. It was a beautiful spot, wild and secret and somehow entirely magical. White lines of surf crisscrossed diagonally in the little bay; apparently the tides here were unwilling captives, fighting the enclosure. I thought that in high winds the entire ocean would funnel into this little half-moon, white and furious and glorious.

"How perfectly beautiful," I said. "How . . . enchanted."

"It's mine," he said, smiling. "I saw it this spring when I first came out to look at the Friedman site, and I mortgaged my soul and bought it the same week. I have two acres. I'm going to put a house here, right along the dune line, with a studio wing that crowns that tallest dune and looks straight out to Madagascar. It will take me about a million years, but I'm going to do it. It's already designed."

I turned away abruptly, and started back down the beach. Water flew under my feet. My heart was triphammering. Whoever or whatever this man was, I wanted no more of this uncanny duplication. Paul Sibley redux would have no place in my life. I would go to Carl Seaborn; I would ask off the project. . . .

He caught up with me and turned me around.

"What's the matter?" he said. "What is it?"

"Paul Sibley wanted the same thing," I said tightly. "You know, Captain Tightass. He's building it now, in fact, on the dunes at Nag's Head. Those interiors Mr. Seaborn told you about, that I did . . . they were for that house. You knew that, didn't you? Didn't you know that?"

He stared at me, shaking his head silently,

no, no, and then he began to laugh.

"Oh, Christ," he said. "Why is it us Jews always get there one step behind the god-damned Golden Goyim?"

I stood still in the climbing sun for a long moment, and then I began to laugh, too. I laughed until I could not stand any longer; I laughed until my sides hurt and I clutched them and sank down onto the sand.

"He ain't your typical Golden Goy," I choked. "He's half Seminole Indian!"

Alan Abrams gave a great hoot of joyous laughter and sank down on the sand beside me, and we laughed and laughed in the new morning, until we were finally able to climb to our feet and make our way back across the dunes to the car. When we rolled out of Bridgehampton toward Manhattan, we were still laughing.

"Okay, Kate Lee," he said, when he let me out at my building. "It's time to go to work."

CHAPTER TEN

It is how my life came back to me that summer, work and laughter. From the first day the Friedman house went so well that I forgot any qualms I had had about being at McKim on sufferance. Ideas and intuitions, colors and textures and details and solutions came bubbling up as they were needed, so effortlessly that I began to get superstitious about it.

"It can't possibly be this good always," I said over and over to Alan as we worked. We worked side by side in his office; he had asked that my board be moved there for the duration of the beach house project, and Carl Seaborn had agreed.

"You're right. It almost never is," he said. "This project makes me nervous, it's going so well. The Friedmans haven't even had a fight since we broke ground. You and I haven't had a fight. Well, not a major one. Carl hasn't yelled. We haven't had a rain delay. The subs are actually fully developed life forms. Let's don't even talk about how well it's going until it's over."

And so we didn't. And the beach house on the dunes at Sagaponack continued to grow under his hands and mine, and I don't think I will ever love another design project as much as that, my first.

I can see now that much of the joy and success of the Friedman house came from the nature of Alan's talent, and how he felt about it. He was enormously talented, perhaps not so much as Paul Sibley, and in a very different way, but greatly gifted, anyhow. It was not a dark, consuming, flaming thing, like Paul's; Alan was always more of the earth than the air. He was easy, methodical, patient, often even plodding in his attention to detail . . . but he lived his projects in a kind of sunlight of pure delight. Sometimes, when something he had done pleased him, he would whoop his pleasure and glee, and people would come running out of surrounding offices to see what he had done. Alan's designs were a kind of communal thing; like the man himself, they enfolded you, wrapped you in safety and warmth, connected you unalterably to the earth. To live in a house of Alan Abrams's would be to feel always the pulse of the earth and the breath of the sea and the cool shelter of the sky, to rest like a ship on the currents of the very air around you. To live in one of Paul's would be to live with a laboring heart and shuddering breath; to live outside one's very skin, stretched to the outer edge of being. You could not rest in a Sibley house; but you could always rest in one of Alan's, and with Alan himself. It was just where I should have been that summer.

We worked from early morning often until late at night. We talked, argued, fought, laughed, yelled, laughed some more. We ate lunch at our desks or at the coffee shop around the corner, and we spent at least one or two days each week at the site, sweating and peeling with sunburn, hair wet beneath our hard hats, driving the crew nearly mad and driving the Friedmans, whose habit it had been to hang around the construction and second-guess the crew, back to Manhattan for the duration. Alan accomplished this by simply telling them one day in July that if they didn't lay off he would see to it their house never saw the pages of *Architectural Digest*. The Friedmans flew home in their little airplane from MacArthur Field that very afternoon, together for once. I upbraided him for it.

"That's blackmail," I said. "How can you possibly affect what goes into the *Digest* one way or another? You're not much more senior than I am."

"It's already in, if we can get it done by December," he said. "Carl told me last week.

Most of his houses are. The Friedmans know that. It's one reason they came to us. We're probably saving their marriage."

As the house grew, we began to forget which of us had done what to it; it was simply, to us and to the firm, Kate and Alan's house. Carl held us up in a design meeting once as a perfect example of the cooperation between architect and interior designer. We took a great deal of teasing after that, but it was true, and the firm began to pair us on other projects. If I had made the choice myself, I could not have picked a swifter, higher-arcing star than Alan Abrams to whom to hitch my wagon.

I suppose it was inevitable that we would carry the relationship over into the other parts of our lives. I for one had few other parts, and so I was perfectly content to let his presence shape all of life for me. It never occurred to me that he had a life independent of me that summer. He must have; he had family I did not know, and friends, but he seemed to have put them on hold. For those months, that season, we might have been Siamese twins. With the emphasis on twins. Never once in all that time did Alan do more than take my hand, and casually at that. Never once did I do more than throw my arms around him in a transport of discovery and delight.

For that was the summer that he truly gave me New York. That was the summer that I really did, with him, all the things I had been saving to do with Paul. Because I was coming out of pain and all things seem new then, and because Alan's presence beside me gave everything we did the patina of laughter as well as the rich warmth of safety and surety, New York bloomed for me that summer as it never will again. Sometime during those months I put away, in my heart, everything to do with the treacherous South and all I knew of its softmouthed, dreaming, murderous men. I knew that I would not go home again, and I did not. Not until many, many years later.

I can scarcely remember what we actually did: I remember a blur of work and music and food and drink and endless walking, and late nights in odd, smoky places, or exotic-smelling bright ones. We ended up in these spots, usually, to eat and drink coffee and listen to music; after that first night we drank very little. We did not need to.

He showed me all the things he said I needed to see . . . the Statue of Liberty, the top of the Empire State Building, the Public Library, Carnegie Hall, Central Park, the Zoo, the Botanical Gardens in Brooklyn, the Aquarium, the Metropolitan and the Modern and the astounding new Guggenheim; we saw plays and art movies and exhibits and circuses and once or twice the Yankees, at Yankee Stadium up in the Bronx. Alan was an avid sports fan. He took me to boxing matches at the Garden, and the races at Belmont, and to tennis matches at Forest Hills, and once, when we were out at Bridgehampton, we rented a Flying Dutchman and went sailing. He was good, quick, and deft.

"Where did you learn to sail? Not NYU," I said, when we came in at sunset that day.

"No. In France, actually," he said. "Where did you? You're not bad yourself."

"On Cape Cod," I said. "And I've hated it since the first day I set foot in a Beetle Cat."

He laughed. "Me, too. Makes me sick and upsets my precious equilibrium for days. I only brought you because you look like you ought to sail, like Grace Kelly in that movie. You know, where she sings."

"Well, then, let's don't do it again," I said gratefully. "Life's too short."

And we didn't. There was enough of New York to fill many more summers than that one. We went up to the Cloisters and spent an entire Sunday; my passion for medieval herb gardens was born that day. We spent many weekend afternoons at the Museum of Natural History, and at the Metropolitan. We saw Shakespeare in the Park, and heard the symphony there; we prowled through Chinatown and hit every ethnic street festival we could find; we ate at least one meal from every cuisine the city offered, or tried to. In all that time, in all those places we went, at all those hours, among all those peoples, I never remember being afraid. New York was a different city then. And I was with Alan.

He undertook to teach me to cook that summer. He had a small apartment in a stained brownstone on East 18th Street, near Gramercy Park, and we produced, from its scurrilous little kitchenette, a succession of sloppy, highly seasoned, wonderful suppers in the late evenings after we'd finished at our boards. Alan's cooking was, like his apartment, the antithesis of Paul's; profound disorder prevailed, and nothing cost much. But both had the complex, slapdash charm of the man himself. Books tumbled and sprawled everywhere, like the bright pushcart vegetables he brought home, and photographs and posters of designs he particularly admired lined the walls and lay scattered on tables and the floor. There was little glass and steel and concrete; Alan loved wood and stone, and the evidence of that love was everywhere. In the center of the living room, on an improvised stand, stood a scale model of the Friedman house. There was little room for anything else. We ate sitting on cushions on the floor; the sofa was given over to teetering piles of drawings and blueprints.

"Where do you sleep?" I said.

"Under there." He gestured at the piled sofa. I giggled.

"Well, I guess there's no doubt you're celibate," I said. "There's not an inch to ravish a maiden in in here."

"It's hard, but not impossible," he said. "There's always standing up in the shower, or then there's . . ."

"Okay, okay," I said hastily. For some reason I was blushing fiercely. I thought of that small, beautiful body, glistening with water, entwined with a woman's in the fragrant steam . . .

"What are we making tonight?" I said.

"Sauerbraten, with gingersnaps," he said.

"Why don't you eat at home more often?" I asked curiously. Alan's father had a kosher delicatessen with his uncle on Fulton Street in Brooklyn, and his mother cooked for it often. She was, he said, a truly wonderful cook.

"Are you kidding? I'd weigh five hundred pounds. My mother force-feeds you her chopped liver like you would a Strassburg goose. Grabs you by the neck and rams it right down you. And then she's usually got Daddy and Uncle Daniel and Aunt Rose and my older brother Eli, the good one, old Eli the rabbi in Astoria, you know . . .''

"Alan, do you not get on with your family too well?" I asked. "You haven't been home more than twice this summer that I know of. Is it me? Do they dislike it that you're working so closely with a . . . a goy?"

"They're not crazy about it, but it isn't that," he said slowly. "It's that they can be so censorious of someone that they haven't even met. It's that whole Jewish thing, that dark old weight of it . . . all the thou-shalt-nots, and the taboos, and the refusal to let any new light in at all . . . the old ways, always the old ways . . ."

"Doesn't any of that matter to you?"

"I'm not sure about that yet, Kate," he said soberly. "The religious part of it doesn't, much. Maybe it will later. I have this funny feeling that the other part . . . the cultural, the heritage thing . . . will come to mean a lot to me. But it's going to have to come in my own time, and fit into my life. You know, there's room in a good life for chopped liver and gray shingle architecture, too. And for loyalty to a family that might include an outsider, children with blue eyes and names like Sally and Michael, a wife with blonde hair and a nose like a Gainsborough painting. There's just too much world to be satisfied with a tiny snip of it."

"I'd hate to think I'm causing any kind of wedge between you and your family," I said.

"Nah," he said. "The wedge got driven in by my first blonde shiksa, when I was about seventeen. The rest is just a matter of degree."

"Well," I said, somehow stung. "Just so it's not me."

"No," he said. "Mostly it's me."

I did not meet any of his friends per se that summer, but I met several people who, one way or another, had ties to Alan Abrams. I met the old man next door, who came at night to get the plate of supper Alan cooked for him when he was at home. The old man was very shy, and did not speak to me; he took his plate and nodded his thanks and scuttled out. When we left the apartment to go back to mine, the clean plate would be set neatly at Alan's door, with a paper napkin over it, and a peppermint on the napkin.

"His daughter is supposed to bring his meals, but she doesn't do his supper," Alan said briefly. "I found him going through the garbage cans once. What's one plate of sauerbraten, when I've made a whole batch?"

I met the black mailman who came by one evening full of smiles, with a sealed envelope and a photograph of a skinny, beaming young black man in satin trunks, posing with gloved fists upraised.

"I helped his boy get a Golden Gloves scholarship to NYU," Alan said. "Which didn't take a whole lot of doing, since the kid is the best natural boxer I ever saw. And I lent him a little to get him started. He's paying me back on time."

I met the rheumy-eyed, half-crazed old woman from upstairs who brought her sad, malodorous old poodle, who looked amazingly like her mistress, down to Alan's apartment to be walked on weekends, and once to be kept for a week while the old woman visited her house-proud daughter on Long Island.

"Won't let me bring Suzette," the woman whined to me, trailing Marlboro ashes down the front of her negligee and onto Alan's floor. "Says she smells up the place. I tell her Suzette smells as good as her house does, all that fish she cooks, but she still won't have her. But this angel boy, this sweetie pie, he takes good care of my precious. Precious loves him, don't you, Precious?"

Precious sighed and lay down in the corner beside the sofa to wait for her dinner. When the old woman had gone, Alan opened a can of roast beef and she bolted it down so quickly that her scrofulous stomach bulged. She was instantly and deeply asleep. A profound and pervasive odor emanated from her corner.

"Now she'll fart for seven days, on top of everything else," Alan sighed. "But I don't think she gets a square meal until she comes to me. When I walk her on weekends we go by the White Castle and both have burgers."

"You're a terrible softy," I said fondly. "You let people impose on you awfully."

"Nah," he said. "I like this old bitch. The furry one, that is. And she likes me. You should see her when I come in after a day at the office. You'd think I'd been gone for a month. 'Oh, God, you came back, you came back, oh God, I'm the happiest dog in the borough. Oh, God, let me fart for you!'"

I collapsed into laughter. He was essence of dog; he was the best dog I ever saw. His gift for mimicry was fey and dead on the money. The old dog thumped her tail in her sleep.

"I know just how she feels," I said, still

laughing. "Safe as a baby, cherished as a lover. You have a wonderful gift for nurturing, Alan Abrams. You take great care of me. How can I show my appreciation?"

"I don't know," he said, looking at me with his bright eyes. "Fart for me, maybe?"

"Hug you," I said, and I did, a hard, long hug. He patted me on the back and pulled gently away.

"Why won't you kiss me?" I teased. Or was I teasing?

"You're not kosher."

"That's not it. Either I'm just not sexy or you're not interested in women."

I did not know why I could not leave it alone.

Alan looked at me for a time, and then he grinned widely. He reached over and picked up my hand and put it on the crotch of his blue jeans. A hard mound strained at the fabric. I jerked my hand away as if it had been bitten. Heat flooded my face and neck.

"Does that feel disinterested?" he said.

Things changed for me after that. We still did the things we had done together: worked, cooked, prowled the city, listened to music, ate, drank, laughed, talked. But I did them, then, with the thought of that warm hardness never far under the light-dappled surface between us. I do not know how he felt. He did not touch me again.

I had told Alan early on about my life in Kenmore, and my mother and father, and about Cecie and Fig and Ginger and Paul. After I did, perhaps sensing that I was done with that part of my life, he never alluded to it. As for me, I cut my ties with care and finality. I canceled the subscription to the Randolph monthly alumni newspaper that came automatically with my diploma. I threw away the appeals for money that came from the development office, and, unopened, the three or four notes from Ginger that came from Nag's Head. When a Tri Omega passing through found my number in the directory and phoned me, I put her off and had my number unlisted. I canceled my subscription to the Tri Omega Alumni magazine. I did not read out-of-town newspapers; indeed, all that long summer, I read few newspapers at all. When my mother phoned in late August and said that she was marrying the deacon in a little ceremony in the Baptist church and would like me to come home for it, I said that I would provided I could bring a friend. My mother said, "Is it that Indian?"

"No," I said. "It's a Jew named Abrams."

"You're obviously doing this just to spite me," my mother said coldly.

"Impossible as it may seem, I never even thought of you," I said, and hung up. I did not go to her wedding; I sent flowers. I knew that I would not go home again to Kenmore, Alabama.

In November, *Architectural Digest* ran a spread of Paul Sibley's studio addition to the house in Nag's Head. Color photos showed it soaring out heartbreakingly over those old dunes, with the blue sea beyond it, and one of them showed Paul inside it, bending over a drawing, with Ginger, in skirt and sweater and pumps, admiring it from the other side of the board. A fire roared in a great gray stone fireplace, and furniture the colors of the sea and sky and ocean storms sat about in the soaring whiteness. I knew that furniture as well as I did the people in the photograph. I looked up at Alan, who had brought the magazine to show me. We were in his office. Outside, in the twilight, the first snow of the season was falling silently onto Third Avenue.

"Uh huh," he said, smiling grimly. "I noticed. You even got a byline."

I looked closely; in tiny type, at the bottom of the page, a line read, *Interiors by K. S. Lee.*

"That son of a bitch," I whispered, tears of fury starting in my eyes. "He took my interiors and built them for her."

"I rather think he built them for himself," Alan said mildly. "He'd never have gotten ones as good anywhere else. It's a perfect room, Kate. It doesn't matter who lives in it. Enjoy the byline and forget it. You'll do better ones for a place of your own, some day."

And to my great surprise, I could and did forget it. Both the photographs of the studio exterior and the one of him with Ginger in the room that was to have been ours. Or at least, I almost forgot. Perhaps they haunted me a bit in those soft, new winter days, but distantly. Like very old ghosts.

Just before Christmas the Friedman house was finished, and the Friedmans gave a little champagne party for the firm and a few friends in it. Outside snow blew like white fog around the dunes, and the surf roared on the beach below, but inside firelight and tree light and candlelight and the clear, vibrant, medieval jewel tones I had chosen lit the big, carved room to radiance. It was a lovely party, with a lot of laughter and music and toasts, and even more champagne. The Friedmans were having one of their good nights, and *Architectural Digest* had indeed been out to photograph just days before, and already four requests had come in from acquaintances and passersby who had seen the house from the beach or from Potato Road, inquiring as to whether the team who had done it was available for consultation.

In the white and gray and sea-green living room, Carl Seaborn raised a champagne glass to Alan and me. We stood in front of the fire simply looking around at the beautiful room we had created, grinning like, as Ginger used to say, 'possums in the middle of a cow plop.' We had both had quite a lot of champagne; I could feel it burning in my cheeks, like flags. Alan's eyes were as bright with it as a squirrel's.

"To the very formidable young team of Abrams and Lee," Carl said, "who give new meaning to the old expression, 'the whole is greater than the sum of its parts.' Long may you be on our team. Long may you *be* a team, as far as that goes."

Everybody clapped and shouted, and Alan reached over and kissed me. It was not a friendly kiss, or a brotherly one. I was so surprised that I simply stared at him.

"We will be a team as long as Kate will let us," he said. "Like maybe, as long as we both shall live. How about it, Kate Stuart Lee?"

"I'd love to," I said.

When Stephen died, someone gave me a copy

of Juliana of Norwich's *Book of Hours,* intending, no doubt, that I should find comfort in the words of that terrible old abbess. It was a long time before I could read that or anything, but when I did, I opened it to the passage that goes, "All shall be well, and all shall be well, and all shall be exceedingly well." I threw the book into the fireplace in a cold, trembling rage, and was about to set fire to it when Alan rescued it and read the passage. He cried then, terrible, tearing sobs that went on and on and on, rising sometimes into a kind of wail I had never heard before. It frightened me badly; I had cried, torrents, rivers, seas of hopeless, anguished tears. But he had not, until then.

We talked about it later, after the awful crying had stopped, and he was calm again, limp and somehow clean and light.

"I hated her for saying that," I said, by way of explaining why I had attempted to burn the book. " 'All shall be exceedingly well.' It's horrible. Nothing shall be well. It's the worst thing that ever happened. How can anything be well again?"

"It's not the worst thing that ever happened, Katie," he said. "It's just the worst thing that ever happened to you. To us. And now, nothing this bad can ever happen to us again. I think that's what she meant.

She wasn't stupid; she lived a godawful life. And my dear love, for a very long time all was most exceedingly well with us. And may be again, who knows?"

I was angry with him for days. I did not want optimism. It was a long time before I saw that it was not that; it was the only way Alan could stay alive in those unspeakable days. But from the moment he spoke the words, I knew in my savage heart that he had been right when he said that indeed, for us, all had been, until then, exceedingly well.

From the beginning we were a fortress against the world. A unit. As Kahlil Gibran said, we two were a multitude. Our world was, from the very first, the small one of our work and the people who shared it with us. For neither of our families would.

My mother slammed the telephone down when I called to tell her that Alan and I were being married; I could picture her, in her mercilessly new brick ranch house in Kenmore, saying to the deacon, "It was a wrong number." I am sure she was afraid that he would leave her if it got about that her daughter was marrying a New York Jew. And Alan's mother wailed and shrieked for weeks; his father came around in the end, and his brother the rabbi, but his mother was inconsolable and unshakable in her conviction that I would bring nothing but ruin to her son. After Stephen was born she allowed herself to be cajoled and lulled, and we saw a good bit of her, but when he died she felt herself vindicated, and closed her door and heart to us for good. Or rather, to me. In her eyes I had kidnapped her son and murdered her grandson. There would be no sufferance for me. Alan saw her rarely and grimly, and so far as I know, her absence from his life was not the profound sorrow it might have been. The two of us together were always enough, sufficient. Sometimes, in the early years of my marriage, it seemed simply miraculous to me that I had found this port, come home to this. I did and do love Alan Abrams with an enduring sweetness and complexity that I did not know myself capable of. And I know that he does me.

I don't know when, in that first year after the civil ceremony in Carl Seaborn's living room in Bridgehampton, I realized that I was in love with my husband. I knew, when I married him, that I loved him, and that he was the best and most constant friend I might hope to have in the world, now that Cecie was lost to me. And I knew that nobody else could ever understand me as he did, or make me laugh as he did, or comfort me and anchor me to the earth as he did. And I knew by then that I adored going to bed with him; that slight, fluid, hard-muscled body sated my emptiness while it fanned my greed for him like a desert wind. But I was not aware, for a long while, that those things were enough to add up to being "in love," for "in love" was what I had been with Paul Sibley, and that drowning, consuming, helpless thing was light-years away from the lighthearted, sweet-fitting, lockstep rightness I felt with Alan. And then one night, when he was away on a project and I was alone in the apartment, puttering restlessly and feeling as empty and wrong as a shoe for an amputated foot, it struck me that I was deeply in love with him and very likely to stay that way forever. A tide of elation washed over me, followed by a dark surge of fear. If I had been religious, I would have been on my knees praying, "Dear God, please don't let me lose this." I think on some level I was, anyway.

When he called later that night, I said, "Do you know that I love you so much that my toes curl up and I can't get my breath?"

And he laughed, and said, "It's about time."

Early in the second year of our marriage Alan bought two lovely old weathered-silver potato barns and had them moved to the top of the dune line on his lot on Potato Road. All that summer we built decking around them, and a breezeway to connect them, and started work on a crow's nest sleeping loft atop one of them. I began my garden that summer, and though it was another year before we were able to move out to the gray house beside the sea that has been our home for all these years, it became the central reality of our life to us. In those first years we shared it with our friends, bringing food out from Manhattan on weekends on the train or in Alan's battered Toyota, and later cooking our sprawling dinners in the small kitchen we built off one end of the larger barn. I know I speak truthfully when I say that no one who ever sat on our deck amid my rioting flowers and watched the surf on the wild beach below failed to feel the spell of the house and the sea. Even Alan's mother, who spent only one night under our roof in all the years of our marriage because, as she said, the sound of the ocean upset her, said also that she approved of the house.

"You've fixed things up real nice, Kate," she said. "If you like this kind of thing, that is."

"Thank you, Golda," I said, managing not

to grin at Alan, who rolled his eyes behind his mother's back and pantomimed stabbing her.

"You're welcome, I'm sure," she said.

"If your mother likes it, it must be some kind of house," I said to him that night. "What makes it so special, do you think? There are grander houses all over the Hamptons."

"It's a happy house," he said seriously. "It was built by people who love each other and it, and it had a good, productive life on this old ocean before it became a house. Everything about it works hard and has a purpose, and works in harmony like a good team. I think you feel that in houses."

"Is that what is known as artistic integrity?" I said, grinning.

"Holy shit, I hope not," Alan said.

That fall Carl opened a branch of the office in Bridgehampton, to handle the burgeoning spate of residential beach work. The Hamptons were starting their great odyssey toward mediocrity and overdevelopment, and the firm was swamped with requests for beach properties. Carl, who loved the wildness of the area, nevertheless saw the potential, and turned the office over to Alan and me.

"If it's going to be done anyway, it ought to be done well," he said, "and I can see

410

the handwriting on the wall. If I don't put you two out there I'm going to lose you to those potato barns of yours. I will anyway, sooner or later, but maybe this way it will be later."

And so we moved into the house on Potato Road, and there took up the life that would sustain and nourish us for all of our years, and there conceived our son Stephen, on a night of wild, moaning November wind . . . I know that, because a Nor'easter blew for most of November, and for a good part of it we were without power . . . and there, the following summer, Stephen Daniel Abrams was born. And then we added the big studio wing over the dunes that Alan had planned long ago, and there wasn't anything else in the world I could even conceive of wanting. The three of us, then, were a multitude.

After Stephen's first birthday party, as we sat on the darkening deck watching the citronella torches gutter in the sea wind, Stephen asleep in Alan's arms, I said, "Five years ago I was getting ready to get married and live in a house on the beach with a brilliant architect, and here I am. Only it's a different beach and a different architect, and now there's Stephen. Everything I ever wanted, and then some . . . and nothing I thought

I would have. It's eerie, how things worked out. It makes me superstitious. It makes me afraid to wish for anything else; my wishes come true, and I must have used all of them up."

"What else would you wish for?" Alan said.

"Nothing," I said. "Except to be able to keep what I have. To keep on keeping on."

And for a long time, we did that. Three years later we left McKim, Mead and started our own design firm, and after that we worked out of the house as well as lived in it. We did well, if I do say so myself; at that time, in that place, you would have had to be very bad indeed not to make an ample living designing beach houses and furnishings. We worked prodigiously, and I hired a housekeeper/babysitter for Stephen, and we made friends with some of the permanent residents of the Hamptons . . . writers, fishermen, nurserymen, artists, a lawyer or two, an overworked GP, the owners of small shops and businesses that sustained the villages during the long winter seasons. We did not know many of the new summer people. I did not mind. Many of them had too much money and too little else; the Hamptons were different places when they were in residence. We built and designed some of their beach houses . . . the best, I think; the ones that today look the least like silos for missiles . . . and we were asked to their parties. I might have gone, dutifully, if Alan had wanted to, but he did not.

"Why should I like them kneedeep in the ocean when I don't like them in Manhattan?" he said. "If we get into that routine we'll have to get new clothes and a new car and start giving parties out here, and then old Stephen will be seduced by one of their snippy, airheaded daughters and marry her, and there we'll be."

I laughed. It was no loss to me. I did not want Stephen to move in that world. I wanted him to live in the one we made for him, Alan and me, in the house by the sea.

He did that, too. For another three years he did just that, my dark little boy, and then, in August of his fifth year, he drowned in the swimming pool of our friends the Montags, in full view of their three children and their babysitter, who thought he was playing at snorkeling with the oldest Montag child's mask and fins. We were at a cocktail party over in Sag Harbor, one of the very few of the summer cocktail parties we had ever been to in all those years. When the call came for Alan, and he came out onto the terrace to me, his face somehow shrunken and mangled in the twilight, I was drinking a gin and tonic and talking to a woman named Haralson about Richard Nixon. She was a nice woman, I remember; we both hated and feared Nixon, and had found in each other a haven in that fervently Republican gathering. After that night I could never remember her name or face, though I ran into her many times in the village shops, and once at the dentist's, and she came to see me the next week with a lovely pot of dusty miller and white philodendrons. I soon came to hate the sight of her, quite literally, and to avoid her. I'm sure she always wondered why. I cannot say, except that in some irrational and arcane way, she was a lightning rod for the monstrous red pain of that moment.

It is useless for me to talk of the year after Stephen died. I do not have the words; no one does. I know that two things got me through the first days: the presence of Alan, who never left my side even in his own crushing grief, and the thought that when the pain got too bad I could end it as my father had. As I have said, the suicide's legacy is not an unmixed curse. It helped save my life that fall and winter. So did my husband. I know that many marriages do not survive the anguish and guilt and outrage of a child's death, but it never occurred to

Alan or me that ours might not. We clung together like survivors in a life raft. I remember something he said to me late in that first night, after they had taken Stephen's little blue body away to the funeral home and I had fought my way up out of the sedative our GP friend had given me.

When I got to the surface, Alan's was the face that I saw, and as memory swept over me like a cold, black salt sea, he held me fast and said, "One thing we will not do is blame ourselves. Of course it wouldn't have happened if we hadn't gone to that terrible fucking party, but I want you to remember this, Kate: neither of us wanted Stephen to die. Either one of us would have died to prevent it. So we can cry, and we can mourn, and we can stand it or not, but we are not going to blame ourselves or each other. And we are going to get through this one minute at a time, and one hour, and one day. Just like that. Together."

And from that moment on, I knew that we would get through it, and just how we would . . . because he had given me the blueprint for it. Alan always knew exactly what I needed in order to live. When he could, he gave it to me.

After that our horizons shrank. Or mine did. I was not comfortable out in the world.

I seemed to have lost all sense of context. I had been Stephen's mother for five years; now that he was gone, my arms, indeed, my very core, felt hugely empty and flaccid and useless. But I could not go back to being just Kate, wife of Alan, designer; it was too late for that, after I had been that other perfect thing. I did not know what I was. The world where I had moved with my son was not only unreal, it frightened me. I often thought, later, that if there had not been that vast, exposed emptiness inside me, the Pacmen never could have gotten a toothhold. It was a stupid fancy, of course; the real truth was that the death that came into my emptiness was more the death of connectedness: I wanted little from the world where Stephen had died, and very gradually I built my secret, walled garden and drew away from it.

"I should have stopped it," Alan said to me much later. "I should have seen where it was leading. I should have just plain made you stay in the world; I should have gotten Carl to ask you back to the firm, or gone back myself, and taken you with me. But we made such a good thing of it; I loved what we built out of that awful time. It was good, Kate, wasn't it?"

It was. After a string of blind, featureless

white days where moving and breathing through the pain were, had to be, my only concern, I emerged into a too-bright, too-large, too-vivid world where it seemed that a little work might be possible, and Alan and I threw ourselves into that. Once in, the old, rhythmic sorcery of form and color and texture and space claimed me, and I let it take me down and under. I worked as I never have before, getting up in the pink sea-dawns, working over my board until far into the night. Alan, in the big studio wing, was working just as hard, just as single-mindedly. He urged me to set up my board there, to use part of the vast, beautiful, light-washed space as my own, but somehow I could not. I needed, at that time, enclosure, small spaces, minute and manageable slices of the world. I set up in the bay window overlooking the deck and the garden. By that time it was almost completely walled away; shielded by house, fences, windbreaks, dunes. There I made a new world for myself, one I could orchestrate and control. There I have stayed.

The firm flourished. We began to win awards, modest ones at first, and then one or two really lustrous ones; I have never ceased being amazed by that. Our work has appeared not infrequently in national design magazines, and once an international one. People with cameras and tape recorders began to come to the house on the dunes; after the first time or two, when I found myself sick and sweating from the intrusion, Alan and I worked out an arrangement. He would handle the interviews and the photographs, and he would do it away from the house. The thought of my face, even my name, on a page for the world to examine, perhaps to remember, terrified me with the same superstitious terror an aborigine must feel facing a camera: the primal and awful fear that your soul will be stolen away.

"Don't you want any credit?" Alan would say. "At least half of it's yours."

"Please," I said. "Oh, please. Don't ask me to do that. We don't need that."

And we didn't. We had all the work we could handle. Our arrangement included other divisions of duties: Alan did the outside contact work, and we designed on the board together, and he oversaw construction, and I stayed in my bay window and did specs and expediting and ordering and the overseeing of models and fabrics and details. When he was away, as he frequently was, I stayed behind and read and listened to music and walked on the beach and gardened. Mostly, I suppose, I gardened. Somehow I only felt completely safe with my fingers plunged directly into the rich earth I had brought to nourish my flowers and vegetables and herbs; I was, then, about as connected to life and living as I would ever be. Only a few very close friends saw the garden by then. I saw little else.

We talked of having other children, but somehow we did not do much about that. We didn't try not to have them; we just never went the route of tests and temperature-takings and calendars and all the rest of it. I've often wondered since if we did begin children, and the Pacmen ate them. They say that most cancers grow for years before they are found. But it is a thought I have not shared with Alan.

"I will not have you anthropomorphize that goddamned thing," he said once. "It's tough enough to fight reality. I'm not going to let you stack the deck against yourself."

He was really very angry, and so, even though I habitually thought in terms of Pacmen and gobbling mouths, I rarely shared them with Alan. As he said, reality was burden enough for him.

Not in those good days after we built the firm, though. Once I asked him if he missed children, the fact of them, too terribly badly.

"No," he said. "I miss Stephen terribly,

awfully, and I always will, but it's the particular little person I miss, Stephen himself, not the idea of a child per se. I don't think I've ever really wanted anything but this, this firm and this house and you, from the minute I met you."

"Really?" I said. We were lying in each other's arms in a flood of white moonlight, on the big double chaise with the faded duck pad, on the deck. It was a September moon, but the air and water were still as soft as summer on our naked flesh. Sweat was drying slowly on our bodies.

"Really," he said. "I still wake up and pinch myself to see if it's all real. Sometimes it scares me, though; sometimes I think . . . I don't know . . . there should be something more in our lives. Other people. Especially for you. This oneness stuff is almost dangerous. It's like it's too perfect, and the gods will take it away from us. I feel sometimes like we ought to share it, just on principle. Just to propitiate . . . them."

"With who?" I said. "Who would you want to share this with?"

"That's just the point," he said. "Nobody."

"Well, don't worry," I said, and nibbled his shoulder at the small hollow place where it joined his neck. "The gods are not going to get you."

* * *

And they didn't. They got me. In my forty-second summer, I had a miscarriage, not even realizing I had been pregnant, and the resulting D&C turned up ovarian cancer. It is a terrible and insidious and secret cancer, and almost always does irreparable damage before it is found; my gynecologist told me that my never-to-be-born baby probably saved my life.

"Or to look at it another way, the cancer murdered him," I said.

"Maybe. I wouldn't have put it that way," he said. "It's more that diseased tissue can't sustain life. You don't want to go putting a face on this thing, and giving it a name."

Which is precisely, and almost at that moment, what I did. The Pacmen were born on that day, and their murderous, cheerful, gobbling images have been by far the hardest things to kill.

For they think they have killed the cancer. Ovarian is a dread and savage cancer because it shows no flags, causes no early symptoms to speak of. Even the later ones are vague and easily misunderstood and misdiagnosed; by then, usually, the cancer will kill you. Mine, though, was caught very early, in what they think of as the second stage . . . involvement in both ovaries, but no discernible metastasis . . . and they went after it aggressively, with a diagnostic laparotomy and a following hysterectomy, and enough chemotherapy to render me bald as an egg, weak and thin and nauseated most of the time, riddled from mouth to genitals with sores and a virulent kind of acne that sometimes seemed the worst of all. All to stop, so far as they can tell, the march of the Pacmen.

I have two doctors, John McCracken, my old, good friend on Madison Avenue, who saw me through my pregnancy and delivered Stephen, and Carter Hilliard, the flamboyant, handsome, immensely gifted medical oncologist who saw me through most of my cancer and delivered me of the Pacmen, and both went after the cancer with surgery and a pantheon of drugs, terrible, pragmatic-sounding things like Leukeran and Neosar and Adriamycin and Adrucil and Folex, that left me in infinitely worse physical shape than before I had had the miscarriage. After more than a year of chemo, there was another exploratory operation to "see where we stand," and two years later still another, and after that I went home to my secret garden and ripped out my perennials and planted annuals and waited to see if I would live or die. Now, in late October, I will have the last, the five-year one, the biggie. By now Alan and Carter and John are euphoric with shared certainty. And I have a blank white wall where November should be, and in that quiet whiteness, if I listen, I fancy that I hear the Pacmen gobbling.

This is not a story about cancer, and even if it was, other women with greater gifts of tongue than I have told about the terror, and the lethargy, and the moments of wild, cheeky elation and the subsequent dizzying plunges into despair, and the fury and depression and denial. I had them all, beginning with the moment in John's office on Madison when he told me, and the air seemed to brighten as if a small, silent, invisible nuclear blast had gone off, and the hanging plants seemed to tremble in the radiant air, and I stared at him for a long moment and then vomited into his wastebasket. But from the beginning I knew three things . . . I knew that the abyss lay under all, and always had; I knew how to find an abyss-denying world and live my way into it; I knew that I could always and literally die as my father had if I found that I could not live. No, make that five things: I knew also that in my house and garden by the sea, under the sun, there is pure timelessness, and I knew that Alan would never, for one moment of one hour of one day, leave my side.

I have had it easier than most cancer victims

because of those five things, and the greatest of them has always been the timelessness. With that I could and can live. Without it, I simply do not think so.

I wish that I had died before Alan asked me to choose between that and him.

When the dew began to fall the little night wind off the sea was suddenly too cold, and I got up and went into the house and lit the birch logs in the fireplace. I made coffee and took the big road atlas down from the bookshelf and spread it out on my board and looked at it, sipping coffee. There it was: Nag's Head. Lying far to my south in all that great, windy blue. And on its bright tan outer dunes a great black house with, now, a seaward wing like a gull in flight rising from it, and in that house three girls frozen like Keats' brides of quiet, waiting for me to come and finish, with them, a book that had lain open and unread for more than twenty-five years.

I studied the map. I could take 95 to below Philadelphia, 13 on to Norfolk, and then over to 158 and finally 12, to Nag's Head. It should take me no more than a day of steady driving. I would take the sports car. It should be a lovely drive; much of the last part of it bordered the sea, or was close to it. There were many bridges. One, the Chesapeake Bay bridge-tunnel, just before Norfolk, was immense. There would be wind, and blue space, and high sun, and under it, like a great tundra, the restless glitter of that other sea. . . .

I saw, suddenly, what I could do. I could go, and I could spend my time in the sun with them, with Ginger and Fig and with Cecie . . . Cecie . . . as much time as I needed, or as little. And then I could get into my little red Alfa Romeo and start home again, home early, so that Alan would not yet be there waiting for me. I would go in the early morning, while it was still pearled and gray outside on the beach, and when I came to that great bridge across the air, I would need only to turn the wheel once, sharply. . . .

I thought that at some point, in midair, I would not be able to tell which was sky and which was sea, and that it might well be like rising up to meet the young sun.

Outside, on the gravel, I heard the crunch of Alan's tires, and I went out to meet him on the front deck and tell him that I had decided, after all, to go to Nag's Head.

CHAPTER ELEVEN

Once I left the Interstate at the Delaware state line a subtle change took place in the air and light, or perhaps I simply imagined it: I was in the South. Imaginary or not, the tenor of the journey eased and slowed, and the light thickened, and I stretched my legs and arms and took a deep breath. I smiled to myself. I had not been South in almost thirty years, but the pace of it still called out to my blood. It might have bothered me once; today, nothing did.

Highway 13 through Delaware down to Norfolk is studded like a cowboy's belt with small towns, farms, fields, and forests. There was something near-magical about them all in that golden September morning, some rare and wonderful thing to see. Perhaps it was nothing more than the light on a weather vane, or a roadside stand utterly scarlet with the first fall apples, or a sign on a sagging rural grocery that said STOP. GAS. SEE BIG SNAKE. But there was no hour's passing that did not give me a gift to enchant the senses. By the time I left Pennsylvania I was singing along with the radio.

Just after noon, almost precisely between

Laurel and Pepper, in Delaware, I saw a vacant field that seemed, at first glance, to be full of marching elephants. I slowed and stared; there were, indeed, in deep green-gold grass, a line of great gray shiplike elephants swaying trunk to tail across the field, and another line of them tethered, fortresslike, off to the side. Then I saw the trucks and the puddled billow of big, dirty tents, and the bustle of workmen in the distance, and saw that the elephants were being led by a man who walked at the head of the leader with a long pole.

I laughed aloud in pure delight.

"Oh, Lordy," I said to the sweet, rushing air. "Circus has come to town. Everybody stop everything and go!"

A great surge of joy swept me, so fierce and pure that my head snapped back and my eyes closed for a moment, and wheeling dots of light swam behind my lids. I remembered the feeling from when I was a very small child; I would sometimes be so overwhelmed with it that I would dance about and hug myself. I had not felt it since then. I thought of something Cecie said once, at school, watching a cat out on the quadrangle lawn suddenly jack-knife from a demure crouch into a wild, stiff-legged leap, spin around twice, and shoot sidewise across the grass before subsiding into a sunny doze once more.

"That cat," she said, "is having an attack of delicious. It's what Aunt Martha always called it. Don't you know just exactly how that feels?"

"I am having an attack of delicious," I said to the elephants, and drove on down the sunny road laughing loudly. Anyone meeting me on the road would think I was drunk, or mad.

And I was very nearly both. I was quite literally drunk on sun and sky and rushing air and the music pouring out of the Blaupunkt, and strangeness and freedom. The top on the little red Alfa Romeo Spider was down, and the sky overhead was steel-blue with oncoming autumn, and the sun was as thick and sweet as poured cane syrup. My hair blew wild around my head and stung into my mouth and nose, and I could feel the top planes of my cheeks beginning to burn slightly with the sun. Under everything there sang a kind of secret glee, a delectable and hidden madness. And of course it was just that; anyone who has planned their death and set a date for it *is* mad, though perhaps not in the commonly accepted sense of the word. Or, at the very least, has left human context behind.

But it was precisely that death . . . or, rather, the idea of that vivid moment of free-floating, and the thought of exultant oblivion in bright air and water . . . that gave the day its wild sweetness. Death blued the sky to crystal and lit the sun to poignant gold; it stopped time like the sea did, and promised that winter did not have to come, or age, or pain. Or, in the odd way, death itself. I smiled again; I was dying so that I would not have to die. That *was* crazy, no doubt about it. No matter. The sense of control was as heady as wine. I was, with this death, finally in charge of the world.

"Death is the mother of beauty," I said aloud. Who said that? Where had I read it? I had a swift sense of a winter classroom, with cottony gray outside tall, dirty windows, and a radiator hissing, and wet wool steaming. Randolph, almost certainly. I would ask Cecie. Cecie would know. It was the kind of quote we had loved; if I had heard it I would have quoted it to her, and she would remember. I did not doubt that she would.

"Half in love with easeful death," I said then. That was Keats, I was almost sure of it. We had been just that, Cecie and I, in those untouched and unknowing days. And now I was again . . .

In mid-afternoon I stopped for a traffic

light in a small town in Virginia. Onacock, I think it was, halfway down the long peninsula between Chesapeake Bay and the Atlantic. The sense of great waters on both sides of me was heavy, though they were out of sight, and the vast bridge and tunnel looming up ahead was like a spot of deep, cold shade on the sunny road. I had been driving since five A.M., and my arms and neck and buttocks were tired. I rolled my head on my neck, back and forth, and saw, in the pickup truck ahead of me, a young woman reach up and touch the face of the man driving. He covered her hand with his, and then put his face down to hers and kissed her. She snuggled into his right arm, and he drove away with her head on his shoulder and his cheek bent to rest on her hair. I felt a single deep trembling pang, as if someone had touched a violin chord within me. How could I be leaving, have left for all time, Alan?

But I knew the answer to that. Far better to let him be anguished and angry at me than torn to death, along with me, by the Pacmen. Oh, far better, and a better love . . . besides, I lived in timelessness now. There was no longer any such thing as for all time, or forever. There was only this instant, this hour, this day. I would, I thought, write

430

him a long letter on the night before I left Nag's Head. He would understand then. I had not said goodbye this morning; we had lain close together all last night, drifting in and out of sleep, and I had gotten up at four and simply put my packed bags in the Alfa and driven away. As I had left the dark bedroom he lifted his head and said thickly, "You going already?"

"Shhhh," I said. "Go back to sleep. If you try to say goodbye to me I won't be able to go at all, and then you'll be mad at me. I'll call you when I get there."

"See you in a week," he said, from the depths of the down pillow. "I'll be here when you get back. Be careful. Love you."

"I love you too," I said, and swallowed a startled sob, and was away from there as the dawn broke. Going around the deck to the front of the house I felt a track of wetness drying on my face. I flung my arm out toward the sea in a backward salute and ran the rest of the way to the Alfa. Until I cleared the Hamptons and was bowling down the tunnel-like banality of the Sunrise Highway, I resolutely thought of nothing at all.

After that it was easy. I had not brought Alan Abrams on this trip. I had not even brought Kate Abrams; in a sense, she had already died. It was Kate Lee driving this

431

car along this September road. Kate Lee, going back at last to find the truth of the four girls who had left each other all those years ago.

I thought, somewhere in those bright, spinning hours, that the truth of us might turn out to be just what we had thought it was then. No more and no less. That would, in an odd way, be immensely reassuring, as if somewhere, somehow, those girls still lived, whole and vivid. But I already knew that it would not. I knew that the instant I called Ginger Fowler Sibley a week before, to tell her I was coming.

Her voice was exactly the same. It was as if she stood in the next room from me, all those years ago. I felt the breath go out of me in a little sigh, and the smallest smile tugged at my mouth. She was Ginger only and fully, no doubt about that. I have read that the voice is the last thing to change with age.

"Oh, my God, Kate," she burbled. "Oh, I can't believe it! Oh, you sound so . . . *good!* And you're coming; your nice husband said you'll come . . ."

"Well, I'm thinking about it," I heard myself saying. Somehow I could not make myself say the words, "Yes. I will come."

"Oh, Kate, please," Ginger said. "I want

to see the others, of course I do, but it's you I've missed most. We'd lost you so completely; nobody had any idea where you were for all those years, until the directory came out, not even Cecie . . . Kate, listen, I've hated it all these years, that we were estranged. I've known how badly I behaved, and how it must have hurt you . . . I've wanted so badly to try and make things right with you. Paul . . ." she hesitated. "Paul won't be here. He'll be at the Norfolk house. It'll just be the four of us. But if you don't want to, I'll understand . . ."

My heart gave a fishlike flop. Remembered love flooded me. I realized that it had been more than a quarter of a century since I had minded about Paul Sibley, but that good, single-hearted Ginger had been suffering because of it all those years. Suffering at my imagined suffering.

"Of course I'm coming," I said. "I've missed you all, too. Oh, I have! Lord, though, Ginger, where on earth did you find Fig?"

There was another pause. Then Ginger said, "Kate, don't you know who Fig is?"

"Who she is?" I said. "No . . ."

"Kate . . . Fig is Georgina Stuart. You know, all those books with the half-naked women on the jackets? All those television talk shows? All that shit in *People* and *Enter-*

433

I could not speak. I literally could not. Fig? Georgina Stuart? Whose string of lurid bestsellers and affairs and public outrages were the stuff of tabloid headlines and national morning and late night shows, whose platinum-streaked mane and half-naked breasts had been in as many magazine pages as the rapturous harlots on the covers of her paperbacks? And whose husbands had been nearly as numerous? Even I, buried in flowers by the sea these many years, knew who Georgina Stuart was. You would have to have lived your life on Uranus not to know.

"Stuart?" I said numbly. I heard my voice squeak.

"Stuart with a U," Ginger laughed. "You know how she felt about you. I always thought she wanted to be you, and I guess she did, at that. I don't wonder she borrowed your name; she borrowed everything else. Don't you remember? She even looks sort of like you, Kate, or like you used to. You wouldn't know her now. Literally. God knows how much weight she's lost, and how much plastic surgery she's had."

"Dear God, old Fig Newton is Georgina Stuart," I said, beginning to laugh. "I wouldn't miss this for anything in the world. I'm going to have to read one of those awful books before I get there. And she'd really bother with the likes of us now?"

"It was her idea," Ginger said happily. "She called one day early this month out of the blue and said she was coming down this way on a book tour, and wouldn't it be fun if we could meet at my house on the beach, like we did that time back at school. You remember. She even offered to pay for it, but of course, I said no to that. And Kate, she absolutely insisted that you come. She said it was a condition. She wanted me to write you because she said she knew she used to drive you crazy and she didn't want to spook you off. She even offered to send a private plane for you. I said I'd bet the farm you wouldn't come in a private plane, but I'd ask, so consider yourself asked. I know she really did bug you awfully at school, but she seems so different now, really nice, even if she is famous all over the world. Don't let what you remember of her keep you from coming. She's bound to have changed . . ."

"No, I don't care about that now," I said. "I'm dying of curiosity." And cancer, I thought but did not say, and giggled. "No plane, though. I'll drive down. I've already looked at the map: I think I can do it in a day. Listen, Ginger . . . what about Cecie?"

"Cecie's coming, if she can get her mother-in-law into a respite program of some kind the government has. She's wheelchair-bound now. There's not anybody else to stay with her."

"Mother-in-law . . ." I said stupidly.

"Have you heard from Cecie at all?" Ginger said. "I've kept up with her a little, but she hasn't mentioned you . . ."

"No," I said softly. "Not at all."

"She's had an awful time, Kate," Ginger said. "She married an Italian policeman in Boston; she was there visiting some relative or other right after you left school, and met him then, and fell for him like a ton of bricks. Vinnie Fiori. Vicente Fiori. I met him once, early on, when we were up there for a convention, a big, blackeyed, good-looking guy with more charm than you ever saw, and just idolized Cecie . . . anyway, they had two little boys, and then when the kids were still small, he got shot in a bank robbery and paralyzed from the waist down, and she stopped work to take care of him, and did that, almost completely, for twenty years, and the old lady for ten, so far. I don't even know when she moved in with them. Vinnie died about two years ago, and the kids left as soon as they could get out of there, and she's been looking after that old harridan ever since, in that miserable little house in Quincy. She never went back to the Tidewater. I don't think she's had one vacation since Vinnie was shot. God knows what she's lived on. They've never had anything. It's been just terrible. I thought maybe you knew."

"Oh, Cecie," I breathed silently. "No, I didn't know," I said.

"Well, she said she'd walk every step of the way if you were going to be here, and I said I'd see that you were," Ginger said. "You know she doesn't drive; she's still scared to death of cars. So Fig's sending the stupid-ass plane for her, and Fig and I are driving in Fig's new Rolls to pick her up at the Currituck airport. I was afraid maybe she wouldn't want to come . . . you know Fig and I are awfully comfortable, and somehow I figured you probably were, too, and she . . . but she said herself she couldn't wait to rub elbows with some success, for a change. And she wasn't being sarcastic. In all this time, in all the times I've called her, or gotten a letter from her, I've never heard her sound in the least bit sorry for herself . . ."

Grief for Cecie flooded me. Cecie, who like me, had once seen the world as Halliburton did, *The Royal Road to Romance*. Cecie, who

437

was to have traveled the world like a migratory swallow and come to rest in a house by the great river, whose light would dance on her ceiling and whose water would sing under her dock. Unworldly little flamehaired Cecie, who lived on wings, all these years a drudge, making life go on for her wounded family, away from the water . . .

I won't think about that, I thought to myself. Not yet.

"I'll be glad to see her," I said. "You too, Gingerrooney. Fig too. Most especially Fig."

"Then hurry on," Ginger Fowler Sibley said, with joy and love in her gruff voice. "Eight more days to Nag's Head!"

"I'm on my way," I said.

I came to the Chesapeake Bridge at mid-afternoon, when traffic was light, so that I could slow down and look about me and get the feel of that great arch into space. Halfway up it, when I could no longer see the land behind me or the glittering water below me, but only the endless vault of the sky, it struck me suddenly that this was it, this was what had waited for me all my life, this was the abyss. Low to the road, with the top down and only warm, high air around me, I could feel it with all my senses; there was nothing, now, between me and it. I slowed almost to stopping and listened: there it was. From far below me came the very voice of the abyss, the breath of it: the formless wind that sang up from far below, seeming to say many things, among them my name. Kate. Kate. Sweat broke out at my hairline and dried in the wind, but my mouth smiled. I had been wrong, then, all those years; it was the abyss that waited for me. Not the Pacmen. Not gobbling mouths, but space, clean and blue and receiving. It would be all right. I could do this.

Not in the car, though; I could see that. The guard rails were too dense and high. The Alfa would never break through. All right, then, just me. I would leave the car and go out into that blueness alone. With nothing wrapping me, not even the fragile red skin of the little car. Just me; just my own skin, clean and still taut and unadorned. I would hold out my arms like a lover, laugh, sing . . . I shook my head and drove on. The spell of space and glittering water was strong; it would have been easy on this transcendent afternoon. Well, it would be easier still in a week. No strings, then, no loose, flying remnants of Kate Lee to catch on the sun, snag on the edges of the world. The last weight flew off my heart and I drove on into Virginia, singing.

The last hundred miles did not go so fast. I left the highway and threaded my way over toward the coast on small blacktop roads, choked with resort traffic. At Barco I picked up 158, that would take me on into Nag's Head, and there got my first glimpse of ocean water: Currituck Sound, off to my left, just beginning to go silver-pink with the westering sun. Parallel to it, further left, was, I knew, the wild, tawny necklace of the Outer Banks themselves. My heart began to beat faster. The palms of my hands were wet on the wheel. Thirty years, almost thirty years, it had been . . .

I crossed the Wright Memorial Bridge at Point Harbor and I was there. I was on the Banks. The great, heaving, dark blue ocean that I remembered stood off my left; I could see it, fleetingly, between tight-packed, stilted beach houses and shops and hotels and restaurants. But I could not get the sense of it. This was not the coast road I remembered. This was not the country of that long-ago idyll. This was a place of condominiums, RVs, antennas, neon, souvenir shacks, motels, shrimp and pizza takeouts. Even in the twilight of a September midweek, the coast road was thronged with traffic, blaring horns and farting exhaust fumes. This might be anywhere too many people come to the sea:

Ocean City, Daytona, Myrtle Beach. Disappointment was so sharp in my heart that I could taste it, like the thin, sour reflux of vomitus.

I passed the great hulks of Jockeys Ridge on my right. On the highest ridge, antlike people lined up black against the setting sun. Great, prehistoric shapes like pterodactyls flew black against the orange sky, and I realized that the people of the Banks still sailed their kites, but such kites as I had never seen or imagined. I ground through Kill Devil Hills behind an RV from Portland that said on its bumper, "Hell, Yes, I Do Own the Whole Damned Road." I passed the fishing pier, clotted with people, and went through Nag's Head, as bad as Kill Devil Hills. The air was thick and warm now, the fresh, streaming salt cut off by beetling condos and highrise motels, and I violated one of my own strictest rules and switched on the car's air conditioner, even while the top was down. It did little good. I hesitated, and then smiled grimly. Why not? What did it matter now? I turned the air on full blast.

Past the Coast Guard Station I turned left onto the narrow sand road that led over to the dune line, bumping between dreadful new raw wood condos and chalets on stilts, and saw, ahead of me, the half-remembered, viscerally known, haglike line of the Unpainted Aristocracy black against the evening sky. My heart soared out of my stomach, where it had fallen, and rode up singing like a lark. Familiarity, *déjà vu,* snatches of pure memory and sensation and images, wisps of long-dead sounds and smells and tastes, all crashed down over me like a tidal wave.

"Yeah," I whispered aloud. "Oh, yeah."

At the end of the line of great cottages stood Ginger's. Ginger and Paul's, I amended, looking up at the sweet swoop of gray shingle that rode the tallest dune straight out to sea. Sunset light dazzled off its windows, and inside, warm yellow light glowed. Otherwise Ginger's house was just as I remembered it. Unlike most of the colossi of one's youth, it had not diminished one iota. It still stopped the breath and heart with its grace and substance and wild old beauty. Tears stung in my nose, but they were not tears of loss. I whipped the Alfa into the sandy, burred little backyard and got out.

For a moment I simply stood there, drinking it in, feeling that peculiar peace and stillness that I remembered stealing over me. I could not see the ocean, but as always before, I could hear it, booming hollowly on the sand below the dunes. The rightness

442

of the place and the moment moved me; even Paul's studio wing, even the big Land Rover and the beach tractor underneath the first floor, that I knew must be his, did not intrude. I remembered that it was here, in this place, that I had first been given that great gift from the sea: timelessness. The thought bloomed in my mind, whole and finished: this place could heal you.

"Almost, anyway," I thought to myself, and started up the sandy path to the back deck.

From the open windows of the studio I heard laughter. General female laughter, at first, and then, magically, wonderfully, a laugh unlike any other in the world. A silvery spiral, that wound up and up and up, hung on the very border of affectation, and then rolled richly down into a bawdy, froggy whoop, and started up again. I began to run, stumbling in the sand.

" 'Oh, life is a glorious cycle of song, a medley of extemporanea,' " I half-laughed, half-wept, as I ran.

From inside the studio came, on the wings of the laughter, " 'And love is a thing that can never go wrong . . .' "

" 'AND I AM MARIE OF RUMANIA!' " we shouted together, and met on the outside spiral staircase.

443

And we stood in each other's arms again, Cecie Hart and I, after a very, very long time, and both of us cried.

The first thing I thought was how little she had changed. I would have known her anywhere on the earth; I would have known her if I had seen her in a group of nuns, of holy women, chanting in a temple in Himalayan Nepal. I could have found her in the throng outside St. Peter's on Easter morning.

The second thing I thought was how small she was. It had been many, many years since I had thought of Cecie in terms of size, but I remembered, in that moment, how her diminutiveness had surprised and charmed me in the first days of our friendship.

The first thing I said to her, stupidly, was, "Cecie, you're so *little*." I had planned what I would say to her all the way down the Atlantic Coast, trying and discarding this pleasantry and that. But I could remember none of them. Idiocy prevailed.

"Yeah, well, what can you do," she said, in the precise, dry Virginia drawl that was as familiar to me, all of a sudden, as my own voice.

We looked at one another for a long time, smiling through the drying tears; we dropped our arms from around each other, and I know that my hands felt huge and clumsy. I did not know where to put them. I think she felt it, too. Her small hands flexed and unflexed. They were rough and red now, but then, so were mine, with wind and salt and the earth of my garden.

All of a sudden we began to laugh again. I don't think either of us could have said why. It simply felt good and right, and was better than silence. It was one of the things that we did together, Cecie and I. We laughed.

"You look exactly, precisely, *totally* like you used to," she said, grinning. "Still skinny. Still got the famous Lee nose; nobody's put it out of joint in all this time, I see. Even still got the celebrated French twist. And the streaks. Do you still put lemon juice on it and sit in the sun?"

"It's gray, you numbskull," I said. "Now I put white wine on it and sit in the sun. But you, Cecie . . . if it weren't for your hair, you still couldn't get a drink in any bar in America. I swear you've sold your soul to the devil."

"Blind, too," she said. "Ah, age, c'est tragique."

It was true, though not literally. The profound and prevailing sense of Cecie was that she was still the redhaired, ardent friend and

445

companion of my college years; that and that alone, wholehearted, unchanged. It may have been solely in my eyes that she was, but nevertheless that truth remained. But the world's truth was that the riotous tangle of Orphan-Annie curls were pure white now, and her watercolor blue eyes were webbed with tiny lines, and deeper lines of pain and endurance cut her kitten-shaped face. She was very thin, as thin as she had been during the terrible siege of mononucleosis, at the end of my college days, and I saw that her small shoulders were stooped a bit. There was no sagging flesh on her face or neck; it was as tight and firm as it had been as a girl, but the soft rose color that seemed to flicker just beneath it was gone. Cecie was pale to transparency. Blue shadows stained the thin skin beneath her eyes. She wore, instead of the horn-rims I remembered, large, round glasses with thin, silvery gray rims. They were very becoming; somehow, even with the lines of pain and exhaustion and the white hair, Cecie was beautiful as a woman as she had not been . . . or as I had not seen . . . as a girl.

"You look beautiful," I said. "You really do. I hope your children look just like you."

"Nope. Just exactly like Vinnie. Which is great for boys, and makes me thankful every day of my life that we didn't have girls. They'd have had mustaches."

"I have missed you so much," I said.

"Me, too," she said, in the formal little way she had when she felt shy. "I have, too."

There was a great whoop and thumping flurry of legs and arms and Ginger was with us on the stairs, capering and squealing, trying to gather both of us into her arms at once.

"Lord, just look at you two," she bubbled, hugging and patting. "You could be hugging hello after spring break. Neither one of you has changed one single bit. It's not fair; I'm the only one who's gotten old and fat. Oh, Kate, God, it's just so good to see you! We've been guzzling gin and counting the minutes till you got here! Come on up; we'll get your bags later. You're way behind."

She turned and loped up the weathered gray stairs to the studio, chattering over her shoulder. Cecie and I followed. Unlike Cecie, it was hard, at first, for me to find the Ginger I had known and loved in the woman who went ahead of us. This woman was very fat, and moved heavily, without the long, vigorous, hip-slung stride that had been young Ginger Fowler's. This woman's flesh was plushy and wattled, though still the deep mahogany that Ginger's went in the summers, and her hair, though still the white-blonde of the girl's, was whorled and carved on her head and spongy in texture, and sprayed into immobility in the vast river of wind flowing off the ocean. This woman wore an elaborate yellow-flowered cotton caftan with wide, loose sleeves and a deep V neck; her great bronze-speckled breasts bobbled in the V. On her brown feet were strappy bronze sandals, and her toenails were painted platinum. Ginger Fowler would never in her life have worn such getup. She would have hooted out of the room anyone who did.

But the warm blue eyes, crinkled with sun and laughter, were the same, though half-buried in flesh, and the sweet, snub puppy face, under layers of makeup, and the freckles and wide white grin, and the endearingly graceless gait and posture. I noticed that, though she wore several large, rather dingy diamonds on her big, shapely hands, the nails were still bitten short. I grinned at her back. The shy colt of a girl who had lost her fingernail in the ADPi's punchbowl and burned a hole in the Tri Omega's sofa was still under there.

"Shit," Ginger said, tripping on the doorsill, and my grin widened. Still under there, and not so far, either.

I stood in the doorway of Paul's studio and looked in. I had been almost afraid to do it; afraid, I suppose, that some lingering essence, not of him, but of me in the days of him, would remain to pierce and diminish me. It had, after all, been my room on the inside. My gift to him, his austere white room. But I need not have worried. There was nothing of me here, and nothing of Paul. There was hardly anything of the sky and sea. I blinked, trying to take it in. But it was not possible to do that in one glance, or even two or three.

The vast room was indeed open to the pink and silver sea and sky, just as he had envisioned, but aside from the great, curved sweep of seamless glass and the panorama beyond it, Paul Sibley's white room no longer existed. This room crawled and teemed and shimmered and writhed with color and form and texture and objects. Many, many objects, so many that you had to concentrate on them one by one to get the sense of them. The white floor had been covered with blue and white vinyl tile, dotted with bright throw rugs like islands in the Gulf Stream. Fat-stuffed furniture, also covered with rugs and throws, stood in groups everywhere: before the great fireplace, in front of the seaward window wall, in corners and nooks and bays. Most of it was plaid or striped or print chintz. Two sets of bunk beds stood against a wall where I had designed bookcases, and boxes and bins and trunks and baskets spilled out children's toys everywhere. Child-sized furniture, tables and chairs and dollhouses and stoves and refrigerators and rocking horses, clustered at the landward end of the room. At the seaward end, before the fireplace, a huge sofa and flanking chairs and a coffee table made a grouping, and a huge built-in bar and a complicated sound system flanked the stone fireplace itself. The lights I had seen from outside came from this end, from great bronze lamps on low tables.

"Well . . . wow," I said faintly. The room inundated and drowned every sense at once.

Ginger looked at me oddly, and then laughed.

"Oh, Kate, I completely and totally forgot," she said. "This was your room; you designed the first one. The pretty white one. Oh, poor baby, no wonder. . . . This has been my place, mine and the children's and the grandchildren's, for so long that I'd forgotten it was ever Paul's. But of course it was . . . well. You can see that it's had a lot of living and a lot of love over the years. The kids adored it, still do, and the grandchildren just live out here. Literally. I do too, when Paul's gone, and he is, an awful lot of the time."

"Where is his studio?" I said, still stunned

by the metamorphosis of this room that had been the first fruit of my first love.

She shook her head ruefully.

"He hasn't practiced architecture in almost twenty-five years," she said. "He did for a couple of years, right here, but for some reason he was having a hard time with it . . . he said the view was so sensational he couldn't concentrate . . . and then Daddy got sick and he started filling in at the mill, and that happened more and more often, and when Daddy died he took over. I don't think he's been unhappy with it; he's tripled the business. There are two more mills now. But sometimes I think it's a shame; he was just so gifted. . . . He's at the Norfolk house, or the one in Alabama, far more often than he is here. So he couldn't very well object when the children and I took this fantastic room over. And he didn't; he says himself it's the answer to a grandparent's prayer. Get them out of the main house. Don't think he doesn't dote, though. He did on our girls, and he does on their kids. I'll be glad when he can retire and spend most of his time with us. I'll bet he hasn't been in this room twice in the past year . . ."

"You have girls . . ." It was not a question. Their photographs were everywhere in the big room, dark, slender, long-limbed girls with brilliant anonymous white smiles and a great deal of hair, caught in cheerleader uniforms and debutante dresses and wedding gowns, posing demurely with small children.

"Three. All of them with two or more children, all of them less than a hundred miles away. This place in the summer is worse than a juvenile and female house of detention. And the oldest, Genie, is pregnant again. Another girl; she's had ultrasound. Paul says one more and he's going to put out on a freighter for three years."

One of the daughters uncurled herself from the depths of the vast sofa and came toward me, smiling. I put on my automatic social smile, but disappointment and faint resentment flared inside me. I had thought it was going to be just the four of us.

"Effie, dear love," the girl said, and threw her arms around me. In a ringing moment of shock I realized that it was Fig Newton. Ginger, looking at my face over Fig's head, laughed aloud, and so did Cecie, behind me.

"My God," I said, putting my arms around her and patting her numbly. "Fig, my God."

"Never," Fig said, "underestimate the power of a woman with a buck or two and a good plastic surgeon."

Even her voice was different, low and throaty and with something like laughter in it, only, not quite. She almost whispered, like Jackie Kennedy Onassis, with the same result: you leaned close in order to hear her.

I put her away from me, and she laughed, and held her arms over her head, and turned around like a mannequin. She wore skin-tight stone-washed blue jeans tucked into highheeled fawn suede boots, and a meltingly beautiful russet cashmere tunic, outsized and hanging down to her knees. Under it, perfect bare breasts pushed at the fabric; I could see her nipples plainly. She wore no jewelry but a wide hammered gold cuff and gold hoops in her ears, and she smelled of something musky and bitter and Oriental. She was still as short as I remembered, but so slender and perfectly proportioned now that she looked like a life-sized doll, and the skin of her face and arms and neck and bosom was flawless and satiny, the color of very pale café au lait. Her face was high-planed and hollow-cheeked and full-lipped; her eyes were green and slanted, and her nose was . . . my nose. Mine to the last dimple, the last curve of nostril. Her teeth were white and there seemed to be a great many of them, and around her face a mass of tawny hair fell, full and leonine and glowing with strands of gold and bronze and platinum. She did not look real, and of course she was not: she was Barbie and Tina Turner and Lena Horne and Michelle Pfeiffer and . . . yes, more than a little . . . Kate Lee. She looked about twenty-five years old.

"Is there any Fig in there?" I said.

"Not so's you'd know it," she laughed again, and hugged me a second time. "Everybody calls me Gina now, or Georgina, of course. You know perfectly well where the Stuart came from. I haven't been Fig since my first book came out, and that's more years ago than I want to remember. But as a special dispensation, just for you all, I'll be Fig this week. In fact, I want to be. That's why I called this meeting, in case you wondered. So we could all be us again."

"I don't know if I can even think of you as Fig," I said. "It's so . . . you're so . . . it's just incredible. I'm going to be tonguetied by your fame and your looks all this week. I never saw such a difference in anybody. Oh, not that you were bad before; it's just that . . ."

She laughed again.

"I was bad before," she said. "I was awful. Don't worry about it. I always meant to reinvent myself the minute I had the money for it, and that's just what I did. I had the works, the minute the first book got on the *New York Times* list. Diet, teeth, face lift, nose and chin job, cheekbone implants, boob implants, contacts, liposuction, collagen, chemical peel . . . there isn't anything you can do to the human form I haven't had done. It took two years. I've never been sorry for a minute of it. You'll never know how much I wanted to be you at school, and by God, I've even gone you one or two better."

"Ten or twelve better," I said. "Lord, Fig, I never looked even remotely like that in college. You must know that."

"I thought you did," she smiled. "That was enough."

We sank into the great soft chairs and the sofa and watched the light go out of the sky and sea, and drank the drinks Ginger brought us. They were outsized and strong, and I thought, from the glitter in her blue eyes and the slight slur in her voice, that she had had several. Her cheeks burned and she chattered. Fig drank white wine and Cecie sipped at bourbon in a balloon snifter, and we talked as if we had broken off this same conversation only a day or two ago. We talked and talked, and the sea went from grape to gray and finally to black, and the fire burned low, and still we talked. We talked of what we talked of when we last sat together: of people we all knew, and things we all remembered, and songs we had all sung, and movies we had seen, and professors we had had, and the clothes we had worn; and we laughed, and we drank some more, and we sang a little, and the years fell away and we were not women remembering the girls we had been, but somehow, those girls themselves. We were nineteen and twenty, and all that was closed to us reopened, and all things seemed once more possible. The pain and disappointments and flaws of our lives since vanished; a strange foreshortening of time took place. It happened over and over that week. We could not seem to dwell long in the present. From that first twilight, we all seemed to know that at some point we must speak of our lives as women, acquaint each other with the roads we had walked to mid-life, catch up with each other . . . but not now. Not yet. We all seemed to want to put off the moment of growing up. When Ginger started to ask about husbands and children and careers, we shouted her down.

"Okay, let's just go around the circle and say who-what-when-where-how," she said, "and then we can go back to libeling our Tri O sisters. I'll start. Ginger Fowler Sibley. Married twenty-eight years to Paul Sibley, mill owner. Housewife, mother, and grandmother. Three daughters, seven grandchildren, winter address Norfolk, summer address Nag's Head, Outer Banks, North Carolina."

She pointed at Fig.

"Georgina Stuart, aka Fig Newton," Fig said. "Novelist. *Best-selling* novelist. Five husbands, legion lovers, no children, four movies, two mini-series, three hundred million talk shows and tabloid interviews. Houses in Manhattan, Aspen, Malibu, and Puerto Vallarta. Current lover, but he's a secret."

There was a pause, and then Cecie said, smiling, "Cecelia Rushton Hart Fiori. Widow of Vinnie Fiori, Boston Municipal Police Sergeant. Mother of two boys, Leo and Robert, one for each side of the family. Grandmother of Susannah Fiori, age two. Living now in the same house I married into, in Boston, with my mother-in-law, Cosima, who is an invalid. Housewife, nurse, cook, cleaning lady, and medieval herbalist."

We all laughed at that. She did, too.

"I am, though," she said. "I've been studying medieval herbalists and herb gardens for years and years. I have a herb garden of my own, in my backyard, and I've been working on a book about them off and on since Vinnie died. It's almost done now."

I looked at her, charmed and intrigued.

"Cece, that's wonderful," I said. "Knowing

you, I'll bet it's an incredible book. I'll bet you anything somebody would love to publish it. How far away from finishing it are you?"

"My time's up. Your turn now," she said, and the others chimed in.

"Well . . . Kate Lee Abrams," I said. "Married twenty-eight years to Alan Abrams, architect. I'm his partner in a design business and we live in a gray-shingled house sort of like this one, on the beach at Sagaponack, Long Island. I'm a gardener and . . . I guess that's it. Designer and gardener."

"Children?" Ginger said.

"No," I said.

Ginger started to bring out photographs of her children and grandchildren, and again we protested.

"We'll get to all that," Cecie said comfortably from the sofa.

"Better still, let's not get to it at all," I said.

Fig looked over at me. In the firelight her face looked like that of a movie star, or a department store mannequin. The strangeness of it brushed me again. She was simply so . . . not Fig . . .

"Oh, but I want to know," she said in her soft purr. "I want to know everything about you, Effie. I want to know every single detail."

"I'm not going to have you put me in one of those books, Fig," I smiled.

"I wouldn't do that," she smiled back. "I'm off duty. Besides, we're all just plain too boring for one of my books. It would never sell in the supermarket."

"You, boring, after all those husbands and things?" Ginger said. She pronounced it "hushbands."

"Oh, God, Ginger, I made all that stuff up," Fig said, grinning. "Well, almost all of it. It's good PR, that's all. What kind of writer would I be if I couldn't invent a glamorous life for myself? You all know I've been writing my life ever since I was eighteen."

"The diary!" the three of us shouted together.

"The diary. And guess what. I brought it with me. The one I kept then. And as a special treat, if you're very good, I'm going to read the chapters about us to you every night, after dinner. Us in the flesh, the way we were. Would you like that?"

"Oh, yes," Ginger cried. "God, what fun!"

"Just like Scheherazade," I said. Somehow the thought of it made me uneasy.

"I hope not," Fig said. "She was all set to die if she ever got finished telling her stories. So, you guys, look out! When I'm all done . . . it's death!"

"Whose?" Cecie said interestedly.

"All of us, I guess," Fig said, smiling at her. It was a sweet smile, full and natural. I could not get over it, or her. "Us the way we were, anyway."

"I'd rather think that it would be just the opposite," Cecie said. "That it would keep us alive . . . the way we were."

"Let's don't talk about it," Ginger said, getting up clumsily out of her chair and stumbling a little. "Let's do it."

And so, that first night, after we had cooked and eaten a mess of spaghetti in the kitchen of the big shingle house, we came back out to the studio and built up the fire, and Ginger poured a round of brandies, and Fig sat down on the rug in front of the fire and opened the familiar, battered old fake crocodile book, and read from it. And in the firelight of the house on the Outer Banks, we all went back.

She read the passage about her initiation into Tri Omega in the new, intimate voice, and I was there, there in every aspect and in all my senses, in that dark, hot, candle-and-carnation-smelling room at Randolph, with the bells and the incense, and the sweat of all those tightly-packed young bodies, and the effluvia of their terror, and the droning on and on of the Latin, and then more bells,

460

and more incense . . . My head swam, and my stomach contracted. I closed my eyes and across the miles and the years Fig's face flickered in close, the face of that other Fig, heavy and fleshy and crazily rapt, great eyes swimming behind the glasses, lips loose and wet, tongue playing in and out . . . those lips, that dreadful hair, the thick waist and nonexistent neck . . .

". . . and at the very moment of the kiss that would make me her sister, she was so overcome with emotion that she fainted, and we had to revive her," Fig read. "My heart sang like a lark within me. I knew that we would be bound together forever, sisters in Tri Omega, and even more than sisters. I knew in that moment that she felt it, too, that great bond between us. Oh, Effie, my sister, I will love you always, and will strive all my life and with all my might to be worthy of you. I will make you proud of me. I will never let you forget me, just as I will never forget this holy night."

There was more in the same vein, and then she fell silent. I could not think what to say. Surely she had seen me vomiting into the sink in the Tri Omega kitchen. She could not have escaped seeing that. Had she really thought, all these years, that I had been overcome with sacred love for her?

"Well . . . Lord, Fig," I said. "That's really something."

"Isn't that a crock of shit?" she laughed, and all of a sudden something within me eased, and I laughed too, and found myself liking this ridiculous, flamboyant mythic creature, whoever she was, very much indeed.

"But God, it was everything to me then," she said. "I've never forgotten that night, no matter if I did make it sound like something Harriet Beecher Stowe wrote on a bad day. I never will forget it."

"Me, either," Cecie said equably. "If old Kate hadn't gotten the vapors I would have. Those goddamned things always did go on too long. I wonder if they still do it that way?"

"Can you doubt it?" I laughed. "Of course they do, bells and kiss and the scales falling from the eyes, the whole nine yards. Listen, can anybody remember the grip, or those terrible words that must never be spoken aloud?"

We all began to laugh, and give each other the Tri Omega grip, and cast about to remember that holy of holies, the secret motto, but nobody could. So we settled for having just one more drink, and singing several explicitly scurrilous fraternity party songs that Ginger knew, and then, finally, we went to bed.

At her own request, Fig was sleeping on the sofa in the studio.

"Can't resist waking up to sunrise over that ocean," she said. Cecie and I walked Ginger down the spiral staircase and into the big house, and saw her between us into the big bedroom that, I remembered, had been her parents' in those long-ago days. She slurred and stumbled, but she stayed on her feet.

"Be okay," she mumbled. "Be fine in the morning. Just need a little nap, and I'll be fine. 'Night, 'night, sleep tight, don't let the bedbugs bite . . .'"

We shut the door and walked down the hall to our room. It was the same one we had shared all those years ago, that looked over the deck and straight out to sea. I sat down on the bed that had been mine, and looked out into the darkness.

"Full circle," I said. "What goes around comes around . . . or something. You want to raid the fridge, or are you sleepy?"

"I'm pretty sleepy," she said, and I knew from the tone of her voice that she was still feeling strange with me, and shy, and that in a moment she would go down the hall to the bathroom and change into her night clothes there. A powerful wave of love and memory rocked me. I wanted, suddenly, to

463

take her in my arms and hug her again, as I had that afternoon, and feel the light bird's bones, and the rapid beating of her heart.

When she came back into the room, I had turned off the light and lay silently, still looking out to sea. I thought of the night of the great storm, when I had seen her far down on the beach, plunging luminous and naked into that awful black surf, swimming far out to sea with the lightning playing around her and the silver rain pummeling her. I remembered that she had turned over onto her back and taken the full brunt of the storm in her face . . .

As on that night, I heard her slip into her bed, and heard for a while her light, even breathing. Somehow I knew she was not asleep.

Presently I said, my eyes still closed, "Did you know I saw you that night, swimming out in the storm?"

"I thought you did," she said. There was a hint of laughter in her voice, but she did not say anything else.

I fell asleep then, and dreamed of Stephen. He was the age he was when we lost him. Five. I dreamed that we were at the circus with him, Alan and I, and that when the elephants marched into the ring in a circle he slipped away from us and was lost in the crowd. I ran after him, crying, but could not get to him through the mass of people. He called back to me, though.

"It's all right," he said. "I'm going to go with the elephants. I'll be back when it's over."

I woke up with tears running out of my eyes and onto the pillow. I lay still, struggling to calm the pounding of my heart, to will the tears to stop. In the next bed, Cecie stirred and sat up.

"You okay?" she said in the darkness.

"I had a little boy," I said. "Stephen. He drowned when he was five."

In the darkness there was silence, and then she said, gently, "I know. Fig told me before you got here. I don't think Ginger knows."

"How did Fig know?"

"How does Fig know anything?" Cecie said. "You going to be able to go back to sleep, or you want to get some milk or something?"

"No, I'm okay," I said. "I'm sorry I woke you."

"It's okay," Cecie said. "I wasn't asleep."

We lay in silence until I thought she had dropped off, and then she said, "We don't lose them, Kate. When you love them they don't die. I have to believe that, and I do. It's the only thing I really know, but I know

465

that. Whoever you love is alive as long as you are."

"Oh . . . I wish so," I said. "I hope so."

"I know so. Go to sleep," Cecie said.

And before I could even answer her, I did.

CHAPTER TWELVE

"Are you mad at me?" Ginger said the next morning. "Have you been mad at me?"

We were walking along the tide line, kicking our feet through the water. The beach was empty as far as we could see; only the two of us and the wheeling seabirds and the lazy tide moved in all that blue and tawniness. The wind was down and the long grasses on the dunes were motionless.

It was mid-morning. The night had been chilly and the fresh coolness still lingered, though the sun on our shoulders and the tops of our heads was hot. We wore sweatshirts over shorts, and had left our tennis shoes and socks on the steps leading up from the beach to the house. The house itself rode dark and imperial against the steel-blue sky. The old cottages stretched away down the beach like old, black-clad matriarchs. Here and there smoke curled from a chimney, speaking of occupancy, but we saw no one on the decks and porches and verandas, either. The water was surprisingly warm; I remembered Ginger's father telling us, long ago, of the gentle current that cut in beneath the colder one along these old Banks, that warmed the water and birthed the great storm seas. The air was so clear that we could read the lettering on the naval helicopters from Norfolk as they scissored over. Their clatter was almost the only sound in the morning, that and the hushhh of the low tide. I was rested and almost idiotically content. Time rocked at a standstill.

"Why on earth would I be mad at you?" I said, smiling at her. "It would be easier to be mad at a Lab puppy."

"Well, I got pretty squonked last night, and I know I'm not a lot of fun to be around when I do that. Didn't you and Cecie put me to bed? Or did I dream that?"

"We pointed you toward it," I said. "You did the rest. Come on, Gingerrooney, you know I'm not going to get mad at you because you got tiddly in your own house. This is me."

She smiled.

"Nobody ever called me that but you and Paul," she said. "And he hasn't, in years. It's nice to hear it again. I guess what I mean is, have you hated me all this time because of . . . him? I know you must have been awfully hurt and mad right after it happened, but I hoped all along that your life would be so wonderful that it wouldn't matter after a while . . ."

"I wasn't mad at you even then," I said truthfully. "I never blamed you for that. I know how persuasive he could be; can be. I couldn't have withstood that, either. I didn't, as you well know. And right after that I met Alan, and then it truly didn't matter. Alan is the best thing that could possibly have happened to me; I should have written you both a thank you note. I can't even imagine a life without him."

"I'm so glad. I really am," she said. "I've felt awful about it ever since. I knew it was wrong; I knew it when I was doing it. But . . . I was so crazy about him, Kate. I'd have committed murder for him. I guess I still would. Sometimes I still can't believe that somebody like me has him. Even if a lot of it was the money. Anyway, I wanted to tell you officially that I love you and I've always been sorry. I'd have told you much earlier; I did write you, several times. I just couldn't find you."

"I know," I said. "I guess I was hiding, for a while. But it was never from you. Come here and give me a hug."

She did, and I hugged her hard, and she held me for a moment, and then let me go. Her body felt slack and somehow ill in my arms, far too soft. But she looked more like my old Ginger this morning. She had left off the heavy makeup, so that the freckles and the beginning age spots showed clearly through the leathery tan, and she had pulled her white-blond hair into a long, fat braid that hung down her back. Her shorts were faded and frayed at the hem, and the sweatshirt was ancient, and said Currituck Yacht Club. Her blue eyes were veined with red, but they danced with Ginger's old deviltry. I thought she seemed years younger than when I had first seen her yesterday.

"It is time," she said, "for a Bloody Mary. The hell with coffee and mineral water and fresh juice. Let's cut through the crap and get our perspectives straight."

"If I start on Bloody Marys now I'll be back in bed by noon," I said. "And I just got up. But coffee sounds good."

We turned and plowed through the soft sand back toward the steps and the house, stopping to collect our shoes. The deck was still empty, but Cecie's tennis shoes and socks, ridiculously small, lay in a jumble under the porch hammock. I wondered if it was the same one that had dumped Paul and me onto this deck, half naked and blind with desire, all those years ago. It looked weathered enough to be. I felt nothing, looking at it.

"Have you seen Cece this morning?" I said. "She was gone when I woke up."

"She's down the beach looking for specimens for her rock garden," Ginger said. "She thinks she might be able to get beach primrose and beach pea and golden asters to grow in Boston. It's the same kind of salt soil, only colder. She's experimenting with a new deep kind of mulch that she thinks will get them through the winter. It's an awful shame she lost the house on the water in Virginia. It would have been the saving of her, after Vinnie died and the boys left. There'd have been room for that old dragon of a mother-in-law, and she'd have had her garden, and her boat, and crabbing and the Bay and all her friends and people around her. As it is, I think they live in two rooms of that awful little house and shut the rest off, to save electricity. Vinnie never managed to buy it; she still rents. Jesus knows how she manages."

Had Cecie not been permitted anything of her life, then? Not even the water of her beloved Chesapeake, not even the big, shabby old house she had grown up in? I knew that she would have stood to inherit it; she was all the family the grandmother and aunts had.

"What happened to the house?" I said. "I thought surely it was hers by now, and that she went there, maybe in the summers . . ."

"The aunt who inherited it from the grandmother went crazy as a loon and left it to some kind of awful fundy preacher," Ginger said grimly. "He seduced her away from Mother Church and the other aunts and Cecie; turned her against all of them, and damned if she didn't leave it to him and his church. Cecie tried to take it to court, but Vinnie was failing badly by then, and the boys were in college and the old woman had moved in, and she just ran out of money. She could maybe have gotten it back, but it's been so long now that she just hasn't tried again. I don't think she can afford to, anyway. Don't tell her I told you. It must have almost killed her, but she doesn't talk about it."

"I'm glad she's had you to talk to," I said, aware of a craven lick of jealousy deep inside me, like wildfire smoldering. "She doesn't talk to many people about things that matter. It really helps."

"Well, I wish she had, but in fact it was Fig who told me, and then swore me to silence," Ginger said.

"God, how does Fig know the things she does?" I said. "There was a time that Cecie would have bitten out her tongue rather than tell Fig anything. I can't imagine them on terms that intimate."

"Fig just knows things," Ginger said indulgently. "She always was curious, you know that. She always could find out anything. And now she's a famous writer used to research, I guess she has her ways. She's been good about keeping up with me. Cecie says she's had a good many letters and calls from her, too. You have to admit, Kate, she's not what she was. Money and reputation aside, she's a whole lot better now than even I ever thought she'd be. Success can make a whole different person of you, I guess."

"I'll say. Success and surgery," I said, only half sourly.

Far down the beach a dot that I knew, even at that distance, was Cecie coming into view, moving slowly along the tide line. When she got nearer I saw that she was carrying a big paper sack, and a small hoe. She walked with her head down as if she was studying the sun-dappled shallows where the green water broke into foam and rushed back to the sea. Occasionally she kicked and foam flew. The sun glanced off her white hair as from spun glass, or sugar.

"She still looks like a little kid, doesn't she?" Ginger said.

"Yes," I smiled. "A little boy in a white wig. Put the red back in those wild curls and you'd have Cecie Hart thirty years ago. It's uncanny."

A big golden dog, a retriever, burst from between the dunes barking maniacally and made for Cecie, and she dropped her sack and hoe and held out her arms, and the dog ran into them, rearing up and putting its paws on either shoulder, licking her face and beating the air with its tail. She hugged it hard, burying her face in the golden fur of its neck; on its hind legs, it was taller than she was. She pushed it down and turned and dashed with it into the waves, splashing and capering, sending sheets of diamond water flying. The dog bayed its joy and I heard, faintly, the glissando of Cecie's laugh. In a moment she came out of the water and trotted up the beach toward us, waving, the dog dancing along beside her. In a bit it gave one last bark and cut sharply away from her and loped off home. Ginger and I were grinning as she came up the beach steps toward us, wet to the waist and laughing. I would have given anything in that moment to wrap her in the sea's timelessness with me, and simply keep her there. Cecie belonged to the water like a fish or a gull.

"Cecilia Rushton Hart, go and change your clothes immediately," she said in a prissy, precise Virginia drawl, looking down at herself, and I heard the voices of the nuns and the old aunts and the grandmother.

"Better do it; you'll get twat rot," Ginger said, grinning evilly.

"Age cannot wither nor custom stale your infinite variety," Cecie said mock-acidly to her. "Nor your foul mouth. Morning, Katie. Thought you were going to sleep forever. I was going to get the *1812 Overture* and blast you out again, but all Ginger has is old Elvis Presley records. Philistine that she is. Y'all scuse me. My . . . you know . . . *is* kind of cold."

As she went into the big house Fig came down the curved stair from the studio. She was wearing soft black leather pants poured over her tiny figure, and a flat-knit red Italian sweater and short scarlet boots, and she had pulled her lion's mane of hair back and tied it with a black and red scarf that, even without the signature, I would have known was Hermès, and large black sunglasses. Like Ginger, she wore no makeup except a slash of red lipstick on her wide mouth and a smear of white zinc oxide on her nose, and even in the pure gold light of morning her skin was as flawless as tawny marble. No lines, no crow's-feet, no furrows, no wrinkles. She did not look like a child, as Cecie did, but something else entirely, both young and old as time. A statue, perhaps, or a painting come to life . . .

"It's Joan Collins in the flesh," Ginger said. "Or do I mean Jackie?"

"Neither one," Fig purred in her new throaty voice. "I'm better looking than Joan and I write better than Jackie, or else I've wasted an awful lot of money. How are you all, chickies? Isn't it a glorious morning?"

Cecie came out in clean khaki Bermudas and a Tri Omega sweatshirt, and we sat at a round wooden table in the sun, as it climbed the vault of the sky toward noon. Ginger made Bloody Marys and brought them out with a tray of shrimp dip and crackers, and we drank them, lulled with sun and salt wind and the seamless perfection of the September day and the cell-deep simplicity that the open sea sings into you. We drank a second round, and then another. We talked a little, lightly and lazily, and laughed a lot, and by one o'clock the air around me had begun to shimmer as it invariably does when I have had too much to drink. I squinted at Cecie and her face swam, and I closed one eye and she came into focus. She saw me, and laughed.

"I'm glad my mother-in-law can't see me," she said. "She'd burn the place down lighting candles for my soul. She's absolutely sure I hit the cooking sherry after I've put her to bed. And I do."

"I'm glad Paul can't see me," Ginger said. She had had four or five drinks to our three, and her face seemed to be melting slightly. Her voice, like the night before, was slurred just a bit. "He gets absolutely crazy when I drink. He watches me like a hawk, and I think he measures the bottles when he comes home from a trip. He's gotten so damned ashb . . . ashb . . . what is it when you're very austere and don't eat and drink much? something . . . stemious . . . that he doesn't even drink wine with meals anymore. I used to love our dinners together, and our drink at the end of the day, watching the sunset. He won't even take me to parties anymore. So I don't drink at all when he's around. But boy, do I make up for it when he isn't!"

She laughed loudly. Fig laughed with her merrily, but Cecie and I did not. The morning lost some of its gold.

"Remember that night we went up on the roof and got drunk, Ginger, the night you made your grades for initiation?" Fig said.

We all groaned.

"That's still the worst hangover I ever had," Ginger said.

"And I think it's still the most glamorous thing I ever did," Fig said. "After all these years, I still do."

The three of us hooted in disbelief. The

night had had a certain naive sweetness to it, perhaps, or at least the part before Ginger began to cry and Fig threw up over the railing. But by no stretch of the imagination could it be called glamorous.

"Come on, Fig," Cecie grinned. "Tell us what the most glamorous thing you ever did was, really. Or at least, the one that can be repeated. There must be some doozies, the life you've led."

"Well," Fig said, putting her head to the side so that her hair hung down over her shoulder like a palomino's tail, "it might have been the time I was in Venice for Carnival, just after *Melissa* came out, and I made love in a gondola with a gorgeous stranger all in black with a Venetian Lion's mask on. I never saw his face. But I sure did see his cod, as the Elizabethans used to say; it was a foot long and had a red ribbon tied around it . . ."

"Fig!" we all cried together, as we used to do at Randolph. Only now we were not exclaiming at her appalling naiveté.

"Wowee," Ginger said, giving a little wiggle. "I wouldn't mind getting a load of that. As the Elizabethans used to say."

"Or maybe it was the time in Morocco when I had lunch in a sheik's tent and stayed for breakfast the next morning," Fig went

478

on, licking her lips. "It is absolutely true what they tell you about the Bedouins, dear hearts."

"What?" Ginger breathed.

"Two feet long," Fig smiled beatifically. "And coated with Tiger fat."

"Or was that camel dung?" Cecie said happily, and Fig laughed.

"No, but really," she said. "I still think that night was it. Listen to this."

And she took the diary from the big leather tote she had brought with her, and read to us the passage from it about the night on the roof of the Tri Omega house.

Again, as she read, we looked at each other, dumbfounded. The flowery words spilling from the book were undoubtedly those of that first Fig; you could actually see the dogged rapture in the eyes swimming behind the thick glasses, see the wet lips forming the words, hear the tremor of ecstasy in the treble voice. But they told of a night that had never happened; could not have happened. This night was so star-struck and enchanted and full of portent and promise, so highminded and purely and cloyingly romantic, that it could not have occurred to human flesh and blood. It surely had not occurred to four drunk, silly college girls who ended up in maudlin tears, or vomiting over a railing. As in the passage about her initiation, I starred in the story of the night of Fig's first transcendent brush with alcohol, and the things that she remembered my saying and doing were not even possible to a medieval saint.

"Effie and I lay together under the stars, in the presence of our dearest friends and sisters, and pledged our silent devotion to each other, and felt in our veins the music of the spheres," Fig finished with a flourish.

"Now how could anything top that?" she said, when none of us spoke.

"Nothing could," I said. "Fig, I just can't believe you ever saw me like that. I sound like St. Joan, or the Little Colonel, or Elizabeth Barrett Browning, or maybe all three. You know I was never that good. Half the time I wasn't even nice to you."

"You always were, Effie," she said. "I know some of the others weren't, sometimes, but you were. You three always were."

"No," I said, thinking ashamedly of those nights that Cecie and I lay in bed, strangling with laughter at her, and at my imitations of her.

"You must have known I laughed at you sometimes, and mimicked you," I said. "I'm terribly ashamed of it now, but it's true, and you mustn't romanticize me. I was never as pure and noble as all that. None of us were."

"Listen, you let me be one of you, and nobody had ever done that before," Fig Newton said seriously. "I didn't care what you said about me. I knew you were just teasing. I even liked that. Nobody had ever even teased me before. You changed my life. All of you did. I'll never forget that."

I got up unsteadily and went around the table and hugged her. The others followed. She hugged us back, so hard that I could feel her long nails digging into my flesh.

When I sat back down, my eyes were wet.

"I'm sorry I was a rat," I said. "I was even sorry then. I'd feel just horrible if I thought I, or we, had really hurt you. But just look at you now."

"Just look at me," Fig said.

We got up and went in on tottering legs to lunch, and then to our beds to sleep off the vodka and the little burst of emotion. Or rather, Fig and Ginger and I did. I left Cecie curled up in the hammock on the porch.

"No sense wasting the ocean," she said. "I think I'll sleep in full view of it. Want to go swimming when we wake up?"

"Sure," I said. "What did you think of that little soul-baring? Very cathartic, wasn't it?"

481

"Ummmn hmmmm," Cecie said noncommittally. "It was really something."

I laughed.

"You still don't take any prisoners, do you?" I said.

"Somebody's got to keep their head around here," she said.

I fell asleep on my bed by the open window, the afternoon wind off the sea blowing cool on me. It was a delicious sleep, sweet and deep, and I woke feeling clean and whole and light, as I remembered feeling when I woke from one of those perfect, dreamless sleeps of adolescence. I stretched luxuriously. And then the thought came, sweeping everything before it: "I have cancer. I am going to die in less than a week."

The shock and surprise and simple desolation of it flung me out of bed and had me running down the hall before I was even aware that I had gotten up. I ran, I knew viscerally, for Cecie. She was sitting in the hammock in a faded old bathing suit that I thought I remembered from school, rocking herself with one foot and humming, looking out at the cobalt sea.

"Well, hello, there," she grinned. "Dr. Livingstone, I presume."

I stood with sweat drying at my hairline and heart hammering, trying to smile naturally around the devastation of that unguarded revelation. I felt it beginning to ebb.

"You said something about swimming," I said. "Let's do it."

She looked at me keenly.

"You look, as my grandmother's faithful old retainer Titter-baby used to say, like you'd been whupped through hell with a buzzard gut," she said.

"I should never drink at noon," I said. "I'm a wreck the rest of the day."

We swam far out in the heaving blue sea. The tide was coming in and the wind was strong and cool, but the water, after the first shock, was lovely, like swimming in brilliant bubbles, or wine. We stayed in for almost an hour, and when we came out we collapsed side by side on our towels, breathing hard, letting the sinking sun dry and warm us, and lull us nearly back into sleep. Once more the timelessness of the sea came into me and soothed me, shutting away fear and outrage and death. This was right; this good moment was all.

Presently, without lifting her head from her arms, Cecie said, "I'm sorry about your little boy."

"It was a long time ago," I said automatically; it was what I said when anyone mentioned Stephen. It meant nothing except,

"Stop. Don't say any more."

"It doesn't make it any less hard," she said. "I know. It's been ten years since Vinnie, and I still hurt for him every day."

I rolled my face toward her. I had never, in all the years I had been close to Cecie Hart, heard her speak so openly of pain. Her face was peaceful, but there were new lines in it, as if simply to speak of the loss brought it forth afresh, to cut and tear anew.

"I wish I'd known him," I said. "Ginger said he was absolutely charming. He must have been really special, to capture you."

She smiled. "He was special," she said. "He was handsome and romantic, and a silly fool; nobody has ever made me laugh like he did, except you. He was also opinionated and frankly not too smart, and maybe the worst male chauvinist pig I ever met. Just a perfect stereotype of the Italian male. I have no idea why I fell so for him. He was everything I thought I hated. In the long run, it just doesn't matter."

"I guess not," I said. "It's a lot simpler when you can feel that way about somebody. That kind of constant love . . . it can get you through anything."

But, I thought, it isn't getting me through. Why is that?

Cecie shook her white head impatiently.

484

"I didn't say it was simpler," she said. "It's not simple. The love may be constant, but it isn't enough for the worst of the times. In the long run you have to do that yourself. I came almost to hate Vinnie before he died; to hate the dependence, and the manipulating, and the out-and-out bullying . . . never underestimate the strength of weakness, Katie. There's an awful power to it. He was a very brave and simple man, and he couldn't forgive life for crippling him, or me for having to help him and support the kids. When he saw he was going to die soon, he invited his mother to leave his sister's, where she'd lived for years, and come live with us; he said she would be company for me after he was gone. What he meant was, it would be another chain to him, even after he was dead. And she is. I know that. I still love him as much as I did the day I met him, and I always will, and I miss him every day of my life, but I hate him for that, and for other things, too. I refuse to romanticize what he was, and what we were. It's like refusing my entire life for all those years. It's like a kind of death in life. The real thing is quite enough for me."

I was silent. Under the old Cecie there was a new one, then. A woman I did not know, and wondered if I could. This woman was very strong. The Cecie I had left in her bed at Randolph on graduation day had not been strong in this way.

"I hate it about the house," I said. "I know what that must have done to you. Cecie . . . are you awfully poor?"

She laughed. It was a free laugh, her old one, a girl's.

"Jesus, am I! Rock bottom," she said. "Flat line. One step above food stamps. His insurance stopped when he died, and his social security is practically nothing, because he didn't work that long, and his mother's barely pays for her therapist and medicines and what not. I don't have any benefits: I never worked at anything long enough. And it wasn't any kind of work, really; I ran the bookmobile in the neighborhood for a while, and did a little tutoring, and I've done quite a bit of sewing, but it's not the kind of thing you get pensions from. Mostly I was nursing him and raising kids, and then his mother came. His brother Gino sends me a little money sometimes, and he's going to pay my tuition at the community college at home, to see if I can finish my degree. I'll pay him back, of course. I may make it through law school yet. The kids will be able to help some in a little while."

Her voice was easy and cool, as it always

had been. Her face was serene, eyes closed against the last slanting rays of the sun. I stared at her.

"You didn't graduate?" I said dumbly.

She opened her eyes and looked at me for a while.

"No," she said. "I thought you knew."

"No," I said. "No, I didn't."

"Well . . ." and she took a deep breath. "I went home the day after you graduated and I had what I guess you'd say was a nervous breakdown. A clinical depression, I think they call it now. I must have had it for a long time, that last year; it was what most of that sleeping was about. I never realized it; I just thought it was the mono. But when I got home Aunt Claire, the one who had just a hair more sense than the others, saw that there was something really wrong, and she sent me to my Uncle William's, in Boston, and he and Aunt Susan clapped me into a discreet and hideously expensive little hospital the same day. I'll always be grateful for that, even though I know it was because Aunt Susan couldn't cope with me staring around underfoot. I was almost catatonic by then. It's an awful thing, Kate, that utter, sucking blackness. You really are sure it will never end. Death looks not only good, but like absolutely the only option there is. They'd just started with the psycho-active drugs then, and they had me on those, and I had a lot of therapy from a woman who seemed to have more sense than most, and after eight or nine months I got where I could leave and go to a halfway house, and that's where I met Vinnie. He lived with his Mama and younger sister next door; I used to see him swaggering off to work in the mornings, singing and looking sideways at me under those foot-long eyelashes. I'd be out working in the garden early. I was still awfully shaky; I think he literally flirted and teased me back into life! We did most of our courting over the garden fence under the baleful eye of Mama, who definitely did not want the apple of her eye to hitch up with a redheaded fruitcake. I think that was one of the things that decided me. We eloped to Elkton, Maryland, the day I got out of there. I had Leo exactly ten months later. So no, I never did go back and finish. I always meant to, after the kids were in college. But of course, by then, he'd been shot."

"And you never got back to the water." It was not a question.

"No," she said ruefully. "Losing the Tidewater house is the one thing I really regret out of all this. That and never seeing the Cloisters in New York. I'd kill to see their herb gardens, and to study with their medieval herbalist."

"Well, I can't do anything about the house, but I can surely by God get you to the Cloisters," I said. "You come this winter and we'll go spend every day for a week there . . ." and then I stopped.

"I'd love to see your house," she said. "The pictures are beautiful. But I've used up all my respite time with Mama Fiori for the year. In the spring, maybe."

"I want to tell you, here and now and out loud, that I think you're something, Cecie Hart Fiori," I said. "Anybody else would be whining or playing the holy martyr if they lived like you have. You make the rest of us look like self-indulgent snips."

"Oh, Lord, Kate, don't you give me that," she said impatiently. "One reason I don't see more people is that I always get that poor-noble-Cecie garbage. Listen, I love my life. It's so full now that I can't get done everything I want to do. And I'm not being noble; I mean that. There's absolutely nothing I want that I don't have, except maybe enough money, and I can probably rectify that, ultimately. Of course, there are a few things I do have that I wish I didn't, like Mama . . ."

"Say the word and I'll find somebody to

put a hit on her," I said. "Tell me what you do that you love, Cecie."

"Oh, Kate. Well, I garden. That's just utter joy to me. I've turned the entire yard into a garden. Flowers in front, herbs and vegetables in back. *Boston* magazine came and took pictures of it a couple of years ago; I'll send you the article when I get home. And then there's the herb book; it's really quite something, Kate. I haven't seen anything else like it in the book stores. I have high hopes for it. And the boys; they're not special, Lord knows, but they're funny and nice, and I enjoy them. I only wish I saw more of them. And I study things: I've studied astronomy, and ornithology; I help with the Christmas Bird Count for Audubon, and I volunteer with the Massachusetts Conservancy. I belong to three different reading clubs; I read constantly. Even, God help me, Fig's appalling and astonishing opi. And I rent millions of videos, and I watch the Arts and Entertainment Channel slavishly. I'm the world's leading authority on "The Jewel in the Crown" and "Rumpole of the Bailey." And I have friends, and I sew, and I have three absolutely worthless and eccentric cats. And other things. It really pisses me off when people assume my mind and soul are impoverished just because my pocketbook is."

490

"I didn't assume that. I just . . . wish things had been better for you," I said.

"Well, they're perfectly okay," she said, smiling. "What about you, Katie Lee? I know about your nice Alan . . . funny, isn't it, us two WASPS of all WASPS, marrying a Jew and an Italian? It's like a bad WWII movie . . . but what about the rest of it? How's your life working out, old Kate?"

"I lead a charmed life," I said lightly. "I'm almost embarrassed to say it, but I really do."

"Oh, Kate . . . nobody does," she said, smiling gently. "Isn't there anything at all you regret? Not, I hope, anything to do with the beautiful and talented Paul, but anything . . ."

"The only thing I really regret in all my life, besides Stephen, and you can't call that regret, is that I never said goodbye to you," I said. "And that I never wrote or called you. I thought I had an excuse, but I didn't."

"I'm not sorry," Cecie smiled. "I couldn't have stood it if you'd said goodbye. That's why I put your bags out in the hall, brave soul that I was. And I could have called and written you, too; I knew what the Paul and Ginger thing must have done to you. But I didn't. I think I needed to keep you just like you were."

"And am I?"

"To an almost remarkable degree," she said.

And of course, she was right. I was. We were. Or rather, Ginger and I were; we worked enormously at it. Fig, though, was simply too un-Fig even to retain a shard of her past Fighood; and Cecie, though on the surface still the delicately dry, unworldly sprite we had known, was something else too, now. Oh, she laughed with us, and sang, and did the dance steps and drank the drinks and swapped the remembrances we did, but that other thing that she was sat apart and watched us, with, it seemed to me, an odd commingling of tenderness and uneasiness. It made me just a hair constrained with her, just a shade puzzled and off-balance. I did not know for what she watched.

Fig watched, too. That, at least, had not changed. While we giggled and romped, bridled and sang and capered on the beach and indulged our clumsy sillinesses in the evenings, Fig watched and watched and watched. And smiled, and egged us on with remembrances of her own and entreaties to tell about this and that that we had done, and of course with the evocative and wildly fanciful entries from the ever-present diary. And watched.

"You look like a little ol' hoot owl perched

over there on that stool, watching away," Ginger said to her once, a trifle owlishly herself, after dinner, after we had howled and protested and giggled at the passage from the diary where I had read poetry to her and changed her life, once again, forever.

"I hope you aren't getting any ideas about writing about us."

"What's there to write about?" Fig smiled. "You act just like you did back in school, and I've already got that down."

"If I'd brought my camera I could blackmail you all with the Junior League and the Welcome Wagon and the Design Council and whatever else you hold dear," Cecie said one afternoon when Ginger and I, in our sandy-rumped bathing suits, were on the beach reenacting Tri Omega rush skits and songs. "I have a revolutionary idea: let's dress up and put on adult clothes and go out to dinner tonight. My treat. I want to see what you're going to be like when you grow up."

"Ringading-ding-ding-ding, ram it up your ass," Ginger and I sang loudly. "Good times are coming soon!"

Cecie got up and went into the house and did not come back. I found her asleep on her bed later that afternoon. I did not mention the little scene. It made me ever so slightly angry, and worse than that, for some reason, it frightened me a little. What was the harm in being nineteen again for a while? There had been a time when she would have danced along with us, had indeed done just that. We had, after all, come to the Outer Banks to recapture each other. Hadn't we?

The weather held in a molten luminosity so perfect that it was almost eerie. I had never seen light like that, never felt and smelled air as soft and pure and heady, never tasted so sharply the savor of freshness and salt and smoke from early morning fires. Food tasted glorious, and we ate like wolves; liquor tasted fine, too, and we all drank more than I supposed we did at home. I hoped that was true of Ginger. Fig had brought several cases of exemplary spirits, and not an evening passed that Cecie and I did not walk Ginger between us to bed. I would have worried more about it, I think, if she had not been so totally Ginger when she was tipsy: sweet and funny and clumsy and endearing, precisely the oversized nineteen-year-old who had come to us all those years ago. Ginger drunk was still Ginger, only more so. I put it out of my mind.

One day melted into another, and except for grocery shopping we never really left the beach. We kept meaning to, kept planning nebulous trips to Manteo, and the Gardens, and the *Elizabeth II,* jaunts in the beach tractor, fishing and crabbing expeditions, a sunset tour of the Sound in Paul's runabout. But somehow we never went. Later, we said to each other. Later. There's plenty of time. I remembered that we had done the same thing that autumn we had come from Randolph. Planned and planned, but never managed to leave the gilded September beach until the last day. The day we had driven far down the coast road to where the ferry left for Ocracoke, and seen the great, haunted dunes and the primeval maritime forest, and that wilder sea, and the awful and wonderful little Carolina Moon Motel. Thinking of it, I grinned.

"Ginger, is the Carolina Moon still there?" I said. "Do you remember, when we rode down there in your father's car?"

"Still there and going strong, Magic Fingers and all. Do you know, Paul Sibley actually took me there for our honeymoon night? Can you beat that for elegance?"

I was silent. So was Cecie.

"Lord, I remember he was going to take Effie Lee there," Fig said gaily. "Look what you escaped, Effie."

"I'd forgotten about that," Ginger said softly. "I really had, Kate."

"Oh, Gingerrooney, so had I," I said.

"Don't even think of it."

"Oh, my dears. I *am* sorry," Fig said remorsefully. "I have an awful mouth."

"True," Cecie said levelly. I glared at her.

"You just aren't going to give her anything, are you?" I said to her indignantly later, when we were alone. "I wish you'd lighten up on her. She's been perfect this trip. She's gone out of her way to make things nice for us; God knows how much she's spent on liquor and gas for that monstrous car, and the jet that brought you down and will take you home, my dear. Where is your gratitude?"

"Not, apparently, where you think it should be," Cecie said unrepentantly. "I just can't get a handle on her. At least, before she was Fig, awful as that was. Now she's . . . I don't know who. Or what. It makes me nervous."

"Maybe, just maybe, she's what she seems," I said. "A very successful woman who had the guts to make herself over completely and worked like a mule and made a mint. And is having a glorious time with it."

"Kate," Cecie said seriously, "Fig is not what she seems and she never has been. You of all people ought to be able to see that."

But I was unwilling to see anything but

what lay light upon the surface of me: sun and stars, water and horizon and golden light, lavender twilights and the girls I had loved long years ago. And I was unwilling to be anything but one of those girls. Later. Later . . .

But there was not much later left.

A night came toward the end of the week when it all blew up. I think we had all been waiting for it, on some level; the days had passed too uniformly in perfection; the laughter had gone on too long. The girls of that long-ago autumn had come too vividly alive. Nothing of that transcendence can last. But we had tried our best to keep it with us.

On this night, we gathered after another day in the sun for the drinks that had become our ritual, and to hear the excerpt from the diary that was, like Scheherazade, keeping our tender ghosts alive. We were, I think, addicted to Fig's fulsome words by then, or at least Ginger and I were. I felt Cecie going further and further inside herself as the days and the excerpts wore on. I don't think the others knew it, but I did. I had seen her do it often enough.

We sat in the sunset in the big studio, watching the sea turn pink, then the silver of crumpled foil, then violet, then gray. Ginger touched a match to the beautiful gray driftwood logs that were piled in the fireplace, and they roared into life, giving a whispering, beating heart to the room. We drew close around it. The night outside seemed, suddenly, very black and full of a vast old silence. I shivered. Endings shimmered unseen in the air like moths.

We drank a great deal that night. A restlessness seemed to have gotten under all our skins, and we could not seem to settle; we changed positions around the fire, and drank our drinks fast, and refilled them often. It seemed to me we worked harder to keep the foolishness going. We were able to keep the skins of those young girls around us, but only just; a fire is not a young thing.

In the leaping light I looked at us. A strange kind of fire-spawned pentimento prevailed in the dusk; through the used flesh of the women the taut, sweet flesh of the girls shone clear, and under that the strong, green young bones. And under those, somehow, the simpler, fresher hearts. At that moment we absolutely *were* Kate and Cecie and Ginger. Even Fig was nearer to Fig. It was as if we had been practicing rites all week to take us back in time, and all of a sudden, to our surprise, while we weren't looking, had succeeded.

Take Ginger. In her cutoff blue jeans with

the hole in the seat, her faded sweatshirt, her sneakers with the toe out, her straw hair in pigtails, her freckles shining clear in the bare tanned face, the battered plastic ukulele with the Arthur Godfrey attachment her father had sent her at school on her scarred knee, there was nothing left of the painted and beringed and caftaned fat woman who had met me on the stairs the first night. Or Cecie. Whether or not she wished it, she had shed the years like a sunburn, and, wearing an old nylon fishing hat over her white curls and a pair of back-buckled Bermuda shorts I knew she had had since college, was that other Cecie, my Cecie, once more. Fig, sitting across from the three of us on the sofa, was not that old Fig, but she did not seem the outrageous, lacquered chimera who had come to Nag's Head, either. She was laughing and singing along with Ginger and me, to the faltering strains of the ukulele, but mostly she was watching. As she watched, she smiled. It was, I thought, a sweet smile, and open. As if, somehow, what she saw pleased and delighted her to her core. I felt a surge of affection for her. Surely Fig had paid her dues with us.

Rising to get a drink I saw my own reflection in the wall of dark windows. I stopped, frozen. I had not seen the face of the girl who looked back at me for a very long time, but I knew her. I had first seen her in a watery old mirror in a bathroom in Kenmore, standing next to the tall, beautiful man who was her father. I heard his voice across all those years: "That girl doesn't belong in this town."

"You were right, Daddy," I thought, on a rising surge of grief. "I didn't. But you forgot to tell me where I did."

I did not want to feel the grief and so I made the drink quickly and drank it down. The grief receded. Hot gaiety ran along my veins.

"What's the dirtiest song you know, Ginger?" I shouted over the ukulele's plonk.

"Is the F word permitted?" she yelled back. Her eyes glittered and red spots burned hectically in her cheeks. She looked as if she had a high fever. I knew that she was on her fourth drink.

"Sure," I said.

"NO," Cecie shouted. "Come on, y'all."

"Oh, be a sport, Cecie," Fig smiled. "I use it all the time and get paid a bundle to do it."

"Yeah, but I have a choice about whether I have to read that or not," Cecie said mildly. "When Kate and Ginger crank up to sing, nobody has a choice."

"Well, then, without the big F . . . I

guess maybe it's this," Ginger said, and struck a chord, and sang: "Tingaling, goddamn, get a woman if you can; if you can't get a woman, get a clean old man . . . oh, she wasn't very pretty and she acted sort of shitty so I hit her in the titty with a hardboiled egg."

Ginger and I shrieked with glee, and Fig laughed too, and cried, "More, more!" Ginger complied.

"Oh, first trip up the Yukon River, first trip up the Michigan shore, there I met the Mistress Flanagan, otherwise known as the Winnipeg Whore. Some were drunk and some were drinking, some were lying on the floor, but I was over in the corner, screwing the hell out of that Winnipeg Whore . . ."

"That's awful," Cecie said, holding her nose. "That's enough. Stop. Have another drink."

"The cabin boy, the cabin boy, the dirty little nipper," Ginger howled. "Stuck a piece of glass right up his ass and circumcised the skipper."

Cecie put her glass down with a thump and got up.

"Enough," she said. "You're regressing five years with every word. If you're going to do that, I'm going to go make a sandwich."

I don't know why it struck Ginger and me as so funny. The liquor, doubtless. We roared with laughter, gasped, beat each other on the back, rolled around on the rug before the fire. Fig, smiling, said, "Don't go, Cecie. It's diary time. Then we'll eat and sober up."

"Why not skip the diary this one time?" Cecie said goodnaturedly. "I think these guys need food more than nostalgia. And I know I do."

"Oh, but this is the best one by far," Fig said. "I've been saving it specially. This is guaranteed to bring back all our golden yesterdays."

"Am I the only one thinking about tomorrow?" Cecie said wryly. "The dawn's early light is going to feel pretty grim to you two."

"Hey, Cecie, remember?" I shouted over the uproar. "Remember Dorothy Parker?

"Oh, seek, my love, your newer way;
I'll not be left in sorrow.
So long as I have yesterday,
Go take your damned tomorrow!"

"Right!" Fig bellowed. " 'Go take your damned tomorrow!' "

"Well," Cecie said, getting up, "I believe I will."

"No, Cece, wait," I said, sobering a bit. "We'll be good. Come on; stay. Let's hear the diary. Please? Pretty please?"

She looked at me.

"Okay," she said, grinning. "I sound like Mother Superior even to myself. Lay on, Fig."

And Fig did. She came and sat on the hearth rug with the firelight falling on her lion's mane, the exotic chimera's face bent over the crumbling fake alligator, the bitter Persian scent of Detchema rising from the V of her white silk blouse, and read to us the passages from the time that I first met Paul Sibley, and about the dinner party in his apartment, where she first fell under his spell. At first we laughed; the words, in the breathy, rich voice, were simply so ludicrous, so unlike what we knew of the truth of that time. But gradually we stopped laughing. Despite the naive hyperbole and the reverent references to Paul as a sort of prince, or young god, and me as his princess and consort, two things emerged with diamond-hard clarity: the fathomless depth of my helpless love for him and my utter, tremulous happiness in those days; and the savage and aching thing that was Fig's hopeless passion for him. When she stopped reading, after the part about that other September on the Outer Banks, we sat still and silent, our heads bowed. Paul Sibley sat with us, warm and living; he and I sat together, wrapped apart in our oneness and absorption like a single unit. I felt no nameable emotion, but I could perceive, on the skin of my arm, the precise, exact heat and texture of his, where it pressed against me. I could smell the warm smell of him, somehow a dark and musky thing. I closed my eyes. I was afraid that I would see him next.

Fig's new laugh rang out into the silence, silvery.

"Lord, I even embarrass myself," she said. "He must have wanted to drown me like a puppy. You, too, Effie. I followed you all everywhere that summer and fall; but you were too wrapped up in each other to notice me. And when you graduated, I followed him like a bloodhound for another year. Did you know that? I bet he never told you, but I did. If Ginger hadn't come along, I think I would have proposed to him. You saved us both a lot of embarrassment, Ginger."

No one said anything, and then, in the silence, I heard the sound of weeping. It was silent weeping, but you could hear the little soft, indrawn breaths, and the sniffles. A child cries like that when it is cranking up for a storm of tears. Stephen used to do it. I opened my eyes. It was Ginger crying. I had known that it must be.

"Oh, Ginger, sweetie, don't . . ." I began.

She lifted her head and looked at me. Her mouth was drawn open in a rictus of woe, perfectly square. She took a great, shuddering breath.

"He never loved me," she sobbed. "It was always you, Kate. I knew it then and I've always known it, and he knows it too. He said he did, but it was my money and I knew it was . . . he still talks about you sometimes, when I've done something that makes him mad, or embarrasses him, and I know he's thinking about you a lot of the time when he's quiet . . ."

"Oh, no, he isn't, he doesn't; don't say that," I whispered in a frail, little-girl voice. It sounded silly even to me. "You were ten times cuter than I was, that was why. He always thought you were just the cutest thing; he told me . . ."

"*Nooooo,*" Ginger wailed. "No, he didn't. No, he did not . . . it was you. And you know, I tried so hard to be like you . . . to be good . . . to be what he wanted, classy and quiet and smart and funny, like you . . . I wanted so bad to be good for him . . ."

I realized she was very drunk. I realized that I was, too. I wanted to end this infantile idiocy, but I did not know how.

505

"Let's don't talk about it anymore. Let's sing some more," I said, smiling winsomely.

"No, get it all out," Fig said from before the fire. She was leaning slightly forward, her lips parted. "If it's been festering all this time, it's better to get it all out and then it can heal. Go on, Ginger, sweetie. It's just us . . ."

From her wing chair Cecie made a small, strangled sound of disgust. Ginger took a deep breath, and whimpered, on a tide of tears, "I always thought if I was a very good girl, everything would be all right. I thought if I was sweet and cute enough, I would have a good life, and be a good mother, and keep Paul. I even thought . . . if I was funny and charming and lovable and wonderful . . . I wouldn't have to know that I'm going to die. Maybe I wouldn't even die. I'm so afraid of that; I always have been . . ."

Something cold and malignant coiled up from my stomach like a snake. I felt it coming and did not even try to stop it.

"Well, then, you lose, Gingerrooney," I said coldly. "You're going to lose this round. You're going to D-I-E, die! Even you can't outcute and outgood a baby, and babies die. Even the cutest and best ones die . . ."

I looked at her blindly, appalled at myself.

She dropped her face into her hands and wailed loudly, scrubbing at her eyes with her fists. Cecie stared at me whitely. Fig looked, in the firelight, interested and sympathetic and rapt. There was a small, curved smile on her perfect new mouth.

"Well, I'm sorry, but that was such a silly thing to say," I began fretfully. Cecie jumped to her feet, her face paper-white, her blue eyes blazing.

"GET REAL!" she shouted. She stood there, fists clenched, tears in her eyes. We looked at her in silence, all of us.

"I'm sick of this and sick of you all," she said. "You, Kate, and you, Ginger . . . you're acting like the worst kind of children and you have been, this entire week. My God, just so cute and funny. . . . There's nothing real about you . . ."

"And I suppose there is about you?" I said angrily. But under the anger, I felt grief, coming fast.

"You're damned right there is," she said. "You bet your cute little Tri O fanny there is, and there has been, for a long goddamned time. Lord, what a drag it is to have to deal with people who aren't real; the work and grief and pain it dumps on the people around them is just . . . enormous! All this effort, all this work . . . just so two middle-aged women can play sorority girls and feel good again. Shit! It makes me furious! You know, I used to wonder what kind of women we'd all be. I thought about it for hours, and I'd fantasize that one day we'd all meet again, years later, and I'd know. And here we are, and I still don't know . . . except about me. Just think about that; that's awful. All those years, all that living, and I still don't know what kind of women you all are! I don't know what you've done with your lives . . . I don't know how you feel about being here, in the middle of them, like we are; I don't know what you've come to believe all this adds up to . . ."

I felt myself begin to cry. I tasted the tears. But I had no sense of crying. Only of deep, weary sadness, and an end to something.

"I think reality sucks," I quavered. "To hell with real life. Life is just too awful . . ." I could not go on.

"Christ, Kate, how would you know?" Cecie said relentlessly. "If this week is any example, you're going to die without ever having lived. I hate death as much as any of you, and I have just as good reasons as you all do, whatever they are, but I hate this kind of non-life more. It *is* a death. It's a chosen death. And that's a sin. That's a sin against the people around you, who have to live a harder reality because you won't live yours at all . . ."

She turned and ran out of the studio. We heard her feet clattering down the spiral stairs, and the door to the big house open and shut. We stood still. Ginger stopped crying, and I did, too. The beginning of shame and a great, whistling white shock lurked just beyond the bell of liquor. I knew when it lifted both would crash down over me.

"Well, goodness, our little cucumber has a boiling point after all," Fig said in a light, amused voice. "Come on, let's build up the fire and have some brandy and I'll read you some more . . ."

"No," Ginger said, and her voice was dull and lifeless. "I want to go to bed. I'm awfully tired and I think I'm going to be sick."

"Want me to help you?" I said.

"No," she said. "I want to do it by myself."

Fig and I watched her down the steps and into the house. She stumbled once or twice, but she did well enough. But the puppy spring had gone out of her step, and her big shoulders drooped. She did not look like young Ginger Fowler now, but like what she was: a middle-aged woman who weighed too much and had had too much to drink, and who had just seen the merciless and banal truth of her life.

"I'm sorry," I whispered after her.

"She'll feel better in the morning," Fig said. "So will Cecie. I have a wonderful idea; it will make up for all this silliness. We'll do it first thing in the morning."

"What?" I said listlessly. I did not care; could not imagine caring.

"You'll see. Something really special. Something magical," she smiled.

When I reached our room, Cecie was not in it. I hesitated, and then padded off in search of her through the darkened house. Somehow I could not sleep until I had tried to make peace with her. Cecie had never been angry with me before.

When I reached the deck facing the sea, I saw that she was lying curled up in the big old hammock. There was a blanket over her, and she was rocking, back and forth, back and forth. The chains that held the hammock creaked steadily, like the stays of a sail in the wind. I started to speak, and then I didn't. I did not know what I could say to her. I knew that she was right, but I was not able to address that, and perhaps I never would be. Perhaps, in the end, it did not matter. Probably it did not.

I lay awake a long time that night, and

heard, until I finally fell asleep, the creak of the hammock's chains as it rocked with her in the little night wind off the sea.

CHAPTER THIRTEEN

It began, that perfect day, with bells and cannons. I heard them dimly at first, and lay curled into a ball with the comforter over my head, trying to work them into a dream. But soon they were simply too loud for that, and I sat up, feeling, under the disorientation and alarm, a frond of *déjà vu* uncurling down deep in my mind. Bells and cannons and Cecie . . .

I opened my eyes and there she was, holding a little cassette player near my ear. Tchaikovsky's *1812 Overture* boomed to its exuberant conclusion and I scrambled out of bed and chased her down the hall. Only when we reached the deck, laughing and gasping, did I realize that I was naked except for my panties. The morning was newborn and washed with pearly sea-light, and fresh with frost. Down on the beach the low tide lapped and whispered in that absolute crystal clarity that the cold brings. I turned and fled back to my room, Cecie behind me. I was skinning gratefully into a heavy sweater before I remembered last night's sad, shabby ending.

I turned to look at Cecie, and she grimaced.

"I know. I'm sorry," she said. "I made an absolute butt of myself. I don't have any excuse at all except that I'd had too much to drink and I was so mad at Fig for setting all that up, and egging you all on. But it's such a great morning I've even forgiven her. And if you'll forgive me I'll shut up and play the '1812' for you again. The tape cost me a fortune."

"Please don't bother on my account," I grinned. "And no apologies are necessary. Really. Let's just pretend it never happened; I'm not sure Ginger's going to remember that it did, anyway."

"I don't think she does, at that. I've already been in to see her and take her some coffee. Come on, breakfast's ready, and then Fig has something she wants to show us."

"*You* cooked breakfast?" I said, in exaggerated surprise. Cecie was by her own admission a dreadful cook. We'd agreed early on that she should handle dishwashing detail, and she accepted with alacrity.

"Now you know just how sorry I am," she grinned.

Ginger was in the kitchen grimacing over toast and coffee. I could not tell if it was the food or the hangover. Probably the latter; Ginger had what Fig called a tin tongue, relishing fast food fried clams as much as

513

she did Fig's exquisite little pâté suppers. An untouched plate of scrambled eggs and bacon sat before her.

"Good morning, sunshine," I said.

"There is absolutely nothing good about this morning," she said. Her eyes were swollen nearly shut, and her hands trembled. She had not yet combed and braided her hair, and it stood about her broad face like excelsior from a packing crate. She wore a fleece robe with a hole in the elbow. Shirley Booth in *Come Back, Little Sheba* came to mind.

"Aren't you going to eat that five-star breakfast I cooked for you?" Cecie said dryly.

"No, I am not," Ginger said. "I'd just throw it up. If it's so bad that I can't eat, I must really have made a jackass of myself, so for whatever it was, I apologize right now."

"It wasn't you that was the jackass," Cecie said. "It was me and Fig, and I've already apologized. I don't think she's going to, but she's got a surprise for us that's probably her way of apologizing. Finish your coffee and get dressed and let's go. I said I'd bring you all over."

"Over where?"

"No more questions. Scoot. Move," Cecie said happily, and Ginger went slumping off.

Cecie and I polished off the eggs and bacon while we waited; they were as bad as I thought they would be. I ate hungrily. There was a rising tide of something in the new morning that felt like simple joy, and after the misery of the previous night, I did not want to examine it, but only to revel in it. Outside, the light over the sea dazzled like a spill of diamonds.

Ginger came back in shorts and tennis shoes and a huge, fleecy brown sweater that I knew must be Paul's. It hung down below her wrists and nearly to her knees. In it, she looked like a benevolent woolly mammoth, or a prehistoric Viking woman wrapped in skins. Her long single braid and fair hair and lined blue eyes heightened the image.

"All you need is a shield and a spear," I said.

"I feel too bad to even guess what you're talking about," she said wanly. "I hope this surprise is a killer. Otherwise I'm going back to bed."

Cecie tossed a set of car keys to me and opened the doors to the big, battered Land Rover.

"I hope you can drive this thing," she said. "I wouldn't try, and I wouldn't ride with Ginger this morning in a kiddie car. Fig said to meet her at the public dock over on the Sound. Do you know where that is?"

"It's just right across the main highway; it's not half a mile," Ginger said. "Why are we going to the dock?"

"You'll see," Cecie said, and laughed aloud, her wonderful gurgling laugh.

I wrestled the big Rover around in the sandy yard and drove it slowly across the main highway and down the little sandy lane to the public boat dock. It was heavy and sluggish; I felt as if I were hauling it physically, rather than driving it; felt awkward and exposed and vulnerable sitting so high up. The road and the lane were practically deserted, and the boats in the public marina rode silently on flat pink mirror water. It was still very early.

We saw it before we saw Fig standing beside it: a trim, blue and white seaplane riding at rest alongside the silvery dock out into Roanoke Sound, bobbling very gently on the satiny skin of the water. Beside it stood Fig in white slacks and a scarlet leather bomber jacket. Her hair was bound back with a red scarf, and she wore the outsized dark glasses that shielded her eyes completely. She looked impossibly exotic and rich among the sea-stained fishing and pleasure boats and the oil and gas cans, and wet coils of dirty rope. She looked like a mirage, or something from a movie being filmed on the dingy little working dock. She was smiling brilliantly, and the low early sun glanced off her teeth. Beside her slouched a very tall young man in filthy blue jeans and cowboy boots, with a baseball cap on his head and mirror aviator glasses covering much of his brown face. He was drinking coffee with one hand; the other held Fig's waist, loosely.

"Holy shit," Ginger croaked. "She's bought a goddamned seaplane."

"Rented. But not just any seaplane," Fig said merrily, trotting up to meet us. "This seaplane belongs to the one and only Poolie Prout, former Nag's Head tight end . . . wouldn't you know . . . and full-time illegal substance runner and all-round Pussycat. Isn't he beautiful? Not to mention his little plane, which is full to the gunnels, or whatever, with French champagne and ready to take us all the way down to Ocracoke. So how do you like them apples, Tri Omegas?"

We liked it. More than that, we loved it. It was just the sort of grand and eccentric stroke that the glorious day-in-the-making called for; just the antidote for the heaviness of the ending to this time that lay in wait for us, at the edges of our consciousness. It wiped last night's shoddy little ugliness completely away; it brought those vanquished

517

young women scampering back. Ginger's rump, as she scrambled into the rocking plane ahead of me, was the muscular, teasing rump of young Ginger Fowler once more; the flash of tanned legs as Cecie skipped aboard seemed miraculously wiped free of scales and scars and the sad little nests of blue veins behind the knee and ankle. My own legs and arms seemed to move in their sockets as if they had been oiled. Fig, who had slipped into the seat beside the elaborately taciturn Poolie Prout, looked like an ingenue in a movie about barnstormers or wingwalkers. She tossed her heavy hair and held a champagne bottle aloft, and gave us the old WWII thumbs-up sign. It would have been impossible not to be charmed by her.

It was clear that Poolie Prout was. He did not so much as acknowledge the rest of us, except for a nod of his head when Fig introduced us. But he cut his mirror-glass eyes toward Fig with regularity, and after he had us in the blue air and droning smoothly down the coast, rested his callused brown hand on her thigh. Occasionally he leaned over and whispered something in her ear, and she laughed and tossed her hair. Once I even saw him smile; when he did, the muscles in his jaw that spoke of regular acquaintance with Red Man tobacco bunched and knotted, and white lines fanned out familiar eyes behind the lenses of the aviator glasses. He had a decal stuck on the plane's dashboard that said, "Born to Raise Hell," and a pair of gossamer black panties rode on an anonymous knob. Every so often Fig would hold the champagne bottle to his lips and he would swig some, not bothering to wipe the foam off his chin.

"He must think he's got ahold of Dolly Parton," Ginger said as we drifted down the long white ribbon of the Cape Hatteras National Seashore. "Look at him; he's in macho hog heaven. He probably thinks we're her old maid aunts, or something."

"I don't care what he thinks, as long as he keeps this thing in the air," Cecie said. "That makes the second bottle of champagne they've opened. Pass that bottle over here, Kate. If I'm going into the drink I want to go swigging Perrier Jouet."

"It wouldn't be a bad way, would it?" I said dreamily. "Blue sky over you and blue water under you, and champagne bubbles in your blood . . ."

"Bad enough so that I'd rather not," Cecie said. "Lord, Kate. Shut up. Drink your champagne and look out the window. Did you ever, in all your life, ever on this earth, see such a day?"

It was true. There never was such a morning; never will be again. Blueness streamed and shimmered through everything; crystal blue edged the horizon and the dunes, and the sky over the sound was perfect cobalt. The air we floated in was liquid radiance; the great, wild dunes and the dark maritime forests and the occasional tiny villages fled beneath us, limned in blue-edged clarity as if by an Old Master's brush. I thought of the perfect, bronze-blue of Van Gogh's Arles paintings, and of Winslow Homer's burning, translucent subtropical landscapes. They were close, but nothing, no human hand, could have captured the radiance of this day. I think perhaps you get days like these maybe twice or three times in your life. I remembered only one: the day long ago when we had come together, with Paul, down the same highway that unrolled below us, to where the ferry left for Ocracoke.

Ginger said the same thing that she had that morning.

"Weather breeder," she said, swigging champagne contentedly. "Too perfect to last. See the blue edges to everything? Something's making up somewhere. And there's no wind at all . . . has anybody seen the news? What's going on in the tropics?"

No one had, but Poolie Prout said over

his shoulder, in a tenor nasal twang that belied the shoulder and neck and jaw muscles and made Cecie grin at me, "Nothing big, but a little blow coming up-coast from across in the Gulf. Small craft warning in Georgia and South Carolina. Headed out to sea before it gets here, though. But the next few days will probably be foggy and sully."

"Then I'm glad we picked today, or rather, that you did, Fig," I said. "I wouldn't want to navigate around here in fog."

"I can fly this thing in fog or anything else," Poolie said remotely, but he cut his eyes over at Fig. "I've flown in force ten gales, with wind blowing the rain into us like machine gun fire. I can remember taking her home when the hurricane flags were flying all along this coast."

"Where's home?" I said. The champagne was buzzing in my head, running sweet and fizzing through my veins. I felt wonderful.

"Down to Avon, just on ahead," he said. "Right before the Ocracoke ferry. Got a dockage at the fishing pier in Pamlico Sound."

Fig giggled. It was a little girl's sound. She had taken off the glasses; her eyes glittered as if she had been taking some psycho-active drug. I wondered suddenly if she was. She had laughed often and gaily and at nothing in particular all morning. We were all giddy from the day and the flight and the liquor, but I had never seen Fig this way before, either that old Fig or this new one.

"Avon," she piped. "Isn't Avon where the Carolina Moon is? Do you know the Carolina Moon, Poolie?"

"Do I know the Carolina Moon," he said. He reached over and ruffled her hair and let his hand trail down her neck to the collar of the jacket, and linger there. "Is the Pope a Catholic? Listen, I've tried out the Magic Fingers in every one of them rooms. They've got a bronze plaque in one of them. Says, the Poolie Prout room. Got a mark on the wall for every time I've . . ."

"Spare me the details," Fig purred. "I've got a mighty wide jealous streak. Well, well. The Carolina Moon. I'd love to see the inside of one of those rooms . . ."

"That could be arranged," he said, smirking. "I could run up to Nag's Head anytime you say. Not more than an hour flight in any weather."

"Even at night?" Fig said in a low, growly voice. In the back seat, the three of us grinned at each other.

"She'll have him lifting the plane when we land," Ginger whispered.

"I doubt if he'll have to," Cecie snorted. "Looks like she's halfway to those Magic

522

Fingers as we speak."

"Even at night," Poolie Prout said to Fig. "Even with no moon and no stars. Even in fog at night. Even in rain at night. I've landed in any kind of weather you can imagine all up and down this coast. You get an itch to see the Carolina Moon by night, you give me a call. I'll get you there."

"I'll keep it in mind," Fig laughed, and looked back at us and winked. Poolie Prout put his hand on her thigh and left it there. She did not move it.

We set down in the little harbor at Ocracoke and had lunch there, at a fish place on the wharf. Poolie vanished into the dark bar, to play video games and frog biceps with his buddies. We could hear their raucous laughter. He was undoubtedly telling them about his conquest of the rich older woman. We four each had steamed blue crabs and cold beer, and a slice of the lemon pie that a handwritten sign on the wall said LaVerle, the wife of the Prop., made herself. If she did, she was not a great deal better than Cecie. We ate the gummy pie, laughing. We laughed a great deal at that lunch; I don't remember at what, now. But I remember the laughter, and under it, the sadness, like chill dew in grass.

When we were finished with the pie and

coffee, Ginger said, her voice blurry with champagne and beer and unshed tears, "I love you all so much. I don't want this ever to end."

"Me either," Cecie said. "But if I'm not back in three days Mama Fiori will have one of her screaming fits and they'll throw her out on the street. Even the government won't keep her one minute longer than they have to by law."

"Why don't you just pack her up and send her back to the brother?" I said. "To Gino. Surely they're better able to handle her than you are. Surely, now that you're alone there . . ."

"Because dear Celeste, my sainted sister-in-law, says she'll leave Gino if his mother comes back," Cecie said acidly. "Good riddance to bad rubbish, I say, but somehow Gino can't see it that way. I keep thinking she'll die any day, but she never will; she'll outlive me, and then my poor sons will probably get her. She's going to be passed down from generation to generation of Fioris, like a family curse."

"Isn't it hard to go back, after something like this?" Fig said.

"It will be the hardest thing I ever do," Cecie said. She was not smiling. I felt tears come into my eyes. I wanted, suddenly, to hand her the moon; to fix things for her; to make her life good again, with one grand, sweeping gesture. I had money enough to do something: get her book published, stake her to a year's study at the Cloisters, hire her a year's respite from the old woman. But I did not, now, have the time . . .

"Let's at least make it an annual thing," Ginger snuffled. "Let's come every year, this time of year . . . the fall is best, I think, don't you all? . . . Oh, let's do! Every year! It will give me something to look forward to . . ."

She fell silent. We did not look at each other or her. The little sentence, broken off, told me much I did not want to know about Ginger's marriage to Paul Sibley.

"Well, we have three more days, and the rest of this one," I said briskly. "Let's fill 'em up. Let's do things we'll remember till . . . next time. Everybody gets to pick one day of their own. Cecie, you're first because you're the smallest. Pick something and we'll do it this afternoon."

"I want to go to Currituck Gardens," she said, smiling at me. "And I want to take the runabout and go out into the sound and watch the sunset from there. Y'all don't have to come, but that's what I want to do."

"You got it," I said.

When we got back to the dock in Roanoke Sound it was just coming on two o'clock. We had drunk the rest of the champagne coming back up the wild, blue coast, and my head spun gently and rhythmically with it. I smiled and smiled, at whatever transpired, at nothing. On the dock we stretched and yawned and blinked around us. The day had warmed like an apple in the sun: on the surface there was a bronze, sweet-smelling heat, but at its heart there was still a crisp coolness. A little afternoon wind was picking up; the tide would have turned an hour before.

"Nap for me, if we're going out to dinner," Ginger said sleepily. "I can just about make it to bed. Y'all drop me off and take the Rover and go on over to the gardens. And if you still want to take the runabout out, it's the one at the end over there, under the tarp. Just tell Bobby in the boathouse. Keys are in the blue saucer on the kitchen counter. Do either of you know how to handle a boat?"

"Are you kidding?" Cecie said. "I was born in a boat."

"Well, then, *Sayonara*," Ginger mumbled. "Bed, here I come."

"Fig?" Cecie said.

"I think," Fig said in a slow, molten voice,

"that I may just run on up the coast with Poolie a little way. He says there's lots up toward Duck and Corolla I ought to see."

She smiled at us and then slid the smile around to Poolie Prout. His face did not change, but his bull neck reddened.

"I'll just bet there's a lot she ought to see," Cecie said, as I wrestled the Land Rover onto the main highway and headed it south toward the causeway over to Manteo. "And she undoubtedly will, the minute he unzips it."

"Cecie Hart Fiori!" I laughed. "I never heard you talk trash before."

"Well, they sure ain't going to play mah jongg," she said. "Lord, she was practically panting. I never saw such a performance. He must be twenty years younger than she is."

"I somehow don't think that's the subject closest to his mind right now," I grinned. "Maybe she's researching a book."

"You're probably right," Cecie said, propping her feet up on the dashboard. "Fig is just not the type to do something without a reason. Even that."

When we got to Currituck Gardens there was only a half hour left until the new autumn closing time, and so we loped around the trails and circles of raked white gravel, drowning ourselves in the flaming splendor of the fall annuals and perennials. The gardens

527

were formal ones, seventeenth-century English, with statuary and vistas and follies and a yew maze, and many leaping fountains. I admired them, but somehow I could not warm to them. They were too tamed, too groomed and controlled and considered. To my eye they cried out for splendid chaos, for randomness and unseemly opulence and the rowdy sweetness of the accidental. I trotted along behind Cecie as she looked, and exclaimed, and knelt to sniff, and cocked her head to consider. At the very back of the gardens, against a wall of warm, rosy old brick, we both stopped, our breath indrawn together.

The entire wall was covered with roses. They were a living fire, a mantle of burning, golden-hearted pure pink. The entire wall seemed to shimmer with life and light and health. The very air around it seemed suffused with radiance. You could, I thought, see that wall of roses for fifty miles in weather like today's.

Cecie looked up at me, shading her eyes with her hand.

"You know where these would be gorgeous?" she said. "On the dunes just outside your garden, the ones in that picture you showed me, that shield the garden from the beach. You couldn't see them from your side of the garden, but from the beach they'd just knock the socks off anybody passing by. And they'd live forever. They're *rosa rugosa*. Nothing kills them."

"What good would they be if I couldn't see them?" I said.

"I don't know," Cecie said, looking straight at me. "I guess they'd just say to the world, 'Hey, I'm Kate Lee, and I was here. I *am* here.' "

I turned and walked away, down the path toward the car. Cecie wanted to stop in the Garden Center for postcards, so I went to the Land Rover and climbed in and turned on the radio, and put my head back and closed my eyes and listened. The mannerly strains of a song I had liked at Randolph swam out into the warm air: "Lisbon Antigua." It had had a revival that summer and fall.

"She knows," I thought. "I don't know how, but she does."

I tried very hard to think of nothing else but the spilling strings on the radio, and by the time Cecie climbed into the front seat beside me, I was submerged in it, gone far away into the country of our youth.

We took the slender little runabout far down the Sound toward Oregon Inlet. Once we passed under the Umstead bridge over to Manteo, we were in wilder country, and the shacky little boathouses and sagging docks and fish restaurants gave way to the uninhabited, undulating gold-green marshes that bordered the warm, shallow water. Salt marsh cordgrass waved in the late breeze, and huge, fierce green stands of marsh elder and myrtle and cottonbush rose beyond it. Cecie cut the motor to its lowest idle, and we drifted on the black surface as slowly as a water bug or a sailing leaf. Sometimes, near the shore, she put her paddle out to feel for the muddy bottom. She was as deft and sure with the exotic little red-hulled boat as if she had spent her life in one. But I felt sure that she had never been in anything as sleek and expensive as this arrow-shaped bauble. Ginger had said that it was new: Paul had just ordered it at the New York Boat Show the previous spring.

I knew that the highway down to the Hatteras National Seashore was just out of sight over the stands of vegetation; we could hear, faintly, occasional cars whining by. But the sense of isolation was acute and all-encompassing. Night was coming on, a purple shelf to the west, over the distant shore, and the slapping gray water was going pink and silver out on its middle. I shivered.

"It feels like the dawn of time out here," I said. "I keep waiting for something huge and scaly to rise up out of that marsh, bellowing."

Just then a great blue heron rose up out of the long spartina, flapping wetly. A big, flopping fish flashed silver in his beak; he lumbered away into the clear air directly over our heads, showering us with drops of blood-warm water.

"Make that a pterodactyl," I said, laughing, my heart pounding.

Cecie lifted her paddle and saluted him.

"Good hunting, *amigo*," she called after him.

"You ought to be a hunting and fishing guide," I said. "Or even better, a white goddess. Boy, wouldn't those little red guys have loved you, with that wild white hair and fierce blue eyes and white skin? They'd have danced around you at the council fires, and given you all the best pemmican. You'd have had it made."

"Pemmican and council fires," Cecie snorted. "Lord, Kate. Those were the Plains Indians. What an ignoramus you are. The Roanokes ate mainly fish and crabs, and were tall and skinny. But I know what you mean. It does look prehistoric out here, doesn't it? A salt marsh like this is probably the oldest and most unchanged part of the earth we have left; it wasn't a whole lot different when the Manteos and the Wancheses were paddling around here. And rich. There's the richest and densest life system on earth all around you here. It's absolutely self-sustaining; it doesn't need anything else. There's more life down there than along the Ganges."

"Looks like plain old mud to me," I said, watching a smokelike cloud of bottom silt rise at the touch of her paddle.

"Yeah, but in that mud there's everything from plankton to all kinds of fish, crabs, shrimp, and squid. Plus oysters and mussels and snails and periwinkles and turtles and terrapins and raccoons over there on the banks, and mice, and about a million birds and herons . . ."

"You could be a marine biologist," I said. "As well as a medieval herbalist. Why don't you write about this?"

"Other people have done it better," she said comfortably. "I just want to live in the middle of it. I'm going to get back to the Tidewater, or some kind of salt marsh, one of these days. I may have to stake Mama Fiori out on a hummock like a goat to do it, but I'll get there."

As we neared the great cut through the ribbon of the Banks that was Oregon Inlet, the water began to move faster down deep, and the surface rippled with motion and purpose. The air cooled, and the sense of the sea's vastness, just across the line of vegetation, was strong and urgent. Cecie cut the motor and tossed the anchor overboard. It settled to the bottom with a silvery sucking, and we rocked on the pinkening skin of the water until the ripples subsided.

"This is far enough," she said. "I don't want to mess with Oregon Inlet at high tide. There's just too much water coming through there too fast. Did you know that there wasn't an inlet here until 1846? It was just the Banks. But there was a huge hurricane in September of that year, and the water just cut right through the Banks and made the Inlet. It's named for the *Oregon,* a sidewheeler that was the first ship through it into the Sound."

"How do you know all this?" I said. "You know more about the Banks than Ginger does, I think."

"I got some books out of the library when I knew I was coming," she said. "Most of them are ghost stories; it's hard to find any hard facts about this old coast. Right where we're anchored there's supposed to be a ghost ship that shows up on winter nights, burning for all eternity. It's on its way down to Ocracoke, but it never gets there. So they say."

"I'd just as soon be about our business," I said, shivering a little. The Sound and the marsh and the sky above it were absolutely empty. The afternoon had turned, for good and all, toward evening.

"Let's wait a little," Cecie said. "There's something that happens sometimes, around sundown, and I wanted to show it to you. If it doesn't, in a few minutes, I promise we'll head for home."

"What?" I said apprehensively.

"Surprise," she grinned.

"It better be real," I said.

"Realer than Dick's hatband," Cecie said. "If it happens. It doesn't, always."

She wouldn't tell me any more, and we sat quietly, feeling the great, inexorable drawing away of the sun, the huge, formless oncoming of the night. The air was still as clear as spring water, and a sunset like a conflagration burned over to the west. It was all purple and red and pink and gold, shot through with streaks of pure, pale green. I have never seen anything so lovely; there seemed no sense in remarking on it, so I did not. Once Cecie turned and smiled at me over her shoulder, but she did not speak either.

There was a long, green afterglow. I knew there would be light for another hour and a half yet, but suddenly, I wanted to go back to the cottage. I wanted yellow lights and the sound of jazz or rock drifting from the studio, and the smell of something cooking, and the ripple of laughter. Anything could happen out here in this flat place where the land slid into the water. Anything could come.

Cecie seemed to sense my mood. She swung around on the seat and said, "You know that you never talk about Alan? You don't talk about him, and you don't talk about what you want to do with him, how you want your lives to be tomorrow or next week or next month. Don't you have any kind of agenda, old Kate?"

She wrinkled her nose at the yuppie phrase, and I smiled. I cast about in my mind for some way to nudge her away from this. I did not want to talk about Alan; could not, in fact. Alan belonged to another woman, and she no longer existed. I intended to keep it that way for as long as I had to. If that woman did not exist, then neither did the Pacmen.

" 'There's no tomorrow,' " I sang. " 'There's just tonight.' "

"Thank you, Jean Paul Sartre," Cecie said sharply. "A nice existential philosophy. Only aren't you curious? Don't you want some say in tomorrow?"

"I'm not awfully sure there's going to be much of a tomorrow," I said. I meant it lightly, but it did not sound that way here on the darkening water.

She shook her white head.

"There were people like you in the hospital," she said, "and they scared me to death. Well, not like you, but they said the same thing. They didn't live one minute ahead, not one second. They had no stake in the future. Didn't want any. And that did scare me. And you scare me when you say that."

"Just tell me what's so hot about tomorrow," I said. "What's tomorrow got that right now doesn't?"

"Tomorrow is when I might see a Canada goose up close, or win the lottery, or one of the boys might marry Brooke Shields, or a man from Venus might land in my thyme patch," Cecie said. She said it intently. "Possibilities, Kate. Tomorrow is about possibilities."

"No, it isn't," I said in a low, furious voice. "It's about death. If there's a tomorrow, then there's death in it somewhere. Tomorrow won't bring back Stephen. Or Vinnie."

"How the hell do you know?" she said, just as vehemently. "It might. You don't know. You never will. You don't have to worry about death, Kate, because you've already had yours . . ."

Something bumped the boat. It bumped again before I could jerk my head around to look. I heard Cecie draw her breath in in a soft little gasp, and then I saw them. The boat was ringed with big, sleek, wet, gray seal-like heads, nudging and bobbling and splashing. I started to scream and Cecie laid a hand on my knee. Two of the heads came out of the water and stared over the gunwale of the boat directly into my eyes, and I saw the bright, wide-set black button eyes, and the upcurved snouts, and the smiles; heard the strange, wet little breathy exhalations from the blowholes, smelled the sea strong on them. Dolphins. We were surrounded by dolphins.

I drew in my breath again, and Cecie said in a low voice, "They won't hurt you. They're the sweetest, friendliest things in the sea. They're curious, and they want to play. Sit still and see what happens."

I did and it was incredible. It was like something out of a wonderful childhood dream, or a fairy tale. There was an element of fright in it, of eeriness, because they were so big and so close, and so wild, for all the bumping, nudging friendliness, and the clowns' antics. These were sea creatures, things of myth and legend, born of wildness

537

and a different element entirely. But mostly it was simply . . . enchanted.

For they did play. There were, we counted, twelve of them, twelve enormous, shining creatures with sleek skins like wet gray inner tubes; I know because I touched one. Reached right over and touched him as he reared himself up out of the sea to look at me, grinning his greetings. He felt sleek as glass and firm and alive, yet unlike anything I had ever touched. He felt . . . transcendent.

"Oh," I said softly. "Oh. Oh."

For fully half an hour, until the last green light began to fade, they put on a show for us. They swam in formation around the boat and then away from it; fell into a straight line and porpoise-dived toward us like swimmers in a water ballet; leaped in pairs and threes far out of the water, sometimes completely, tossing their tails, and splashed down again, still in their sets. They swam backward in formation, their bright faces staring at us; I had the sense that if they had been on land they would have been dancing backward on their tails. They dived and surfaced directly under and around us, smacking the water with the gray, rubbery tails; they arced and capered and soared, and slapped the water flat with their beautiful big bodies, sending silver sheets of it over us in the boat. If we clapped our hands, they shot out of the water in unison, like underwater missiles. If we shouted and applauded, they raced away and came booming back down the Sound in twos, fours, sixes, and once, all in a line. Twelve of them. They put their faces up to ours, and squeaked and whistled and chittered their strange, unearthly little cries, and sometimes lay still in the water with just their heads on the boat, gazing soulfully at us. If we had wanted, I think we could have slipped out of the boat and mounted them and ridden away. We laughed and sang to them, we shouted and clapped, we whistled and petted them, and once Cecie reached over and hugged a massive gray head. "Ondine," I thought. "She is Ondine."

And just as suddenly they were gone. There was a last fillip of tail, and they submerged, and in a moment the dark, satiny sea was as still as if they had never been there. We looked at each other. Neither one of us had said a word. Both of us were crying, silently.

"That's why tomorrow," Cecie sobbed. "That's why."

"I love you, Cecie," I said, and reached over and kissed her, and hugged her close.

"I love you, too," she said. We sat for a moment with our wet cheeks pressed together. We had never said it to each other before.

I felt an enormous sense of peace.

She flicked on the motor and the running lights, and we headed up the Sound toward the dock in Nag's Head. We said very little on the silent, deep-blue trip back. Soon the lights of Nag's Head began to appear on either side of us, and the world of people leaned in close once more.

"Shall we tell them?" Cecie said, as we turned east and began to cut in toward the dock.

"No," I said. "I don't think so. I think I want to keep this for us."

"Me, too," she said.

She began to whistle through her teeth, and then she chuckled, in the dark.

"You know Maslow? The peak experience guy? What he said about a real peak experience: that it told you something about your relationship with the harmony of being? He'd have loved those guys," she said.

"That's nice," I said. "That's a nice thought."

"Fuckin' aye," Cecie said.

As we drew close to the dock, she pointed up toward the east.

"See that light? That top one? That's in the studio at the cottage. Ten to one old Fig's up there with the telescope, looking at us. Hi, Fig!" And she waved gaily into the darkness.

I laughed.

"That's ridiculous. How do you know? Why would she do that?"

"Because I went up there and looked one day when she wasn't there, and she's got Paul's telescope pulled over to the window where she can see the house and the yard and the road and the dock. And because that's what Fig does. She looks at you. She watches you. Stand up, Kate, and let's give her something to look at . . ."

"What on earth . . ." I said.

"Stand up!" Cecie shouted, and I did. The boat rocked wildly. I staggered, and braced myself.

Cecie threw her arms around me and kissed me on the mouth and hugged me hard, and then turned to face the light and shouted, "Looky, Fig! Kate and I are queer for each other! Queer as three-dollar bills, gay as geese! Just what you always thought! Look ahere, Fig Newton!"

And she held up her hand and shot a bird into the darkness.

I began laughing. I laughed so hard that I could not stand, but slumped, my arms still around her, back down onto the seat, pulling her down. The boat wallowed wildly. She was laughing, too. We wept and howled and roared. I had not laughed so hard since those nights at Randolph so long ago, and

541

then it was, as it was now, at Fig Newton.

"L'chaim, old Kate," Cecie gasped as the dock rose up before us in the darkness.

"L'chaim, old Cece," I said.

When we got out of the Land Rover in the sandy yard of the cottage, still giggling, Ginger came unsteadily down the wrought-iron staircase from the studio to meet us. She wore the yellow silk caftan that she had on when I had first gotten there, and her hair was snailed and lacquered into a gleaming helmet atop her head, and vermilion lipstick leaked crazily up the small furrows around her lips. She carried a full glass, and she stumbled twice.

"In the bonds, Tri Omegas," she said, slurring, and giggled. "I have a surprise for you. Come on up and see."

Something prickled at the back of my neck. My skin felt as if a little cold wind had rippled over sunburn.

"What?" I said.

"Paul. He came in while you were gone," Ginger said merrily. "He's waiting for you in the studio. For y'all, I mean. Of course."

And so it ended.

CHAPTER FOURTEEN

Late that night the outriders of the storm came in. I saw them stream slowly across the high white moon, the mare's-tail clouds that Ginger's father had shown us long ago at just this time, in just this sky. From where I lay, my face turned on the hot pillow so I could see the sky and sea, they looked like long, wind-blown tresses of silver hair flung across the sky. Mermaids' hair, maybe. Paul had said, as we all left the studio for bed, that the mermaids had gone from the Outer Banks, but perhaps, after all, they had not. Surely, if you were to hear them singing, it would be on a night like this, riding the slow silver sea before a storm. I rolled over on my other side and then back to the window, and flung the covers off me. The night was thick and still, even with the window wide open. There was no wind off the sea. The moon-bright room was airless. I had been lying awake since before eleven. I knew by now that I would not sleep.

The week was over, of course. The girls of September were scattered even before we parted physically. We might stay on for our appointed three more days, but now it would be middle-aged women who slept and ate and drank and laughed in the big house on the Outer Banks. Other people entirely. Well, I thought, surely it would have ended before it ended, anyway. I can't imagine how we carried it as long as we did. The center could not hold, and didn't. I lay under the weight of the moon, not young Kate Lee anymore, and not Kate Abrams, either. I did not know this woman . . . for woman she was. Desire dark and mature and fierce flamed along her veins and made her toss in the hot bedclothes, desire with nothing in it of tenderness or wit or subtlety. Simply, I wanted to go up to Paul Sibley in his dark studio and make love to him until there was nothing left of either of us. Until we were consumed and gone.

If it had not been for the utter shock of seeing him when I had thought not to, I think I could have kept the fragile skin of timelessness and content around me. I think, if there had been any warning, I might have kept it intact no matter what. But I had had no warning at all. Ginger's words shattered the shell, and the sight of him blew the shards away. And ever since I had been as I always had in his presence: naked, skinned, vulnerable to anything and everything in the world. Vulnerable to death: the

Pacmen and the waiting bridge shimmered and sang. Vulnerable to the life I felt leaping in his flesh when he touched me. Vulnerable to the answering thunderclap of life in my own.

He had only kissed me lightly on the cheek, as he did Cecie; brushed my burning cheek with his mouth and said, in the voice that I had not remembered except in the marrow of my bones, "My God, Kate, you've struck a deal with the devil. Get out of here and age twenty years before you come back."

And I had said, my ears roaring, "Well, hey. Fancy meeting you here."

And he had laughed, because after all, where else should I meet him but in his own white room above the sea, even if it was no longer white? And I had blushed because it had been a stupid thing to say, and he had said, still grinning, "You still do that, don't you?," and gone back to his seat in the wing chair by the fireplace. And this new woman was born, whole and vivid and hungry, and I feared and hated her. She was all hunger and thirst and fear and anger; she gnawed and raged and shrieked inside. Outside her, I smiled cheerfully and chattered, and drank my scotch, and laughed as Cecie and Fig and Ginger told him about our week. And sat as far across the room from him as I could get, in a deep leather armchair, with my knees drawn up against my chest and my arms wound tightly around them so he would not see the beating of that other woman's heart.

I watched him as he listened to us, amused and attentive. He had changed; you would not mistake this man for the hawklike young architect I had left behind at Randolph. He was heavier, massive, now: it was as if even his long bones had thickened. But he was not fat. Muscle played along his forearms and in his neck. There would be enormous power in his grasp. He was deeply tanned, as tanned and leathery as Ginger, but of course it looked right on him, and the Kate I had known felt a flicker of annoyance at the unfairness of that. His thick black hair was striped with pure white. It was startling and theatrical; you would remember him. He would stand out in any crowd now. Well, he always did. That had not changed. The presence of him smote the air around us four women like something not heard, but felt: the percussion of an explosion.

"You look like an aristocratic skunk," Cecie said.

He laughed. His teeth gleamed white. There were deep, sallow circles under his eyes, and long furrows in his forehead and cheeks, but he was, somehow, still the young Paul who had overwhelmed them all with French cooking and wine and music at that long-ago dinner for them. It was, I remembered, when Ginger and Cecie and Fig had first met him. It changed a lot of things, that night.

"And you look like Peter Pan grown a little older but still not up," he said. "You look just like I thought you would. You and Kate. Me and Ginger, we haven't managed so well. And Fig . . . what can I say? Is this a Fig I see before me?"

"In the flesh," Fig said. It was the throaty purr she had used with Poolie Prout, and Cecie grinned at me. I made myself grin back. I wondered where Poolie was, and in what condition. Fig looked languid and creamy.

"In the very considerable flesh," Paul said. "I was prepared for you, though. I've seen you on about a million book jackets and talk shows. But Cecie and Kate . . ."

He looked from her to me. His eyes stayed on me.

"Fix us another round, honey," Ginger said. "I'll go get some munchies."

He looked levelly at Ginger, and I did, too. Somehow it was hard to do it. Looking at her was not good; looking at Ginger had always given me a little surge of warmth and safety, but there was nothing of that Ginger here. Even less than there had been of her when she had met me on the stairs. Was it only a few days before? I had thought we had lost that sad, wrecked, lacquered woman for good, but here she was back. She smiled widely and fixedly at her husband, her jewelry flashing in the firelight, her heavy face painted and strange, her hair impenetrable and dreadful. Her eyes glittered under the beading of mascara, and there was sweat on her upper lip and forehead, and crescents of it stained the yellow silk caftan under her arms. She swayed slightly on the gilded sandals.

"I'll go get the munchies," Paul said. "I don't want you taking a header down the stairs. We just got your leg out of a cast after the last one. Fix yourselves another, girls; I think I'll pass. I have to get up early tomorrow; I've got a long drive ahead of me."

"You're not staying?" It was a wail of disappointment, from Ginger. I thought that tears as well as liquor glistened in her eyes.

He shook his head. "Can't, I'm afraid. I've got to be in Alabama for a directors' meeting day after tomorrow, practically at dawn. I just came by to get some proxy forms. I'll be driving till midnight tomorrow night as it is. And the weather doesn't look good; there's a tropical something or other coming across the Carolinas from the Gulf, that should hit in the afternoon. They thought it would go the other way, but it didn't. You all might think about cutting it short and leaving in the morning, if you can bear to; it could just be a day's blow, but then again, it could hang around for two or three days and kick up all kinds of fuss. You never know about the Banks in September."

"Oh, no! Oh, don't any of you go," Ginger cried. "Even if it lasts, we could just dig in with the fire and the booze and the records and have a wonderful time. The Banks are famous for their hurricane parties . . ."

"I'm not going anywhere," Fig said languorously. "I'd love to see a real storm from this room. Or some room." And she smiled, silkily.

"Fig has become a close personal friend of Poolie Prout," Ginger giggled. It was a silly giggle, high and artificial. "I do believe it is to him she refers."

"My God, Fig, Poolie Prout is pond scum," Paul grinned. "The surest way I know to get busted for something unfunny and unsavory is to hang around him. He's been flirting with the Feds up and down this coast

549

for years. It's only a matter of time."

"I like a little salt with my . . . ah . . . meat," Fig said.

"So I hear and read," Paul said, the grin widening. "Well, on your head be it. Whoever doesn't have a big, solid car better skedaddle, though. Whose Alfa is that?"

"Mine," I said. "But I really don't think . . ."

"You'd better be on the road early, Kate," he said, and he was not smiling. "I'm not kidding. I've seen the coast road three feet under surf in bad storms, and as it is it'll be following you up the coast if it doesn't blow out to sea . . ."

"I'm not leaving," I said loudly. My heart was pounding, and my ears rang with pure fright. I saw, as clearly as I saw him across the room, watching me, the great bridge arching into air in the dawn over the Chesapeake Bay. The bridge, and rain blowing straight across it . . . The girl who had not feared the bridge, who had been half in love with it, was gone now. The new woman went cold at the thought of it. No, I would not leave. To leave would be to go to the bridge.

Deep inside me the Pacmen gobbled and gnawed.

"No," I said.

"Oh, it is going to be just so perfect!" sang Fig in a new voice. We all stared at her. Her face was radiant, and her eyes glittered; her whole small, carved body seemed to vibrate, to shimmer. You could practically feel the heat coming off her. No one spoke.

"So wonderfully, totally perfect; just like at school in winter, all closed in, just the four of us sisters, remember, Effie, the time we had the ice storm and we couldn't even leave the house, and we didn't have any power, and we wrapped up in blankets in yours and Cecie's room and ate apples and drank tapwater coffee and you read poetry to us by a flashlight . . ."

It was Fig's voice. Not Georgina Stuart's, but Fig Newton's. Long-ago Fig, shrill and skewed and . . . wrong. What had called her back, I wondered? The storm? No, of course, it was Paul. I thought then that she was probably still in love with him. Why, I thought bitterly, should that change?

"Well, then, it's settled. Let's drink to that," Ginger chortled, and snatched up the heavy Waterford whiskey decanter and dropped it. It flew into a cloud of stinging crystal shards, and amber liquor splashed everywhere. I saw it spatter over Fig's white silk breasts, and drip slowly off Paul's brown face. The silence was long and terrible. I

551

saw Cecie close her eyes. Fig smiled and smiled, looking about her interestedly. Ginger began to cry.

"I'm sorry," she whimpered, her eyes on Paul's face. "I'm so sorry . . ."

"Come on, Gingerpuss," he said neutrally. "Let's get you to bed before you wreck the joint."

"Oh, no, please . . ."

"Come on. Party's over," he said, and took her forearm in his brown hand. I saw Ginger wince, but she did not pull away.

"I'll probably read a little and turn in, too," he said, looking around at us pleasantly. "You all carry on. I'll make pancakes in the morning if anybody's up early enough. Specialty of the house."

"You got a deal," Cecie said, and I nodded. Relief flooded me; under it, the new woman wailed, "Don't go!"

"Do you remember the mermaids?" Fig said in her old-new voice. "Remember, Ginger, about the mermaids who sang in the storm, for sailors who were going to wreck? Maybe we'll hear them. Have you ever heard them, Paul?"

"Nope," he said. "Nary a trill. I think they must have relocated. Maybe up to Long Island. What about it, Katie? You ever hear the mermaids?"

"Nary a trill," I said.

He turned and was gone down the outside stairs, marching Ginger before him. I heard her voice all the way down, pleading like a small girl's. I did not hear him speak at all.

"Anybody for a nightcap?" Fig said brightly.

"Maybe I will, just one," Cecie said.

I was surprised; she drank seldom, and I had never known her to seek out Fig's company. But the surprise was dulled and blunted under the howling of the new woman.

"Shut up," I said to her aloud, out in the still, thick night, and went into the big house and down the hall to my bedroom, and shut the door, and crawled into my white bed without washing my face or putting on my nightgown. I did not sleep. I did not think I would.

At three A.M. I got up and slid into my robe and went out onto the deck. I know it was three because I heard Ginger's foolish little cuckoo clock strike the hour in the kitchen as I tiptoed past Cecie's bed. She had come in an hour or so earlier, and had whispered, "You awake?"

I had not answered. Neither young Kate nor the new woman had anything to say about this night. Over, just let it be over . . . Cecie slid into her bed and did not speak again. Presently I heard the familiar small sigh that meant she had slipped into sleep. Now, as I went softly past her bed, she stirred but did not waken. She usually did not, once she slept. I wondered how Cecie handled those heart-sickening, breath-sucking night horrors of middle age, whether she simply made dreams of them, or even if she had them at all. I thought that if anyone could avoid them, it would be Cecie Hart Fiori. The night honors are about death. Cecie was more about life than anyone I have ever known.

Out on the deck, the night was dark. The clouds had curdled over the moon and cobbled the entire sky now, flying, ragged gray, shot with silver from behind. Where the sea had been burning cold silver it was now leaden, pewter, tossing. The wind was strange; it whispered and moaned, then fell still, then crooned again. The night air was chilly, but the wind was warm and thick with wetness and, somehow, the odor of tropical trees.

I had thought I might walk down to the edge of the sea, but with the moon gone and the rags of gray clouds flying and the eerie little moan of the warm wind the beach was suddenly a fearful place. I remembered a strange little horror movie I had seen when

I was a child, called *I Walked With a Zombie;* through it all a warm wind keened over a black tropical sea, while a giant emaciated black zombie came on and on down the silent beach, his monstrous feet dragging in the sand. This wind was like that. I turned away from the dunes and the sea and went around the end of the deck to where the big hammock hung, far under the porch eaves. I would finish the night there, and wait for the morning.

He was there, of course. I had known he would be; or at least the new woman knew; knew it on the backs of her hands and in the loosening joints of hips and knees. I saw only the bulk of him, black against the blackness, and the slight motion of the hammock. But there was no doubt who it was. I turned to go back into the house, in blind flight, but my naked feet hung back, and he saw me.

"Don't go back," he called softly. "I've been sitting here for two hours, willing you out here. Stay and talk a little while."

"I can't, really," I said. "I was just . . . I was on my way . . ."

"You were on your way here, and here you are," Paul said, smiling. I saw the gleam of his teeth in the dark. "Come sit. I'm not going to molest you. No nose dives out of hammocks this time. It's a different hammock."

I went over and sat down in an old green-painted Boston rocker across from the hammock. He was stretched out full length, his arms crossed beneath his head. He wore shorts and a white sweater, and was barefoot. In this thick darkness, he looked perhaps thirty years old. He did not sit up, but he turned his head to face me.

"You couldn't sleep," he said. It was not a question.

"No. It's sultry tonight, and the wind sounds funny. It's the first time since I got here I've been too warm."

I thought that that sounded suggestive, and reddened. He could not have seen the color, but I heard him laugh softly.

"It's the tropical air coming in from the gulf," he said. "It always leads a storm about twelve or fourteen hours. This one doesn't smell like a big one, but still, I wish you'd get on out of here in the morning."

"I'll be okay," I said. "I can always wait it out here with the others. But I can drive that car in anything. We have some pretty hairy Nor'easters on Long Island."

"You and your sports cars," he said. "I've never forgotten that little MG. Long Island . . . somehow I never really pictured you in that part of the world. You were always the quintessential Southern woman to me. But at least you got your ocean, didn't you? And your house beside it. I'm glad I didn't do you out of that, too."

"Paul . . ."

"Don't worry, Kate. I'll keep my midlife crisis to myself. I just meant that I'm glad you've had the life you deserve. The man you deserve. From what Ginger tells me, you've made it all work for you. I'd like to know your Alan. I see your credits and your awards: Abrams and Abrams. It's really nice stuff, Katie Lee. Way beyond nice. You know, for the longest time, I didn't know that the second Abrams was you? I'd lost you completely . . ."

He broke off. Then he said, softly, "Completely."

Warmth flashed in my groin and ran along my legs and up into my arms. My wrists felt heavy. His voice had always done that to me.

"How did you find out?" I said chattily. Stay away from that . . .

"Oh, I guess Fig told Ginger and Ginger told me. Fig's been tracking you for a while, I think."

"What do you think of her?" I said brightly. This was safe. "Of Fig as a living legend?"

"What is there to think about a woman who completely made herself over from scratch, including your nose? It is, you know. I think that on the eighth day she rested. I think, in a way, you have to admire it, but in a way it scares me. She's so totally singleminded. She always was . . . inexorable, I guess. I never doubted that she'd get just what she wanted."

I laughed. It sounded almost natural.

"She didn't always," I said. "For a while there, she wanted you more than anything else. From the way she carried on tonight, I think she still does. I thought she was going to jump your bones in front of all of us."

He laughed.

"So did Cecie," he said. "She sat up with old Fig until close to two, just to keep her in line."

Revelation and amusement and new love for Cecie flooded me.

"She did, didn't she?" I said. "I wondered about that. Little old Cece, sitting up there choking down booze and trying not to fall asleep, looking out for Ginger's interests."

"I don't think," Paul said, "that it was Ginger's interests she was looking out for."

"I don't want to do this, Paul," I said.

"I know, I'm sorry," he said. "Tell me

about your life. Tell me what you're like now."

"What you see is what you get," I said. "Nothing much has changed." I was having difficulty breathing. His body, barely visible in the dark, was like a magnet to my flesh. The space between it and my hands felt huge and cold and alien.

"Oh, Katie, it has," he said. "It has all changed."

"Tell me about you," I said desperately. "Tell me what you do. Besides being a captain of industry, I mean. Ginger has told us about that. You've just about tripled the mill operation, she says. Are you terribly rich?"

"Terribly," he said. "What do I do? Well, when I'm not in Alabama or Norfolk, I do things around here. I do an awful lot of fishing and hunting, and I run on the beach, and I hang-glide up at the ridge, and I stay out on the water a lot. Mainly, I fish. You remember that old motel we saw the first time we came up here?"

"The Carolina Moon," I said.

"Yeah. Well, it sits right in the middle of the best fishing banks on the East Coast. People come from all over the world to fish Pamlico and the ocean there. I have a permanent room at the Carolina Moon, and I come and go when I please. There's really nothing else in the area. There are guys from Miami to Bangor who'd kill me for the key to that room."

"The Carolina Moon has loomed large over my stay here," I said lightly. "The incomparable Poolie Prout said this morning he has a permanent room there, too."

"Yep," Paul said. "Nobody pays any attention to him; Ed Tinsley, the owner, knows damned well what he's hustling in and out of there — besides women — but he's not about to bother him. Half the time Ed isn't even there. We just come and go when we want to, and pay him a chunk annually. I'm just as glad I'm at the other end of the crescent from Poolie. I don't even want to know about it when the Feds finally get him."

"It's hard to think of you as a sportsman, a hunter or a fisherman," I said. "You were so absolutely singleminded in school. Talk about Fig . . ."

"Well, you know us Native Americans," he said. "We got it in our blood."

"Do you design at all any more?" I asked.

He was silent for a while, and I knew that I had reached inside the dark, weathered skin and put a finger on the heart of him. I could have bitten out my treacherous tongue.

"I never could, after I had money," he said. His voice was remote, and he had turned his head out to sea. "It took me a long time to get over the realization that I was on fire to make money, not buildings. I was pretty bitter for a while; I blamed everybody else. I blamed Ginger for a while. It was hard on her. I blamed the girls. It wasn't easy on them either. But I finally worked the blame around to where it belonged. I only wish I'd known myself better earlier. I could have studied accounting and saved us all a lot of grief."

His voice was dry and somehow dead.

"I think you knew yourself pretty well," I said. The dead voice sent pain flooding through me. "You were the best natural architect I ever saw."

"I'm better at making money," he said.

We sat silent. I cast about frantically for something to say that did not lead down into that warm, sucking darkness at the core of me. I could think of nothing safe. But it was even less safe to sit here silent together, in the darkness and the sea-sound.

"It isn't enough, you know," he said presently. "It never has been."

"Don't . . ." I whispered. He could not have heard me.

He turned his face to me and smiled. I

saw his teeth flash again, and I saw something else: the glimmer of tears on his face. I was beside him in the hammock before I even realized I had left the rocker. I put my arms around him and pulled his face down against my breasts, and he simply put his hands on them, through the thin stuff of my robe, and sat still. I felt his mouth pressed to my skin, and his hands, moving slowly at my nipples, and I thought that I would die from the utter exquisiteness of the feel of him. I remembered this feeling; it had never left me, but had lain at the core of me, like the bulb of a plant that blooms many, many years apart. I felt his breath in the hollow of my neck and smelled the dark, warm smell of him, and felt everything inside me loosen, go liquid, begin to burn.

"I made the worst mistake of my life when I let you go, and I've paid for it every minute of every day since," he said. His voice was thickened by my flesh, and I could feel the little puffs of breath as he spoke. Don't-don't-don't, the Kates I knew keened. Yes, the new woman screamed, in ecstasy and triumph. Yes. . . .

"I tried to make Ginger into you," he said. "I tried to make her be to me what you were, but she couldn't; she can't grow up, Kate. I can't make her. It's nearly killing both of us, and I can't seem to stop riding her. Look at her; see what I've created, trying to get you back? And on some level she knows it; but she can't let herself, and so she drinks, and she drinks . . . if she stops, if she grows up, she'll have to know who it was she married, and why he married her . . ."

He raised his head and looked at me.

"I would give the rest of life on this earth simply to fuck you right now," he said.

I leaped out of the hammock and backed against the railing of the deck. My robe fell away from my body, and he looked at it. I could feel the impact of his eyes.

"My God," he said. "My God."

My rubbery legs would not hold me up. I hugged the robe around me. I could have pulled him down onto me on the rough boards and taken him into me at that moment, and died of the shuddering completion on the instant; I wanted it so violently that I shook all over as in a bone-deep chill. But my voice, hoarse and cracked, seemed to come through my hot throat from somewhere else.

"No. I'm going back inside. This is wrong. I'll go home . . . You forfeited this almost thirty years ago, Paul. I have a man I love. You have a woman you love. You can't go back . . ."

"No," he said, his voice coming out on a long breath. "I can't go back. But we could go forward, Kate. We could do that. We could . . . I've lived thirty years without living. What the hell do you think Ginger can give me? Money? I don't want any more money. Whatever time is left, I want to live it. I want to live it with you . . ."

"No."

"I know you want me like I do you. I can feel that in every inch of your body."

"No."

"You do. At least one night, then, Kate. At least that. Something I can live on the next thirty years . . ."

"No. No. No."

"Listen, Kate. Tomorrow morning . . . I won't go to Alabama. I'll call them and tell them I can't get through the storm. I'll go down to Avon, to the motel. I'll leave early; everybody will think I'm going on to the mill. You tell them you've decided to beat the storm, and leave about noon, and come there. It will only take you a couple of hours; the storm shouldn't be too bad by then, only some rain . . . come, Kate. Come to the Carolina Moon with me. I meant to take you there on our wedding night. We'll have this night instead. This afternoon and night, and the next morning, in the storm, all alone . . ."

"I won't do it," I said.

"Pull around to the last cottage toward the ocean," he said. "You'll see my car. You don't have to go by the office. Ed won't be there, anyway. He always goes inland and drinks when there's a blow. Probably nobody else will be, with the storm. I'll be waiting for you."

"No."

"I'm going anyway," he said. "I'll be there by eleven. I'll go, and light a fire, and chill some champagne, and I'll bring some sandwiches and a radio. And I'll take off my clothes and get in the bed and I'll wait for you. And when you get there . . . do you remember, Katie Lee? You used to scream out like a crazy woman. I'll bet you don't scream anymore. I'll make you scream, Katie Lee . . ."

I turned and ran into the house and down the hall.

"Come, Kate," I heard him call, softly, behind me.

I got into bed and pulled the covers over my head and lay there, rigid as a wood log petrified, body racked by shudders and the simple, terrible wanting of him. I sweated profusely in the still, hot night, and I think that I cried, but I did not move from beneath the covers. Beside me in the other bed Cecie slept gently, turned toward the sea with her fist beneath her cheek. I would lie there, I thought, until she dressed and left the room in the morning; I would feign sleep; I would not move. I would continue to lie there until past the time he would leave. I would not respond if anyone called me. I would lock the door after Cecie, so that no one could come in to wake me. Only when I knew with utter certainty that he was gone would I get up and dress and come out into the house. And then I would pack and go home. Or . . . to the bridge. All right, then, to the bridge. This trip was over.

I did not think that I would sleep, but finally, in the gray dawn, I did.

I waked to gray light and erratic rain peppering the roof, and a knocking on the door, and Paul's voice calling, "Kate. *Kate!* Dammit, get up! You have a phone call . . ."

His voice was both annoyed and amused, an ordinary morning voice. I stretched every inch of my body, cracking the cartilage luxuriously, smiling, my eyes still closed. Paul's voice in the morning, and rain on the roof . . .

I came awake.

"I don't want any breakfast," I called, my heart beginning to pound. "I want to sleep

566

some more . . ."

"Your husband is on the phone and he's not calling from home," Paul shouted. "He said to drag you out. He needs to talk to you."

"Oh . . . just a minute," I said, annoyed and frightened. I did not want to see Paul. I did not want to talk to Alan. Alan . . .

I pulled on sweat pants and shirt and went barefoot into the kitchen where the wall phone was. I was pulling my tangled hair up into its knot with automatic fingers when I entered, and Paul said, "Leave it down. I want to see if there's any gray in it."

He grinned. It was a pleasant, light little grin. He wore gray flannel slacks and a crisp blue oxford shirt under a gray crewneck sweater, and his hair had damp comb tracks in it. His sharp-planed tanned face glowed from the razor. His eyes were clear and mild. He held a spatula in his hand. At the butcher block table Cecie and Fig sat, eating pancakes. Ginger was nowhere in sight.

He pointed the spatula to the phone and I picked it up. "Pancakes?" he mouthed, and I nodded.

"Alan?" I said.

"Kate," Alan said, in the clipped, no-nonsense voice he used when he was full of plans and arrangements and the sweetness of controlling things. It was the voice I liked least. "Kate, I want you to come home today. This morning. Start as soon as you can. I want you back as soon after dark as you can get here, and with that storm . . ."

"Well, good morning to you, too, darling," I said. "Yes, thank you. I'm having a wonderful time. Wish you were here."

"Oh, for God's sake, Kate, I'm sorry, but I'm in Manhattan, and there's somebody waiting for the phone, and I don't have time . . . can you get on the road by ten? It's past nine now."

"Why, I suppose I could," I said languidly. "But why on earth should I?" Alan knew I hated it when he hustled me like this. What was the matter with him?

"Because there's a goddamned hurricane or something headed right straight for you — A. And because I have an appointment for you with Carter Hilliard at noon tomorrow, in his office — B. It's the only time he can see you until late November, and we're not going to wait that long."

"Carter Hilliard . . . no. I'm not coming," I said. "I'm not going to see Carter Hilliard. It was John McCracken I'm supposed to see, and not till the middle of next month. You had no right to make any appointment for me with Carter Hilliard . . ."

"I ran into John at lunch yesterday at the Yacht Club, and I told him about this foolishness with . . . the stuff coming back," Alan said. His voice smoothed into the one he used when he thought I was being a fractious child. I like it second least. "He said he thought it was just that, too: foolishness, but he wanted you to see Carter anyway, instead of coming to him first. Said sometimes these vague feelings had a kind of body wisdom behind them. So he called Carter, and Carter said he could see you, but only tomorrow morning. He's going on vacation the day after. So get it on the road and let's get this thing behind us, Kate. I'll be at the house when you get in tonight. I'll take you in in the morning."

"I'm not coming," I said. "Not for another three days. Nobody else is leaving; I can't just run off . . . it's not going to be a bad storm. Nobody around here is worried . . ."

"Carter can't see you after tomorrow, Kate; didn't you hear me?"

"Then I'll wait and see John when I was supposed to," I said. "I don't understand you, Alan. You weren't worried; you said you were sure there wasn't anything, and now you're jerking me out of here like my life depends on it . . ."

And it does, I thought. Just not the way

you think. I thought again of the bridge, the bridge in the rain, the bridge in the wind, the bridge in the pink of dawn, and beyond it, the wild, sour-honey sweetness of space. . . .

Not now, the new woman said to me and to the man on the telephone. Not now. Not before I've lived once more, and burned up with living and blazed out with it. Not until then . . .

"I want to stay until Saturday," I said. "I meant to stay until then, and that's what I'm going to do. I'm sorry. Call Carter back, or I will."

"Is that how long he's staying?" Alan said.

"Who?" I said, honestly.

"Come on, Kate. Your old friend there. The one with the voice, who answered the phone. Little Beaver, or Paul Perfect, or whoever. I thought he wasn't going to be in residence. I gather he changed his mind. I wonder if you have."

Rage flooded me. My eyes filled with angry tears.

"I hadn't, no. But I have three days to decide, don't I?" I said furiously, and hung up the telephone. I turned to face Paul and Cecie and Fig.

"Sorry," I said. "He wants me to come home this morning, and I really don't want

570

to. What a charming little marital vignette to treat you to before breakfast . . ."

"Compared to Vinnie and me when we disagreed, it sounded like a Japanese tea ceremony," Cecie said comfortably. She was eating pancakes and drinking hot chocolate.

"Hand me that plate, Kate, and I'll dump these new ones on it for you," Paul said. "I think he's right. You ought to get cracking right after breakfast."

I ate the pancakes and drank coffee, not looking at him. Fig sipped coffee and looked around at us raptly. She still moved in the shimmer of something . . . barely contained, licking at her like heat lightning . . . that had played over her the night before. She was humming something this morning, over and over, just under her breath. When I had hung up the phone she had smiled at me as brilliantly as if I had done something lovely for her benefit, something delicate and special. When Paul spoke, she nodded enthusiastically, tossing her head up and down so that the heavy palomino hair swung up and down, as a child would nod.

"You listen to Paul, Effie," she burbled. "You listen to your husband. We love you dearly, but you need to beat this storm home. That silly little car will float away if you wait much longer. Listen, the wind's picking up."

It was. Outside, a spume of sand rose off the top of the dunes and whirled away on a gust. A violent spatter of rain followed. Then it subsided. But I could still hear the strange little moan that had begun last night. The sea was still flat, dimpled now with rain, but it was moving in great, slow, roiling heaves far out, as though, down deep, something monstrous struggled to be born.

"What about you, Cece?" I said. "How do you vote?"

"Stick around," she said. "This will be over by this time tomorrow. I'll beat you at chess this afternoon and make you pasta a'fagioli tonight."

I looked back at Paul. He smiled at me pleasantly, and took my empty plate.

"Up to you," he said. "You know what I think. Well, ladies, I've got to get out of here if I want to beat the worst of it inland. I'm not going to say goodbye, because I hope this is the first of many such. I'll collect a smooch from you, though. For the road."

He walked from one to the other of us, kissing us lightly, hugging us. Cecie smiled and averted her head very slightly. Fig's face, as she held it up, made me think of a young novitiate's as she became the Bride of Christ. Or of that young Fig, holding her face up to me during her doomed initiation into Tri Omega. It burned with transcendence, with a still, fierce flame. His lips brushed hers and she closed her eyes.

He came to me, and hugged me, and kissed the top of my head. "See you, Katie Lee," he said, and patted my behind, and picked up his raincoat and briefcase and went out of the kitchen. In a moment we heard the big Mercedes purr into life and bump away down the rutted drive.

We looked at each other in the quiet, bright kitchen. We smiled. There was a sense of atoms torn out of their orbit, rearranged, by something enormous and elemental that had swept through and passed on.

" 'When I'm calling you — ooo-ooo,' " Fig shrilled out suddenly, in a tremulous soprano. "'Will you answer tru-uuu-uue?'"

She looked around at us and smiled enigmatically.

"I have heard the mermaids singing," she said. "And so have you. So you be careful going home, Effie Lee. Don't get shipwrecked."

She giggled. Then she laughed aloud.

Ginger came shambling into the kitchen. She wore the silk caftan over nothing; you could see the softness of her big body bobbling beneath it, and the big, dark aureoles of her nipples. Her hair was wild and her face puffed and pale. She wore sunglasses. The odor of stale whiskey was powerful in the thick air.

"Has Paul gone?" she mumbled, opening the refrigerator door and looking in. She did not look at me. She did not look at any of us.

"Yes. You just missed him," Fig said. "And we're trying to persuade Effie Lee she ought to get going, too. Alan called her and practically ordered her home."

"Good move," Ginger Fowler Sibley said, her head still in the refrigerator.

There was a little indrawn breath from Cecie, and a wider, even more beatific smile from Fig. I felt my face go stiff and hot. She could not have heard, last night. She could not have . . .

I turned and went into my room and packed. It took me only a few minutes. When I came out again, Ginger was gone.

"She got sick," Cecie said, looking at me worriedly. "I told her to go on back to bed, you'd understand, and you'd call her when you got home. You will, won't you?"

"Of course," I said. "It may be a few days, though. Alan has an appointment for me in Manhattan first thing in the morning, and I'll be very late getting in."

Fig hugged me hard and kissed me quickly

on the lips when I left the kitchen. I felt her nails go deep into my ribs, and her lips part slightly against mine. Then she stood back, smiling, shimmering, humming.

"Godspeed, Effie Lee," she said. "Now that we've found you, we'll never let you go."

Cecie came into my arms and we stood holding each other silently. My chin rested in the white curls on top of her head.

"Toujours gai," I said into her hair. I tasted the sun in it, and the salt of my own tears.

"Toujours gai," she said. "And all that. Call us. And be careful, old Kate. It's a long trip."

"Tell Ginger goodbye," I said, and went out of the kitchen and around the deck and down to the car. The rain and the tears were warm on my face, and the wind sang. I could not see the horizon now. That far out there was no way to tell the sea from the sky. I tossed the bag into the back of the car and stood for an instant, looking up at the big black house. Except for the bright kitchen, no lights burned. Standing this close, it shut out the sky.

I got into the Alfa and drove out of the driveway and down the sand track to the road. And there, instead of turning right for the mainland and the Interstate, I turned the car to the left, down the old coast highway, toward the Cape Hatteras National Seashore.

CHAPTER FIFTEEN

It should have taken me about four hours to get there. It is seventy-eight miles from Nag's Head to Avon on the narrow blacktop National Park road, and the rain was gusting horizontally by then, so hard that the windshield swam continually, the little wipers laboring at top speed just to keep a thread of vision possible. The wind prowled high overhead, and the moaning rose occasionally to a keen. It was not dark, but rather strangely bright; it was as if the entire world was immersed in a radiant, flying spume. There must have been sun somewhere out to sea, but the storm, coming in from the east, was eating it alive. It was another element entirely, not wind or water or air, but a crooning melding of the three. I could see little but the teeming silver-pewter and the occasional white shafts of oncoming headlights, and could hear nothing but the roar of the storm and the hollow boom of the surf, hidden by the dunes to my left, and the frying static of the Alfa's radio. Those, and the profound staggering of my heart. I should have been afraid; I should have hugged the right shoulder and crept along, and stopped periodically to clear my windshield. I should, of course, have turned around and gone back. But I did none of those things and I was not afraid. I made the trip, finally, in two hours and fifteen minutes, and I drove those howling miles in a consuming and immutable flame of rage as bright and hot as the vanished sun.

There were two of us in the car that morning, and the rage belonged to the new woman. The old Kate hung on and whimpered and begged ineffectively for her to stop, to go back, to turn around, to go back along the coast road to the quiet bridge and the quiet dawn and the quiet death. But the new woman, sizzling and shimmering with the delectable rage, overrode her.

I was angry at my whole life, of course, angry at my father and mother, angry at that young Paul, angry at Ginger, angry at Stephen for dying, angry at Cecie and angry at my vanquished, never-born self. The anger filled the world and the car and my head. I did not attempt to understand it, or to mitigate it. Anger is its own excuse and its own reward, and needs no assistance from its owner. It was all the anger I have never felt, all the anger I had been afraid to own, all the anger I had abjured for my cherished timelessness and peace. Over it all rode the two great, sustaining tides of this rage. Anger at death. Anger at Alan.

I flew down the wild coast road on invulnerable wings of anger. I could, that morning, have driven the Alfa Romeo into and through hell.

Madness rode with me, singing; oh, yes, I knew that. I knew that it was never far from the two Kates. It rode the wind over the little car like a stormy petrel. It set us, the old woman and the new, to humming and singing through the lava of anger, and to speaking aloud to each other, and even, once or twice, to laughing.

We sang "Waltzing Matilda" and "Once I Had a Secret Love" and "Ebbtide." We sang, choking and gasping with secret laughter, "The Man That Got Away" and "Stormy Weather." We shouted Yeats and Dylan Thomas, and Dorothy Parker:

"Death's the lover that I'd be taking;
   Wild and fickle and fierce is he.
Small's his care if my heart be
      breaking . . .
Gay young Death would have none
      of me."

and:

"You will be frail and musty
   With peering, furtive head,
Whilst I am young and lusty
   Among the roaring dead."

We conducted Wagner, the great, booming storm overture from *The Flying Dutchman*, and sang wordlessly along with it. We shouted aloud, from *Ulysses*, Molly Bloom's wild, joyous cry of surrender:

". . . and then I asked him with my
   eyes to ask again yes
and then he asked me would I yes, . . .
and first I put my arms around him
   yes
and drew him down to me so he could
   feel my breasts all perfume yes
and his heart was going like mad
and yes I said yes I will Yes."

And from Shakespeare:

"O wonderful,
   wonderful,
and most wonderful wonderful!
and yet again wonderful . . ."

"You're nuts," we said to each other. "Certifiable. Where are you? What is the date?

Who is the president?"

But under and over and through it all, the blazing, sustaining anger.

"Why are you so mad at Alan?" I said to the new woman.

"Because he didn't come and get you, if he wanted you back so damned bad. Because he didn't stop you from coming here. Because he didn't stop Stephen from dying. Because he didn't stop you from getting cancer. Because he can't stop you from . . ."

"What?"

"You know."

"Say it."

"Dying, then. Dying."

"It's not his fault . . ."

"It's not yours. To hell with him. To *hell* with him. He can't even make you come."

"That's not him. That's the Pacmen. You know it is. They eat the sperm, they would eat him . . ."

"Bullshit. It's him. You can have that again. You can have that for as long as you want it. We're going down there now, to get it. That's what this is all about . . ."

"I can't go down there. I have to go to the bridge. You know that . . ."

"Then," shouted the new woman, "go to the goddamned bridge fucked like a lioness or a cat! Go fucked like a whole woman, one more time!"

"I've never been that, have I? Whole?"

"We're going to get that now."

Far ahead, through the solid, radiant rain, I saw the frail flashing of red lights. We were coming up on the narrow spit of land where Oregon Inlet poured through from the sea to Pamlico Sound, and I slowed the Alfa automatically. With the dropping of the engine, I heard a new sound: the deeper, wilder boom of angry surf, near at hand, of furious water crashing on concrete, instead of sand. I inched the car closer; without the forward motion, the rain was a solid, impenetrable sheet on the windshield; it was like being totally submerged in a maelstrom.

I got out of the car and shielded my eyes with my hands and peered ahead. The force of the wind pressed me against the car and drove stinging needles of rain and spray into my face and arms. The wind was still erratic; when it steadied into its storm force, I knew the car could not go forward through it. Ahead, dimly, I saw that the Herbert C. Bonner Bridge over Oregon Inlet was two or three inches under white water, and that every third or fourth wave that broke on the piling seas trying to crowd through the inlet surged over as though no bridge existed. The sea was a great, gray and white animal battering at the bridge. There was no one about, no police or emergency vehicles. Just the lights, on their sawhorses, flashing in the rain.

I got back into the car. I was sodden with rain and spray. I tasted salt. Standing still as it was, the car was rocked by the wind erratically, like a demented child with a rocking horse.

"I can't get this little car over that," I said to the new woman. "I could get washed right off that bridge if one of those big waves hit while I was on it. At the very least the engine is going to drown out."

"What difference would it make if you did?" she said. "You were going to go into the water anyway."

"It has to be the other bridge," I said. "The one over the Chesapeake."

"Why? A bridge is a bridge is a bridge."

"I have to choose. It has to be my choice."

"Go on. Ram the gas and take this thing over."

"No."

"Go on!" she shouted. "Go on! Who knows, maybe this man can do it, maybe this man can fuck the Pacmen right out of you! Alan Abrams couldn't do it; what have you got to lose by trying? This man . . . this man just might scourge you clean inside!"

I knew we were at the heart of it. For this I had come to the Outer Banks, for this I drove the coast road in a raging storm. For this. To be purged empty of death and filled with life.

Paul Sibley owed me a life.

The surf crashed over the bridge and withdrew, leaving a sucking wash of white bubbles. The wind keened. I revved the powerful little engine up as high as it would go. I closed my eyes. And I heard the singing.

I was mad; of course I was. At that moment, I was madder than a March hare. But I heard it. Far out at sea, pure and clear and impossibly thin and high, it floated over the storm like a white bird, the voices of the mermaids, singing to me.

" 'Human voices wake us, and we drown,' " I whispered, and rammed the car forward. We hit the sheet of water on the Herbert C. Bonner Bridge like a small red projectile, and then I felt the Alfa fishtail, lift, plane, and soar, riding the water like a racing shell. We crossed the bridge to the sound of the silvery singing out at sea and the scream of the wind and the shrieking laughter of two women who became, finally, one.

I was still laughing, off and on, an hour later, when I parked the car beside

Paul's Mercedes behind the end cabin of the Carolina Moon Motel.

He had the door open before I knocked. I stumbled in on the wings of the wind and a fierce spatter of cold rain, and he caught me in his arms and drew me away from the door.

"God, look at you, you look awful, you look beautiful," he said, holding me against him and rocking with me. He kicked the door shut and the tumult outside dropped to a low, dreamy roar, like a waterfall. In the silence I heard my heart, a rapid triphammer, and his, deeper and slower, and a little crackle of static and jazz from his transistor radio, and the soft snicker of a wood fire. I heard my own breathing in my ears, and the little puff of his breath on my wet face. I heard the rhythmic, faraway bronze lament of a bell buoy out at sea. I heard the little liquid chuckle as ice shifted in a bucket, and the spatter of rain on the small-paned windows of the little cottage. I heard the occasional secret sigh of the fire as a raindrop from the chimney found it. They were the sounds of peace and safety, profound and enfolding. I sighed, a long, bleeding sigh, and ground my face into his soft sweatered shoulder.

"Hold on to me," I said. "I almost didn't get here. The bridge is under water up at the Inlet. I haven't seen another car since

I came over it."

He held me away from him and looked at me.

"How'd you get through?" he said. "They close it once the water comes over the road."

"I just came through. I put the pedal to the metal and came on through like gangbusters," I said, and began to laugh. I laughed and laughed and laughed.

"I was going to give you a drink by the fire," he said, turning me toward the bathroom. "But first, I'm going to give you a hot bath. You're about to lose it, Katie Lee."

He walked me through the crowded little room and into the tiny bathroom. He turned on the shower and it coughed and bucked and spat, and then hot water streamed out in a comforting shower and dimpled into the bathtub. The tub, washbasin, and toilet were a violent pink, and the tiny-tiled floor was pink and burgundy. The shower curtain swarmed with Disneyesque roses. The ruffled curtains that shut out the wild sea beyond the little window were filmy pink net over deeper pink vinyl. The thin chenille bath mat and towels were faded candy pink. I laughed harder. By the time he had peeled the sopping clothes off me, the bathroom was swirling with steam and I was weeping with laughter.

"I'm going to wring your clothes out and put them by the fire," Paul said. "When you've finished, yell. You can have my bathrobe."

He opened the door and the steam gushed out and cool air streamed in.

"Paul," I said. He turned back to me.

"Wash me," I said. I stood in the swirling steam, still gasping with laughter, my legs and arms weak from it and from other things, and held my arms out to him.

"Oh, yes," he said, and came into them.

I ripped the soft sweater dragging it over his head, and I ripped buttons getting his shirt off him. I whimpered and pulled at him while he struggled out of his socks and shoes, and I had him in the shower with me while his shorts still clung about his knees. I met him as he came to me and climbed up his body and wrapped my arms and legs around the warm, wet length of him; I pulled his hair and bit his mouth and clawed his back and shoulders and left deep scorings from my fingernails on his buttocks as I pulled him into me. I could not be still and I could not wait; I found his center and opened myself to it and thrust myself up to him to take him inside me; I screamed out like a falcon when I felt him slide deep, and felt the hot water pound and pound,

587

and fought and clung and bit and licked him. He braced himself against the wall and I rode him like a tiger, clawing and screaming. We slid down the wall and into the tub, water pounding down over us, and finished it there, thrashing, screaming, exploding. I felt the molten core of me surging out into the water, and felt the life and heat of him pounding into me. When at last we lay still, I was bobbing slightly between his opened legs as he lay back in the cooling water; I said: " 'Would you like something to read?' "

He lay back, laughing, his hands covering my soap-slicked breasts from behind. We bobbed there for a little time, until the water began to be uncomfortably cool. Outside the storm lifted a notch or two in intensity, and the lights flickered.

"Dylan Thomas. I remember," he said. "You know, that's what I missed, that I never knew I did. That's what I haven't had in all these long years. Besides your incredible long, skinny body, I haven't had your poetry and your laughter, to light me up. I haven't had laughter and love at the same time since you."

"How could you live with Ginger and not have laughter?" I said.

"You can laugh at Ginger," Paul said. "It's hard to laugh with her."

We got out of the bathtub and he wrapped me in his big terry robe, and I bound my hair in a flimsy piglet-pink towel and we sat on the heart-shaped braided rug in front of the miniature fireplace and drank the wine that he had chilled in a plastic motel bucket. He had brought cheese and a baguette and some good pâté from somewhere, too, and we ate that, and fed lumps of coal from the dingy scuttle to the sputtering fire, and listened to the storm take the Banks in its teeth and shake them. We did not talk much, not then. I knew we would, but not yet. It was like the beginning of the week, when I had just come to Nag's Head, and the four of us women had talked little of ourselves and our lives. I had the sense that should we start to talk, Paul and I, we would talk until dawn broke the next day. I thought we would say, must say, things that would change things, things that would start engines that could not be stopped. Somehow I shrank from that. What we had done together already had the force of an inexorable phenomenon, like the storm; words that we chose and set adrift into the air were acts of deliberation, of affirmation and intent. Later for those. For now, peace and depletion and languor; wine and wind and fire and perhaps sleep; cleanness and lightness and rest. For now

. . . now. I could not hear the Pacmen and I could not feel them.

"Down the drain," I thought drowsily. "Washed those suckers right down the drain."

"I didn't think you'd come," Paul said. "I really didn't. I thought I'd just hole up here until the storm was over and go on down to Alabama and that would be that and I'd never see you again. But somehow when you came I wasn't surprised. God, it was like Easter morning or something, seeing you walk in that door out of the rain and wind. Or no, like watching some amputated part of yourself come back and hitch itself in place after years and years. What now, Kate? Don't you see that things have to change now?"

Fatigue, simple and white and whispering, swept me.

"No talking," I said. "Later, maybe, but not now. Now I want to sleep, and then I want to drink some more wine and then I want to do that nice thing we just did again, and after that maybe once or twice more, for good measure, and then maybe . . . *maybe* we'll talk. Although I don't guarantee it."

We fell asleep spoon fashion, my back fitted into his stomach, with the thin, fuzzy, antiseptic-smelling pink nylon blanket pulled up over us and the fire whispering and sparking in the grate. I slept deeply, thickly, dreamlessly; I do not know how long. Sometime during the afternoon the storm came down upon us in full: the air outside blackened and the wind rose to a shout that reached deep and dragged me up from sleep. Just as I raised my head the lights flickered and went off, and the sound of the surf on the beach outside seemed suddenly much closer. I got up and padded to the window and pulled the curtain back. I could see nothing through the slanting black rain, but the wind was so vast and alive that you could almost see the shape of it, prowling outside. The little cabin shook with it, and the roof squeaked and tugged, and lightning and thunder struck simultaneously. In the constant green light I could see the dark, fussy bulks of the other little cabins and the office, but no lights glowed; lantern, candle, fire, nothing, and our two cars were the only two I could see. I shivered. Kate . . . young Kate . . . put her head out momentarily and thought, wildly, what am I doing here alone at the end of this frail earth in this storm, with this man? With that monstrous ocean out there? It's not even the right ocean. Where is my ocean? Where is Alan?

When Paul came and stood behind me, as naked as I was, and put his arms around me, it was the new woman who turned into his arms and said, "Gentlemen, start your engines."

We did it again, did it twice and three times, on the bed and on the floor, and before the fire, and even under the silly, ill-made burn-scarred tea table that sat before the windows. We bumped our heads and carpet-burned our buttocks and bruised each other's flesh and rasped our throats. The new woman knew things that Kate did not know, had never known, and did them shamelessly and with joy and greed. The man Paul knew things that the young Paul had not discovered, either. The man Paul did them all to the woman, found new sources of heat and light in her thin body, stroked new chords altogether, called out new urgencies of muscle and blood and pressure. I took what he gave me with absolute, savage appetite, and asked for more, and got it, and when at last we fetched up once more before the fire, hair and faces and necks and legs slick with sweat, bodies emptied out and trembling, it was near eight o'clock at night. I could see the green glow from Paul's Rolex clearly. There had been no abating of the wind and rain and hollow-booming surf, none of thunder and lightning, but it had not risen, either.

"Is it stopping?" I said. My throat was so raw that I could barely whisper the words. I was as sore as if I had been in some physical accident. I remembered that I had felt this same soreness after Stephen was born. Who, I wondered, what, had been born this day?

"No, it'll blow and rain and so forth for another six to twelve hours," Paul said. "But it isn't going to get any worse. It isn't a real hurricane. The wind will start to drop very gradually now; by morning the bridge will be open. You could probably get through it by midnight in a four-wheeler. But I wouldn't want to try. Does it really matter? We're not going anywhere yet."

"Not yet," I said. I drank some tepid wine from the bottle he had just opened, while he built up the fire. The ridiculous, rococo little room leaped into shadowy life.

"I will never, as long as I live, forget the Carolina Moon," I said, nestling back into the tumbled covers of the bed. They smelled of him and me and salt and love.

"It'll be our place," he said, smiling and tracing his fingertip lightly from my chin down to my navel, slowly. My flesh rippled like a horse's when a fly lights on it.

"We'll come here at least once a year," he said.

I did not answer. He pressed close to me in the fire-shadowed darkness. I could feel all the bulk of him, the knobs and long bones and flesh and heat, the fine tangles of dark body hair. He seemed very large.

"Kate," he said into my snarled hair, "what is it? There's something . . . I don't know. Something not right yet. What is it? Tell me so I can fix it."

I sighed. Something inside me that had been knotted and frozen, some last small ice-shut lock, opened. I could tell this man. There was nothing I had held back from him this day. I could tell him.

"You can't fix it," I said. "Nobody can."

"I can. I will. Only you have to tell me."

I stared into the darkness and felt his arms and his weight and his blood, coursing calmly and strongly.

"I'm sick," I said. It was not at all hard to say the words. Easy, in fact. Easy.

"I've been sick a long time. I don't think I'm going to get well."

I felt his muscles freeze. It was uncanny. I had the idiotic thought that if I had had my fingers in his hair I could have felt it lift from its prickling roots and stand aloft. I went still, too.

He was out of the bed and around it, standing on my side looking down at me, before I even realized he had moved. I looked up at him, speechless, breathless. His face swam whitely in the darkness above me, and there was white around his eyes. I could hear him breathing, and hear his heart beating fast and hard, even over the wind and the surf. Beyond us the bell buoy off Diamond Shoals cried and called in the dark.

"What do you have, Kate?" he said. His voice was nearly inaudible. "Do you have AIDS?"

"AIDS?" I said stupidly. "AIDS?"

He looked down at me, my naked, oldest love, and it seemed that despite the fire-red blackness, I could see him very plainly. His spectacular black and white hair was in his eyes, and his mouth was open. I could see the tip of his tongue, moving on his lips. They were bruised and pulpy where I had bitten them. I said nothing; I simply looked at him.

"You do, don't you?" he whispered. "You do, and you let me do that, all afternoon, all night . . . you were getting even, weren't you? Kate, goddamn you, tell me . . ."

"Cecie was right," I said mildly. "You do look like an aristocratic skunk. AIDS. Yes, well, as a matter of fact, Paul, I do. That's just precisely what I do have. AIDS."

"Christ almighty, Jesus, Joseph and Mary . . ." He was across the room skinning into his clothes when I began to laugh. It was like vomiting, that laugh; it pumped out of the deepest part of my stomach and flowed out from between my lips, and I could not have stopped it if my life had depended on it. In a way, I suppose, it did. I laughed and laughed; I rolled back and forth in the bed and gasped and wheezed for breath, and when it came I laughed some more. I pulled my knees to my chin and ground my knuckles into my mouth and roared and howled with laughter. I was still laughing when he slammed out of the cabin, his half-buckled suitcase trailing a red and blue striped tie. I was still laughing when the Mercedes roared to life and screed around in the gravel and slewed out into the rain. I had not stopped laughing when he had looked back at me from the door, with a terrible face, old and caved-in, and said, "Kate, you bitch. Even if you're lying you've killed me." I did not stop laughing until long after the sound of the Mercedes had died in the wind.

But I did stop then. The laughter segued into weeping without missing a breath, and I lay in the bed with the Magic Fingers in the Carolina Moon Motel and cried without stopping and without hope until I fell asleep. The last thing I remember hearing was the clamor of the drowned bell buoy off Diamond Shoals.

I was dreaming. I was dreaming that I stood in the shower in the cluttered little bathroom that had served our suite in the Tri Omega house at Randolph, and cold water poured down on me, and I was late for a final examination, but I could not seem to wash myself clean of the stickiness that covered me. I was in a panic about the examination and a sick agony of shame about the stickiness: I knew it was seminal fluid, and I could not let them see it on me, Cecie and Ginger and Fig. But they stood outside both doors and pounded and pounded, and I could not remember if I had locked them . . .

I woke abruptly, but the pounding went on and on. And the water went on pouring. I pushed myself up on my forearms, the covers sliding off me. It was cold in the room. I shook my head, hard, and my hair flew about my face. The pounding continued.

I realized where I was and that the knocking was at the door at the same instant, and fury flooded me. So he had come back. For what? To apologize? To have the truth out of me? To resume our lovemaking? Let him knock all night, let him pound his hands bloody; let the rain drown him and the lightning char him . . . I would not unlock the door. I would not answer him if he called out.

"Kate! Kate, are you in there? Open the door, Kate . . .

The voice rode eerily over the sound of the wind and rain, but it was not his voice. I stood still, wrapped in his terry robe, and stared at the door. My mind slipped out of its tracks and wandered loosely in time and space for a moment. I could not move or think.

"KATE! LET ME IN!"

It was Cecie's voice. I ran across the room and jerked the door open and she stumbled in, much as I had done almost twelve hours earlier. The wind drove her nearly to her knees, and the rain poured in as if someone had thrown a bucket of water in at the door. I slammed and locked it and simply stood, looking at her. She looked back, her chest heaving and her breath coming in huge, tearing sobs, unable to speak. She wore her old yellow slicker and rain hat from school, and her face was blanched gray and running water, and the fringe of white hair showing under the hat was plastered to her forehead. Her glasses ran with rain, and blue veins beat in her temples. She made a funny little sound, a whimper like a small animal might make, and her knees buckled, and she would have gone down if I had not caught her. I shoved the flimsy carved chair under her and pushed her head down. The hat slipped off and lay on the scarred yellow pine floor, puddling there.

I brought towels and dried her face and hair, and eased her out of the slicker and draped the blanket from the bed around her shoulders, for she had begun to shiver violently. I saw that she still could not talk, although she tried a couple of times. I looked out the window to see if anyone had followed her there, or come with her, but there was nothing but the cabins and the blowing rain and my Alfa and now the bulk of Paul's big Land Rover. Was he here, then, waiting in his car? But he had been driving the Mercedes . . . A forked branch of lightning showed me that the Land Rover was empty.

"Is Paul with you?" I said.

She shook her head, but could not manage words. Her breathing was still deep and shuddering, but it was beginning to slow. I built up the fire and gave her a glass of red wine, and when she could not hold it against her chattering teeth, I held it to her mouth and steadied her chin with my hand, and she drank it. I had never seen Cecie in anything remotely resembling this panic. Somehow, incredibly, it did not really alarm me; I observed her with a kind of objective anxiety, and a mild clinical interest. As soon as she could talk, she would tell me about this night, and we would talk about it. I would understand. All would be revealed.

"Now will the scales fall from my eyes," I said aloud.

Cecie raised her head and looked at me, and took a deep breath.

"Have you seen Fig?" she said. Her voice was weak and thin, a sick child's. "Has Fig been here?"

"Fig? No. How would Fig get here?" I said. "Did she bring you? Did she drive the Rover, then?"

Cecie shut her eyes and shook her head. Her lips were absolutely bloodless. She breathed deeply again, and said, "No. I drove it." And then she began to cry.

I knelt beside her and held her like a child, and she cried like a child worn out with terror, her head pressed against my shoulder. I could feel the sobs bucking at her ribs, and feel the racketing of her heart. I rocked her in my arms, back and forth, back and forth, and whispered into her wet, matted hair, "It's all right now. Everything's all right now. You're safe and I'm here and the storm is going to end soon, and we'll stay here safe and warm till it does. We won't go out again until it's gone."

She shook her head violently against me,

and wailed, "No! No! We have to go . . ."

I patted her back, feeling tears start in my own eyes once more. How much worse those endless miles must have been in the dark, with the full force of the storm savaging her. And the lightning, and oh, God, the surf . . . the surf at Oregon Inlet . . . and she could not drive. So far as I knew, she had never driven. To drive that great, plunging car in that . . .

"Shhhh," I said. "Shhhh . . . whatever it is, it's not bad enough for me to make you get in that car again in this storm. Whatever it is, we'll fix it, in a little while . . ."

Cecie took a great, sobbing breath and pulled herself erect, and fought for control of the tears. She stared into my face and held both my hands in her cold white ones, and said, "Paul's gone." It was not a question.

I nodded.

"Ah, yes. Like a scalded tomcat, hours ago. Tell me now, Cece."

She drained her wine glass and said, "Come over by the fire. I can't get warm. And listen and don't ask questions until I finish. I don't think we have much time."

And so we sat on the rug in front of the coal fire and I watched as it burned bluely down, and she told me. She drank wine steadily, and occasionally she shuddered, a

601

great, profound ague, and her sweater and jeans steamed in the heat from the grate, and she told me about Fig Newton. She kept glancing at the locked door as she talked, and once, when the coal shifted and a lump fell to the bottom of the grate she jumped like a nervous cat. And she kept looking at her watch. It was nearly midnight when she began to talk.

"Kate, she's crazy, and we didn't know. I mean really crazy," Cecie said. "She has been, all these years. Since the beginning. And since the beginning, almost, she's been after you, and now I think she's coming . . ."

"Cece . . . sweetie . . ."

"No!" she shook her head violently. "You promised! Don't talk. Let me finish . . . Kate, all afternoon after you and Paul left she was . . . just on fire, just burning up. Jittering around, talking a mile a minute, not making real good sense, almost . . . glowing. Like last night, you remember, only worse . . . and she made Bloody Marys before noon and started Ginger on them . . . Ginger wasn't in real good shape; you saw her . . . and by two Ginger had crashed and it was just Fig and me. The storm was really getting bad and I was getting worried; I never saw such wind, but she was just drunk on it, running outside in it, and singing, and yelling . . . said she heard the mermaids singing . . . and then she went up to the studio and did something or other up there until about five, and I took a nap . . . and then she came back and Ginger was up and we started on the scotch. I should have noticed something, but I didn't; everything was just too strange . . . but I did notice she wasn't drinking, and that she was making the drinks herself and bringing them to us . . . well, Kate, I think she drugged us. I mean, I'm sure she did. Ginger was out like a light on the sofa by seven; nothing could wake her, and I went out, too, and if I hadn't thrown it all up after a couple of hours I'd be there on the rug by the fireplace. It was about nine when I came out of the bathroom, feeling just awful, and I tried to wake Ginger and I couldn't, but she was breathing okay, and then I tried the phone, to call Fig in the studio, and it was out, and so I started out there after her and . . . I saw her come down the stairs carrying her bags, and kind of look around, smiling this . . . *terrible* smile; God . . . and then she got in her car and drove off. So I went up to the studio; I really don't know why, and there was this note for Ginger saying she'd decided to go on home and beat the storm, and thanking her for the week. I knew that wasn't right; the storm was already here, nobody would drive in that . . ." Cecie smiled a watery, rueful little smile. "So I sort of . . . looked around. And I found the stuff she'd used on us in the bathroom; she'd left a lot of stuff behind. It's Dalmane. Makes you sleep like the dead, if you take enough. I know she gave it to us in the scotch because they tried it on me in the hospital and I threw it up every time, about two hours later. There was other stuff there; Percodan and something I think might be dexamine, and one or two antidepressants, and other stuff I never heard of. She must have been on it yesterday, and today, and maybe the rest of the time, too . . ."

I simply looked at Cecie. What was this madness she was telling me? Perhaps it was she who had become unhinged from reality; it had happened before . . .

"Oh, *shit*, Kate! I'm telling you the truth," Cecie shouted at me. "You goddamned well better listen to me . . . so, okay, then I looked around some more and I found her diary. And I read it . . . all of it; I sat there and read it . . . and then I knew about her being crazy. Because it was all lies. You know what she read us this past week? All the sweetness and light, all that stuff how much she loved us, about you being her soul sister, and Paul being a god, and all that? It was lies, Kate; it's not in the diary, that isn't what she wrote at all! What she wrote . . . God, she hated us! She hated me for being closer to you than anybody; I was right; she did think we were gay. Lezzies, she called us . . . and she hated Ginger, and she hated you most of all. For laughing at her and mimicking her; she heard all that, through the wall. She used to lie there and listen, night after night, oh, Kate, I *told* you . . . and she hated you for looking like you do, for having an aristocratic nose and name, for God's sake. She just *hated* that. She even hated you for trying to be nice to her. And most of all she hated you because she knew it was always you Paul wanted. She knew he only married Ginger for the money. She's the one that threw Ginger at him after you were gone, so he'd drop you, and rubbed it in to him about the money . . . and then she hated poor Ginger when he married her. Oh, Katie Lee, I knew that then, and I never told you . . ."

I shook my head silently. I looked at her. I did not know what to say, and so I said nothing.

"I read the rest of it," Cecie said, looking down at her clasped hands. "She tracked you all those years in New York, Kate. I don't know how. She doesn't say. But she knows all about your life, and I know how she got you here. Or at least, I know why right now, and not some other time. She's been having an affair for years with your doctor, and he told her. She knew . . . she knew your last checkup was next month. She knew all about your . . . illness; she knew everything. She said that it had to be now because you might find out you were going . . . not going to make it, and she couldn't let you get away with that. 'This one's on me'; she wrote that. Oh, my dear Kate . . . why didn't you tell me? I knew there was something, but I didn't know what . . ."

I looked at her, still shaking my head.

"Well, so anyway, she engineered this week, and then yesterday . . . or no, night before last . . . she called Paul in Norfolk and told him you still loved him and that you said for her to tell him to come to Nag's Head. And . . . she was listening and watching you last night. In the hammock. Just like she did before, all those nights . . . She knows you came down here, Kate. It's in the diary. She wrote it last night. I wouldn't have known otherwise. I wouldn't be here otherwise."

I said nothing; I watched her.

"She's coming here, Kate," Cecie said. "I

don't know how. I didn't see another car on the road, she may have had to stop, to wait some of it out. But you've got to get out of here. We've got to go now . . ."

I heard the wind outside in the silence, and the voice of the surf, and the bell buoy. All sounded further away. Lightning still bloomed, but the cracks of thunder had grumbled on past, up the coast toward the Tidewater. Cecie's breathing was even now, but light and fast. The coal fire snickered.

Far beneath me the abyss howled. Something down deep in it sang. Well, of course.

"Have you ever heard the mermaids singing, Cecie?" I said.

Her shoulders slumped and she closed her eyes.

"You don't believe a word of this, do you?" she whispered.

"Well . . . I know you do," I said carefully. "I know you do, or you wouldn't have made that terrible drive . . . but Cece, it's just crazy. This is bad horror novel stuff. Fig's not coming here. How could she come here? You know she's a fiction writer . . . and listen to that outside . . . nobody could drive in that . . ." Color came back into her blue eyes, and she looked at me levelly. And I thought, "Cecie just did."

For a fraction of a moment I could feel

it, the danger prickling in the air around us, the full extent of her sacrifice for me. But then disbelief flooded back, and a deep, sweet, limb-numbing lassitude: too much, I don't care, so what, let it happen then . . .

"What will it take?" Cecie said, beginning to cry again. "What will it take?"

"My doctor would never do that," I said, and felt, suddenly, an invincible raft of certainty solid beneath my feet, buoying me up. "John McCracken would never on earth have an affair with her and tell her about . . . all that. I know that, Cecie."

"It wasn't McCracken," Cecie said. "It was somebody named Hilliard. Your specialist, I think . . ."

I sat for a long time, it seemed, though it could not have been; sat looking into the fire. I saw us, the four of us, in a booth at Harry's in Randolph, drinking coffee. I saw us piled into my car, top down to the moony whiteness of a summer night. I saw us lying in the starlight of the Tri Omega house roof, drunk and singing. I saw us in winter night-clothes, sitting on mine and Cecie's beds, drinking hot chocolate. Each time, in all the pictures, we were laughing. We were laughing, and we were very young.

"Give me the diary," I said through stiff, numb lips, and Cecie did.

"I marked some places for you," she said.

I picked up the shabby book. The pages were coming loose from the binding; crumbs of glue fell over my hands, and flecks of yellow paper showered down. Fig's childish, looping handwriting covered the pages, closely and densely. There must have been hundreds of thousands of words in this book and the others like it, I thought. Words and words and words, a bridge of words stretching back into those years and forward into these . . . stopping last night. . . .

The first passage Cecie had marked was the first one Fig had read us this week, the one she had written the night of her initiation into the sorority. I stared at the page. I remembered what she had read to us, the cloying words that had made us giggle and squirm, words of adoration and sisterhood and that strange, canted love she bore for me.

This passage finished up: "She almost vomited on me. I raised my face for the kiss and I saw her; she couldn't look at me. I made her sick. My face made her sick. The thought of my mouth on hers made her sick. She ran into the kitchen and vomited in the sink. And she thought I didn't know why. Well, I know. I've always known. I've always known everything about her. I always will.

I'll never lose her and I'll never let her go and she'll wish she had died before she almost vomited on me. The day will come when she'll wish she had died before that."

The second was the passage written the night we had gone up to the roof to celebrate Ginger's making her grades. She had read that one to us, too. About the music of the spheres and the holy bond between us. About my face in the starlight, and her yearning to live up to my faith in her, to live for me.

"Effie's face in the moonlight looks like an effigy on a Crusader's tomb," she had written. "Pure and chaste and perfect; nobody has a face like Effie's. But she doesn't want me. She's told me a thousand different ways. She only wants Cecie. I know about that; I know what they do together after they turn their lights off. I hear them. I hear them every night. Effie isn't pure. Effie is a devil whose flesh burns with the unclean passion for another woman's . . ."

I raised a sick face to Cecie. She shook her head and looked away.

The last passage was the one she had read us last, about the night that she and Ginger and Cecie had come to Paul's to have dinner. I remembered that we had all laughed about that, and Fig had said, laughing herself, "Lord, I embarrass myself. He must have wanted to drown me like a puppy. I followed him everywhere that year . . ."

"I heard them through the wall again to-night," the passage said. "She was doing it again. Mocking me. Talking in my voice. Saying what she imagined I said to Paul, and what he said to me. Saying what she thought I wanted him to do to me, and what he would say and do if I asked him to . . . what does she know? What does she know of love? She thinks that what he says to her and what he does to her is love, but it isn't. What he says to me with his mind and his eyes when we are alone, that's what love is, and she will never have it . . . so she mocks it. She laughs. Well, she won't laugh long, because I know him better than she does or anybody else in the world, and I know what he wants and I know how to get it for him and I will. And I will kill her. One day I will kill her for laughing. And him. When it's time."

Cold started at my fingertips and ran up my arms and down my legs. It reached my heart and froze it rocklike and dead. I kept on thumbing pages. All of them were the same. All those years. Hate, venom, obses-sion, rage. Madness. Madness, clear and real and alive as the flames in front of my face.

I found the last page. Written this very

night, only a few hours earlier. It was as Cecie had said, all of it. It was there. Fig's handwriting had grown larger and more erratic as she wrote, until the last few lines covered whole pages, and the point of her pen had torn through the flimsy paper. I could read the lines, though.

"It's time now," they said. "Everything's right. It all worked. They're down there together and it's time. I can be halfway to Manhattan before the others wake up. She never should have laughed at me. She never should have. Oh, yes, it's time. And past time. Twenty-eight years past time."

"What a book this would make," was the last sentence.

I put the book down very carefully and put my hands on my knees and looked at Cecie without seeing her.

"Wow," I said.

"Kate," Cecie said, standing up, "get up now, and put your clothes on. We're leaving. You're going to have to drive, but I'll navigate for you. Come on, I'll hand them to you . . ."

"This can't be happening," I said serenely.

"This is happening!" Cecie shouted. "I know how: I just figured it out, while you were reading; it's Poolie Prout, of course . . . she called him to come for her, and he did; he said he would, remember? And she drove

over to the dock in the Sound to meet him
. . . get dressed; she's coming, she'll be
here . . ."

I stretched and let my head roll around
on my neck.

"I don't care," I said.

Cecie slapped me. She drew her arm back
as far as she could and slapped me so that
my head bounced on my neck. I put my
fingers to my face and stared at her. She
grabbed my shoulders and shook them and
screamed into my face.

"You want to die, don't you?" she shouted.
"You're planning it, aren't you? I should
have seen it; I've seen it before, in the hospital
. . . I know what you're doing; you're going
to go home and do it some nice, neat, seemly
little way before you have to see the doctor
. . . you've been telling me you were all
week, and I didn't hear you . . . goddamn
you, Kate! What is it, the cancer's back? Is
that it? Well, let me tell you something: so
the fuck what? You think it's going to be
better for Alan to do it rather than let the
cancer do it? You think it's going to be
better for me? You think your little boy
would thank you for this; you think your
friends will? Did it make you feel better
when your father did it; did that help you
live your life? Death is bad, Kate, but to

go courting it . . . that's obscene! If you kill yourself you've killed all there'll ever be on this earth of Stephen. And you'll kill Alan. And me. Kate . . . I'm not going to lose you again. I simply will not do it. Get your clothes and come on, now. Kill yourself on your own time; as long as I'm in this place with you I AM NOT GOING TO LET YOU DIE!"

She hauled me to my feet and tossed my clothes at me, and stood thrilling like a wire while I put them on. I looked at her while I did. Her face and body seemed wrapped in flame, shimmering in the dimness almost as Fig's had last night. I thought again that she was a beautiful woman.

We started for the door. Lightning and thunder flashed and boomed, close once more.

"Wait, get the diary," she yelled over her shoulder at me.

"Why . . ."

"GET IT!"

I turned back and picked up the diary.

Cecie jerked the door open. The lightning forked again, close and greenish-white. The wind howled, and I heard it once again, far and pure and silvery out on the black sea. The singing. The singing . . .

Fig stood in the door. She stood very still looking in at us, as silent and sodden as a drowned woman. Her hair was pasted to her skull and her lipstick was eaten off her wide mouth and her cheekbones seemed carved from the dead white skull of something wild. Her eyes stared at Cecie and at me behind her, in the doorway, but I did not think that she saw us. I did not know what she saw. She might have been there a very long time; she looked as if she had just risen from the bottom of the sea. The lightning flickered again and she gave us a small, formal smile. In her hand was a ridiculous little snubnosed pistol with black and white calfskin on the handle.

I thought, very clearly, "It's only a toy. One of Fig's little pieces of theater. We're okay, because it's only a toy."

"In the bonds, Effie Lee," Fig said, and fired the gun. I saw the white spurt of flame before I heard the report. Thunder cracked then; I have never been sure that I heard a report at all. But, of course, I must have.

Cecie fell. Fig looked down at her. She shook her head slightly, as you do in annoyance when you have made a trifling mistake.

"Get it right, Newton," she said, and fired again.

When she fell, it was backward, out into the rain.

CHAPTER SIXTEEN

It is nearly noon, though from the angle of the sun on the back of my neck, you might think that it was mid-afternoon. It is strange, how different the light is just this much further north, and what a difference two weeks makes. The last time I knelt in the sun among flowers, in the Currituck Gardens on the Outer Banks with Cecie, the light hit me almost full in the face. Today it strikes my shoulders and neck and dapples the old blue sweater of Alan's that I wear for gardening in the autumn. We had frost this morning. The wind, before it dropped, was almost cold.

It fell only a few minutes ago, and now there is that profound hush that I love, that means the turn of the tide. I hear the earth hum again. I had not thought I would do that. I hear the earth hum, and the soft slap of the waves on the beach below my garden, and that is all. I do not hear the wind off the abyss. And I do not hear the Pacmen. This time tomorrow, I will know whether or not they are still there. I think John McCracken will tell me that they are not. Somehow, I think they are gone; that they went with that other Kate when she died on the Outer Banks. For she did die. Just not from a small lead pellet. Not in a cold sea.

But if the Pacmen are still here, it is hardly important. I know something else about living and dying now. It is something entirely new to me. It changes everything.

Right now, just at this moment, the world is timeless again. The world stands still in high sun, waiting for the blue wind of autumn to come with the turn of the tide.

I know I will never see them again, my sweet, punished Ginger, and Paul. Paul: less than nothing to me now. Less than zero. I know that we will not even speak of that night on the telephone, or write words about it in letters. We are done with each other. That died, too, on the Outer Banks. I will mourn Ginger. I have already forgotten Paul.

And I find I can remember nothing of the woman I left lying in the cabin at the Carolina Moon that night. Neither the sad, terrible, vulnerable young Fig Newton that she was, nor the even more terrible, mad, beautiful Georgina Stuart who came to Nag's Head. Nothing. When I think of her, I see darkness and a spurt of white fire. And that is all.

I saw a truly strange thing toward the end of that night, even stranger, somehow, than everything that had gone before: I saw a woman grow up before my eyes. I wish I had liked the sight better, or my part in it. When I got to the house in Nag's Head early the next morning, before dawn, Ginger was still asleep where Cecie had left her, on the couch in the living room, and it took me several minutes of shaking and calling to waken her. When she did, her face crumpled with grief and rage at me. When I finished speaking, it was another face altogether: much older, somehow harder, and with the child that I had loved irrevocably gone from behind the eyes.

I still do not know what she thinks. I know she knows that I was somewhere with Paul, but she also knows that it came to nothing and is over now. What she made of Cecie, gone away without her clothes, I do not know. Neither do I know what she made of Fig, dead in the Carolina Moon Motel down the coast near Avon on the night of the great storm, dead and alone and without a car, in a room permanently kept by Paul Sibley. I do know that Paul was in Alabama by the time that Fig was ascertained to have died and could prove it and was cleared, and I know that there is no official doubt that Fig fired the gun that killed her. Powder burns and fingerprints and all that grisly arcana saw to that. I think that no matter what she eventually comes to believe, Ginger will not speak of it. She has her husband back, and from the look on her face when I drove away from there, she is going to keep him on a short leash from now on. He is going to need her attention and her protection; it was that I went to tell her that night. That, and to tell her that I loved her and would miss her.

No, I do not think she will speak of it. So I think that, despite the blaze of publicity that followed . . . NOVELIST FOUND DEAD IN SEASIDE MOTEL IN HURRICANE, DEATH WEAPON FOUND, etc. . . . . we are done with it, if we want to be. Paul Sibley isn't going to mention it. Neither is Ginger, most likely. If Alan does, it will be when I am ready to talk of it, and only then. It is unlikely that Poolie Prout will, wherever he might be. I try to imagine how he must have felt, awakening in his room at the other end of the motel, the taste of the drug in his mouth and her gone, perhaps finding her there, perhaps hearing sirens . . . I feel sure that once he got the drift of things, he found it expedient to move his base of operations to a more hospitable climate. I imagine he left, as I did, before dawn that same morning.

It was first light as I drove over the Chesapeake Bay Bridge. Just as I had planned before I started out for Nag's Head. A long time ago; so long . . . I had driven most of the way in the rain, and for a great deal of the trip I cried. I thought of Cecie and of Stephen, of Paul and Ginger and Fig — the young Fig — and of Alan, and I cried and cried. There were many people in the little car that night; I rode with the living and the dead beside the black sea, in the dwindling rain. By the time I came up on the big bridge, the rain was only a soft mist. I thought of the poem that Cecie and I had loved:

"Oh, let it be a night of lyric rain
  And singing breezes, when my bell
    is tolled.
I have so loved the rain that I
    would hold
Last in my ears its friendly, dim
    refrain . . ."

Grief doubled me over the steering wheel, and then I raised my head again. She was with me and would always be with me. I would see to that. I would never let her go. I thought of what she had said to me on the beach in Nag's Head: "As long as we live, they do."

All right, then, I thought. While I live, she does. While I live, Stephen does. While I live, we all do. We live as we did then, we four, whole and clean and laughing. With all our hopes and dreams and that foolishness still ahead. That's enough. That's more than enough. That's everything.

I learned the central lesson of my life from Cecie Hart Fiori that night: that life can only be kept by giving it away. But then it will bloom.

When I came to the highest point in the arc of the bridge, I stopped the car and got out and walked to the railing. I knew just how to do this; hadn't I rehearsed it, only a scant week before? Yes, I knew how to do this. Down on the water the last of the rain dimpled the flat, oily gray swells of the great bay, but out at sea the sky was bright. Morning was coming up fast. The day would be fair.

I raised my arm over my head and threw the diary far out into the misty air. I did not leave the rail until I heard it hit, far below.

Georgina Stuart was buried a week later in a private cemetery on Long Island. The Abramses and the Sibleys did not attend. But *People* magazine did.

I hear the screened door slam and look down from the dune line to see Alan waving at me from the deck. He is carrying a tray of Bloody Marys, and he is smiling. Everything looks good from up here, where I kneel surrounded by the rich black earth that I have hauled up in the wheelbarrow. Everything looks simple and good and very clear: the house, the deck, Alan, the scarlet drinks: everything.

"What are you doing?" he calls.

"Planting *rosa rugosa*," I reply. "Beach roses. They came this morning from that garden I told you about, in Nag's Head. Currituck. Cecie had them sent when we were there; they're a surprise. There's a card with them that says, 'L'chaim.' Only it's spelled, La Hime. You never could spell shit, Miz Fiori."

"It wasn't me," Cecie calls from the chaise in the sun at the end of the deck. "I can too spell L'chaim. I can spell shit, too, as far as that goes."

She is looking much better now, a little heavier, faintly tanned from the days on our back deck, with only the thin white line of the bandage on her shoulder showing under the collar of her shirt. John McCracken, who took the bullet out and lost it and the record of her visit without raising a sandy eyebrow, says she can "resume normal activities" next week. She was ferociously adamant about my taking her to him, enduring the long drive and the pain with serenity. "Anybody else will report it," she said. "It doesn't hurt." And I don't think it did, not then. Cecie had simply gone away inside herself again. The bleeding was minimal, and stopped by the time we cleared Virginia.

So we will start with the Cloisters. And we will go on from there. Cecie has given me back my life, for a little while or a long one. I am going to give her hers now.

"We can't see the roses if you put 'em up there," Alan says, but he is grinning.

"Maybe not, but they'll be spectacular from the beach," I say. "And they'll live forever."